www.united-pc.eu

Jack Walton

War in the Pripet Marshes

Book 1

The Hammer Falls

(June 22nd to October 10th, 1941)

The Hammer Falls

Chapter 1 – Awakening

Yuri Petrovsky was cold, very cold. The creeping shivers emanated from his feet and coursed with ever increasing strength around, down and through the dense, impenetrable fog that swirled endlessly within the dark recesses of his mind. Feeling began to pervade into his limbs and his right leg twitched in a spasmodic gesture of impatience, as his reviving body fought against the sweet, peaceful, grip of unconsciousness. Slowly, as a spring thaw unlocks the icy doors of an endless winter, his brain began to function.

Pain. His whole being seemed to be awash with pain. He tried to raise his arms, but they seemed somehow stuck and immovable. His legs were the same, nothing was working. He appeared trapped within his delirium. Again, he tried to move and this time he succeeded in moving his right leg, but the effort brought a gasp from his throat, as a stab of agony coursed up his back and into his chest. Something told him that he was lying on his back with a great weight pressing down on him from above. He lay there momentarily stunned while he attempted to take stock of his situation.

Gritting his teeth against the pins and needles of returning blood flow, he came to a sudden and violent dawn of realisation. He couldn't see. His eyes were blind, the lids caked with some glutinous mucus and what, he thought suddenly, is that stench? Panic rose like a volcano in his chest and he tore his right hand free of the cloying grip that threatened to overwhelm him and with a superhuman effort, broke his arm away from whatever was rendering it immovable. His hand groped for his eyes, rubbing and gouging the sickly smelling ooze away until he finally could make out a little of his surroundings. To either side chinks of light showed him that he was at least not fully covered, but he still couldn't fathom where he was or how he'd got there. His body was now becoming hotter by the second, as the shivers of returning circulation gave way to a growing heat that warmed and soothed his fragile mind. But as his eyes became accustomed to the dim wavering light of his strange environment, he stared intently at his right hand and a high pitched wail broke from his throat as he gawped in disbelief at his ooze covered fingers. Blood. His Blood? Who's blood? Was he injured? He strained his head gingerly and peered down to what he could see of his body, regardless of the shooting pains that blasted into his skull. Holy Mother of God, what's happening to me! His mind, sure now that he was seriously injured, was going into overdrive and he felt his jaw trembling with a jabbering fear as he moaned deep in his throat. Strange convulsive tics assailed his arms and face and in a moment of revulsion, he forced his head to turn to the left, away from his blood soaked hand and he found himself able to twist his body to where stronger light was shining. Rolling his eyes around in their sockets he came to the conclusion that something, perhaps another body, was laid on top of his own. He blanched, unable to comprehend his predicament, until realisation swept like a lightning bolt into his befuddled brain. War. War had erupted. The German Fascists had dared to invade Mother Russia and he, Yuri Petrovsky, had seen it begin. So why was he here, laid beneath some other body? Desperately he tried to extricate himself from the ponderous weight pinning him down, until he finally broke free of the restrictive encumbrance and pulled himself gingerly onto his knees. The body had sunk downwards now that it was free of Yuri and he turned on his hands and knees towards the space that opened before him and crawled out into the light of day.

He raised his right hand against the glare of hazy sunlight, squinting between his fingers as his eyes became focussed and then he was able to make sense of his surroundings. He turned his head and stared at the body that had imprisoned him and realised he was looking at the fat, bloated corpse that had once been his Sergeant, Boris Maslak. He knew it was Maslak, by the ring he wore on his right hand. His left arm and right leg were missing, torn off by some unknown force and as Yuri strained to look further, he saw that the head had been ripped from Maslak's shoulders. With a strength that belied his previous attempts at movement, he scrabbled away to his left and ended up gazing across the bodies of nine of his comrades, all still and silent in a tangled mass of death, until finally, fifteen feet away, against the top lip of the trench, he gazed into the flat reptilian eyes of Boris Maslak, staring out of the grotesquely severed head. Tearing himself away from those baleful eyes he stared disbelievingly at the carnage surrounding him. Nothing in his young life could have prepared him for this. Grigori, his older brother lay staring into heaven with his arms outstretched as if welcoming the fading sunlight. Yuri forced himself onto his knees and dragged his body over to that of his brother. He gently shook the inert lifeless form, pawing at his face, willing his brothers eyes to open, to hear him speak, to hear him admonish Yuri for failing him. "Grigori, Grigori" he moaned piteously. But nothing could have survived the bullet that had torn through the left cheek and exited upwards through Grigori's skull. The gaping wound in his chest caused by the thrust, twist and removal of a bayonet would have had no effect, Grigori would have died instantly. Tears coursed down Yuri's cheeks and he buried his head into his brother's body, lost in his own misery.

After what seemed an age, Yuri finally lifted his head and gazed around him. Vlad and Ivan, his old village friends lay side by side, their faces turned towards each other, Vlad's arm resting across the body of his friend. Together in life, inseparable, and now, together in death. The remaining bodies were those of his troop, all pierced again and again with bullets and also, with the single bayonet thrust, just to be certain. It appeared that the enemy were thorough. His eyes finally came to rest on the head, leering at him fifteen paces away. He had never liked Boris Maslak, even before he had become his sergeant. A fat, conceited pig of a man, always bragging what he would do and what he had done. Their father, Joseph, had warned him off when he had come sniffing around his daughters, talking big and making a play for their affections. His drinking and brutality were well known around the region, in an area where hard life bred hard men. But, as Yuri conceded, he didn't deserve to die like he had done. As it was, his sacrifice had no doubt saved Yuri's life. The shell that had propelled him into the air, ripping his body apart, had dumped him unceremoniously right on top of the unsuspecting Yuri, rendering him unconscious and oblivious to the eyes of the enemy. The enemy. He had forgotten about them. What if they were still about? A hurried look around him was enough for him to realise that no weapons were available. He felt around his waist to where his knife was still sheathed in its leather scabbard and the touch of the handle brought a small thread of comfort to his isolation. At least he had his knife. Most of his troop had modern rifles and the machine guns were in reasonable condition, even though they included some well used Russo – Japanese war relics. Yuri's job was to keep ferrying ammunition to everyone and this, he remembered finally, was what he had been doing when Maslak had made his leap of faith.

Concentrating as best he could, Yuri listened intently, but could only hear a distant rumbling, as of thunder across the marshes. The stench, however, was beginning make his head ache and the fetid air of a summers evening lay heavily within the trench. Slowly, he heaved himself into a standing position, pushing upwards with his legs, while gripping the remains of the wooden posts that had served as part of the defensive parapet of the trench. Once upright, he leaned backwards against the crumbling mud walls, gathering his strength. The ache in his head was beginning to subside a little and he tilted his head back, raising his nostrils to breathe in the cooler evening air that seemed to have deserted the lower levels of the trench. He gazed upwards into a blue sky, interspersed with grey and black clouds that seemed to drift up from the earth itself, melting away towards the west. He blinked, mesmerised by the flickering shadows that played across the dark clouds, shadows of fire and sparks that would suddenly flame brightly and then fade into the dark rimmed halo that surrounded the setting sun. But these were no ordinary clouds. His eyes widened. His mind had been playing tricks. Smoke. He recognised it now. Clouds of thick black smoke rising from behind him in the east. Fire, fire in the east.

Carefully, he scanned the trench, looking for a foothold. The smoke was beginning to sting his eyes and he raised a bloodied hand to wipe away the tears that spilled down his cheeks. Finally, he caught sight of the remains of a ladder that had survived partially intact and propping it against the side of the trench, he managed to raise himself, cautiously, until his eyes cleared the lip and he stared, wide eyed and disbelievingly, into hell's kitchen.

Before him, all was death and destruction. Yesterday's fields of growing corn, stretching for as far as the eye could see, were now so much smouldering black charred stubble. The shattered corpses of men and horses were randomly sprinkled across the killing ground of smoking craters, burning wagons, crumpled field guns, crashed aircraft, abandoned tanks and blasted half-tracks. Dismembered limbs littered the ground, hovered over by the constant drone of millions of flies, gorging themselves on a devils feast of butchery. Peering along the trench to his left he could make out the huge holes in the defensive parapet where tanks had battered their way through. The relentless procession of caterpillar tracks criss-crossed the area in front of him and onward to the distant horizon. Nothing had been able to stop their passing, not even the minefields and anti-tank ditches, the cunningly placed field guns and, as Yuri remembered, the coming of the enemy infantry.

He found it impossible to believe that yesterday, he and several of his unit, had journeyed to the bridge across the River Bug, which at that time, was the border between Poland and Russia. They had watched the stream of horse drawn traffic ambling slowly along the road from Minsk and disappearing westwards towards Warsaw. Stalin was keeping his bargain, struck with Hitler, to supply goods for the Reich. Throughout the night they had listened to the sound of distant explosions. Warsaw was getting pummelled again. Just another night like so many nights over the last month. They huddled deeper into their blankets and cursed the Nazi guns. Then, sometime about three o'clock, all hell had broken loose. The endless salvos had screamed down on them in a torrent of death and destruction. Yuri had never witnessed anything like it before. The shelling had started to land about fifty yards away from the trenches and crept closer and closer until finally it was ripping the trenches apart from within and smashing great holes in the concrete pill boxes and trench walls. Deafened and frantic with fear he had curled himself up into a ball and pressed himself deeper and deeper into the trench wall, trying to escape the shrapnel shards that zinged all around him until the shell that shattered the machine gun and dumped Boris Maslak's body over him.

His ears were becoming accustomed to the various noises going on around him. There was the constant drone of aircraft flying overhead and he watched as bombers and fighters streamed from the west and disappeared eastwards on missions, he knew not where, only that they displayed the black crosses. Where were the Russian planes? All he had seen of the Russian air force were several wrecks littering the battlefield. Was the enemy so superior in everything? He shook his head, slapping absent-mindedly at the flies that swarmed around him, unable to unravel the events of the last twelve hours. Twelve hours? The westering sun told him that it was late afternoon so yes, perhaps twelve hours since it all began.

He slid down the trench wall and padded softly towards the area where the tanks had battered their way through. The field guns that had seemed so powerful and unyielding yesterday now lay shattered and twisted, their barrels pointing uselessly skywards. The concrete pill boxes, seemingly so solid and insuperable, were blackened, shattered and eerily silent. Bodies and bits of bodies lay everywhere. Feeling morose and defeated he slowed as he neared the churned up gap and then suddenly, he was flat on the ground, heart pounding. Germans. Not more than half a mile away and moving towards him. His heartbeat thumped loud in his ears as gingerly, he risked a look above the torn earth and saw not only Germans, but what appeared to be brown uniformed Russians too. Ducking back down he maneuvererd himself backwards towards where the height of the parapet allowed him to stand again, out of sight for the moment. Slowly and carefully he scrambled up the incline of the trench and raised his head between the spokes of a smashed gun carriage wheel.

The Germans were, as he had initially surmised, moving across the area of no man's land. They were spread out across the battlefield, in no particular order, herding what appeared to be two or three hundred or so Russian prisoners. These men were silently picking up dead Russian corpses, two men per body. Once each had hold of one end of the corpse, they carried it to the edge of the trench and tipped it over the lip, the body disappearing into the bowels of the earth beneath. When their grizzly chore had been completed, they turned to go and collect another one. All the while, the German sentries hovered, rifles slung at the ready, watchful and alert. Every so often a sharp command was meted out to any would be slacker and the words backed up menacingly with a gesture of a bayoneted rifle. Further afield, others were stacking bodies onto a series of horse drawn carts led by armed German handlers. Once full, these carts made their way to the top of the trench and the contents were disgorged into the depths. Yuri watched with grim fascination as a pair of prisoners picked up a body, moved over to the cart and after one, two, three swings, threw it on to the pile. Others were picking up body parts and slinging them on in the same gory way. About a mile behind the burial detail two huge Bulldozers were clanking and snorting along on either side of the trench. Their diesel engines growled and chugged, pushing the earth into the trench and creating a communal burial plot for the unfortunate Russian dead. Every so often, one would straddle the area where the trench had been and so flatten the top to blend in with the undulating terrain of the area. Yuri shook his head, grudgingly admiring the efficiency of the enemy. They would not want the chance of an epidemic resulting from corpses left to rot in the sun. Even the dead horses were being bulldozed into the trench.

Spellbound, Yuri watched as the German soldiers chivvied and drove the prisoners on with shouts of 'Raus, Raus' and 'Schnell, Schnell,' with malevolent gestures from the bayoneted rifles. Suddenly, there was a shout, a prisoner had made a break for it, thinking he could outrun the bullets that now peppered his body. He crumpled, face down on the edge of a smouldering crater. The nearest guard marched over to him and plunged his bayonet once, twice into his back. Then he hawked and spat at the body, muttering obscenities under his breath and beckoned menacingly at two prisoners to come and get the inert form. They reluctantly obeyed, holding their hands up in front of themselves as if warding off any thought the Germans might have of them chancing an escape attempt. They then picked up the body and threw it into the nearest cart along with the rest. The whole episode was over in minutes and the sweepers went back to work, ferrying the dead. Yuri was sickened. Such instant retribution for one brave stupid fool.

At the rear of the column, the German Sergeant smiled grimly and shook his head. Maybe now they would learn, although he doubted it. There was always one willing to give it a try. He looked up as another flight of Heinkels and Messerschmitt's sped across the smoke stained sky. This lot had delivered their payload and were heading west to their airfields in eastern Poland for refuelling and rearming. No doubt there would be another mission for them before the end of the day. He had been impressed by the way the Luftwaffe had gone about their business dealing with the Russian planes. He had witnessed several dog fights during the course of the day and he had seen many planes shot out of the sky. All were now smashed up wrecks on the battlefield, all with the Red Star insignia on the wings or fuselage. He had not seen a

German plane shot down, nor had he heard of one. Again he nodded to himself, satisfied with the day's results.

"Unteroffizer," he yelled. The corporal hurried over, snapped to attention, clicking his heels and gave the straight armed, Nazi salute.

"Jawohl Herr Feldwebel."

The sergeant spoke unhurriedly. "Tell them to get a move on. I want this lot bedded down behind barbed wire for tonight. No more escape attempts hmm! Time is pressing."

"Jawohl Herr Feldwebel," came the reply.

"And corporal, have you seen Private Gruber?"

The corporal's face betrayed no emotion as he replied. "Nein, Herr Feldwebel, "he said innocently.

"Well corporal, when you do see him, tell him that I want to see him immediately. He may be the company's crack shot, but he just can't keep wandering off without telling anyone. Carry on corporal."

"Jawohl Herr Feldwebel, at once sir." The corporal saluted once again and turned, heading back to inform his men. One thing you don't know Herr

Feldwebel sir, he thought to himself, is that Private Gruber is, above all things a thief, a dirty stinking shit stealing thief. I have a very shrewd idea where he is at the moment and it probably involves bodies.

Yuri had no idea what the altercation between the German NCO's was about, but decided he had better not hang around much longer, as his chances of sneaking away into the woods were diminishing with every yard the prisoners cleared. He slid gently down the bank glancing around him and listening intently for any problematic sound that might lead to his discovery. Then he made his way around the corpses and detritus of the shattered trench until he arrived back at where he had started. He gazed down at Grigori and sighed. Would Grigori prefer to be with his comrades, or would it be better to try and take him somewhere quiet and away from here so that Yuri could return with his family and show them where Grigori was laid to rest. He glanced skywards as another flight of aircraft headed towards the east, the black crosses stark against the blue of the summer skies. He decided to go and check out his escape route while he pondered over what he should do with his brother but as he turned to go something moved on the edge of his vision. He melted into the lengthening shadows now dappling the trench and furtively glanced towards the woods.

Coming down through the trees and finally into the trench itself was a German soldier. He moved with a steady purpose but apparently unconcerned about the proximity of immediate danger, as his rifle was slung over his shoulder by the strap. He carried a large pack on his back and moved easily up to the first of the Russian corpses. At this point, he unslung his rifle and his pack, laying them against the side wall of the trench, took off his helmet, undid the buttons of his jacket and removed his webbing belt with its over-the- shoulders accoutrement straps and laid them down next to the pack. He then removed his jacket, laid it on the ground and placed the belt with its accoutrements onto it. Folding it all neatly together, being secured to the top of the pack with a couple of webbing straps, he then stood and rolled up his sleeves. Casually, he began to fleece each body in turn. He went through pockets, searched around the neck and wrist areas and then finally dragged open their mouths and inspected the insides. Each time he found something of interest to him he grunted with satisfaction, totally oblivious to anything but the matter in hand.

Realisation of what the man was doing dawned suddenly on Yuri. He was robbing the corpses. A fucking trophy hunter. The man reached into his breast pocket and pulled out a pair of pliers. Yuri winced as a tooth was extracted with a bone crunching snap. He's after the gold fillings in the teeth thought a shocked Yuri. Then he tried to extract a ring from a finger, failed and so reached into his pack bringing out some large barbed wire clippers and simply hacked the finger off above the knuckle. The finger was then thrown away and the ring placed in a muslin bag, which was also produced from the pack. The bag looked heavy, so Yuri surmised that many more victims had given up their rings through the course of the day. Chains were ripped from necks and more teeth extracted as he moved from corpse to corpse. Yuri was incensed. What kind of vile creature would desecrate a human body so? What warped mind took satisfaction from removing a man's most private possessions? He felt the blood rising into his face, but before the red mist consumed him, his brain screamed caution. He fought down his loathing and concentrated on his own dire predicament. A German in front and more Germans to the rear. Think you stupid shit!, there has to be a way out. He couldn't charge the man, it was much too dangerous, yet he was trapped between the hammer and the anvil. Think. The man was now on the move to the next bunch of corpses, not more than fifteen yards away. Once these were dealt with, then Yuri would be next. He racked his brain, but all he could come up with was a long shot, a really long shot. It was a faint chance, with little hope of success, but it was all he could come up with, given the time.

Silently, he lay down on his right side at a wide part of the floor of the trench, slid the knife from its sheath with his right hand and held it concealed by the side of his body. His left arm he draped behind him. It was a shit plan, but now he was committed. The German carried on with his exertions, humming to himself as he worked. The seconds slowly ticked by into minutes and Yuri began to feel his muscles cramping up. He knew he was nothing like 100%, but forced himself to concentrate. The air in the trench bottom was cloyingly fetid and rancid, he could almost taste the aroma of death. Sweat ran down his back and dripped from the side of his face. Flies swarmed incessantly around him, but he steeled himself against their itchy presence, as he tried to slow and control his breathing. He heard the footfalls behind him, sensed the pack and the rifle being laid down. Any second now. He felt the Germans knee touching his back as he knelt behind him, felt his breath on his cheek and then the fingers gripped Yuri's shoulder and began pulling him backwards to expose Yuri's front.

As Yuri tilted over he exploded into action. The right arm clasping the knife sped upwards and out as the left hand clawed for the back of the Germans neck. Surprise was a total success and the German gawped stupidly as the knife arrowed for his throat. For a split second realisation crossed ghost like across his face, then the knife slit and ripped through the wind pipe and out through the back of the his neck, severing the spinal column on the way. Yuri twisted the blade, yanked out the knife and lunged to his feet. The German slumped slowly backwards, blood pumping from the gaping wound, mouth soundlessly trying to form a scream, fingers groping towards his almost severed throat. Yuri fell on him, knees astride and with both hands raised the knife high above his head and then slammed it into the man's abdomen, just below the sternum. He heard and felt bones splintering. Blood was pumping all over the man's shirt front. Then the Germans body relaxed for the last time. He lay there, oblivious to the flies that fluttered onto his staring wide open eyes. Yuri pushed himself up onto his feet, his breathing coming in ragged gasps and gazed down at his handiwork. Groggily, he staggered sideways, leaning against the side of the trench and retched uncontrollably. He had never killed a man before, but he felt somehow elated. Grigori had been avenged in some small way. He,

Yuri, had killed his first German. He swore it would not be the last.

As his breathing returned to something like normal and the adrenalin ceased pumping through his veins, he took stock of the situation. He knew the other Germans were not far away, so how to dispose of the body? He could drag it into the woods, but then……., why not just leave him here, amongst so many other corpses. He liked the idea, but first he had to make the corpse appear like all the others. Quickly, he knelt, slid out his knife and wiped it clean, then returned it to its sheath. He undid and took off the man's boots and socks, unfastened the waist belt and trouser buttons and pulled the trousers off. Then he dragged off his own boots and trousers and hurriedly slipped the Germans trousers on to himself. Surprisingly, they fitted quite well, even though he was now wearing field grey. He tried the Germans socks and boots. Again they fitted and were so superior to his own army issue. The socks felt wonderful, he had never really worn socks before, only in the army and his issue socks were coarse and itchy, making them uncomfortable to wear. He then clumsily put his own trousers on the dead German. Then his own boots, but he kept the socks for the future. Autumn would not be long in coming. He was aware of more shouted commands coming from the direction of the burial detail, but there had been no more shots.

He grabbed the corpse by the arms and dragged it over to where Grigori and the others were laid. He moved Grigori out of the way and laid the corpse face down against the side of the trench so as to conceal the slashed throat from would be prying eyes. At least the hair was dark brown in colour, much the same as his own. This was no Aryan blond that he had heard so much about. He would merge in nicely. Just for added effect, he cascaded soil from the trench wall to partially cover the features and stood back to admire his work. There was no doubt now that he would have to move Grigori, no way would he leave him with such a vile creature for company. He could see no reason why anything but a close scrutiny would reveal the truth about the corpse. It was just another brown uniformed body in a trench full of them. A shouted command from the burial detail galvanised him into action. He moved over to where the blood was thickest and kicked mud and soil over it. It would have to do. He picked up the rifle and pack, but what to do with the helmet. Hide it. He picked it up and crossed over to where Maslak's dismembered body had shielded Yuri from detection and shoved the helmet behind it and out of sight. It was the best he could come up with. Then he made his way to the end of the trench, to the area where the trench stopped and the trees of the wood began. There was a small patch of open ground where he would be out in the open before entering the security of the trees and he paused to check that no eyes were aimed in his direction. Luckily, the trench walls masked any view of the burial detail and satisfied, he walked off into the trees for about 30 yards and laid down the rifle and pack. Then, he crept forward to his right through the trees, until he could see out over the battlefield. The scene was much as before, although they were moving much, much closer. He still had time, but only just. The two Bulldozers were working the flanks of the trench. Only if they moved onto the top would there be a chance of him being seen as he emerged with Grigori and carried him into the woods. Quickly, he retraced his steps, sat Grigori upright and with a heave, lifted him onto his knees, then he bent forward, allowing the body to fall over his right shoulder and powered himself upright. Grigori was a heavy man, more so in death, a dead weight. He shrugged the body further over his shoulder to achieve a better balance and then marched purposely out of the trench and into the woods, until he arrived at where he had left the rifle and pack and laid Grigori gently down. He was sweating profusely as he breathed out a long sigh of relief. There had been no cry of alarm signifying that he had been spotted, but he was not in a position of safety yet. In the trench he had done all he could and now it was up to providence.

He also knew that he was almost spent, the ravages of the day's events had taken their toll, but he needed to find somewhere to hole up for the night and hopefully to get some sleep. With that in mind, he steeled himself for one last effort. Grigori and the rifle and pack he hid away from the path and out of sight. Then he marched off into the deeper woods. The air in the woods was so much cooler and sweeter than the confines of the trench. He walked along between towering pines and groups of oaks, alders and scrub brush. In some places the trees thinned out into grass covered glades. Dense thickets of thorny bushes gave way to marsh and bog and he was careful not to leave too much of a trail for others to follow. The path rose gently ahead and he moved by rocky outcrops with gnarled pines and stunted aspens, interspersed with thorn and thicket. After about half a mile he found what he had been looking for. The marshes were riddled with small streams which by various means found their way into the River Pripet and on into the Dnieper and the Bug. One of these streams had, in time of flood, carved out the rock wall to afford a long fissure about twelve feet long and perhaps, four feet high. The outcrop above it rose vertically up about fifteen feet and atop stood a stunted, gnarled oak, its hoary lichen covered roots spread in all directions, in search of water and sustenance. Yuri rested for a few minutes, squatting on his haunches and saw that a watcher could only see into the fissure from the low boggy ground on the opposite side of the stream. It fitted the bill almost perfectly.

So gathering up his strength, he made his cautious way back to Grigori plus the rifle and pack. It took him all of forty minutes to carry Grigori back to the hide, having to stop three times for rests. Finally, he was able to squeeze Grigori under the overhang. Then he returned for the rifle and pack. All the time he had been in the woods he had been listening and watching, always aware of the danger that lurked all around him. He had heard nothing untoward, apart from the distant burial detail and the drone of aircraft. He now drifted stealthily through the trees until he could see over the battlefield. The German troops were herding the Russian prisoners back towards the road and were well over a mile away. One of the Bulldozers was also clanking its way back, while the other finished the job of flattening the trench. There had been no hue and cry, no warning sounds of discovery. The evidence of his killing was buried forever within a bulldozed trench. Within three months no-one would know it existed.

He took one last look and turned on his heels, picked up the rifle and pack and wearily trudged back to his brother. The last twenty-four hours would be forever imprinted in his brain. Today was his eighteenth birthday.

Chapter 2 – The Island

For Yuri, morning came late and grey. When he finally opened his eyes, the whole area was blanketed in mist, a mist that clung to the trees and made visibility next to nothing. He lay still, allowing his ears and eyes to become accustomed to his surroundings. Satisfied that the morning posed no immediate threat, he adjusted his position to allow his cramped muscles to flex and then settled down to allow the sun to work its magic on the mist. He had slept fitfully, assailed by strange dreams and visions, until he must have finally drifted into exhausted oblivion. How long he had slept he had no idea, but he felt better and rested. Before settling down for the night, he had rummaged through the Germans pack and found a greatcoat tucked away at the bottom. This he used as a blanket, with the rolled up jacket as a pillow. His own blanket had disappeared from the trench, as had everyone else's and he presumed that the enemy had claimed them. He had also found a drab coloured Poncho that would be very useful come the sudden summer downpours that regularly sprinkled the area. The Germans water canteen was almost full and he drank thirstily while he munched on some hardtack biscuits that he had also found. It wasn't much, but for a man who hadn't eaten for twenty-four hours, very welcome. He had put off searching for any other treasures in the pack pockets until today, as he was almost out on his feet.

The thought of the remaining water and biscuits prompted him to locate the rest now, but as he was about to move, something stirred at the edge of his vision. Very slowly, he swivelled his head and saw, across the stream, a large furry shape emerge through the tendrils of mist. The bear hesitated on the other side of the stream, not more than twenty yards away. It sat back on its haunches and cast its head about from side to side, nose raised, to sniff the air. Yuri remained stock still. The bear was obviously curious and could probably scent Yuri's presence. It made a strange kind of whining noise as it dropped back onto all fours and appeared very agitated. Then Yuri realised, he was not the subject of the bears discontent. It was Grigori. Yuri was beginning to tell, that his brother was not smelling too sweet. The bear growled deep in its throat and rocked back and forth, fearing the man smell, but hunger was playing its part. What to do, thought Yuri? He daren't shoot the creature, as noise was the last thing he wanted. He had no idea who could be around the vicinity, so he determined to wait it out and hoped that eventually, the bear would relent. Time crept slowly by. He was aware of the sound of the gently flowing stream that eddied and swirled over the rocky stream bed. Somewhere a water droplet fell noisily into a puddle and in the strange murky silence it sounded loud and foreboding. Eventually, the bear let out an exasperated snort, turned and disappeared back through the mist portal, its fear of man overcoming its hunger, at least for now. Yuri ruefully reflected that had it been springtime, with young cubs to feed, the outcome may not have been so fortuitous. However, it meant that he had better dispose of Grigori's body sooner rather than later.

The sound of dripping water was becoming more pronounced and frequent and as he looked upwards into the distant trees he saw the ghostly circular spectre of the sun haloing above the tree tops. Before long it would be full light he thought and he had better prepare for the task ahead. He came to his knees and shrugged off the greatcoat, laying it carefully to one side. The night had been cold and the dew had laid a damp sheen of condensation over the coats surface. He brushed his hand over it, wiping away the silver droplets. Forget it, he thought. The sun will dry it soon enough. He took another long survey of his surroundings, listening intently for anything to cause him concern. In the distance, he heard the distinct sound of a woodpecker hammering away at some tree. The realisation pleased him. It was a normal sound opposed to the unnatural tumult of the previous day. He smiled to himself as he moved over to the pack and set it near to the edge of the fissure where he could inspect more of the contents. He sat with his legs dangling over the edge to where the stream gurgled six inches below his feet. The sound of the running water was a salve to his spirit and after another careful look around, he undid the strap on a side pocket. Reaching inside, he pulled out a long cylindrical object that was wrapped in a soft muslin bag. He carefully stripped open the cover and gazed in awe at a pristine, black metallic, telescopic sight. He marvelled at the precision and delicate detail of the piece, rolling it between his fingers. Lifting it up, he placed it to his right eye, the rubber lens cap sitting comfortably and easily in his eye socket. He scanned the area with it, moving upwards and outwards until he settled on a clump of trees on a knoll, maybe half a mile away. They appeared quite blurred so he fiddled with the dials and moving parts of the scope until suddenly, the trunk of a tree leapt into sharp relief. He could make out the bark of a twisted oak and as he panned upwards, spotted the culprit of noise he had been hearing for the last few minutes. The woodpecker filled the scope and Yuri revelled in the simplistic beauty of the bird, as it hammered away searching for grubs. So, he thought, the German had been a sniper. Laying it gently down in its wrappings, Yuri pulled out another two cylindrical bags, one of which proved to be another telescopic sight, albeit a few inches shorter than the other. Perhaps, he thought, one is for distance and the other for close up's, although he had no idea, never having come into contact with a scope before. He had heard about them and recognised what it was instantly, but that was all. The other bag contained what turned out to be a sturdy metal two legged bipod, which would clip onto the rifle barrel near the end of the muzzle. When in place, it would give a very stable platform for a laid down sniper looking to execute opponents when the opportunity arose. Yuri shivered involuntarily. If the enemy had these, then nobody was safe, even at a distance. He carefully wrapped up the three pieces and put them back into the pack pocket, but then, on a hunch, kept out the long scope. It would come in handy for the day ahead, as he knew he could not carry the rifle with him. Rummaging around in the bag he found a lanyard. He thought he'd seen it earlier and it would be perfect for carrying the scope. He removed the scope from its muslin bag, popped the bag back into the side pocket and deftly slid the noose of the lanyard around the scope and tightened it. Perfect, he thought. Then he placed the other end around his neck. The scope swung freely and safely.

He put off any more searching as time was pressing. The sun had all but burnt away the mist. He reached into his breast pocket and pulled out a silver pocket watch. He had found it last evening, along with about a dozen others, in another part of the pack. More of the Germans ill-gotten gains. It was a beautiful time piece, delicately engraved with swirling concentric circles around a flower, complete with stem and leaves. Yuri had no idea what the flower was, but admired the ornate pattern. On the reverse were three Russian characters which spelt out V.A.L. Someone's initials perhaps, thought Yuri, although he didn't recognise them. When the cover was opened, it revealed a simple clock face and he noticed that the time was ten thirty-five. Time to move, he thought and admonished himself for falling under the spell of the scope and watch. He snapped back the cover and slipped it back into his breast pocket.

Quickly, he packed away the jacket and greatcoat. Abruptly he realised that he had forgotten all about eating anything, so he pulled out another two hardtack biscuits from the Germans provision tin and in doing so, unearthed a couple of bars of chocolate. He consumed half of one of the bars after the hardtack and washed it down with the rest of the water. OK, he said to himself, time to go. He tightened up all the straps, picked up the Germans entrenching tool which had hung from the webbing belt. It was light but strong, with a solid sharpened blade and the handle folded in half to allow for ease of carrying. A simple nut and bolt held the handle in place when extended. Yuri reflected that it was a little short in power and surface area for the kind of job he had to do, but it was all he had. It would have to suffice. He bent down and refilled the canteen, whilst scanning the area for any unwelcome guests. Satisfied, he clipped the canteen to his belt.

Cautiously, he peered around the edge of the overhang. Then he stood and searched all around for any sign of movement. Hopefully, the bear was long gone, but he daren't leave Grigori for any length of time in case the creature returned. Stealthily, he climbed up to the path and again searched around. Nothing. He could see nor hear anything. Turning, he dropped back down to where Grigori, the pack and the rifle lay. He picked up the pack and humped it onto his back. Then the rifle was slung over his shoulder. He climbed up to the path again and turned towards the gnarled oak, searching for a place within the branches to leave the pack and rifle. He thought he'd spotted a place and began to climb the tree. Sure enough, about fifteen feet from the ground he found the perfect hiding place. The oak split here into two distinct trunks which afforded an area where the pack could sit quite safely. He knew that bears could climb trees, but hoped that the man scent would keep it away. Anyway, there was nothing more he could do. The rifle, he hung from a short protruding branch. Only if someone looked directly at them from the base of the tree would they be seen. He nodded, satisfied and clambered down. Then he went for Grigori. He eased his brother out from under the overhang and pulled him clear of the fissures entrance. There's nothing for it, he thought, I'm going to have to pull him up the bank by his arms. There's just no way I can balance down here by the water's edge. So, he took hold of Grigori's hands and unceremoniously dragged him up the bank. Yuri lay him down in the dust as he caught his breath and scanned the area. All appeared OK. As yesterday, he sat Grigori upright then raised him to his feet, bent over double and let him fall across his shoulder. Then he adjusted the balance and set off to find his brothers burial site.

The path wove in and out between the boggy areas and the woods. He paused several times to view potential sites, but decided that all were unsuitable. He was looking for somewhere that offered protection from the spring and autumn floods, an area of height, although it wouldn't be considerable. That was the main criteria. He couldn't stand the thought of his brother in an area immersed in water. It never occurred to him what an area of marshland tended to be. However, he was only on the edge of the immense Pripet Marshes and there was a certain amount of high ground where he now stood. It had to be somewhere where flowers would grow and the wind could blow through the trees unhindered. Grigori had been a lover of the great expanses of Mother Russia and it had to be a spot where the view stretched for mile upon mile in all directions. He laid Grigori down while he took a breather and he pondered upon a suitable place. It dawned on him, that perhaps he had seen such a place this morning, when he had been looking through the scope. He needed to find Woodpecker Knoll. He had a general idea where he would find it, so he loaded Grigori onto his back once again and trudged off down the path. After about half an hours travel, he arrived at the place where he believed the knoll to be. It was a peaceful area, the sun shining down, dappling the leaves and branches, as he laid Grigori flat and stepped out into a small meadow. Before him, the ground sloped steeply upwards, the grassy banks waving gently in the summer breeze. He looked around, always fearful of being caught unawares and listened keenly to what the breeze told him. He could neither see nor hear the imminence of danger. Quickly, he climbed up the grass matted bank and crested the summit between two tall pines and walked into a tiny clearing awash with wild flowers. He gazed around in sheer reverence at the beauty of the place. Surely God lived here. Without further ado, he strode back down the bank, picked up Grigori by the arms and dragged him through the grass, up the hill and finally, into the glade between the trees. Then he removed the scope from around his neck and moved to the edge of the clearing, belly down in the long grass. Cautiously, he scanned the whole area north, east and west, both short and distant. The scope was a huge aid to spotting anything that moved and he could see plenty moving. About ten miles away the road to Minsk was clogged with traffic, all heading east. The dry summer conditions, caused clouds of dust to rise chokingly around the advancing columns and the scene looked desperately chaotic. He could make out a few mechanised trucks and many horse drawn vehicles, with soldiers marching along on foot. To the west he spotted what remained of a deserted Russian village and he could just make out lines of trucks and various wagons lined up there. He surmised it was some sort of field headquarters and the thought logged in his mind. Anyway, there was no immediate threat to himself as far as he could see. He pulled back from the edge, moved over to Grigori and put the scope down. Then he chose an area to begin his task.

Yuri had helped to dig graves in the past. It was a hard fact of life that death came often in a large community, where he lived. The young men of the town were always on hand to help their neighbours in times of crisis. Now, he stood surveying the terrain and began to map out an area with the entrenching tool. He dug down to a depth of a few inches and lifted out a six inch square sod. This he placed to one side. Then he dug out more sods, arranging them in order until he had cleared an area roughly six feet by three feet. The summer sun was at its peak now as he started to dig down. He paused often for rests and to have a drink of water from the canteen which he used sparingly. An hour passed and he suddenly hit bedrock. Maybe five feet or more. It will have to do he thought. He clambered out of the grave and strode over to Grigori. He suddenly thought, I have nothing to wrap the body in. He sighed. There was nothing for it. Grigori had to be laid to rest. He picked him up under the shoulder blades and moved him over to the graves edge. Then he let him lie while he got into the grave itself. Drawing his brother into the grave, he laid him down, face pointing to the sky. He had deliberately dug the grave in an east-west direction, so Grigori's head would be pointing towards home and the sun would rise at his head and set at his feet. He knelt and reaching below his brothers shirt, removed the chain from around Grigori's neck, which held the large plain silver cross, the cross that had been handed down to the eldest son of their family for generations. Then he folded his brother's arms across his chest and climbed back out of the grave. He knelt at the edge gazing down at his brother for the last time. He muttered a few words of the old psalms he remembered from his childhood, signed the cross and closed his eyes in silent prayer. Minutes passed, then he opened his eyes, stood up and gazed down at his brother through tears that streamed and tumbled down his heartbroken face.

"Grigori," he croaked. "I will avenge you a thousand fold." With that, he turned and started filling in the grave, never once looking into the depths, until all the soil had been replaced. He flattened it down as best he could and then re-arranged the sods in the order that he had extracted them. Finally, he searched around the edges of the knoll for some rocks which he placed as a small cairn around two feet high in the graves centre. Fashioning a small cross of oak, he draped the cross over the three points. This he placed in the middle of the cairn and pushed it down into the soil until it disappeared below the cairns surface. Then he placed a final rock to cover the cairn's centre. In a few weeks, the area atop the knoll would appear as untouched and the flowers would grow in profusion. As if to help the healing process, clouds appeared and the area was drenched in a sudden shower. By then, Yuri had picked up the entrenching tool, fitted the scope back onto the lanyard and placed it around his neck before leaving the site. He was now well on his way back to where he had left the rifle and pack.

The path meandered gently downhill through thick stands of trees and numerous boggy areas. He walked purposefully but watchfully, until he spied a turn in the trail that he had not perceived when coming from the opposite direction. It was a small gap between two pines, but it seemed to offer an alternative route to where he had left his things. Before long, the path widened and moved southwards and he seemed to be heading into a much denser part of the woods and marsh. The sunlight struggled to penetrate the thick overhead leaf filled branches, but they came in handy when the shower arrived. Yuri decided to rest a while under the canopy of a giant oak while the rain passed. There were actually two oaks straddling the path, huge gnarled and twisted forms with long limbed branches. He sat down with his back against one of the trees. Suddenly, he detected movement up ahead, to the right of the path. He froze, waiting for whatever to happen, until a small nose squeezed out of the tree trunks, attached to a Roe deer. The little doe stood listening and sniffing the air until apparently satisfied, she skipped over the path and disappeared into the trees opposite. Yuri breathed a sigh of relief. What had made him leave the rifle behind, when he was in such close proximity to danger, he had no idea. Anything could have come out of those trees. After ten minutes or so, he noticed the little doe returning. She once again tested the air before skipping over the path and back into the trees from where she had originally come from.

Yuri was curious. From where he sat, not ten yards away, the thicket wall on the left seemed impenetrable, yet she had obviously been somewhere. He got to his feet and hesitatingly walked over to where she had done her vanishing trick. There was nothing, no way through that he could see. He searched the ground and saw a track, then another. He was determined to follow them even though he had no idea why. Call it a hunch, he mused to himself. He moved between two trees and a space opened up to his right which he followed, then between two more trunks and then a left. It was quite dark here where the thick tangle of brush and thorn merged into the trees and overhanging foliage. He was forever catching his clothing on thorns until he became irritated and tried to smash a path through them. Inevitably, some drew blood and he winced several times. His feet kept slipping on tree roots and he tripped twice, painfully cracking his knee on the second occasion and he swore repeatedly. Finally he staggered out from the restrictive trees into a clear space, where the path was more defined and this he followed. He now had a definite goal in sight, as he could see water ahead through the tangled branches. Looking down, he saw more tracks and followed them until he emerged at the water's edge. The little doe had obviously come down here for a drink. Looking around him, he realised that the journey through the thicket had been well worth it. He beheld a large expanse of water which lay to both left and right. To his left, thick reed beds lined the water's edge for about a hundred yards, before curving round in a steady sweep, then onwards towards the south with more reeds and thick stands of pine and aspen. To the right, it was almost a mirrored image, with, after two hundred yards or so, a gentle curve to where the reed fringed banks stretched also southward. Effectively, like the horns of a bull. But what fascinated Yuri the most, was in front of him.

Seventy-five or so yards across the water was what appeared to be an island, and an island of some size? It was covered in trees and the leaf laden aspen branches, hung down until they touched the water, forming an impenetrable screen. The foliage was so thick that he could only guess at what lay within the confines of the islands interior. But some inner voice was telling him that he must explore its beguiling presence. At the west end of the island, he could see the gradual rise of a huge slab of rock. Here the trees were sparse and stunted, clinging on to the rocks with a tenacious grip. Many had succumbed to the ravages of the bitter winds that frequently lashed their way across the steppes of Mother Russia and lay smashed and forlorn down the rock sides. Yuri likened the island to a large ship with the deck to the east and the bridge to the west. He knew he had to explore it. Tearing his eyes away he studied his immediate surroundings. The water seemed deep with an appearance of washed out blue reflecting the wide open summer skies. He searched around for a branch and managed to drag one out of the thicket which was about eight feet long. Moving to the water's edge, he shoved the branch down into the watery depths, but even by extending the length by immersing his arm up to his bicep, he couldn't touch bottom. It was deep, he concluded. Moving to his left along the bank he tried again and again to find bottom, but it was always beyond his reach. He finally came to where the reeds began and here, he found the depth to be a few feet. The reeds themselves were tightly packed and stretched out into the water for about ten feet, providing an almost impenetrable barrier between the land and the water. To his side, the trunk of a huge oak towered into the sky, the gnarled roots spreading out like giant tentacles searching for sustenance and stability. The branches, just above Yuri's head were thick and lichen covered, stretching all around and even out over the reeds. The trunk, steepled upwards towards a magnificent leaf screened crown. Yuri was impressed.

He glanced back towards where the path would run, parallel to his position and realised that a line of pines marched downwards to meet the oak. He counted four in the line, their bases set in a rocky, watery channel that ran down to the open water. The scrub and thorns had grown across the water channel and reached upwards around the pines to about ten feet above the ground. The bottom branches of the pines he could see were short, many having broken off into tiny stumps, but the trees rose gracefully towards the sky. Yuri determined to find where they emerged once he got back to the path. He walked back along the lakes edge thinking yes, it must be a lake or mere, but he couldn't be sure. His view was too restricted. He carried on past where he had first tested the depth. The ground here was rocky and slippery, but he carried on cautiously, until he reached the area where the right hand stand of reeds started. Here, was a kind of bay, with a muddy, sandy surface. He spotted several sets of tracks in the mud, mostly deer and water fowl, but then his eyes fastened on a couple of sets of large prints. He knelt down and studied them. They could be human tracks, he thought, but they were ill defined and appeared old. He looked around, suddenly nervous, nonetheless, he was quite alone. He looked back down at the tracks, but they gave no clue as to their origin. Then he noticed a long groove through the mud that started by the water's edge and ran inland for about eight feet. The groove stopped abruptly before the edge of the bay. He racked his brains, but nothing made sense. The groove was virtually symmetrical with a depth of about three inches, the sides almost square. A fallen branch, mused Yuri? But where has it gone? It couldn't just jump out itself, could it? He shook his head in bewilderment. It didn't make sense. And the tracks, were they somehow connected? Nothing would come to him. He shook his head frustratingly and made his way back to the entrance to the thicket and set about trying to find his way out. This time, he realised that had taken a wrong turning, when he had initially forced his way through. The intricate way the path squeezed through the trees and brush was compounded, when coming from the path's direction, by the thicket to his left. He realised that he had taken a right when he should have taken a left and the way out proved much easier, without the drama of the thorns. He peered out between the two pines, saw and heard nothing to alarm him and stepped back onto the path.

He studied the area where he thought the pines from the water's edge led up to and discovered that they did indeed lead up towards the path, but the final tree in the line was an oak that stood at the head of the column abutting the pathway. Again he noticed the branches fanned out all around and a thick one ran right over the path about three feet above Yuri's head. The sun dappled down through the leaf filled crown. It's as well to know something of your immediate area thought Yuri. The afternoon was passing now and he still had to find his way back to the pack and rifle. Looking at his watch he saw that it was three fifteen. Time enough for a little more exploration. He set off along the path in the hope of finding out where it led and if it tied in with the other northern path at some stage. By his reckoning, the place where he had hidden the pack and rifle was almost due north of him now. If that was the case, then at some point, he must reach and have to cross the stream. The path wound in and out through bog filled clearings and tree filled woods. The late afternoon sun was still dappling the woodland floor and all signs of the rain shower had evaporated away. He knew the lake was somewhere south and east, but the terrain had hidden it from his sight. Eventually, he came to the stream and by a series of randomly placed rocks, acting as stepping stones, he crossed to the other side. The path had been turning increasingly northwards for the last fifteen minutes and then suddenly he was back on the path that led down to the trench. He turned and studied where yesterday's path angled left and realised that the new path he had just come up, was quite difficult to make out when walking up from the trench, as he had done yesterday. Again, it passed between several close fitting trees and would have not appeared as a likely route. Well, he thought, now that I'm here, I may as well have a look around. He cautiously made his way down the path, to the opening in the trees which led to where he had exited yesterday. After a careful scan of the immediate area, he settled down, with his back to a tree and lifted the scope.

To his left and centre, the battlefield was laid out before him. The pockmarked landscape brought the memories flooding back. He sighted on the spot where the Russian soldier had tried to escape and realised that he was trying to make for a brush covered hillock and then on into thick woods. Once in there, he could have run a long way without being noticed by anyone. Such a waste, he thought, it's all such a waste. Some megalomaniac of a German Corporal, decides he wants to expand his little empire and all this death and destruction is down to him. Who knows where or when it will end? Having said that, he thought, is Stalin and Communism any better? He very much doubted it. Only time will tell. As he sat there soaking up the evening sun, he slapped absently at a mosquito on his neck. Another three had landed on his leg and he leaned forward lazily to swish them away. The movement undoubtedly saved his life. A bullet smashed into the trunk of the tree where a second ago he had been resting, followed by the sound of the shot, echoing through the air. Yuri was momentarily stunned and then reacted by rolling to his left and coming to his feet in a rush. Another bullet cannoned into the tree by his head, showering his face and eyes with sharp wooden splinters, before ricocheting off into the woods. He clawed at his eyes trying to brush away the splinters as he ran full pelt up the path between the trees. He had felt the wind of that one and it can't have missed him by much. Another two shots zinged harmlessly past him and he heard shouts from the direction of the woods to his right. He had a vague recollection of a group of armed soldiers in field grey running towards him, as he turned from the shock of the first bullet. Now, he was running for his life. He reached the point where the paths diverged and took the one down towards the lake. Another bullet smashed into a tree a yard away from him and he careered onwards towards the stream. He took the stepping stones at break neck speed, slipped on the second to last one and crashed into the water, banging his head on a rock. Blood streamed down his face and he was momentarily stunned, until terror gripped him and he staggered to his feet and forced himself to keep going. He ran as he had never run, legs and arms pumping, the entrenching tool swinging manically behind him, until he heard a sound that filled him with terror and foreboding. Dogs, he could hear dogs. Men he could outrun, but dogs? He heard more shouts to his left, some men were on the other path, but then he heard the dogs barking behind him. Fear coursed through his veins giving him more speed, his breathing ragged and strained. Think, his brain screamed, dogs will follow scents and you're leaving a fucking big scent, because you've been here before today. Think.

It came to him in a flash of inspiration. Dogs can't follow a scent in the air. He knew what he had to do, even though he had no idea if the plan was viable. Coming round a bend he saw the oak with its branch crossing the trail and at full speed leapt into the air and grabbed it with both hands. His natural momentum carried him upwards and then he swung back. Somehow, he powered himself upwards and threw his left leg over the branch. Curling the right leg up to join it, he steadied himself and hauled his body arm over arm until his head touched the main trunk. Releasing his left arm and leg, he swung downwards and turned to face the tree. Managing to find a foothold and a higher handhold, he dragged himself up onto a thick branch which stretched out towards the first of the four pines. He was at least fourteen feet above the ground by now and he steadied himself before leaping across the gap. Flinging his arms around the pine's trunk he searched for and found a foothold and pushing off on it, he leapt for the next tree in line. Again he grabbed the trunk and somehow managed to push off to the next one. He grabbed it and held on, breath coming in rasping gasps, as his strength was waning. Again the dogs, ever closer and more shouts. This galvanised him into an all-out final effort. One to go and then the oak. He pushed off again towards the final pine, but the short stubby branch one of his feet was on, snapped as he tried to take off. He made the gap but only just, ending up well down the trunk as his feet and then his lower legs bit into the thorns and scrub. Grabbing hold desperately to the trunk he clung on, scraping and sliding, fighting for purchase to stop his downward momentum into the thickly packed thorns. Scrabbling and scrambling, his hands and fingers bleeding from the many cuts and bruises, he hauled himself, bit by agonising bit from the gripping grasp of the thorns. They tore and scratched at his legs until he reached a point where he broke free of their snagging grasp and he found a handhold and foothold to raise himself upwards. Another few feet and he would be able to reach a thick branch of the oak at the water's edge, which leaned down towards him. Wearily he struggled upwards and finally tugged himself up onto it, grabbing for smaller branches above and around him as he fought to stand upright. Side stepping along the branch he rounded the trunk hand over hand, and stepped out onto a thinner bough that stretched out over the reed fringe. He moved sideways along the bough as quickly as he dare, grasping at short twigs for some sort of steadiness, swaying dangerously back and forth as he fought to maintain his equilibrium. Alarmingly, the branch began to bend under his weight, though he was still short of the water at the edge of the reeds by three or four feet. Unable to put it off any longer, he took one long desperate step, pushed off and launched himself at the water. The branch held, and his feet just clipped the reeds as he fell rather than dived into the cold blue water.

Chapter 3 – The Cave

As Yuri hit the water, surfaced and struck out for the island, the dogs, in the form of two Dobermans, arrived at the place where he had lunged up onto the overhanging oak branch. They skidded to a halt, unsure as to which scent to follow, padding around in circles, moving between the two places where the scent was strongest, whining to themselves. One went to where Yuri had rested earlier, whilst the other concentrated on the area between the trees which led, eventually, to the lake edge. A soldier arrived, followed by another and then the corporal from the burial detail, the day before. The Doberman by the tree where Yuri had earlier watched the little doe, was pacing about and whining in an obviously agitated manner. One of the soldiers ran over to him.

"Unteroffizer," he shouted, "over here."

The corporal rushed over, leaving the other Doberman to its deliberations. "Where the hell is he?" he snapped at the private. "Have the dogs found him?"

"I don't think so Unteroffizer," came the reply, "but the dog is certainly onto something. Look, what's he doing," exclaimed the private.

The corporal looked and saw that the dog had its front paws on the tree trunk and was looking upwards, sniffing the air. "He's up in the branches," yelled the corporal. "Everyone fan out and search the trees." The soldiers did as the corporal ordered, just as another two ran up followed by the sergeant.

"What's happening corporal," demanded the sergeant breathlessly, "have you found him?"

"Nien, nien, Herr Feldwebel," the corporal replied exasperatedly. "We think he could have taken to the trees."

"So get your arses up there and find him," snapped the sergeant, "if he's there he can't be far off'."

"You," he sapped at the two soldiers who had arrived with him. "Get on up the path and keep searching." "Jawohl Herr Feldwebel," came the reply and the men rushed off.

"Schmidt," yelled the corporal, "can you see anything up there?" The soldier up the tree shook his head.

"Quiet," whispered the sergeant. "If he's up there the dogs may hear him." Everyone stopped and listened, the dogs whining their way back and forth, tossing their heads in the air, but both showed no signs of anything other than the fact that the scent was on the ground.

"It's hopeless," muttered the corporal, "he's long gone."

"OK corporal," said the sergeant. "Send someone to bring back the other two. We've wasted enough time over this. It looks like he's given us the slip. Get the others to search around for a bit longer, but we need to be back at base camp before the next batch of prisoners arrives from the front. There'll be hell to pay with the Major if we're late."

"Jawohl, Herr Feldwebel," came the reply. The corporal gave out his orders, Private Schmidt coming down from the trees. The dogs continued to pace around, still keen on the scent. One of them was sniffing and whining around the area of the path between the two trees.

"Call the dog off corporal," said the sergeant. "There's no way anyone could get through that thicket. The thorns would tear you apart."

"But Sir," replied the corporal, "there are tracks."

"There may well be," said the sergeant pointedly, "but only from small animals. A man couldn't get through there."

"But sir," insisted the corporal, "there's a boot print over here, come and look."

The sergeant wandered over disinterestedly. "Well, yes corporal," he admitted showing slightly more interest. "There is a print, but are there any others? Deer tracks are not enough."

"Sir," cried the corporal excitedly, "there's another partial track here, between these two pines."

"OK corporal, see if it leads anywhere," muttered the sergeant. "Schmidt, go with him. The rest of you wait here." The corporal and private moved off into the trees. After much thrashing around, they emerged in the clearing and saw the dog down by the water's edge.

"Sir," hailed the corporal, "you'd better come through and have a look." After a few minutes, the sergeant arrived in the clearing.

"That was a bit hairy corporal. What was it you wanted?"

"Well sir," said the corporal. "There are quite a few tracks around here. See, over there and by that big oak."

The sergeant inspected the prints and mused, "Well, they are boot prints corporal and quite recent, but where could he have gone from here? As far as I can see, there's only where we came in. Could he have swam over to that island?"

"Yes, he could sir," replied the corporal, "but not if it's who I think it is."

"Go on corporal," said the sergeant.

"Well sir," the corporal replied. "I was thinking that the tracks were from Private Gruber. I caught a glimpse of the man when he bolted into the trees after our shots missed him and I could swear that he was wearing field grey pants sir. The boot tracks look like German army issue as well."

"But you said that the person you were thinking about couldn't have swam over to the island," said the sergeant. "Does that mean Gruber couldn't swim?"

"That's correct sir," replied the corporal. "You remember the river crossing yesterday?" The sergeant nodded. "Gruber was in one of the follow up boats, the one that a Russian shell landed close to and pitched some of the men out into the water. He went in with Schmidt and three others. Schmidt told me that he had to haul Gruber back into the boat, after he had almost gone down twice. He was just thrashing about, screaming that he couldn't swim. So Gruber couldn't have swum over to the island, he wouldn't dare."

"Interesting," said the sergeant, "I hadn't realised Gruber had caused so much fuss. Do you think he could have deserted?"

"I can't answer that sir," said the corporal, "but we know of no other person at large in the area."

"A mystery corporal eh?" said the sergeant, "but we can't spend any more time here. Find your way back through those trees and get the men sorted out."

The corporal obeyed, slipping the leash onto the dog and handing it over to Schmidt. They made their way back to the path. The two soldiers who had been searching up the path came jogging back with the private sent to collect them. At the sergeants unspoken glance they chorused, "No sign of him, Herr Feldwebel."

"Right," said the sergeant, "get them formed up corporal and let's get back to base. This has been a total washout." The corporal busied himself with getting the men together and leashing the other dog. Then he gave the command to move out. The unit trooped off with the sergeant and corporal bringing up the rear. "Bad business corporal," said the sergeant in a low voice, "bad business."

When the sergeant and corporal were mulling over the whereabouts of the unknown felon, down by the water's edge, Yuri had his scope trained on them from the shelter of the trees on the island. Miraculously, the scope had stayed with him, although it was scratched and tarnished from water and tree branches. However, his passage across to the island and subsequent landing on it, had not been without its problems. It was a long way for him to swim in his present condition, but thankfully he had made it. The far side of the island, for he now knew it was an island, had a rocky foreshore that extended out into the lake for a few yards, affording him a relatively easy way out when he most needed it. He arrived soaked, battered and bruised but intact. He had crawled up onto the shore and collapsed with sheer exhaustion, while his breath retched achingly from his tortured lungs. He spat out bits of debris from his mouth, aware that he had gulped down many mouthfuls of lake water. He felt disgustingly sick and stomach cramps assailed him until he finally threw up. Nauseous and light headed, he just lay, watching the bile run in tiny rivulets over the rocks. If someone had heard him throwing up, he just couldn't have cared less. There was no more escape left in him. Finally, the cramps ceased to be as powerful and he slowly raised his head and looked around. To his right, the rocks petered out towards the end of the island, the magnificent cascading branches of the aspens took over and formed an impenetrable barrier to the east. In front, the land rose steeply to what appeared to be a flat plateau, where the pines grew in serried ranks, marching upwards towards the western end. To his left, the rocks continued for a few yards until they merged into a small bay of sandy mud, similar to what he had encountered earlier that day. Strangely, there also seemed to be the same sort of square sided three inch deep gully in the mud. He raised himself up on his arms and knees and peered through the trailing aspen branches. What he saw made his blood run cold.

Under the screening branches and nestled in an out of the way corner was a boat, the handles of two paddles sticking out from the prow. So he was not alone. Someone else was on the island. Someone who was, or could be, watching him now. He glanced nervously around, all thoughts of safety destroyed by his discovery. He listened, and heard noises from the mainland, shouts and commands and the bark of those damned dogs. Were those sounds really from the mainland, or were some of them from his immediate vicinity? No matter, he had to move, here he was too exposed. He searched upwards, listening intently for anything untoward and hostile. Sliding his knife from its sheath he moved, upwards and onwards, towards the sentinel pines. He noticed that there were footholds, seemingly carved out of the rock, making his ascent much easier than he had imagined. Someone had been busy, someone somewhere in front. Feeling totally naked and vulnerable, his eyes nervously crested the top of the rock plateau and searched meticulously around for any sign of life. A shout from the mainland scared him, making him jump with fright, but nothing appeared to be an immediate threat to his wellbeing. Unsure and terrified, he raised up behind a pine and moved gently from tree to tree until he came to the edge of the plateau above the east shore. The adrenaline was back, pumping through his veins, as he searched across the island towards the west.

Nothing. No movement, no signs and no tracks. He moved on, across the edge of the island, making for somewhere to observe the German presence. The aspens afforded him cover from prying eyes on the opposite bank, as he rested by a tree trunk and again looked cautiously around him. Nothing. His attention was dragged back to the mainland and he could make out figures in the trees by the water's edge. He groped for the scope, but found he could not keep his hands still enough to look through it, such was his demeanour. Taking deep breaths, he fought to control his ague–like symptoms. Eventually, his breathing returned to something like normal and lifting the scope, concentrated on his pursuers. He could make out three men, two of which were NCO's. These two were conversing together and gesticulating towards the island. Whatever they were talking about was lost on Yuri. He had a smattering of German phrases in his head, but these were general things like 'Halt' and 'Who goes there? Conversation was out of his league. After a few minutes, they turned and disappeared from the water's edge and he heard them form up on the path. Eventually, the noise of their presence abated and he hoped, they were probably going back to their base camp, wherever that was.

His thoughts now returned to his immediate problem, the other mysterious inhabitant of the island. All he could do was search around and see what he came up with. He moved back to the plateau and scrutinised the area to the west. The plateau itself comprised of bare rock, a few wind blasted tree trunks and several small pools of water. The surrounding pines would be most susceptible to the ravages of the wind, as they clung precariously to the shallow soil above the cap rock. Feeling anything but secure, he scoured the trees, searching for anything that might conceal a potential enemy. Nothing. So he eased his way around the clearing, making the most of any kind of cover, until he reached the point where the ground rose up towards the west end. Here, there was what appeared to be a cave, or at least an opening in the rock face. He studied it for a while, but he could discern no movement from within, so he crept along the rock wall until he reached the opening and peered inside. Nothing. No sign of anyone. The rock floor disappeared inwardly, so he could not see too far inside the opening. The sun was sinking lower in the west and the cave remained obstinately in shadow. He backed off and began to climb the huge slab of rock that ran the rest of the length of the island. Here, he was exposed again, as the trees refused to grow on this inhospitable soil free surface. But several largish rocks and boulders provided some sort of refuge, should anything suddenly manifest itself. As he reached the far end of the island, he noticed several pools. He studied them and realised that the top one emptied into the one below and so on until the fifth one where it disappeared under the surface. What struck Yuri was that someone had caused these pools to fall as they did, because at various points along the pool lips, something had chipped away the rock to form a gully, so that each would empty into the one lower down. Why the bottom one disappeared underground, Yuri couldn't fathom, but someone had thought it important. He shook his head, unable to work out the reasoning. The south side of the rocky precipice fell away almost vertically to the lake below. Broken jagged teeth of rock leered up from the water and Yuri gulped, not enjoying the feeling of dizziness that made him reel back from the edge. He steadied himself and made his way back down across the top to the cave entrance, coming to it from the opposite side. Again he peered inside. This time he managed to see a pile of sawn logs just inside the entrance, but hidden away from the elements. Sawn logs, he mused. So where is the owner of the saw and the boat for that matter? He could make no sense of it, only the fact that he appeared to be alone. Was there more than one boat? Had someone left the island intending to return later? He shook his head. Nothing made sense.

The day was fast disappearing. Soon night would be upon him. He sat down wearily with his back to the rock wall, unclipped the entrenching tool from his belt and laid it to one side. Then he replaced his knife in its sheath and suddenly, he began to shake and shiver. He tried desperately to control the spasms that racked his body, but to no avail. He understood. He was exhausted, physically and mentally, on top of the fact that he was still wet, especially his trousers and socks. There had been no time to dry himself in any way and he realised that his socked feet squelched soggily as he flexed his toes in his boots. No wonder I'm cold, he thought to himself. I need to get out of these damp clothes and into something drier and warmer, because I know the night will be cold. But any dry clothing was hidden away up a tree in the pack and between him and it was the lake. He would have to swim back to get it. No, he murmured to himself, I can't. I just can't. But then he remembered the boat. You stupid shit, he intoned to himself. Use the sodding boat. He knew it was the only way, but firstly, he needed some comfort for his feet. Unlacing the boots he wrenched them off, poured out the excess water trapped inside, then pulled back the tongue and placed them face down on the rock in front of him. His socks, he dragged from his wrinkled white feet, wrung them out as best he could and laid them near to the boots. Oh sod it, he thought and took off his trousers and underpants, giving them a wring out too. Then he sat back on his bare rump, the skin feeling oddly strange against the clammy coldness of the rock. He then remembered the watch, tapped his breast pocket and it was still there, although he had no idea how it had survived the lake crossing. It was working too, showing five fifteen. Anyway, he thought to himself. Ten minutes.

He lay back and tried to make sense of the last forty eight hours. The attack, his survival and escape from the trench. The night spent in the rock fissure with Grigori, the bear this morning, Grigori's burial and his so very close brush with bullets and subsequent pursuers. His arrival on the island coupled with the fact that the boat signified another was here and yet, there were no recent signs. His stomach growled with hunger. He couldn't survive on a few biscuits and the odd piece of chocolate. What he would give for a decent hot meal. But, he thought with alacrity, no-one's going to give you anything for nothing. You're just going to have to go and get it yourself. His mind now made up, he felt better and barely noticed the dampness of his clothes as he replaced his trousers, tugged on his socks and laced up his boots. Let's get this over with, he told himself. Then we'll see. He stood up slowly, looking carefully around, then stepped out purposefully across the clearing and down the hollowed out steps, to the bay and the boat.

Intrigued, he inspected the craft and was impressed with what he saw. The frame was of wood, probably aspen or alder he thought. The internal skeleton framework was evenly laid with smaller boughs and fastened to the main frame with strips of rawhide. The keel was a solid plank of adzed timber, beautifully shaped and the rib bones of the bough ribcage, were nailed individually into this piece. Stretched around the outside of the hull was a single tanned length of hide, probably an ox hide thought Yuri, because of its size. This had been stitched into place around the main frame with thin twine. Spanning the centre was a seat, around six inches wide, which was supported by a couple of legs that were nailed onto the keel to give it stability. All in all, thought Yuri, a nice piece of kit. There would probably be enough room in the boat for four or five people, although they would be packed in tightly. Worryingly, there was a certain amount of water in the boat bottom, but hopefully, that was from the odd summer downpours that had sprinkled over the area recently, thought Yuri. Anyway, time for the acid test.

He went to the upturned prow and released the rope anchoring it by a clove hitch to a stout aspen bough and pushed it down the gully and out into the water. As it left the land behind, he scrambled in, making a clumsy attempt to board, almost capsizing it. But he managed to grab hold of the rim on each side, swivelled his body and gently sat himself down on the seat. So far so good. Picking up a paddle, he maneuvererd the boat around and began to make way forward. Skirting the eastern edge of the island and mindful of any rocks that might be waiting for him close to the bank, he slowly paddled his way across the seventy yards or so of open water, lining himself up with the little bay he had spotted earlier that afternoon. The hairs on his neck were standing proud all the way across, as he knew that any hidden watcher would have him dead to rights. Thankfully, he breathed a sigh of relief, as he grounded the boat and ran it up the gully, tethering it to a secure tree branch. The lateness of the evening meant that finding his way through the thicket and between the screening trees was exacerbated by the lack of light, but he made it remarkably easily. Pausing before stepping out onto the path, he listened, straining his ears for any problematic sound. He heard and saw nothing, so without further delay, he made his way along the path towards where he had buried Grigori. After half a mile or so, he came to the point where the paths diverged and heading left, sought out the scooped out stream bed where he had spent the previous night. The moon was rising into a clear sky as he found the tree above the fissure. Hoping upon hope that the bear was somewhere else, he climbed up the tree, rescued the pack and rifle and headed back to the boat. Wearily, he pushed the boat out into the lake, paddled around the east end of the island and made landfall just as a shower of rain began to fall. Securing the boat, he climbed the hollowed out steps and made furtively for the cave. All was quiet, all was still. He reached into the pack, took out the greatcoat and jacket, decided to shed his boots and socks, slipping on his old socks he had saved from the trench. Then wrapping up against the cold of the night, he placed his head upon the rolled up jacket and fell into an exhausted sleep.

Morning came in radiant splendour. The sun was shining directly into the cave entrance as Yuri became aware of a new day. He squinted his eyes against the rising sun and rubbed them briskly, as he always did, to wipe away the sleepiness of the night. He had slept soundly and felt much better for it. However, the rock floor had proved to be hard and unforgiving and he stretched expansively to remove the kinks from his back and sides. He lay back and luxuriated in the warmth of the early sun, listening and watching for anything which may cause him alarm. Beside him lay the loaded rifle and he felt comforted to behold its presence. At least he had something to defend himself with, apart from his trusty knife. His stomach growled with hunger, reminding him that he needed something to assuage the pangs that rumbled from within. He was warm and comfy, so he delayed rising for a little while, until the sun had risen further into the sky and he needed to think. What was he going to do now? Firstly, he would go through the pack properly, to find out what other secrets it held within. Then? He didn't know what to do after that. One thing at a time, he told himself. I'll decide later. His tongue rasped in his throat and his mouth tasted like a sewer. Something to eat will change all that, he thought. Time to get up.

Reluctantly, he eased out from beneath the greatcoat, rose to his feet and stepped to the edge of the entrance. Searching and listening from side to side, he neither heard nor saw anything, so he stepped out from the confines of the cave entrance, gazing around and alert for the slightest hint of alarm, then turned and put on his boots. They seemed to have dried off a little overnight and felt much more comfortable. The Germans socks he laid out on a rock in the sun, so to dry properly. He would need them later. Then he lifted the water canteen and drank sparingly, swilling out his mouth and spitting the contents onto the rocks. That felt a little better, he thought. Time for a scout around, he told himself, so picking up the rifle, he felt for the scope around his neck and set off up to the high ground at the west end of the island. A faint breeze rustled through the branches, as he came up to the water pools. Painstakingly, he panned a full three hundred and sixty degree traverse of the area with the scope, searching out any cause for alarm. Nothing. Faintly, away to the north, he could hear traffic moving along the main highway and he recalled a mental picture of what he had observed the previous day. You're welcome to the dust, he thought and grinned to himself. Away to the east, he picked out the silhouette of Woodpecker Knoll. Biting back a pang of inward pain, he reminisced over yesterday's burial, but then he reminded himself that Grigori was at peace in a beautiful place. Thinking of beautiful places, he gazed about him with real pleasure. The island was unquestionably remote, but oh, so intoxicating. It was his island now. He needed it as he had never needed anything before. From here, he would begin his counter offensive against the German Fascists. To seek out and destroy them in silence and savagery. He may be only one against many, but he would wage war as best he could. Firstly, he needed a plan.

Putting all thoughts of plans from his mind, he determined to explore this end of the island more thoroughly than he had yesterday, but firstly, he needed food, so he made his way back to the cave. He noticed that the socks were drying well on the rocks, propped up his rifle against the cave wall, selected a sawn log to act as a seat and placed the pack in front of him in the sunshine. What hidden wonders will you reveal, he thought expectantly. Firstly, he delved into the side pocket that he knew contained the hardtack biscuits and chocolate, selecting three biscuits and a chocolate bar. Leaving a few for later he placed them near to his side, as he crunched his way through the rest, while he went through the main compartment. He pulled out the drab, camouflaged poncho, another pair of socks, a field grey cap, two pairs of gloves, one pair leather, and the other pair woollen, a wool pullover and two new pairs of underpants and vests. Then a leather aircraftsman's type of hat with ear flaps and a chin strap, fully lined with wool. Well, thought Yuri. The man was a sniper and would probably need warm clothing as he waited somewhere in the grass for targets. At the bottom were the pliers and wire cutters, that the German had used so disgustingly on the Russian corpses. Handy tools to have around. There was a pocket knife with several attachments and several tins of what turned out to be food. He couldn't read what the labels told him, as they were all in German, but he guessed at meat, corned beef perhaps. He put them to one side for later. He pulled out a small leather pouch and inside found shaving equipment, with a brush, soap and cut throat razor, honed to a fine sharpness. Putting them to one side he pulled out another, larger leather pouch, which contained, wonder of wonders, a pair of field binoculars. Then out came a small cooking pot, a tin plate, mug and mess tins, all neatly folded within themselves. There was also what appeared to be a Paraffin Stove. He shook the stove and heard the slosh of liquid inside. Finally came the rolled up accoutrements belt. It was a substantial leather belt with over the shoulder straps. Several clips and straps hung down for attaching items of equipment to it. There was a Gas Mask holder, again of leather, but inside he found that the Gas Mask had been replaced by more food. There was bread, butter, tins of what looked like jam and a bag of sugar. Another small pouch contained medical equipment. Two stick grenades hung from the cross shoulder straps, the bayonet in its sheath and also several ammunition clips for the rifle. He sat back speechless, an unbelievable haul.

Then he opened the side pockets. One long pocket held a one man camouflaged tent, with metal poles, guide ropes and securing pegs. Another held the other scope and bipod in their muslin bags and a gun cleaning kit containing grease, oil, wadding, wire brushes and cleaning cloths. Yet another contained a leather holster and in it was a German Luger pistol. There were three boxes of ammunition for it, plus another lanyard and a whistle. The final pocket contained the results of the Germans corpse robbing. There was a bag of cigarette lighters, a bag of necklets, a bag of watches, a bag of finger rings and a tin containing about one hundred gold teeth. At that point he selected a lighter and put it into his breast pocket. He shook his head in revulsion. What kind of sick individual would rob the dead? Then he remembered the jacket. Maybe there is some form of ID he thought. He stood up and stretched his legs and arms, then went and picked up the jacket. He went through the pockets carefully, each revealing something new. He found another lighter with three packs of cigarettes, more ammunition clips and loose bullets. Then a compass and a pair of fingerless gloves. One of the breast pockets held a wallet. Another, a Ration book, ID card and a

German/Russian phrasebook. There was also a map of eastern Poland and western Russia and a sketch map of the immediate area.

So, thought Yuri. Let's reveal your identity Mr Robbing German bastard. He opened the ID card and the Germans photographed face stared out at him. His name was Hans Wilhelm Gruber, by all accounts and he hailed from Dusseldorf, as far as Yuri could ascertain. There were several stamps of military districts showing he had been to Berlin, Munich, Krakow, Warsaw and Lublin. The wallet contained a wedge of banknotes and some loose change, a photograph of an old couple, presumably his parents, ticket stubs from a theatre in Munich and a train ticket from Dusseldorf to Berlin. Not much of a social life, reflected Yuri and there was no picture of a girlfriend. But then again, he thought. Who would have him?

He sat back and viewed the treasures at his feet. So much more than he could ever have expected. At least there was enough here to begin his task and to survive for a little while. He busied himself packing all the items away again and then took another look around the area but this time, he used the binoculars. They were superb, of Austrian manufacture and although quite heavy, they would be a welcome addition to his armoury. The pistol and holster were also placed onto his belt by the leather thongs and the long scope put back into its muslin bag for later. He still had the entrenching tool which he had left in the cave entrance. He took a long drink from the canteen that emptied it. He would get more from the pools at the west end later. He placed all his kit back inside the cave entrance and put the log back with the others. He stared around the inside of the cave and reached out to run his hand along the side wall and then the rear. He suddenly flinched. The rear wall moved. Impossible, he thought. He reached out again and the wall did indeed compress as he pushed into it with his hand. He stood back agog. Flicking on the lighter, he saw that the rear wall was made of stretched animal hide, secured all around by a framework of aspen boughs. In the restricted light of yesterday evening he had failed to notice anything different about the inner wall, only that it was grey and blended in with its stone surroundings. How amazing. So what lay behind it? More Cave? He shook his head, dumbstruck by its seemingly innocent façade. He studied the screen all around. It fitted perfectly in between the rock walls. No wonder he had failed to see it. On the right, there appeared to be a handle. He pulled on it and the screen silently opened towards him, attached somehow on the left hand side by strap hinges. He peered inside, all was darkness. He took a few halting steps forward until the guttering flame from the lighter picked up a wooden bench on his right and upon it stood two candle holders, one having a candle protruding from its middle. He picked it up and held the lighter to the wick. The candle flamed and bathed the immediate area with a soft glow of light. He then snapped shut the lighter cover, the sound echoing shrilly through the haloed darkness. He looked around at the hide door and saw that the inside was covered with bear skins, fur facing the entrance, with about three inches protruding from the edge all around which left a tight, almost windproof seal against the elements. It would not stop a direct physical assault, but it would help to keep the inner cave warm, when the bitter Russian winter blew in across the steppes. He took another two faltering strides and the walls widened as he passed along revealing more benches and cupboards. On the walls were hung tools. A crosscut and a bow saw, long cloaks of bear skins and hammers and axes on rawhide thongs. He suddenly realised with alarm, that he had stepped, uninvited into someone's living room. Perhaps the person from the boats living room.

The air was still and the candle showed no sign of movement. The room smelt old and musty with a tinge of dank decay and old cooking fires. The silence was oppressive and his brain screamed caution. Yet, he took more steps forward and the walls widened again outwards. He was into a large area now. The roof rose above his head for two or three feet and a whole aspect of space stretched out before him. Again, another two steps and he came to a sudden, abrupt halt. In front of him was a table, on which were several plates, pots and cups, laid in haphazard abandon. The flickering candle cast eerie shadows across the walls and floor in front of him, but it also revealed a dark, hooded figure, slumped in a chair behind the table. The figure sat motionless, the hood disguising any chance of making out the intent of the eyes beneath it. But what concerned Yuri more than anything else, was the muzzle of a rifle that lay rock steady on the surface of the table. That muzzle was pointing directly and deliberately at his belly.

Chapter 4 – The Compound

Yuri stood stock still, unable to move or speak. The barrel still pointed mercilessly at him. The seconds ticked into minutes. A tic suddenly manifested itself on the left side of his face and he twitched involuntarily. A bead of sweat ran down from his right armpit, the sensation causing him to shiver. His hands shook and he felt beads of sweat forming on his upper lip. The candle flame gutted momentarily, as a faint zephyr of air breathed down from the roof above. A drop of water plopped into a pool somewhere to his right, the sound like a gunshot in the tense stillness. He jumped, with the overwhelming shock of it all. More seconds ticked by. The ominous barrel never wavered an inch. It looks an old barrel, he thought to himself and he had the sudden urge to laugh out loud at the absurdity of his observation. It may be an old barrel you stupid shit, but it will make a nice round new hole in your crap filled belly. He tried to open his mouth to speak, but his lips were glued together with fear. Eventually, he prised them apart and raised his tongue to moisten them. A dribble of saliva eked from the corner of his mouth and hung precariously from his chin, refusing to fall to the floor. Speech though, was beyond him. His muscles were beginning to flex and contract and his legs shook with the unnaturalness of having to stand so rigidly and helplessly. The seconds ticked by. The barrel never moved from its intended target.

Suddenly, something shot past him on the floor, then another disappeared between his legs, then two others. Urgh, thought Yuri, rats. He hated rats. The suddenness of his reaction caused him to fall off balance and he took a hurried, involuntary step to his right. His head swivelled round so that his eyes could follow the rats progress, but they had already reached the outer doorway and scurried off outside. He turned his gaze back to the source of his original fear, but the hooded figure had not moved. However, the gun still pointed towards the cave entrance. He realised with a shock, that when he had made his step to the right, the gun had not moved to cover him. What does it mean, he thought tensely? Something was gnawing at his brain. Was it false hope or dire stupidity? He opened his mouth and something resembling speech shattered the silence.

"Hello," he croaked. "I'm Yuri and you are?" Silence. No reply was forthcoming. He tried again.

"Sir, I'm a Russian soldier, escaping from the Germans. You must have heard the attack two days ago mmm." Nothing. His confidence was slowly returning and he took a step forward, then another and saw in the glow of candlelight the reason for his subconscious decision to break the spell. What gazed out from beneath the hood had been dead for a quite a while. The skeletal bones were still holding what was left of the body together, the arms resting forlornly on the table. The skin, organs and tissue were gone, rat food, as well as other voracious creatures had seen to that. How long he had sat here and how he had died, Yuri would never know. His heart reached out to this poor unfortunate, who had died so mysteriously alone. Without question, he had found the owner of the boat.

Something like normal was returning to Yuri's relieved body and mind. He wiped the saliva from his chin and peered into the far recesses of the room. By even the slightest foresight, Yuri would never have been prepared for what lay around him. The cavernous cave dome towered above his head, blending into the darkness of the far corners of the roof. Hanging from the roof were two chains, from which were suspended what appeared to be two paraffin lamps. Another water droplet dripped loudly into some receptacle. There were wood carved and woven rush fronted cabinets, all along the wall to his left. Above them, metal pegs had been hammered into the bare rock, holding an assortment of hammers, knives and a couple of adzes. Between the cabinets were two large drums. Yuri wandered over to them and shook them. The inside contents sloshed about and Yuri sniffed at the lids. Paraffin he concluded. To his front, behind the skeletons chair, was a huge cast iron stove with circular recesses for pots and pans. What looked like an eight inch copper or bronze tube, emerged from the back of the stove and disappeared into a kind of chimney in the rock. Pegged above the stove in the rock wall were different sized cooking pans, all neatly arranged from smallest to largest. This man had been very fastidious. To the right of the stove, was a wooden bench holding a large, tin, rectangular bowl. There was scummy water in the bowl with several plates, pots, knives and forks showing below the murky surface. In the far right corner, Yuri found the culprit of the noisy drip, a deep pool of water, once again, hollowed by hammer and chisel out of the natural rock. Above was a copper pipe which ran from somewhere up in the roof space and Yuri knew exactly where the pipe led to. It would be the series of pools, so cleverly arranged, at the west end of the island. There was even what appeared to be a copper overflow pipe at the surface of the rock tank, which exited out through the side rock wall, to prevent flooding of the cavern floor in times of heavy rain. Yuri shook his head in astonishment. Surely this is all too much for one man? So had there been another? It suddenly dawned on him, that this particular man could well have had a wife. Yet the area seemed so remote, inaccessible. But then, perhaps that's how they liked it. Yuri crossed over to the left of the stove and here, was another of the stretched skin doors like the one at the front. He opened it and stepped into a long corridor room. About three yards down to his right was a big open fire place, the chimney again exiting up behind it. To his left were two beds, both with horse hair and straw mattresses. The beds were simply made from aspen or alder, but sturdy nevertheless. Blankets and bear skins were neatly arranged between the beds, on a set of shelves. But what really fascinated Yuri, was further along the wall. Here were tables and chairs, the tables with neat piles of writing materials, pads of paper and what looked like, books for sketching. There were pens and inks, charcoal pencils and coloured crayons. At the far end was a tall bookcase, filled with books. But the real highlight, as far as Yuri was concerned, were the four windows, hewn out of the rock walls. They were about two foot square, with cleverly fitted thick panes of glass. They could not be opened, but around each one were solid wood shutters, bear skin backed, to keep out winter draughts. Yuri was again amazed at what he had found. The room itself was about twelve feet wide and ran for perhaps twenty to twenty-four feet. Living space for a married couple? He had not seen any sign of the second occupant's presence in the cavern, it was just the way everything was set out, in other words, a woman's touch. Yuri knew his mother and grandmother were very particular about the way in which his own house was set out and woe betide any male member of the family who failed to keep it so.

Under the windows were three long tables and on these tables were hide cases and larger wooden boxes with removable tops. He peered inside one such box and found piles of drawings. They were all of animals, insects, birds, and fish. Another box held pages of writings, written in an elegant Russian script. These were descriptions of, well, the flora and fauna of the western Russian area, thought Yuri. This man was obviously a scholar, even an academic and an illustrator. Then he found it, his benefactor was Aleksander Dobrovolsky, formerly of the University of St Petersburg. A naturalist, who seemed to have spent his life studying and documenting all aspects of the natural world. Yuri had only scratched the surface, as far as going through all the detail, but he estimated that here was a lifetime's work, which should be available for all to see in one of the big city Museums. One day, he hoped to deliver all of this to some, academic institution. Meanwhile, he could only try to not let it fall into the wrong hands.

He now tore himself away from his discovery and went back to more pressing matters. The skeleton could not remain within the main room, especially if he, Yuri, was going to live in it. Therefore, he must dispose of it but where? He went back into the main room, the candle fluttering gently and surveyed the corpse. If I could wrap it in the hooded fur coat, I could possibly find a place to bury it thought Yuri. His train of thought was interrupted as the candlelight fell upon the wall which he had missed. There were two long handled felling axes, a double handed crosscut saw, a spade, a shovel and what looked like a snow shovel, all neatly laid out on wall pegs. Next to them were two rifles, quite modern and well looked after, a long bow with a sheath of arrows, all suspended on pegs, with two bare pegs, where the gun on the table must have rested. But what really caught Yuri's eye, were the two, handmade and beautifully carved Crossbows. He stared in disbelief. Crossbows, the silent killers. Did they work? He would have to see. Next to them, along the wall, were four large earthenware pots. They stood three feet high and would be two feet diameter at their widest point. Each had a tight fitting lid and Yuri found that they contained about a foot of salt. This would be where meat would be stored against the coming winter. His mind whirled at the resourcefulness of the person or persons who lived in such splendid surroundings. This was no peasant. He was a man with huge capabilities. His engineering skills alone, spoke volumes about his ability to create something such as this.

Yuri checked his watch. It was now midday and he needed to organise himself. He went outside, searching around carefully. Nothing. So he hefted the rifle onto his shoulder by the strap, picked up the binoculars and set off to explore further. The east end of the island was a mass of trees, pines and alders. Here the soil was relatively sparse and the trees were so thickly compacted that he would never find a suitable place. He carried on, along the north edge, the sun warming him and colouring his mood. Nowhere could he see a suitable site, so he climbed up towards the west end. The high point at the western tip, was sparsely covered with brush and the odd stunted pine. However, there were a few pines and small aspens in a grove to the south side. He had not explored this part of the ridge yesterday, only coming as far as the water pools. With water in mind, he made for the pools and, cupping his hands to lift out the water, slaked his thirst. Refreshed, he reconnoitred the small grove he had seen from above and here, tied securely between two pine trunks, was an eight foot bronze pipe. He had found where the smoke from the fires in the rooms below exited to the atmosphere. He shook his head in wonder. Nothing was too much trouble for this man. On top of the tube was an Asiatic conical hat shaped top, which fitted snugly around the rim, with vents slotted into the sides. The smoke would then dissipate up through the leaves and branches. Ingenious, he thought. Passing along by the grove, he reached the far end of the ridge. Here, the ground sloped away westward down to a flat semi-circular headland. He searched around for a way down and spotted a pathway of chiselled stone steps leading towards the headland floor. He followed them and emerged in a clearing. Pines and aspens surrounded the headland. It was, he thought, a beautiful place, reminiscent of where he had buried Grigori. He turned and walked along the base of the rock wall, the aspen leaves rustling gently in the slight breeze and he knew that he would find her here, if she had existed. Sure enough, at a point towards the southern edge of the headland, he came upon a grave. Rocks and stones were laid out in a rectangle, facing south east, and in the centre was a cairn. Atop the cairn was a slab of rock. Carved intricately on this rock was 'Anna Katherine Dobrovolsky – Born Odessa 1882 – Died here September, 1939.'

Yuri bowed his head and muttered a little prayer. Here she lay, the wife of the skeleton in the chair. Fifty seven years old and died almost three years ago. He looked off towards the south east. Yes, he thought, Odessa will lie in that direction. Now he had to place the two of them back together. With a sense of contentment, he returned to the cave. Lighting the candle, he walked through into the main room. The tense atmosphere of the morning had been gentled and soothed away the sheer beauty and tranquillity of this place and now, all he could think of was doing what was right. He picked up the spade from the wall peg and hefted it. The spade had been well maintained, with no rust and a deep sharp blade. He ran his hand over the cold metal and realised it had been oiled. Without further ado, he returned to the western headland and dug out a grave, next to the other. He only got down about three feet before he hit bedrock. So, it would have to do. He returned to the skeletal remains, took down one of the other fur coats from the wall and laid it on the floor. The candlelight cast a strange glow as he picked up the remains as best he could and placed them on the coat. Odd bones had fallen off as he had moved it and he picked them up and placed them with the rest. He knew they were out of order, but hoped the man wouldn't mind. Then he bundled up the bones, lashed it all together with twine, picked it up and carried it, with as much reverence as he could muster, to the newly dug grave. He stepped in, laid it down and quickly filled in the hole. Flattening it as best he could he then carried stones and rocks to lay in a rectangle over the grave. In the centre, he built a small cairn and in it placed a rough wooden cross. He hadn't the skills to make a better job. It would have to remain simplistic. Going down on his knees, he put a hand on each grave and prayed that they might be entwined together for all eternity. Then he turned, satisfied and trudged off back to the cave.

The afternoon was passing, the shadows beginning to lengthen. Yuri checked his watch. Five o'clock. Time for something to eat and then he would decide on his next move. He rummaged around in the pack and pulled out two of the tins he had seen earlier. He scanned the labels, hoping they were meat of some sort. The Germans pocket knife had a can opener on it he recalled and fished that out of the pack too. The first can revealed steak with onions and vegetables, so he opened another, seeing it was labelled the same. The two tins he emptied into the field cooking pot and fired up the field stove. Soon, he had his first hot meal in days spluttering on the stove. Using the same sawn log as a stool, he wolfed it down greedily, with some slices of bread. The bread was hard and chewy, but not stale. These Germans live really well he thought, as he finished off the meal with a can of condensed milk. Sitting back, he burped contentedly. Gazing around him, he took in the beauty of the island and its surroundings. However, he knew that the sight laid out before him, although beguiling, could not be misconstrued. Danger lurked within the mind of anyone who failed to recognise that the woods and marshes were merely a curtain, one that masked the savagery of those who would destroy its serenity. The past days had been the most difficult of his life, but somehow he had survived and come through it. Now he had the chance to make use of his new found confidence and he realised that he appeared to have the ability to cope when under real pressure. Disposing of the German in the trench had not been easy, but he had thought it through quickly and put a plan into practice. That had delivered a real boost to the assessment of his abilities. There was no-one else to help him and he had triumphed. Even when he was trying to outrun the fascist patrol, his brain was functioning and he had formulated a plan to outsmart the dogs and the following soldiers.

He also realised that he had never been alone before. There had always been someone around to guide and help make the decisions for him. His parents had been strict, but not to the point of being abusive towards he, Grigori and his sisters. Both sets of his grandparents had been vast storehouses of knowledge and he realised that he had learnt a huge amount from them. Grigori had been his hero, his idol and Yuri had basked in Grigori's attention, whether in praise or reproach. Now he had gone, it was up to Yuri to honour Grigori's life, by being the best he could be. His thoughts then turned to what he was going to do about the war. He could not, in all fairness, stay here and allow his fellow countrymen to fight and die, while he sat out the war in luxury. But what could he do? He felt he had two options. One, he could seek out and destroy individuals with his snipers rifle. Two, he could try and find where the German supply dumps were and maybe steal some explosives. Then he could really cause some damage. He thought it through and came to the conclusion, that option two was his only recourse. He needed more destructive material. Tonight, he thought. Tonight I'll go out and find the nearest army dump. There must be one somewhere reasonably close, at least this side of the River Bug and then he remembered seeing the deserted hamlet yesterday from Woodpecker Knoll. Yes, he thought, where Grigori and the others in our squad had visited the day before the invasion. I'll bet that's where the dump is. Being high summer, the night would be short, with darkness lasting five or six hours. He had to locate the place, suss it out and get in and out, before the dawn. A tall order, he knew, but he had to try. It's six o'clock he thought. An hours rest and then I'll leave.

Yuri pottered around the cave, tidying up by candlelight. By seven o'clock he was ready. He would have to carry the rifle, with a few spare clips and to this end, he had fathomed out how to attach the long scope and bipod. He knew he hadn't had the time to zero in the sight, but hopefully, he wouldn't need to use the weapon in anger tonight, only the scope. As an afterthought, he decided to take the Luger with him, strapping the holster securely around his waist. He would leave the binoculars here, they were too cumbersome. He shrugged into the pullover against the night time chill and rolled up the poncho, tying it up with the lanyard. Then he clipped it to his belt. Rummaging around in the pack, he located the pouch with the medical supplies in it, pulling out two bandages. He would need to find his way back in the dark and he reasoned that a piece of bandage, tied to a stick and left in full view, should be fairly easy to spot, even in moonlight. If anyone else spotted them, well, it was a risk worth taking. He shoved the woollen gloves into his pocket and also the tight fitting skull cap with the chin straps and with a last look around the cave, closed the hide door behind him and made his way to the boat. He suddenly came to his senses. Stupid shit, he thought. I haven't even bothered to reconnoitre the area. The islands serenity had lulled him into a false sense of security, exactly what he had surmised earlier and he reproached himself for not taking more care. After all, it was only yesterday, that German troops were on the north bank and they could still be there for all he knew. Within a few miles radius, men were killing each other with vicious ferocity. He must tread carefully. He was no use to anybody dead. Well, perhaps the Germans he thought and grinned to himself. He reasoned that the binoculars would be a better bet at seeing around the area, so he went back to the cave, picking them up off the table inside the door and made his way towards the west end of the island. Small clouds drifted slowly across the evening sky, the sun on the wane to the west, as he swung the binoculars back and forth, searching for any sign of movement. Nothing. He then concentrated his attention to the south, trying to see how far the water stretched. His view was only a quarter of a mile or so, before the all concealing trees and reeds blocked his progress. Yes, he thought, the water seems to go on for quite a way, but it was only a presumption. One day he would have to discover the lie of the land in more detail. On a hunch, he did a tight study of the reeds on the western bank and found, to his surprise, a gap in the reeds, where a boat might conceivably make landfall. The gap appeared like a balloon, with the neck in the reeds and a circular open bay stretching out behind and out of sight. The hunch concerned the previous owner. How had he ferried such large items across to the island from the mainland? Even wood for winter burning, would be difficult to carry on such a small craft as the boat in the bay where he had landed. It was possible he had floated the logs across, but what of the stove and earthenware pots? There had to be a bigger boat, or maybe even a raft of some sort. The man had been too switched on to miss such an obvious trick. Did he have the time to investigate tonight? Yuri thought, yes. He was curious and it would provide an alternative landing area, to the one across in the north shore trees. With a final look around the whole area, Yuri went back to the cave, popped the binoculars on the table just inside the door, closed everything up for the night and descended the steps to the boat.

He pushed off, paddling easily west, to where he had spotted the gap in the reeds. The reeds were taller here than on the opposite side, rising to at least ten or twelve feet. High enough to hide another boat thought Yuri. The gap appeared before him and he stroked his way through into a horseshoe bay. The bay was perhaps fifty feet in circumference, with deep sheltered water and as Yuri gazed around, he spotted his hunch, tied to a stake on the northern shore. It was a raft. He grinned with delight, as he realised how right he had been. That man would always be one step ahead, he thought. Paddling over to where it lay, he ran his eyes over the solid wood frame. The prow, was pointed with an animal hide cover, to allow easier passage through the water when heavily laden. Underneath, were lashed six, fifty gallon drums, to give it stability and a large load bearing capability. The deck was flat and open. So, one in the boat, towing the one on the raft, who would be paddling too, with the large oars, laid on the stern. It would be difficult, thought Yuri, but not insurmountable. Pleased at his discovery, but conscious of the limited time available, he beached the boat by the side of the raft and tied it securely to it. He didn't fancy an early morning swim. Then he made sure he had everything to hand, did a quick scan of the surrounding countryside with the rifle and scope and marched off towards the north-west. There was a semblance of a path to follow, which drifted easily through the fairly open terrain, passing bogs and clumps of trees. He placed his first marker at a point where the path deviated west sharply, cutting a six inch length of bandage and knotting it to a stick pulled from a thicket. He also laid a stick on the trail, pointing to where he had come from. Hopefully, it would be enough, he thought. He carried on, over streams and through more dense areas of woodland, placing markers and guide sticks at various points, until he reckoned he had travelled about four miles. The woods here were mostly pine, with tiny glades and sparse boggy areas and he figured he must be getting close to where he reckoned the compound was, because of the gradual increase in noise generating from the road running east to west. The woods began to thin out and he moved carefully from tree to tree, taking advantage of any cover he could find. The sound of heavy traffic was increasing by the minute and he tarried awhile, to put on the poncho and leather cap. Then with the rifle cradled on his outstretched arms, he crawled through the long grass, up to an area of tree covered raised ground. He crested the rise and slid forward on his belly, until he could make out the road and compound ahead. The compound was virtually opposite, about a hundred yards away and he smiled grimly to himself, at the accuracy of his sense of direction. Hopefully, he would be able to follow his markers back to the island.

The scene laid out before him was one of disorganised chaos. From the west, German troops were walking eastward along the sides of the mud road. The road itself was clogged with military traffic, again heading east, with a steady flow of Russian refugees, trying to flee westward across into Poland and so away from the fighting. Their pathetic carts, some dragged by horses, some being pulled manually, were piled high with their remaining possessions. They looked frightened and beaten, staring uncomprehendingly at the massed lines of horses and vehicles ferrying the weapons and munitions of war eastward. By comparison, the German enemy appeared haughty and aloof, passing disdainfully between the pitiful Russians, sometimes even brushing them aside. Any breakdowns were summarily shoved off the road, their conquering ears deaf to the wails of protest. Yuri felt his hackles beginning to rise, but fought back any attempt at intervention. His time would come. Everyone's head turned and looked upwards, as returning squadrons of enemy planes droned overhead at only a few thousand feet, their last mission of the day completed. Strange they should be so low, thought Yuri. Maybe their bases were not too far away. He panned the scope slowly along the length and breadth of the snaking columns. It would appear that the enemy go to war with lots of horsepower, as opposed to mechanical means, observed Yuri. There were many vehicles, but the vast majority of munitions were horse drawn. Teams of horses, with their handlers, were pulling everything from field guns to food and ammunition. German Officers rode horses alongside the troops and as targets, they stood out clearly. Away to the west, he heard the growing rumble of tanks and presently, about twenty feet from the road itself, they pounded their way past his position, their tracks churning up the dust into clouds that drifted up and then settled on the occupants of the road. He counted forty of these metal monsters, powering their way to the front, wherever that was now. Yuri was not too alarmed at their numbers, as he knew his own army had thousands of tanks themselves. But these tanks did look very new and ominously capable. How do you inflict damage on this relentless juggernaut, thought Yuri? He would have to try.

The compound itself was adjacent to the road. The enemy had taken over a small Russian settlement of eight houses, arranged in a circle, with a large open space in the centre. The settlement was typical of millions of such places, spread across the whole of Mother Russia. The inhabitants of this place had moved long ago, after the Russians had started to build the defensive trenches and earth works. His earlier recollection had been correct. His squad had visited the area to watch the trucks ferrying supplies across the Bug into Poland. When the German war machine blitzed its way across the river, they needed some form of transport and holding area, where supplies could be stockpiled and then moved onward to the front as and when required. On the far side of the road were huge stock pens, where horses were being cared for, their handlers bedding down next to them in their small tents, or sleeping out under the wagons that were loaded with forage. Other stock pens held cattle, pigs, sheep and goats. The army had to be fed and the German butchers would be working around the clock to feed them, augmenting their combat rations. It was a huge undertaking and probably one of many along the roads to the east, thought Yuri. On the western side of the compound was a large, petrol dump. Thousands of fifty gallon drums were stacked up high to feed the voracious appetite of the tanks, half-tracks and lorries. Petrol bowsers were lined up being filled from the drums by hand pumps and every so often, one would leave and join the never-ending column heading eastward towards the front. With so much going on, thought Yuri, how the hell am I going to be able to do anything in this mayhem? Surely it will tail off as the night progresses. Even the Germans will have to sleep sometime, he mused.

His attention then switched to the east and his jaw sagged. Coming down through the fields near the road, was an enormous detachment of Russian prisoners. Formed up in rows of eight or ten, this gigantic snake of human misery wended its sorry way through the grassy fields, bossed by heavily armed German guards, driving them on. Officers riding on horseback moved up and down the flanks of the column keeping a watchful eye over the whole proceedings. The prisoners shuffled along as only beaten and bruised men can. Some were barely able to walk, being helped by others. Most were bandaged in some sort of way, many had missing limbs. The whole sad cavalcade, streamed past Yuri at no more than two hundred yards. He could feel their remorse and dejection, it was palpable in the extreme. Thousands walked past him that evening, on their way to captivity in some detention camp, probably in Poland. If this was endemic of the way the war was progressing, then Yuri could not see any hope of victory for his country. How many armies did the Russians have in the field? He knew there were many, but…………, so many captured. How many had died? He could only guess. They must fight on regardless. The Germans were only men, weren't they?

Tearing his gaze away from the fast disappearing column, he concentrated on his own predicament. He had to help. Even in some small way, he, Yuri Petrovsky, could help. All he needed were the tools to do it. This was not bravado, he told himself. This was sheer bloody-mindedness on his part and the part of all free-thinking Russians. These filthy fascists would rue the day they had dared to attack Mother Russia. He glued his eye to the scope and searched for a way in. Dusk was fast becoming night, as he worked out the basis of a plan. He had watched the comings and goings of the compound for the last hour and felt that he knew where the best place for his needs now lay. There was a long, wooden building at the south end of the village. He had seen many officers and enlisted men enter the building from the main central area, emerging after a few minutes carrying all forms of kit, food and armaments. He thought that it could be being used as a quartermaster's store. He had seen horse drawn wagons led into the central area and watched as the contents of the wagons were taken inside. He could only surmise what the wagons carried, but it seemed the right sort of place. The Germans had either not had time to erect a barbed wire fence, or didn't feel the need to. However, armed sentries patrolled the outer circle of the encampment and he had to work out a time frame to get in and out while the sentries were patrolling other buildings. Night was now upon him and the moon bathed the area in a grey half-light. In the west, clouds were gathering and with a bit of luck, could obscure the moon at some stage, maybe even drop a rain shower. Now the night was working in his favour and he needed to shift his position, so he could align himself with his escape route and be able to observe the building at close quarters. He backed off the small rise and crawled westwards through the grass, making for a couple of blasted pines which would afford him shelter, but at the same time, allow him a close up view of his target. He crept into position and saw he was only fifty feet or so from the large, closed double doors of the house. Perfect. He arranged himself behind a blasted log, which offered some protection from prying eyes and silently removed the scope from its mountings. It would be much easier to use it loosely. Turning his head, he was pretty sure he could make out where his first marker was. It meant crossing open ground for about three hundred yards, but hopefully, the darkness would mask his presence. Satisfied, he turned his attention to the house. On the right of the building, was a wooden lean-to, which was probably where animals were kept. Maybe pigs or cattle, thought Yuri. There was an entrance door on the side of the lean-to and he hoped that it offered a way in to the main building, perhaps through forage stalls. Anyway, he thought, that seems to be the only way in for me. The two large doors would expose me too much.

He hadn't really noticed before, but lights were showing all over the compound and in most of the buildings that he could see. The enemy were obviously confident that they were safe, coupled with the fact that the light would deter any would be thieves within the German ranks. As he made this observation, a sentry appeared from his right, the torch he held, making steady sweeps of the buildings and surrounding fields. Here was the acid test. The German passed him by, humming tunelessly to himself and continued on his clockwise route around the compounds exterior.

Yuri glanced left as another sentry appeared, following an anti-clockwise route. Both men met and chatted together, before carrying on in different directions, the anti-clockwise man passing Yuri, as blissfully unaware of Yuri's presence as the first sentry. Yuri breathed a sigh of relief. As long as he kept still and quiet, he should be OK. Lights were going out in the other buildings. Men would be sleeping. Yuri would give the sentries another couple of circuits to make sure of their regularity, before committing himself.

The noise from the road was lessening, only the odd vehicle passing through the night. He could hear the horses blowing from the other side of the road, the handlers probably sleeping too. More lights in the houses were being extinguished, as the sentries appeared again for a second pass. They passed each other, as before and Yuri noted about twenty minutes since they were last here. One more circuit, he thought and then I'm going in. Suddenly, one of the large doors in the house swung open and a man appeared carrying a bucket. Short, bespectacled, balding and running to flab around the belly, his trousers held up by thick braces. His grey shirt, open at the neck was collarless, the sleeves rolled up revealing flabby, hairy forearms. He seemed unconcerned, glancing around disinterestedly, while he threw the contents of the bucket on the grass. Placing the bucket down, he spread his legs, unbuttoned his flies, pulled out his dick and urinated a steady stream. His bladder relieved, he gave his dick a few shakes, shoved it back into his trousers and re-buttoned his flies. He put his hands on his hips and gazed around myopically. Then he burped expansively, patted his chest a couple of times, picked up the bucket and disappeared back inside, closing the door behind him. Yuri heard him replace the locking bar and thought, not much of a fighting man this one. More a clerk, a pen pusher. A quartermaster? The replacing of the locking bar had now decided Yuri's course. It had to be the lean-to. The sudden appearance of the man had caused Yuri to freeze, but he managed to snap out of it in time, to have a quick look at the inside of the house. He then realised it wasn't a house, but a long barn, with stalls down each side. It appeared well lit and he could see the stalls were filled to overflowing with boxes, sacks and drums. He'd come to the right place then.

The minutes ticked by. He glanced at his watch, twelve-thirty. Where were those damned sentries? Presently, the light appeared, followed by the clockwise sentry. He passed unconcernedly, met his fellow sentry coming the other way, nodded a greeting, and then carried on with his tour. The anti-clockwise sentry sauntered past and disappeared around the corner of the compound. Right, thought Yuri, twenty minutes and they'll be back. He had already removed his skull cap and put it in his pocket. He needed to be able to hear properly. The scope had been attached back onto the rifle, and this he laid to one side where it could be easily picked up. Time to go. He moved purposely forward in a crouched trot arrowing straight for the lean-to door. There was a small fence surrounding the lean-to which he silently climbed over. Reaching the door, he lifted the sneck as soundlessly as he could and opened the door a fraction. A faint glow of light bathed the inside of the lean-to from the main barn. The smell was rank. Pigs. His eyes, now becoming accustomed to the gloomy conditions, made out three fat shapes by the outer wall. All three were snoring contentedly. He crept inside, closing the door behind him, and made his way across the manured straw past the sleeping pigs, to the place where the light peeped through from the main barn. Good thought Yuri, forage troughs. The long, rectangular troughs, ran the width of each stall. About six inches above the trough, was a V shaped hay rack, running the width of the trough. Horses and cattle would feed from this. All he had to do was climb over and he would be in. Silently, he raised himself up, grabbed the top bar and pulled his body upwards. He swung his knee over the top and settled himself. At that moment, a slight breeze funnelled down from the top end of the barn. Someone had entered the building. Then he heard voices in a language he didn't understand, but it appeared to be only conversation. Someone laughed and it was answered by another. Bugger off, thought Yuri. After a few minutes, the voices moved away and he heard more laughter and what appeared to be people saying 'good night'. He understood those words well enough. Then the sound of the door closing and someone sitting down heavily on a chair. Peace returned and he slid off the hay rack and down, onto the straw covered ground. All appeared quiet. He lay down and peered around the edge of the stall. The lights were strongest at the far end of the barn and there, sat on a chair with his back to Yuri, was the fat German quartermaster, poring over some books and papers on a table. On the left of the table stood what appeared to be a large radio and as Yuri watched, the man leaned over, twiddled a few knobs and soon the unmistakable sound of music drifted down the barn, interspersed with hissing static as the man tried to tune the station to his liking. Eventually, the static ceased and the not unpleasant sound of a lady singing filled the air. The main thoroughfare through the barn was perhaps twelve feet wide, uncluttered and for Yuri, disturbingly open. How the hell am I going to get anywhere in here, he thought dejectedly. There's too much light and too many easily watched areas. He racked his brains, but it would appear that he could only steal from the stalls around him.

To this end, he stood up and silently moved around the edge of the stall into the adjacent one. There were sacks in here, piled high against the walls.

They were all labelled, but Yuri couldn't understand the German writing. Shit, he thought, maybe flour? He moved into the next one up. These were all back packs, hundreds of them, piled against the wall. Well, I suppose I could do with another, he thought. Where were the weapons, the explosives? After another careful check on the man in the chair, he eased around the end of the next stall. Boxes this time, piles of them, but what's in them thought a frustrated Yuri. He looked quickly at his pocket watch. He'd been in the barn for eight minutes. As he scanned the boxes, his ears detected the sound of the front door of the barn being opened. Straining to hear above the gentle music, he could only hope that whoever it was would leave quickly. But it seemed that the newcomer was deep in conversation with the quartermaster. Sliding silently along the stall edge, he risked a peep around the corner in their direction and felt a chill of fear. The newcomer was a soldier who sat contentedly on the edge of the quartermaster's desk, his rifle laid casually across his knee, as the pair conversed affably.

At this point, Yuri suddenly became aware that all was not as it seemed in his immediate area. Some strange feeling infused into his brain and he shrank back into the deeper shadows that the stall provided. What was it? There's just two men, isn't there? Fear was now beginning to take hold and he began to sweat. What the hell? What about the other side of the barn? He had been so focused on the man in the chair and his new companion that he had completely ignored anything other than the stalls he had been in. Idiot! He looked across to the stall opposite. Was that a movement? He slid out his knife, ready, but felt completely vulnerable. Again he sensed movement opposite. Risking all, he leant forward, his whole being straining to make sense of the movement in the gloom. He realised he was staring into another pair of eyes. The shock caused him to recoil and his right hand sought out the comforting feel of the Luger. Then a leg was tentatively pushed out into the light of the main thoroughfare. He could now make out the figure of a man, his eyes staring intently at Yuri. Completely off balance, Yuri deliberated. It could be a trap, he thought, but surely there would have been some kind of challenge, some sort of warning cry. He edged forward and peered around the end of the stall. The guard and quartermaster were still conversing animatedly. Yuri's gaze returned to the opposite side. The man's eyes had followed him, but there had been no alarm raised. On a hunch, Yuri decided to act. He moved so that he was well into the light and surveyed his watcher. The man nodded and then lifted his arm. From it, hung a chain and as Yuri watched, he realised that the chain was connected to another two men, who both seemed to be asleep. Or dead. The stall they were in had large metal rings bolted onto the stall side, which would have been used for tethering cattle, but now the chains running through the rings were utilised for the internment of prisoners. Yuri could make out shackles that ran around the men's wrists and feet. The three were well secured. They can only be Russian's, thought Yuri, so that's why the soldier is here. As a guard. Risking another glance around the corner of his stall he studied the two Germans. The quartermaster was donning headphones and as he did so, waved the soldier away. The soldier picked up his rifle and as Yuri hurriedly pulled his head out of sight, marched purposefully down the barn towards him. Yuri put his finger to his lips. The man across from him nodded. Then Yuri motioned towards the oncoming soldier, raising the knife and running it across his throat. The man again nodded, the glint in his eye now evident. Yuri faded into the deeper shadows, his pulse racing. Fighting down his initial terror, he prepared himself for what he was about to do. The singing on the radio had ceased as the quartermaster began to tap out a message to someone in Morse code and Yuri knew that the fat little German would be engrossed in his message sending for a while at least. Yuri heard the German guard approaching, a torch beam preceding him. The German stopped with his back to Yuri, his rifle now slung by the strap over his left shoulder and shone his torch into the faces of the Russian's.

"So my little shit kicking Ivan's, aren't you asleep?" the man enquired. The Russian parodied drinking. "Ah, its water you want is it? Tough shit Mr Ivan. You won't get water until tomorrow and only then if Hauptmann Lientz says so. The Hauptmann is coming to interrogate you three little arseholes and he hates Ivan's almost as much as he hates Jews."

With that the German threw back his head and laughed uproariously and in that instant, Yuri made his move. Silently and stealthily he crossed the five or six paces between him and his enemy. At the last moment, the German heard or sensed something, but it was too late. Yuri's left arm wrapped itself around his throat, choking off any chance of screaming a warning and his right hand drove the knife into the mans unprotected back, right up to the hilt. He slid it out and drove it back in again and then again, a third time. Glancing nervously towards the fat German, he breathed a sigh of relief as he saw that he was still tapping away at his key. The guard choked and died. Yuri allowed him to fall backwards towards him and then dragged him as soundlessly as he could into the stall that Yuri had just vacated. He wiped the knife clean and returned it to its scabbard, then slid out the Luger. Peering nervously around the corner of the stall, he saw that the quartermaster was still busy at his Morse key, so he crossed over to the three wide awake Russians. Two of them were about Yuri's age, the third, a lot older.

"There's still another one to contend with," he hissed. "I'll be back in a minute." Clutching the Luger at high port, Yuri crept along the left-hand stalls, eyes riveted on the back of the fat German. The distance between them narrowed imperceptibly as Yuri fought to control his breathing and mounting panic. Slowly the gap lessened until Yuri was about six feet away. If the German moved or someone came through the door, that would be it. He would be involved in a shooting war. Tap, tap, tap. The key stuttered out its message, but then it ended abruptly. The German pulled off the headphones, laid them on the table and turned right into the pistol, gripped at the limit of Yuri's extended arm. The fat jowls sagged as his face took on a deathly pallor, his flabby arms and hands raised up in a gesture of pitiful defence. Instinctively, Yuri knew that this man would not make a play for the pistol. Neither moved nor spoke. Then Yuri acted.

Taking a swift step forward, he bought the barrel of the pistol down hard on the fat Germans exposed temple. The blow was enough to render him unconscious and his body slowly sagged to the floor like a sack of battered jelly. Yuri gazed impassively at the stricken man. Blood was beginning to ooze from the deep cut inflicted by the Luger, but the man was still breathing. Yuri raced to the doors at the courtyard end of the barn and opened one of them a crack. There was a sentry on guard in the centre of the courtyard, but he seemed static and unmoving. Probably asleep thought Yuri. However, he did notice that rain was beginning to fall. Then the sentry moved, shrugging into a poncho. Not asleep, thought Yuri, but not particularly alert, either. He silently closed the door, but this time, he put the locking bar in place. Then he ran back to the table and over to the body of the unconscious quartermaster, grabbing for the key ring that hung from the man's belt. Unclipping the keys, he ran down to the three Russians who were straining to look around the end of the stall to see what was happening. Giving them the keys, they began to unlock the chains binding them together as Yuri said, "Look, I came here for supplies. If you want to come with me, I have a hiding place in the woods. It's safe there for the moment. You want to come?" The three nodded, massaging their hands and legs as circulation returned once the cruel chains and shackles were released. "Right," said Yuri. He looked around and a thought came into his mind. "Over there are some stretchers. Get two of them and we'll load everything onto them and carry them between us, OK?" They nodded. "Kit yourselves out with weapons and clothing and get a back pack each. We'll have to tie up the quartermaster and make sure he's gagged. Don't forget poncho's if you can find them, it's wet outside. I can't read German, so I'm not sure what's in the boxes and sacks."

The older Russian spoke up. "I can, I'll sort it out."

"Good," whispered Yuri. "What I need most is explosives, detonators, food, sugar, paraffin, lubricating oil, medical equipment, water bottles, ropes and camp stoves. Try and get rifles for yourselves with telescopic sights and bipods. I'll go and check the end door and we probably have less than ten minutes max. OK?"

The three men nodded and went off to find the things on Yuri's shopping list. The far end of the barn was in semi darkness as Yuri approached. He glanced at his pocket watch, then slid the locking bar off the door and opened one side a crack. By my calculations, thought Yuri, the sentries should be at this point of their circuit about now. After a couple of nerve racking minutes, he saw the light from the anti-clockwise sentry, slowly appearing through the rain. Closing the door, he listened as the sentry passed, but where the hell was the one coming the other way? His nerves were beginning to fray around the edges as the moments passed. Then he saw the light approaching and waited until the man had disappeared around the adjoining building. Satisfied, Yuri returned to his new friends. The stretchers were full to overflowing with all sorts of boxes, sacks and drums. The three were busy roping them down as he approached. The quartermaster was trussed up like a chicken for roasting, his mouth gagged. What really pleased him were the two heavy calibre machine guns roped on top of each pile. He nodded to them. "Fine," he said enthusiastically, "well done. Now we've got to go."

The two young men picked up one of the stretchers and carried it down the aisle to the far doors. Yuri and the older man picked up the other one and followed them. At the door, Yuri had a quick look around and then beckoned out the two young men.

"Look," he whispered and pointed. "Over there where that blasted tree is laid. Take the stretcher there and then come back for the other one." The two men nodded and set off at a brisk, crouching walk. Yuri and the older man brought out the second stretcher and put it down. Yuri went back inside and put the locking bar in place. He then walked up to where he had dumped the dead German guard. The corpse lay on his back, his sightless eyes staring into space. Yuri felt no pity, the man had come here uninvited and paid the ultimate price. Yuri slid over the hay rack into the pig sty and exited through the side door. Anything to delay entrance to the barn, he thought. Desperate now to be off, he saw that the second stretcher was being carried by the two young men to where they had left the other one, the older man tagging along behind. Yuri covered the distance to the blasted pine quickly and the three men waited until he'd crouched down beside them.

"Right," said Yuri. "I'm Yuri and you are?"

"I'm Alexei," said one of the younger men, "and this is my brother Valery. The older man is the Colonel."

"OK," said Yuri, "Follow me as best you can. It's probably about five miles to my camp. I've left way markers to guide me back and hopefully I'll be able to find them, even in this murk." The three nodded. Yuri shrugged into his poncho, picked up his rifle and threw it over his shoulder by the strap, then tugged the piece of white bandage off the branch and put it in his pocket. The others had also donned their ponchos and slung their rifles. Then he and the Colonel, picked up the lead stretcher and followed by the brothers carrying theirs, walked off south-westwards through the now pouring rain.

Chapter 5 – The Brothers

The rain fell steadily as the four fugitives trudged on into the night. After about a mile, Yuri called a halt. With no immediate threat of pursuit apparent, they took a short break to rest their weary arms. They were up to the third marker and Yuri had ripped off each one as they went along, making sure that the stick markers, on the path, were also scattered. The rain sluiced down out of a moonless sky, making the tree rooted pathway treacherous underfoot and consequently, progress was slow and laboured. They continued on, but Yuri was becoming increasingly aware that the Colonel was suffering. His breathing was ragged and several times he slipped on tree roots and swore and groaned with pain. Eventually, he called for Yuri to stop. The two younger men put down their stretcher and rushed over to him. He was bent double, his breathing coming in rasping gasps, as his bloody hand clutched his right side.

Valery turned to Yuri and said, "He took a bayonet thrust in his side when we were captured. It's stitched and bandaged, but it looks like he's torn the wound open with all that slipping about. How far have we still got to go?"

"Another three miles at least," said Yuri, "can you walk if we spread the load?"

The Colonel nodded. "Sorry," he said, "but I just can't carry the stretcher any further."

"OK," said Yuri. "If we lash branches across the lifting handles, two of us can carry one stretcher at the front and the other, both stretchers at the back. If we rotate from front to back as we go along, we'll try and keep going back to my place. If not, we hide some of the gear and come back for it later. Will that do?"

The two younger men nodded. "Yeah, let's get it all back," they chorused. They searched around for suitable branches and lashed them into position. Then with Yuri taking the rear and the two young men up front, they started off for the next marker, the Colonel following along behind.

The rain was beginning to ease as they approached the tenth marker. They had rotated the load every five hundred yards or so, but now they were becoming weary and their arms were aching. Doggedly, they pressed on, the sky now moonlit after the passing rain. Yuri checked his watch at the next break. Three-fifteen. Not long now until the sun puts in an appearance, he thought, but also, not far to go. He knew that the next two markers were quite close together and there was a stream to cross. This particular stream was quite wide, but by taking their time, they managed to cross over by using a series of rocks as stepping stones, which afforded fairly easy passage. Once the twelfth marker was reached, he remembered that the next one sent them south instead of the direction they had been travelling, which was south-east. The Colonel was keeping up, but he looked terrible and was almost out on his feet. They crossed another stream by wading through the shallow water, it being impossible to cross by the rocks in the half light. Finally, as the sun was beginning to chin itself over the eastern horizon, they arrived at the inlet with the two boats. All four men were totally spent. The ravages of the journey in such wet conditions had taken its toll and even the two young men were clearly shattered. However, Yuri knew that whilst out here in the open, they were still totally exposed to anything by way of pursuit. They had to get to the island. There would be time enough to rest fully when ensconced within the confines of the cave. Another five minutes, he thought, then we have to go. How far away is the pursuit?

At the same time as the four were taking a well-earned breather, the sentry on the clockwise route around the compound was getting bored. The night had passed slowly and quietly since he started his shift at two o'clock. Three circuits of the compound every hour or so and he was on his sixth circuit. Halfway, he thought. In another couple of hours I'll be tucked up in bed and the war can go to hell. The mundane monotony of sentry duty was not lost on his idea of going to war. France, Belgium and the Scandinavian seaboard countries had all fallen so easily to German arms. All were nullified within months and even Britain could not hold out for much longer against the Luftwaffe. The central European states of Hungary, Greece, Czechoslovakia, Yugoslavia and Poland were now dominated and in some cases, allied with the all-conquering Nazi machine. The Finns had renewed their offensive against the Russians in the north as they try to get back their Karelia. All is good, he thought, all is so easy. We shall sweep these Russian clodhoppers into the wastes of Siberia and build our Lebensraum, our living space, here in the east. The Fuhrer has spoken, it is enough. In six months we'll all be back home and Christmas will be wonderful. He has said it in Mein Kampf and then we can rid ourselves of all these Jews, Slavs and Gypsies for the greater good of the world. He nodded to himself, pleased that he understood the implications of this great national quest. He switched off his torch, no need for extra light now, he thought. The sun is rising on another glorious day for the German people. He was passing the huge oil store, amazed at the amount of drums and cans that were stockpiled high into the brightening sky. The bowsers were being filled as he sauntered past, the camp was coming awake. The horse herders were tending to their stock and the road was becoming busier by the minute. The pathetic dregs of humanity that stumbled slowly past him towards the west, brooked no sympathy from his callous appraisal of Russian peasantry. Fucking shit eating rubbish, not human at all, he thought. Soon they'll realise that nothing can stand in the way of progress. Nazi progress. He hawked and spat in the general direction of the refugees.

"Shift your arses you fucking Ivan's," he shouted. "This is what it will feel like for the next thousand years." He then snapped to attention and gave the Nazi salute. The empty faces stared back at him. Just another inhuman example of Nazi tyranny, they thought. Where is God in all this suffering? The sentry laughed at their intransigence, turned and carried on with his round, feeling all was so good with the world. His reverie was interrupted by the arrival of a breathless soldier.

"Klaus," he said tersely, "the Major wants a word in the Officers' Quarters. It looks like those three Russian prisoners escaped during the night and the shit's hit the fan."

"What," stammered Klaus? "I saw nothing, heard nothing."

"Don't tell me," said the soldier, "tell the sodding Major."

With that, he marched off on the clockwise route, leaving Klaus to his fate. Klaus ran into the central courtyard which was now swarming with troops and shouldered his way through the heaving mass to the building which served as the Officers'

Quarters. The doors were wide open, lights blazing, as orderlies and NCO's scurried about like headless chickens. The Major stood in the centre, arms behind his back, his face contorted with rage.

"Sergeant," he bellowed, "get those troops moving. I want the whole place searched now and send four squads to search all the surrounding area. They may be hiding with those refugees, or in the woods. Find them, find them now."

The sergeant rushed off and a senior orderly became the Major's next victim. "You," he screamed, his face apoplectic. "Where are those guards that were supposed to be on duty?" The man quailed under the manic glare, his mouth opening and closing but no words were forthcoming.

"I'll find them sir," he eventually whimpered.

"Then go," railed his leader, "Go". The orderly scuttled off and found Klaus and the other sentries who were standing just inside the door trying not to be noticed.

"You men," the orderly blustered, "the Major wants to see you now." The guards padded across the floor to where the Major stood and came to attention. His head was bowed and he rocked backwards and forwards on his outstretched legs. These men of his were good soldiers, but fate had dealt him a massive problem. How to deal with it, how to bolster their confidence? He needed answers now. They waited until his head finally looked up and were pinned by the baleful stare of their Company Commander.

"So," the Major began gently. "How could this happen? Who is at fault? Mm. Is it I?" The guards were rigid, eyes looking anywhere but at their leader. "I said, is it I?" he bellowed.

"No sir," was the unanimous answer.

"Then who is responsible?" the major chided. The guards stuck rigidly to silence.

"You," he blasted at the unfortunate Klaus. "Report your night's activities."

"Sir," Klaus muttered. "Everything was quiet. All night sir. I saw no-one, heard nothing out of the ordinary. Talking between us sir, we're all of the same opinion."

The Major nodded. "We checked all the doors on every pass. There was nothing sir."

The Major surveyed the trembling guards and swore exasperatedly. "I believe you, up to a point," he said. "I realise that our security is not as it should be, too many open spaces, but we have only just arrived here and it will take time to reinforce the outer perimeter. However, as you know Hauptmann Lientz is due here within the hour and we have no prisoners for him. The Hauptmann is SS and I fear he will not be best pleased. The three Russians were high ranking and of aristocratic birth. They would have been a huge propaganda coup for Goebbels. As it is, I must try and find a way of conciliation with the Hauptmann. The prisoners cannot be that far gone." He shook his head and said gently. "Go and catch some rest, I'll deal with you later. This must not be allowed to happen again."

The relieved guards saluted, turned and marched off. The Major watched them leave and went back to what he was going to say to Hauptman Lientz. Damn those bloody Russians, he thought. Where the hell could they be? And who was it that released them and stuck a knife into the guard and then hogtied Schiller, the quartermaster? He shook his head. The guard was only young, but a good soldier and Schiller was too old a hand to be bamboozled by chained up communists. There had to be someone else. But who? Could these tales about Gruber be true? Was he out there, had he switched sides? All he knew was that someone had released those Russians. The escape had been discovered when the dead guards relief had tried to enter the building just before four o'clock and found the door barred from the inside. No amount of hammering on the doors provoked a response from the inside and eventually, the bar had to be smashed from its hinges. Schiller was found bundled up and still unconscious, whereas the guard was found in the stall opposite to where the three Russians had been shackled. Of the prisoners, there was no sign. The general alarm was then raised, Schiller untied and attended to by a medical orderly and a search of the immediate area, put into effect. By the time Klaus had been summoned into the Majors presence, Schiller was conscious, but unable to recall anything of the night's events. Perhaps, thought the Major, Schiller will remember something as he recovers. There must be something he remembers?

For the next hour, the compound hummed with barely supressed activity, as every nook and cranny was meticulously searched. Reports were filtering back from the search parties. No sign of the missing Russians, no tracks to follow in light of the nights heavy rains and no clue as to the whereabouts of a fourth collaborator, who may or may not have assisted their escape. The Major and his staff awaited the coming of the SS with trepidation. Lientz was not one to be trifled with. Eventually, the blaring of car horns signified the arrival of the SS's main Officer in the east. A small cavalcade of two half-tracks and a beautiful open topped Mercedes staff car swept into the central area of the compound and halted with a screech of tyres. The black uniformed SS guards swarmed out around the central area forming a barrier between the regular troops and Hauptmann Lientz's staff car. They stood facing outwards, machine pistols in hand looking deadly serious and the assembled regular troops were both cowed and terrified by their presence. The Major stood rigidly to attention outside the Officers' Quarters, flanked by his senior orderlies. He knew that he outranked the Hauptmann, but the SS were a law unto themselves. He would try and remain calm and focused for the benefit of his staff.

The SS Master Sergeant nodded to the Mercedes driver, confirming that all was well and the stage set for his leader. The driver stepped out of the car, marched around and opened the passenger side door. He snapped to attention and cried, "Hiel Hitler". The assembled throng returned the gesture, arms outstretched in deference to their Fuhrer. The Hauptmann arose from his seat, stepped out of the car and stood silently watching the assembled gathering, inwardly, acutely aware of the effect his appearance was having on them. He was tall, six foot three, with blond wavy hair and deep set blue eyes, completely confident of his superior aristocratic upbringing and Aryan heritage. His father had been a General, as had his Grandfather and Great Grandfather. His Teutonic Germanic lineage pulsed through every vein in his body. He was a warrior of the old school. Brushing away an imaginary speck of dust from his immaculately tailored uniform, he raised his arm in the Hitler salute and strode forward towards the assembled senior staff. It's all an act, thought the Major, a theatrical contrivance, but he too, was wrapped up in the melodramatic odyssey. The Hauptman strode up to the Major, his blue eyes boring into the Major's soul.

"Well Herr Major," he intoned in a gentle aristocratic voice. "You have three prisoners for me Mm?"

The Major stared back, his mouth suddenly dry and coughed nervously. "I am sorry, Herr Hauptmann, but the prisoners escaped during the night and for all our efforts, we have been unable to find them."

The Hauptmann's brow furrowed and he took a quick intake of breath. "What did you say?" he snarled ominously. "Escaped?"

The Major flinched from the malevolent tone and felt his eyes unable to look directly into the Hauptmann's, such was the intensity of his gaze. "Yes sir," was all he could offer.

The Hauptmann glared at those around him. "You have let the prisoners escape?" he shrieked. "A simple task of incarceration. These men were important, you understand, vitally important. What am I to tell Herr Goebbels?" Flecks of spittle accompanied the spat out words and the whole compound was assailed by his demonic rhetoric. "Imbeciles, dolts, the Fuhrer will have to be informed and it will not be me who tells him this news. If I had my way, you would all be shot for your gross incompetence." He turned, right arm flailing as he pointed at the assembled troops. "Get out of my sight you motherless cretins. Shooting would be too good for you idiots. Officers inside. Move!!"

The Officers retreated into their Quarters lashed by the furious Hauptmann. "I want a full explanation of the night's events, a comprehensive assessment of the circumstances surrounding the escape and a doubling of the efforts to find them, do you understand?" The Officers nodded abjectly. "Do you understand?"

"Yes sir," they chorused.

"Herr Major?" The Major went over the nights proceedings, how the sentries' had not seen or heard anything, how the prisoners were chained and manacled to the forage stalls, how the guard had been knifed to death and how Schiller, the quartermaster, had been beaten unconscious and tied up. Then someone had used his keys to release the prisoners from the chains. As he spoke, Lientz's demeanour softened as the Hauptman became engrossed in the main fact that a third party must have assisted the prisoners escape. At length, he raised his hand for the Major to be silent.

"So, you are certain that a third party was involved in this affair and that this Gruber is a suspect?"

The Major nodded, his heartbeat having returned to something like normal after the Hauptmann's vitriolic tirade. "We believe that Gruber may have gone native and has switched sides. There is no other explanation that we can come up with," said a perplexed Major.

The Hauptmann nodded. "Then, Herr Major, we must follow this line of enquiry," said Lientz. "I am now going to Minsk to oversee SS operations and you can be assured, that we will root out this turncoat once and for all. He will wish he had never been born."

The Major shivered at the savage outburst and knew that this man would accomplish all that he said he would. Then with a final glare aimed at the assembled Officers, Lientz turned on his heel and strode haughtily back to his limousine. Once the Hauptmann was seated in the car, the SS Guards vacated the compound, climbed onto their half-tracks and the cavalcade headed off towards the east in a swirl of dust and grinding motors. Lientz settled back into the thick leather seat, produced a cigarette holder from his tunic, then a cigarette from a beautifully designed cigarette case. He lit it and inhaled deeply. He was ecstatic. Gruber, for it could only have been Gruber, had managed to effect the release of the three Russians. Now he was perfectly placed to carry out his mission. Infiltrate the Soviet hierarchy. Lientz had never met him, but Himmler and Heydrich were sure he would be an asset, even though he was a totally despicable member of the human race, being a convicted thief and corpse robber. His personal foibles were not in question, only his total loyalty to the Nazi cause. Gruber was not German but Finnish. He had come to Berlin with a pathological hatred of all things Soviet, after his parents and sisters had been murdered by a Soviet hit squad following the Soviet invasion in 1939. His father had been a prominent member of the Finnish parliament, with a strong connection to the royal house and also an avid supporter of re-establishing the Romanov dynasty. Their home, just outside Kuhmo had been a target for Beria's NKVD and the family had been wiped out. Young Gruber had been with the Finnish army at the time, but deserted and waged his own personal war against the Commissars. His intimate knowledge of the lakes, bogs and woods in eastern Finland, coupled with the short length of the days at that latitude, enabled him to move around at will. He became a terrain specialist, the perfect predator. Fluent in Russian, German and English, as well as his own tongue. By his admission, he had accounted for twenty-four officers within the Soviet regime in the area, six for each of his family members. He was known as the Kuhmo wolf, an incredibly accurate sniper, which was also the call sign for his covert activities now in western Russia. After the Finnish-Russian war ended, he made his way to Berlin and was snapped up by the Gestapo and eventually, the SS, as perfect espionage material. All Lientz had to do now was wait for him to get in contact, once he had infiltrated the Soviet system. Lientz nodded contentedly to himself. The SS had arrived in western Russia.

The four fugitives had finally found their way to the island. Yuri had initially explained how he needed to transport the purloined goods from the compound across the water and showed them the two craft. They had loaded the stretchers onto the raft and with the two brothers manning the paddles, he and the Colonel had taken to the boat and the four of them had powered their way over the water. Yuri ran the boat up the landing area and secured it with a rope. Then he had helped to haul in the raft. The raft was cumbersome, but immensely useful for the work it was designed for and once the stretchers were transferred to the landing area, the two brothers hauled it safely away from the water's edge and onto the rocks. It tended to screech and scrape its way across the bumpy surface, but it was finally secured and covered with aspen branches to conceal it from inquisitive eyes. Yuri led the exhausted threesome up the stone steps, carrying the two stretchers between the three younger men and across the open area in front of the cave entrance. He could see their disappointment as they surveyed the size of the front part of the cave, but the three ex-prisoners were wide eyed with wonder when he showed them the door and, with the aid of a candle, the expanse of the space inside. Alexei was the first to react.

"Shit," he raved. "This is some fucking hidey-hole." He beamed at Yuri, waving his hand around expansively. "How the hell did you find all this?"

Yuri explained that it had been mere chance after his escape on the second day and that he had not discovered the inside of the cave until the morning of the third day.

"I slept outside, that first night," he explained. "Until I touched the back wall, I had no idea that the rest of the cave existed."

He then told them of the discovery of the original owner's body and subsequent burial, including the finding of the man's wife's grave. "I decided I needed more firepower and that's why I chose to break into the Compound, where I found you three. The rest, we're making up as we go along."

Alexei shook his head with wonderment and laughed out loud. "A place to hole up and strike back," he enthused. "A base for battering the fascist bastards. Shit, this is good." He grinned infectiously around him and then lunged forward to grab the staggering Colonel who almost fell over with exhaustion. They laid him gently on the floor while Valery rummaged through the medical supplies. Yuri put some water on to boil and then removed the Colonel's clothing exposing the wound. The bayonet cut looked ugly and inflamed and it was obvious that the Colonel had lost a lot of blood, but it seemed to have missed any major organs. His breathing was ragged and he grimaced and groaned with pain, as hot water was applied to the wound. He was clearly suffering and eventually fainted. Valery came up with a bottle of Brandy which he poured liberally over the wound in an attempt to cauterize it. Then he dressed the wound with a fresh, clean bandage having first doused it with ointment from the medical supply. They then lifted the inert Colonel and placed him on one of the beds in the side room, wrapping him with a blanket and bear skin.

"He needs rest now," said Valery, "then food and hopefully his strength will return." They left the Colonel sleeping peacefully and started to strip the stretchers of all the booty they had carried back with them.

"I'll take the first watch," said Yuri. "I know where to watch from and I'll wake you in a few hours. Use the stretchers as beds, they should be comfortable enough with the bracing pieces."

"I'll sleep in there with the Colonel," said Valery. "I need to keep an eye on him."

Yuri nodded, Valery disappeared off into the side room and the other bed while Alexei laid a bear skin over the stretcher and lay down for sleep.

"Thanks Yuri," he said. "We were due to be shipped out this morning by the SS. Who knows if we'd have survived that? The Colonel certainly wouldn't. Wake me in a couple of hours."

Yuri nodded and turned, picking up his rifle and binoculars and with a parting glance at the now snoring Alexei, made his way quietly outside. The ferocity of the morning sun's rays dazzled him and he lingered in the shadows of the outer cave while his eyes became accustomed to the glare. Now they were four, he thought. We need a plan and a way forward, but first, we need to be safe from pursuit. He reconnoitred the area from within the confines of the cave entrance, until he was satisfied that there was no immediate danger. Then slowly and methodically he made a complete sweep of the island. On the western cliff he paused and listened, feeling sure that he could hear movement on the paths to the north. Every so often, he could pick up low whistles. There were troops on the paths. Then his ears picked up a new sound, gradual at first and then building as the sound neared the island. It came from the south, from over the marshes and he slid deeper into the shade offered by the aspens and pines. Skirting the tree tops a tiny aircraft droned into view, the black crosses on its fuselage easily seen against the drab painted body and wings. Yuri recognised it immediately, a Fieseler Stork. He had seen enough of this tiny spotter plane during the days leading up to the invasion to know its capabilities. Very slow moving, the two-man crew were able to pinpoint movement and liaise with ground control using radio or hand signals. This particular plane was quartering the marshes to the east of the island and moved closer and closer to Yuri's position. It turned west and banked over the island, the co-pilot sweeping the area with his binoculars. Yuri felt somehow exposed and vulnerable as it cruised slowly above him, then it banked north until it was over the northern paths, then north-west towards the compound. Eventually, the sound faded and Yuri puffed out his cheeks and blew a sigh of relief. They were going to have to be very careful with one of those around. His new friends must be important if the Germans were using a Stork to hunt for them. He found a comfortable place within the trees on the north side, passing away the hours until he felt too tired to keep awake. Cautiously, he made his way back to the cave and stepped inside. All was quiet, the others still sleeping. He was going to have to do something about the south side windows. They could be easily spotted from the air, being too uniform in shape and the glass would reflect light. Anyway, that would be for later. What he needed now was a few hours rest. To that end, he shook Alexei awake. The young Russian was almost instantly awake and followed Yuri outside.

When clear of the cave entrance Yuri said "It's all quiet as far as I can tell. Familiarise yourself with the island. The north is probably where any danger will come from." He then explained to Alexei about the noises he had heard from the path and the coming and going of the Stork.

"Don't worry," said Alexei, "I'll be discretion itself," and smiled hugely. Yuri was impressed by the young man's attitude and devil-may-care demeanour. This was going to be an interesting partnership.

After several hours of sleep, Yuri was awakened by Valery. The young Russian looked rested and gave Yuri an account of the Colonel's present condition.

"He's still sleeping. The feverishness of this morning has given way to a more settled state and I think he should be OK now, given time. What we need to do is get some food into him and the rest of us. It's been a while since we last ate anything."

"That's good news," replied Yuri. "I was going to suggest we ate something, especially as we have lots of food at our disposal. Time to see what you came up with and then later, we can check out the hardware."

The two men busied themselves with food preparation. Hot steak and vegetables with a couple of tins of corned beef chopped in. Black bread with butter and three tins of peaches. Yuri went and collected Alexei from outside while Valery catered to the Colonel's needs. Then the three of them sat down and ate steadily. The meal was eaten in silence, as they were ravenous and talk would just have got in the way. Eventually, when everything was consumed, the three of them moved out of the cave and sat on logs outside, taking in the afternoon sun. Yuri had made up a pot of coffee and handed out cigarettes. The three of them smoked in silence.

"Tell me," enquired Yuri, "what happened to the three of you?"

The two brothers looked at each other and Valery finally spoke. "We were billeted just on the outskirts of Minsk. The initial attack had taken everyone by surprise and we were in the process of rushing more troops in to fill the gaps that the attack had created. However, the German tanks were upon us so quickly, that our positions were overrun. We tried to break out towards Smolensk, but they were too fast for us and we lost a lot of men and equipment. Our party was surrounded and it soon became futile to go on. The Colonel was all for a suicidal charge to break through, but when he was taken out, all we could do was try to protect him from further harm. We were separated from the other prisoners because of our rank. Somehow, they seemed to know that we were more than just serving officers. We presumed that one of our captured soldiers had, under duress, told them of our circumstances. The Colonel was formerly General Sergei Berezovsky. His rank had been reduced in one of Stalin's purges, although he and General Timoshenko had been instrumental in readying our forces, again due to Stalin's meddling. His family are of ancient lineage and he was one of three officers in charge at Leningrad at the time of the Communist takeover. He was a great protector of the Romanov's, but swore allegiance to Stalin. The civil war had been a huge drain on men and resources, one faction fighting another, Reds versus Whites and he was sick of the whole uselessness of more and more bloodshed. He reasoned that a Communist takeover could only be as bad as his present situation and would hopefully stop the endless killing. Only time will tell if he was right. Has he chosen an even worse regime than a sovereign state? Who knows? Then he allied his Cossacks to the Communist cause. His knowledge and tactical knowhow, make him a formidable enemy to the Nazi's. They will be extremely keen to recapture him."

Yuri nodded. "Where do you two fit in?"

"Well," replied Valery. "We are Valery and Alexei Avseyenko, late of Riasan, south west of Moscow. We both made Lieutenant six months ago and were assigned to Colonel Berezovsky's staff in Moscow. His family and ours go back many centuries and have served under various leaders' right back to Catherine the Great. I presume that with our connections and standing, we could also be classed as being a good catch for the enemy. The SS were about to interrogate the three of us until you became our liberator."

"So where do we go from here?" said Yuri. "We have to hit back in some way, or would it be better to try and get the three of you back to your units?"

Alexei spoke up. "Well Yuri, these things will have to be discussed, seeing as you know our backgrounds. What about yours?"

Yuri smiled and told them of the first morning of the attack, the unexpectedness of it and the shattering, overwhelming barrage followed by the tanks and infantry. How he had been hidden by Maslak and awoke to find his brother and comrades dead or missing. The Russian prisoners dumping the corpses into the trench and the subsequent filling in of the trench by Bulldozers. His escape and killing of Gruber, the burial of his brother the following day and his narrow escape from the dogs and soldiers of the German patrol, which led him to this island and its promise of sanctuary. How he had not noticed the cave entrance until the following morning, the confrontation with the original owners corpse and subsequent burial with the owners wife. The way he had reconnoitred the compound and had effected their escape. And all within just a few days.

The pair sat in silence as he ended with, "My brother, Grigori, was sergeant of our unit. I was just a lackey basically, a bringer of supplies and ammunition, as I was still only seventeen and not old enough to be classed as a soldier. My home is far away, near Kazan. My father and grandfather were of peasant stock and we supported the Red Russian cause in the civil war. Our village was quite large as villages go and my father was head of the local Soviet, making sure that everyone was looked after and provided for. We lived quite prosperously, as our parents knew how to use the land that we were allocated. I was educated locally and my maternal grandmother was a source of great inspiration and knowledge, as she had travelled extensively during her youth and these things she passed on to me and my brothers and sisters. Hopefully, one day, I will be able to bring them all here to see Grigori's grave."

The two men silently acknowledged Yuri's account of his baptism of fire and his lineage. Finally, Valery spoke. "Yuri, we're all in this together and Alexei and I will not be dictating what we do from now on. We may have been officers in the army, but here, I am one of a unit of four and we will decide between us how we conduct ourselves. The enemy can be targeted in many ways. We just have to decide what's best for us, to maximise our resources."

The rest of the day was spent touring the island. Yuri was keen to show the brothers where everything was situated in regard to their immediate surroundings. The paths to the north, east and west were studied and there were still sounds of activity emanating from along these areas. The three of them understood the need for silence and the fact that here on the island, they were safe as long as they remained within its protection. The Colonel needed time to recover from his wound and then they would all be able to decide on what course to take. Yuri showed the pair the raft and boat and between them they saw how cleverly they had been put together.

Once back in the cave, Valery saw to the Colonels needs giving him hot soup and some black bread. The wound was healing nicely, but rest for all of them was the main ingredient to health. Once the others had also eaten, they made for their beds.

Two days later, the Colonel was able to get up and walk around, albeit with support from Valery. The days had been difficult for the three young Russians and they had sat around reading and chatting, while the search for them continued over on the mainland. This morning, it appeared to be fairly quiet and it was decided to hold a council of war outside. The sun shone in brilliant splendour, as they arranged some upturned logs for seating plus one of Aleksander's chairs for the Colonel. Yuri elucidated to the Colonel about his escape from the trench on that first day of the invasion. He also explained how he had sifted through the contents of Gruber's pack. The Colonel was intrigued and questioned Yuri.

"This Gruber," said the Colonel. "I heard his name mentioned when we were held captive. Several Germans made reference to him and it's possible that we could utilise this information."

"In what way?" enquired Yuri.

"Well, apparently he had gone missing on the first day, obviously you know where and why, but they believe that he has deserted and has gone over to our side. I did hear that they thought it was Gruber that they chased and lost on the second day, the day when you escaped from the soldiers and ended up here. Perhaps you may have found ID or papers in his belongings, that I could look over and see what I could glean from them. If they believe that he is at large, we could make it work in our favour."

"But how?" said an incredulous Yuri. "Surely they'll class him as a renegade, a turn coat?"

"That may be," replied the Colonel, "but who knows what we may find. Anyway, until I dig deeper, it's pure conjecture and will remain that way unless something comes of it. So let's talk of other more pressing things. The war has not been going well for us, especially in these initial stages. My idea would be to attack their supply system."

"Basically, that's what I had in mind," said Yuri, "that petrol dump at the compound seems awfully tempting. As far as I'm concerned, its destruction would be a huge blow. If we could destroy it, the devastation would be enormous taking out the village, all forms of transport and men. My idea would be a covert attack, very soon before they reorganise their security."

"I like the sound of that," said the Colonel, "but we need to be in and out quietly, to give us a chance of escape."

"I have an idea," said Yuri. "Inside the cave are two Crossbows with several bolts. If we could get close enough at night, a few bolts in a petrol bowser creates a pool of liquid and a fire arrow into the petrol provides the spark."

"Even better," laughed Alexei, "would be a fire bolt straight into a bowser. Why piss about with making holes. One fire bolt and bye bye compound."

"Just a minute," interjected the Colonel. "How close would you need to be with one of those Crossbows Yuri?"

Yuri considered. "Probably fifty or sixty yards," he estimated.

"Then it's a suicide mission," said the Colonel bleakly. "You'd be vaporised in an instant. We need something better than that, something to give us time to get away."

"We do have detonators," interjected Valery. "We just need a plan to get one of us in close."

"OK," said the Colonel. "Firstly, we need to reconnoitre the area. We need to know exactly what's involved regarding sentries, defences and areas of approach. Once the hue and cry of our escape has died down a little, we'll have to monitor the situation on a daily basis. These Germans are a very resourceful lot, but their Achilles heel is a rigidness of sticking to times and schedules, this much I do know about them. Once we know their schedules, they won't detract from them. Then we can formulate a plan that should give us an advantage."

The four men looked at each other. "Sounds good," offered Valery.

"It'll sound better when the whole of western Russia blows up," grinned Alexei. "Who's for roast horse and fascist?" The others laughed, but deep down, they all knew that this was going to be a tough nut to crack. Nevertheless, this was a sure fire way to help their comrades and maybe slow down the advance. Firstly, they needed to utilise the time before striking back and secondly, they needed an awful lot of luck.

Chapter 6 – Strike back

The days that followed were spent in preparation for the attack on the compound's petrol supply dump and for the three newcomers to get to know the immediate area around the island. Valery had broached the subject of food supply and wood for the stove come the onset of winter which, as he pointed out, had a nasty habit of catching people unaware. To this end, he and Alexei volunteered to go out and hunt down some game and source wood for the fire. At first, Yuri was sceptical saying that these sort of things could wait until later, but the brothers argued and with some degree of accuracy, that their continued existence was down to the fact that they would probably need to hide away for extended periods, if their plans for destruction bore fruit. After all, the island was reasonably secure from meddling eyes and only when the snows came would movement and tracks be easier to follow for a vengeful enemy. Therefore, it made sense to prepare now for those times ahead. The Colonel listened to their arguments and gave his blessing, saying that he and Yuri would stay on the island and work out a strategy for the attack, while the brothers hunted for food and wood. The attack would be at the end of the following week, so for the next few days, the brothers would explore and hopefully expand their food and fuel supplies.

They spent the rest of the day collating their haul from the compound and Yuri was mightily impressed. The two large machine guns were brand new and air cooled beautiful examples of German engineering. Then there were several machine pistols, rifles and hand guns. They had managed to get bipods and scopes for the rifles and ammunition for all the weapons, as some differed in size to others. There were three boxes of dynamite with a selection of detonators, a box of medical supplies, four boxes of assorted foods and a large container of Paraffin. In fact, the only thing missing from Yuri's original shopping list was lubricating oil, but there was enough in the packs. They had also brought a couple of gross of candles with matches. The Colonel then produced several maps which he had grabbed off the quartermasters table and two pairs of field binoculars. Finally Alexei reached into his pocket and pulled out the huge set of keys that Yuri had used to release them, plus many more.

"I thought they may have a use, you never know and anyway, they would be very pissed off when they found everything locked. I made sure of that before we left," he added impishly.

Yuri shook his head and laughed. "I think they would be very, very pissed off. I would never have thought of that."

"It comes from having a twisted mind," laughed Alexei in reply.

Then Yuri showed them all the things that he had found including the crossbows, long bow and rifles. The two brothers weighed up the crossbows and pronounced them superb in every way. The previous owner had kept them in meticulous condition and both men couldn't wait to use them. To that end, they took them outside, like a couple of excited children and using a log as a target, proceeded to fire off a couple of attempts.

The Colonel watched with a knowing eye and eventually spoke. "All right you two, that's enough for today. Tomorrow we start using them for real and if Yuri doesn't mind, the pair of you will be in charge of them for our assault on the compound." At Yuri's disappointed expression he then followed up with, "I want you, Yuri, to plant the charge. Will that be OK?"

Yuri nodded. "That's fine," he answered. He then went back into the cave and brought out Gruber's pack. He opened it and produced the bags of rings, necklets, watches and teeth, showing them to the others. They all agreed that Gruber had been a despicable and disgusting individual, who deserved to die as he had.

Finally, Yuri said, "I took a watch to use myself and so take one each. We need to be able to tell the time and also we'll need them to co-ordinate attacks." The others nodded and picked out one each. The rest were put away for the future. By now, the evening was beginning to draw in and after a quick meal and a thorough scout around the area, the four men turned in. Sleep came slowly to Yuri, his head was full of the day's events, but eventually, he drifted away.

Morning arrived. The four men awoke from their slumbers relaxed and rested. After much yawning and stretching, the three younger men wandered outside. The mist was thick, clinging to the lakes surface and the surrounding trees. The eerie stillness enhanced their mood, even though the morning chill made them shiver and rub their hands together for warmth. The rising sun haloed its presence in the eastern sky, but so far there was no sound of drips, in fact there was no sound at all. Yuri closed his eyes and breathed in the crisp air. Where was the war now he thought? Have our troops rallied or is the enemy still in the ascendancy? There's no real way to find out. All we know is that the Germans are still in our country and therefore, must be a threat to our national existence.

The brothers were also silent, until Valery spoke. "Come on Alexei, breakfast and then we'd better be off. No time like the present and there's lots to do."

Alexei shrugged and grunted a reply. "He's always the same," he said to Yuri. "Always in such a damned hurry. Can't we at least have a little time to wake up?"

"You've had long enough," said a suddenly appearing Colonel. "Valery knows that it would be better to set off across the lake while the mist is still thick. There may be watching eyes."

"Yes, he's always bloody right," replied an exasperated Alexei. "No peace for the wicked, or for me," he added with a smirk. Consequently, after a quick breakfast, Alexei and Valery prepared for the day ahead.

"We'll take the crossbows and the long bow," Valery said. "We're not sure if anyone's still around, so we want to be as quiet as possible."

"Good idea," said the Colonel, "but make sure you carry the rifles as well. Don't forget, it's an exploratory trip and we need information as much as anything. Just see what you can come up with." The two men nodded, picked up their gear and the four of them left the cave and went down to the raft and boat.

"We'll just take the raft," said Valery. "You may have need of the boat and we're going to be bringing back more than such a small craft will take, hopefully." Yuri and the Colonel nodded in agreement.

"Remember," said the Colonel. "No need to do anything stupid like getting yourselves spotted. Don't forget about that Stork, it could still be about. Find out what you can, but come home safely,

Mm?" The two young men nodded, both looking quite serious, removed the covering aspen branches from the raft and lifted it, rather than dragged it, down to the water. Settling on board, they paddled out into the mist without a backward glance and after twenty yards, had disappeared from view. The silence returned to the island as Yuri and the Colonel made their way back to the cave.

The Colonel made coffee and sat outside watching and listening as the sun burned its way through the mist. All was quiet and Yuri did a thorough scan of the area with his binoculars before joining him.

"I'd like to have a look through the previous owner's things," said Yuri, "especially that large box of drawings. I have a feeling it could turn up something quite interesting."

To that end, he and the Colonel brought out the boxes into the sunshine and keeping close to the cave entrance, began to go through them. As Yuri had found is his initial quick scan, there were many drawings of animals, birds, fish, flowers and trees. All beautifully drawn, each having a signature on the reverse, either A.D or A.K.D. with the date and year. Aleksander or Anna Katherine Dobrovolsky. They both marvelled at the detail and dexterity with which the drawings had been compiled. Eventually, they found their way through them and came upon several cardboard tubes. Here was the hidden treasures that Yuri had predicted. Inside the tubes were maps. One tube contained a large scale offering, which encompassed the area between the Rivers Bug and Dnieper, showing the main towns and cities, roads and railways. Other tubes held much larger scale drawings of specific areas, especially the Marshes. When all laid out together, they created a map of around twenty feet by fifteen. The maps showed villages, towns and in some cases, individual dwellings, with detailed diagrams of paths, tracks and small waterways, that crisscrossed the Marsh area and beyond. Other tubes held even more detailed analysis of specific areas, where compass bearings and distances in yards were plainly laid out. The immensity of the maps detail and clarity were almost too much to take in, coupled with a seemingly faultless accuracy. This man had obviously been some sort of Cartographer.

The Colonel was the first to break the silence. "Incredible Yuri, such attention to detail. I'm totally overwhelmed. We have to remember that the border between Poland and Mother Russia has been tremendously fluid for centuries, as has the Finnish - Russian border. When Hitler invaded Poland, Stalin was quick to gobble up eastern Poland as far as the River Bug and also the Baltic States. We are now in what was eastern Poland up to a few months ago. Aleksander's work shows the border as it was before Hitler and Stalin's intervention. This man was so articulate, so fastidious in his attention to detail, that I'm totally lost for words. Even so, we are very, very lucky to have inherited this. Incredible".

Yuri nodded his assent, delved into the bottom of the box and brought out a small tin container, which on inspection, held three compasses. "Now we have the tools to navigate the whole area," said Yuri. 'We can quite clearly see the compound as it then was, a cluster of wooden huts and dwellings. There would appear to be an alternative route to it, which I hadn't spotted before, including the ways to get to the River Bug. All the crossings are marked as well. These maps will be invaluable".

They decided to pack all the things away, but left the maps for future use. "The boys could have done with these today. I wonder how they're doing?" said the Colonel.

"They'll be fine," replied Yuri. "Valery seems too savvy in the ways of the world. Did you want to look through Gruber's papers?"

"Good idea," replied the Colonel, "who knows what I might find."

Yuri fetched the Colonel all that he had found regarding Gruber, including his jacket and pack.

"I'll give it the once over," said the Colonel, "although I may have to look in places where it doesn't appear obvious. I'm looking for anything abnormal."

Yuri left the Colonel to his deliberations and did another sweep of the island. At the western end he sat down with his back to a tree and thought about the compound and its petrol store. To his mind, it would be reasonable to assume that security around the compound would have increased since the three Russians made their escape. Petrol would be a much needed commodity and the Germans would make sure it was as safe as possible before tankering it forward to the thirsty tanks. He couldn't really formulate a plan until he had seen around the compound's immediate area, both by day and by night. That would have to be soon and then several times after that. All he knew was that it was a dump central to the invading armies continued progress and its destruction would certainly inhibit that progress. Get in close, take out the sentries, plant the charge and get out undetected. It sounded simple enough, but he knew there were so many things that could go wrong. The Colonel would be an enormous help in planning such a venture, but it would be he, Alexei and Valery, who would be at the sharp end of the actual attack. He had never faced a challenge like it before and was excited by the prospect. All he could do was keep his end up and trust to his new friends. Suddenly, his reverie was interrupted by movement along the eastern side of the lake. He flattened himself between the rocks and peered out through the binoculars. Moving up through the trees, he counted twenty German soldiers, spread out in search formation. They were dressed in camouflage clothing and moved silently and relentlessly between the trees and reeds, on a course that would take them past the eastern end of the island and onto the path at the north end of the lake. Was this just a routine patrol, or were they after something specific, thought Yuri? As he watched, he became aware that they were all wearing the SS flashes on their helmets. So, the SS were combing the marshes, he thought. And where the hell are Alexei and Valery? He had heard nothing, but had no idea where his friends were, or if they were OK. The patrol passed the end of the island and continued into the trees by the path. It was unnerving for Yuri. They moved with a formidable purposefulness that ordinary troops just wouldn't have. Whatever the four Russians did in the future, they must be aware that this class of soldier could be about at any time. He shivered at the thought. Good God, he thought, I'm getting paranoid. After all, they're only men.

Swiftly, he made his way back to the cave and found the Colonel in the entrance, the large calibre machine gun loaded up and pointing in the patrols direction. He nodded grimly to Yuri and whispered, "That was close, were they SS?"

"Yes," said Yuri, "and a mean looking bunch. Do you think the boys are alright?"

The Colonel shrugged. "Time will tell," he added noncommittally. They stayed together and watched for about half an hour. Nothing was apparent, so the Colonel went back to Gruber's papers and Yuri put a meal together. The waiting was getting to both of them and the meal was eaten in silence. Yuri checked his watch, seven thirty. When could they expect the brothers to return?

The Colonel saw his concerned expression and offered "give them another couple of hours. Once the light starts to fade, they'll be coming."

Yuri shrugged and smiled grimly. "Yeah," he said quietly.

At nine-thirty, Yuri and the Colonel ventured outside and made for the high west end of the island. The sun was westering fast and the evening shadows dappled the gently rippling lake surface. Nothing moved wherever Yuri trained the binoculars. Ten o'clock came and went, but still no sign of the brothers. Then the reeds parted and the raft glided out from the bay. Two paddles propelled the craft towards the island and as it neared the landing area, Alexei's hand was raised in greeting, his wide grin signifying that all was well. Yuri and the Colonel helped drag the raft ashore, staring in wonder at the mass of wood and logs piled on it. On top of the logs were the carcasses of a couple of wild pigs, with two deer thrown in.

"Well," crowed Alexei, "what do you think?"

"I hope you didn't lose any crossbow bolts," muttered the Colonel.

"No, no," replied Alexei. "We brought them all back. Mind you, some are still stuck in those carcasses. Anyone for a spot of butchery?"

The tension seemed to fall away from Yuri and the Colonel as they laughed at Alexei's remarks. "We were worried you idiot," said the Colonel "We watched an SS patrol go past earlier and knowing how you two are so easily caught, we assumed the worst."

"Bloody cheek," sneered Alexei. "We were following them. Thought they might be lonely and just tagged on behind. Put it this way. They were in our sights for several miles, but we got fed up in the end and let them go, isn't that right Valery?"

Valery nodded his head and grinned at his younger brother. "We thought the odds were a bit unfair, so we let them off this time. Mind you, they did look very smart, like proper soldiers. Couldn't bring myself to shoot them. Much too pretty."

He and Alexei laughed and the Colonel took a playful swing at them, missed and shooed them off to the cave. "Go and get something to eat, you reprobates," growled the Colonel. "Yuri and I will see to these presents you have brought us."

 The two brothers strode off, arms around each other while Yuri and the Colonel beached the raft and unloaded its contents. The pigs and deer carcasses were lifted into the cave entrance and hung just inside the door. The wood and logs were randomly scattered around the cave area, so as to give no hint of order, should the Stork pass by overhead. By the time all was finished and the raft safely hidden, darkness was upon them. Yuri and the Colonel returned to the cave. The Colonel rummaged around for some containers before slitting the carcasses throats, allowing the blood to run through the bodies and for the meat to begin to cure. The brothers had eaten their meal and were now both tucked up in bed, snoring heavily. Yuri bid the Colonel goodnight and took to his own blankets. Sleep was good for them all.

Morning came in its usual misty way. The four men had slept deeply and awakened later than had been usual. Valery and the Colonel busied themselves with breakfast, while Yuri and Alexei toured the island, scouting for anything out of the ordinary. Finding and hearing nothing, they returned to the cave. Breakfast was taken with coffee and afterwards, the four of them began to talk about the previous day's events. Yuri explained to the brothers about the maps and showed them several examples. They were suitably impressed and sifted through them looking for where yesterday had taken them. Finally, they spread three of the maps out on the ground and Valery spoke while Alexei showed Yuri and the Colonel exactly where they had been.

"Once we reached the bay and grounded the raft," began Valery, "we split up for a quick look around. Alexei went north to the path we had returned on from the compound, while I went south along the edge of the lake. After an hour we met up again and Alexei had found many tracks, but nothing coming towards the bay where the raft was tied. I had found a small hut about two hundred yards from the bay. On inspection, it held a couple of sleds which obviously had been used for hauling timber. The sleds had ropes which were attached to a yoke, which fitted quite easily over a man's shoulders. There was another which was for horses. We decided to utilise the smaller sled and dragged it off to locate the wood that we brought back with us last night. This took several hours, but we managed to fill the raft. Once that was completed, we decided to head south to see where the path would take us. After about a mile, we noticed that the lake sides began to come together and found that the lake narrowed to about fifty feet. There's a rock ledge across the neck of the lake which holds the water back. This obviously overflows in the winter, down to a fairly wide stream which travels west towards the Bug. There is a wooden bridge across the stream at this point. It's a bit rickety, but safe enough for men to cross. The stream is fordable at this time of year, but we took the easy route."

 Alexei was showing Yuri and the Colonel exactly where these things were on the map. "Anyway," continued Valery. "As we moved into the woods, Alexei spotted a couple of deer, so we tried out the crossbows to good effect. Both bows seem very accurate and at fifty yards, we made an easy kill. We hid them up in a tree for collection later and then headed southeast into hillier and densely wooded country. After a few miles we both smelt smoke, and after a while, we came across a clearing with the remains of what appeared to be a cooking fire. There were several carcasses spread about and it looked as though around fifteen to twenty men had been here and not long ago, as the embers were still warm to the touch. The carcasses had been stripped and there were wolf as well as bear tracks around the clearing. The party had moved off towards the Bug, so we decided to head in the opposite direction. We think they were like us, soldiers separated from their units and sleeping rough. However, we weren't too keen to meet up with them at this stage. We travelled east for about four miles and came across a road. This road ran east to west and showed signs of recent use. Lots of horse and lorry tracks with troop movement alongside. You can see where Alexei is pointing as to its location. We followed it for a few miles east, seeing and hearing nothing, until it seemed to veer off southwards. At this point, we came across that SS patrol you spotted yesterday. They had come up from the south and then taken a northward path. It seemed odd to us that they would deviate from the road, so we followed them, hanging well back once we had them spotted. They'd come upon a couple of houses, but no-one was at home, so they moved on. We're not sure exactly where they were headed or why, but they did seem to know where they were going, as they never deviated from due north. Once they got to the path above the lake, they headed east. We tracked their progress as far as we could. It looked like they were heading towards Minsk. Then we retraced our steps, picked up the deer, crossed back over the bridge and came across a heard of wild pigs rutting in the bogs. The crossbows accounted for two before the others got the wind up and vanished into the scrub. We decided then to wait until the light faded before coming home."

After Valery's account of the previous day, the four of them checked over their findings on the maps. The brothers had discovered quite a lot regarding the southern surrounding area and had proved themselves adept at evading detection and sussing out the lie of the land. The road was an interesting find and was an obvious highway to somewhere. It was logged away in their memories for future use.

The Colonel explained that he had been through Gruber's belongings and papers and had come up with a few anomalies. As he explained to the three young men, "I found some odd things in his possession. Apart from the ID card and combat group papers, I also found a letter of introduction, claiming that he was a member of an organisation called the Aryan Freedom Fighters based in Leipzig. Now I was privy to clandestine operations being carried out by the Gestapo and SS, when I was based in Smolensk over the last couple of years and this group came up regularly in our anti-Semitic investigations at Government department levels. Our spies in Berlin were attempting to find the amount of national hatred towards the Jews, Slavs, Gypsies and us. They referred to us as 'Untermensch' which translates to 'Sub-humans'. We concluded that in the event of war, all these ethnic groups, including the 'Untermensch', were to be systematically exterminated."

He held up his hand for quiet as the three younger men interrupted in astonishment. "Wait," he said, "let me finish. You can have your say later." The others relented and he continued. 'We were particularly interested in three individuals who, we found out, were to infiltrate the Communist system once hostilities began. They would report on troop movements, logistics, morale and army concentrations, where our main defences were and where they were at their thinnest etc. In other words, to bring about our destruction from within. The three main thrusts of the German invasion were Army Group North, which aimed to capture the Baltic States and move on to Leningrad, Army Group Centre, which is aimed at Moscow, via Minsk and Smolensk and Army Group South, whose main target was Kiev. We never got to find out the identity of one of the insurgents, but the other two were a shoemaker from Munich and a naturalised Finn. The shoemaker is in our country now. He came on the first day of hostilities and is still at large, somewhere between here and Kiev. This I know from the maps and radio traffic copies, I picked up from the compound. His code name was 'Rhine Maiden'. The other, who as I say, we didn't know the identity of, is now somewhere between here and Leningrad. His code name was 'Brandenburg Gate'. The Finn was also sent on the first day. He disappeared once he was within our borders. His code name was 'Kuhmo Wolf'. Now we don't know his real name, or his naturalised German name, but we do know that he was imprisoned for stealing, not long after he arrived in Germany. During the Winter War of 1939, there were two Finns who excelled in taking out our forces with sniper rifles. One was called the 'White Ghost', the other was called 'Kuhmo Wolf'. The 'White Ghost' is still in Finland, but 'Kuhmo Wolf', as far as I can make out, is lying at the bottom of a trench, killed a week ago by one, Yuri Petrovsky."

At this, Yuri's mouth dropped open and he stammered, "Are you sure?"

"Pretty much so on the evidence I have," replied the Colonel. "It looks like you've taken out the Germans main spy for the central area."

"Shit," offered Yuri, "a spy you say. Gruber was a spy? Well, that's good isn't it?"

"It is," replied the Colonel, "but it also opens up possibilities for us that maybe we can exploit."

Valery chipped in with, "Are you thinking of counter intelligence sir?"

"That I am," replied the Colonel, "but first we would have to make contact with his handler. If it works, we may be onto something really big. Lives could be at stake here, depending on what we pass on, but we won't know that until we do. I have some ideas about contact, so leave that to me. What it must not do, is cloud our thinking over what to do next. That has to be the destruction of the petrol dump at the compound."

"Too right," said Alexei, "this covert crap is all very well, but sending a few coded messages will not stop the tanks rolling, dynamite will."

"Come on Alexei," pleaded the Colonel, "surely even you can see the big picture?"

"Oh, I can see it all right," replied Alexei, "but my picture has a fucking great bang in the middle of it. Stick that on your wall and frame it."

The others collapsed in laughter. "You're impossible," giggled the Colonel, "the three of you can go check it out this afternoon. It's about time we had a look and times pressing. You can all bugger off and leave me in peace." That final statement had the desired effect. The three young men grinned at each other and went to get their gear together. The Colonel watched them ready themselves and wondered at how easily they bonded together. I have no concerns about these three he thought. They're a sensible bunch, even Alexei when he's not taking the piss. I for one am glad they're on our side.

"Listen," he said as they were about to leave. "No heroics, do you hear?" They all nodded.

"Don't worry sir," said Valery. "Information it is. We'll be prudence herself."

"Huh," muttered the Colonel. "And make sure you announce yourselves when you get back, or I may fill your bodies with bullets."

"Yes sir," they chorused as they made their way to the boat. "It'll be dark when we get back, so don't wait up," added Valery as they paddled off.

"God speed," muttered the Colonel under his breath. He watched them pass through the reeds into the bay, then turned, had a quick scout of the surrounding area, before going back to the cave and beginning the butchery of the pigs and deer. He was not worried. They would be fine.

The three young Russians made swift work of getting into position to observe the compound and the comings and goings of the road. The six miles were covered smoothly and unobserved, but as soon as they got up close, they saw a very different compound to the one they'd left earlier. The Germans had been very busy. Two sentry towers had sprung up, one at the northeast corner and one, directly opposite the petrol dump in the northwest corner. Another two were in the process of being built in the southeast and southwest corners. Barbed wire had also been erected up to a height of about twelve feet, on fifty percent of the outer edge. Large metal gates were apparent at the entrance to the inner compound, adjacent to the road at the north end. Through the binoculars they could make out that the wire was not yet electrified, but all that could change in the near future. The three would be saboteur's stared in dismay at the hive of activity. The woods had been decimated in an all-out quest for timber. No way would they be able to get close, not during daylight anyway. The scene was a mass of men and horses. Most of the physical work was being done by what appeared to be Russian prisoners. They were cutting down trees with axes and saws, while teams of horses with their German handlers dragged the logs down to the compound perimeter. Others were digging deep holes for the fence posts to be placed in, while another group mixed an endless supply of concrete. Armed guards patrolled around the sweating prisoners. German carpenters were fixing cross beams and stays to the two towers under construction, others making ladders for access to the towers. Everywhere the three young Russians looked, they were met with work in progress. It looked as if their predicted date for action would need to be brought closer. They decided to split up, with Yuri going towards the north end, Alexei and Valery would work their way around the south side and then Valery would get as close as he could to the western corner. They reasoned that work on the perimeter would cease as evening and night fell. Then they could move in closer and work out some sort of strategy. Valery would be the one who would have a direct view of where they hoped to enter the compound and plant the charge. The plan was to observe and write down as much information as possible about their allocated area. Valery would pick up Alexei on the way back and then the two would pick up Yuri. It was going to be a long afternoon and probably most of the night. Still, it had to be done if there was ever going to be a decent chance of success. Yuri wriggled his way forward into a grove of trees, perhaps half a mile or so from the edge of the compound and a few hundred yards from the road. The road was alive with movement, soldiers on foot, officers on horses, lorries carrying piles of equipment, horses pulling field guns and ammunition, their handlers chivvying them on. All moving east towards the front, wherever that was. In the opposite direction, refugees were battling against the tide, desperate to get away from the fighting. Old and young, lots of mothers with babies, horses and carts, hand pulled carts, prams and hand carried luggage, their desperation etched in the blank expressions on their faces. Yuri felt a curious detachment from all their suffering. After all, he was part of the resistance to these German invaders, he was a hope for them all in their fight against tyranny. And yet, he knew that he was witnessing a mass migration and none of it voluntary.

He tore himself away from his countrymen's agony and concentrated on the matter in hand. He ran his binoculars over the sentry tower and felt a sickness in the pit of his stomach. The tower stood twenty feet high, with a chest high parapet around the top and a wooden roof to keep out most of the rain. There was also a searchlight in place, which could be adjusted to sweep all around the area, both without and within the compound. He could also see the barrel of a fixed machine gun protruding over the parapet wall. A long, wide, wooden ladder provided access to the parapet and at the moment, one sentry was on guard, arms folded across his chest and leaning over the parapet, staring abjectly at the hubbub on the road. He looks bored stiff, thought Yuri. There were also lights fitted to the tops of the barbed wire fence. They would cast a downward and outward glow, reckoned Yuri. Lights aren't too bad a thing, he thought, because they do provide shadows as well as light. Shadows can be utilised. He could also see that even though trees had been felled, the bottom couple of feet had been left. This would provide cover when he was able to move closer. He was writing down everything he could think of, it helped to pass the time. The hours slipped slowly by. I wonder how the others are doing, he thought. Same as me, waiting for darkness. As the day drew on, work was beginning to cease. The tired prisoners were rounded up and trooped off towards the west. There must be some sort of holding pen for these prisoners, thought Yuri, either this side, or the western side of the River Bug. Perhaps Valery could see where it was. The German sentries had stood to and were assembling inside the inner courtyard, where he could make out some sort of feeding station. The horse handlers were leading their charges across the road and into the fields opposite the main gates. The compound was beginning to calm down for the evening. The road too was becoming less busy and as night fell, traffic in both directions began to ease, as tired troops and refugees made camp for the night. Yuri noticed that the wind had picked up and was blowing in a few clouds from the northwest. All in all though, the frantic pace of daylight hours had passed and in its place, the sentries began their tours of the perimeter fence. Yuri checked around him before creeping forward until he was within a hundred yards of the fence, nestled between what remained of two chopped down tree trunks.

The clockwise and anti-clockwise sentries began their circular patrols. Yuri timed them and found after a couple of hours that they were still on the same twenty minute schedule, as they had been when he was last here. There was just one sentry in the tower and every so often, he would swing the searchlight around the trees and scrub in front of him. Whenever he did this, Yuri ducked down, but he was fairly sure that he could not be spotted within the shadowy confines of the two stumps. The main difference this time to before, was that the inner courtyard was patrolled by a dozen men and every so often, they would walk between the huts and houses, torches shining the way. Worryingly, there seemed to be no particular schedule, more a random check whenever the mood took them. This was going to be difficult. The night wore on and at two o'clock, the early shift stood down and the late shift took over. He watched the sentry in the tower descend the steps and have a few words with the new one coming on, who then ascended up the ladder while his mate wandered off to find his bed. The clockwise and anti-clockwise patrols began again, but Yuri noticed that the time gap from when the early shift handed over to the late shift created a gap of half an hour, opposed to the twenty minutes between sweeps up until that time. Perhaps this time difference could be utilised to their advantage. However, the central guards were still drifting between the buildings and Yuri was sure that they would pose the most dangerous threat to his detection, when he moved in to set the charge. The covering crossbows would have to be good, if he was to get in and out undetected. The light was beginning to rise in the east, when he heard a low whistle from behind him. Alexei was beckoning him to fall back and he crept slowly backwards until Valery tapped him on the shoulder. They all grinned at each other.

"Time to go," whispered Valery. "I need my sleep."

Chapter 7 – Alexei's big bang

Slowly and carefully, they made their way back to the bay of the lake. The mist which had been so prevalent every early morning thus far, was not in evidence until they began to near the lake. The wispy tendrils clung to the trees and the almost complete silence, gave the morning an unreal atmosphere, almost like a damp, clingy sponge. Once on the boat, they paddled out across the grey lake surface, until they reached the landing area. The Colonel was there to greet them and Yuri threw him a line, which he used to beach the boat. Once ashore, they made sure the boat was hidden and then they made their way to the cave. All three were tired out and the Colonel hurried them off to bed.

"We'll talk it through later," he said. "Get some sleep and I'll keep an eye out." The afternoon sun was streaming through the cave entrance when Yuri threw off his blankets and groped sleepily into his boots. He turned his head as Alexei and Valery wandered out from the side room and gave them a cursory grunt of greeting which they replied to equally abruptly. The Colonel had been busy heating water for coffee and poured out three large measures into tin mugs which he offered to the three young men. "Let's sit outside," he said, "while the sun's so warm and cheerful." They found themselves logs to sit on and the Colonel told them

167

of his day, while they absorbed the coffee and sunshine. "I managed to butcher those carcases that Alexei and Valery brought back and the meat is now stored in the large pots, liberally covered with salt. It's a start and hopefully, we can add more to it later. I wrapped all the waste and entrails in the hides. They're down by the water's edge and sometime they'll need to be ferried over to the mainland and buried out of harm's way. I also chopped a few logs and gathered sticks for kindling. I presume you managed to do something with your day too?"

"Bloody cheek," retorted Alexei. "We now have more than enough information to carry out our attack, isn't that right boys?" The other two nodded pointedly.

"OK, OK," smiled the Colonel, "so let's discuss our options. Yuri, you want to kick off?"

"Well," began Yuri. "When we arrived at the compound, we noticed that there had been quite a few changes made since we were last there. There are now two sentry towers built and two under construction, with a twelve foot fence covering maybe fifty percent of the perimeter. This fence is mostly barbed wire, no electric wire as far as I could see. The construction was being finished by German carpenters, but the tree sawing and chopping was being done by Russian prisoners. There are lights on the fence and they cast a glow around fifteen feet from the perimeter edge. This I managed to estimate as night fell and I could get in closer. The same clockwise and anti-clockwise sentries, passing each other every twenty minutes, but I counted a dozen sentries in the central area and these could wander anywhere at any time, amongst the buildings and houses. All the sentries carried torches which they used often. The road quietened after midnight and the horses and their handlers still bed down across the other side, where the grass and forage is easier for them to utilise. I did notice that at two o'clock, when the late shift took over, there was a delay of half an hour or more before the two perimeter guards appeared. The sentry in the tower came down to hand over to his mate and the new one climbed up straight away and began to have a good look around initially, but his keenness was only temporary, he probably just got bored I guess. That's basically it."

 "Thanks Yuri," nodded the Colonel. "What about you two?" directed at Alexei and Valery.

 "Well Colonel," began Alexei, "Valery and I left Yuri on the eastern side of the compound, while we made our way round the south and west side. It was impossible to get too close, because of all the work going on. So, we decided to have a look towards the River Bug, to see what we could find and whether there was anything of interest. The woods were very sparse and it became much boggier the nearer we got to the river. We found the main road bridge, which is still intact, but the Germans have also built two pontoon bridges. The main bridge is for heavy stuff, mainly tanks and field guns, while the pontoons cater for the rest, one going east, the other west. They seemed quite well guarded with sentry boxes and pill boxes on both sides. We also spotted another compound, but this would appear to be a holding pen for prisoners, as we saw the prisoners from our compound being marched back to there at the end of the day. Five huts with a barbed wire fence and numerous guards. The refugees camp along the side of the road for the most part, at the end of the day. It may be a thought to give them some sort of warning, when we go to blow the place up. Anyway, we moved back to our compound as soon as darkness fell and I left Valery on the west side as I returned to the south. There wasn't much happening on that side. The fence there is incomplete and the two perimeter guards, with odd visits from those in the centre, is all that I could really make out. My times agree with Yuri and I also noticed the longer gap at two o'clock. But then, I was nowhere near the petrol store. That's for Valery to expand on."

"The petrol store is growing," stated Valery. "I estimated at least three thousand fifty gallon drums, two thousand Gerry cans and twelve petrol bowsers parked up for the night. There was a large delivery arrived at about eight o'clock which was left on lorries and horse drawn wagons, just inside the main gates. These gates were locked with chains at ten o'clock, presumably to be emptied this morning. There were two guards on the road side of the gates, who stayed in position all night, except when relieved at two o'clock. They were always facing outwards, checking any road users. The two perimeter guards described by Alexei and Yuri were as they said, every twenty minutes, a full sweep of the compound. The central guards again made random sorties between the stacked drums, there was no particular pattern. The drums are stacked in neat rows of ten, piled four high, with a passage way between them every eight drums. However, the tower held two sentries at all times. They appeared to be reasonably fastidious, but they did chat a lot and when they did, they tended to look outwards, into the woods where I was. There is quite a bit of cover, in the form of tree stumps and old chopped logs and these would let you get to within thirty or forty yards of the fence and tower. The tower sentries would be a difficult shot, because of the lack of light above the parapet wall, but when they did look over towards me, there would be an opportunity, as they leaned on the parapet walls to chat. Yes, they have a searchlight, but they didn't use it much. I tend to agree with the others. Two o'clock would seem to be the best time, and soon, within the next few days, before they come up with any more surprises."

Valery finished and the four sat in silence for several minutes, digesting the information. Finally, the Colonel spoke.

"This is going to be a tough call," he said. "Those crossbows are the key to this whole operation. How confident are you with their use?"

"Very," answered Valery. "We've used them quite a few times and they're extremely accurate. We could hit an apple at fifty yards, just like William Tell did. The only problem I can see is if it's windy. Otherwise, Alexei and I will take out any target you like."

The Colonel nodded. "OK," he said, and you Yuri?"

"I would say that as soon as the tower sentries are nullified, I make my move," Yuri replied. "I will have to cut the wire sufficiently enough to crawl through, get to the drums, place the charge and set it, then get out the same way. Any sentry problems will have to be addressed by Alexei and Valery as and when they arise. I presume that you will be somewhere near, covering the whole event Colonel?"

"That was my idea too," replied the Colonel. "If the crossbows fail, or if there is any other problem, hopefully I will be able to deal with it. I cannot really add too much to the plan, as I have not seen the area and am not as aware of the problems as you three are. Nor can I advise as to when it happens.

All I will say is, the sooner the better." Yuri glanced at each of his new friends in turn, trying to read their faces. Alexei and Valery exuded confidence, they would be ready. The Colonel smiled in that enigmatic way that he had. He would be their guardian angel and would make sure that they survived. For Yuri, he knew that his time had arrived.

"Then it's tonight," he said with a note of finality. "God be with us all."

Yuri and the Colonel went back into the cave and went over the arming of the explosives. "The device is very simple," assured the Colonel. "Six sticks of dynamite, bound together. You place the detonator here, in the centre. Once you have found a suitable hiding place, remove the safety strip and the detonator is now armed. You will have eight minutes to exit the compound and get the hell out of there. We will be with you all the way." Yuri nodded. It sounded simple enough, but there was always sod's law. Not to worry, he thought. Think of Grigori and all those refugees. This is war, not a Sunday bloody picnic. They rested away the afternoon and early evening, all within their own thoughts. After a good meal, at ten o'clock, they made their way to the boat and pushed off across the lake. Yuri took a brief look back. The die was cast. Alexei would have his big bang. The Colonel had insisted that the animal remains, wrapped in the skins, would have to be buried and away from the island. To that end, Yuri had brought a spade and as the others were tying and securing the boat, he wandered off and found a suitable place, dug a deep hole and buried them, out of reach of roaming carnivores. Then they set off in a silent and determined mood. Midnight found them close to the compound. Thankfully, the wind was only blowing a little and from the west. Low clouds were scudding across the moon and the scene was one of tranquillity and peace, the compound standing out like a tiny island of light within a dark satanic, fascist sea. All appeared quiet, with just a little traffic moving along the road. As they neared, they could hear the gentle snorts of horses in repose and the distant echo of an owl, as it searched for food on silken wings. Yuri was as ready as he had ever been. The darkness would be their friend. Silently they moved around towards the western side of the compound, utilising all the cover they could find. Stealthily, they approached the sparse trees on the edge of the woods, about seventy yards from the fence. Then they waited, binoculars and scopes sweeping the vista before them. The clockwise and anti-clockwise sentries were on time, making their circular sweeps around the perimeter, three times in an hour. The guards in the central area were active, moving between the houses, huts and petrol drums, as and when the mood took them, while the two sentries in the tower, chatted away, whiling away the time.

Alexei slipped off into the darkness to check out the main gates. When he returned, he was grinning hugely. "Just outside the gates," he whispered, "are six fucking great tanks, parked up for the night, crews sleeping beneath them. I think it's time for their early morning wakeup call."

As two o'clock approached, the three young men began to move into position. Valery had identified a stack of logs, no more than forty yards from the fence and perfectly positioned to bring Alexei's and his crossbows to bear on the two sentries in the tower. Yuri took up position ten yards to their right behind a couple of tree stumps. They had already worked out that Yuri would move as soon as the crossbows had done their work. He stroked his hands along the wire cutter grips. He would have to be quick and as silent as possible. Their freedom would be severely jeopardised if he failed. No-one must know that they had been here. The sticks of dynamite, slung in a bag on his belt, weighed heavily on his mind. His mouth was suddenly dry and his hands shook a little. Come on, come on, he thought, get a fucking move on. He suddenly realised that one of the two sentries was coming down from the tower, followed by the other. They waited until their replacements appeared and then stomped off to find their beds. Their two replacements climbed up the ladder and stood looking around. Then one of them leaned over the parapet and beckoned to his friend. They both then looked out towards the west and in that instant, both of them died. Yuri gaped as one of them collapsed over the parapet while the other, clawed at his throat and Yuri hadn't heard a thing. The silent killers had done their jobs. Suddenly, the silence was shattered by the sound of a grenade or mortar going off, somewhere to his left by the road. It was followed by a gunshot and then another mortar exploded somewhere by the main gate, then another shot and the compound came alive with running feet and shouted commands. He looked up at the sentry in the tower, the man was staggering sideways, hands at his throat, until his left foot stepped into space and he fell backwards. His body described a perfect arc, as he turned over in mid-air. His head, somehow slipped between the ladder steps and as the rest of his body continued downwards, his chin caught. The weight of his fall continued until brought up sharply by his neck looped over the step. There was an audible crack as his neck snapped and his body hung suspended by his chin. Yuri froze, his mouth open, staring uncomprehendingly at the sentry's demise.

Then someone slapped him on the shoulder. Alexei knocked him out of his lethargy, pointing to the compound. "Get a fucking move on," he hissed.

"Someone's attacking the compound from the road. Go, go."

Yuri raced over to the fence, kneeling down by the base and snipped away at the wires. Within seconds he had fashioned a hole big enough to muscle his way through. Frantically he crossed the ten yards to the drums, conscious of the mayhem surrounding the main gate. Bullets were lashing across the road as the defenders searched for their would-be assailants. What the hell was going on, he frantically thought? He groped for the dynamite, found a space between four Jerry cans and shoved it between them and out of eyesight. Ripping off the safety strip, he armed the device and turned back towards the hole in the wire. After two paces he came up short. Running towards him from the south, not ten yards away, was the clockwise sentry, rifle at the ready. The man saw Yuri come out from behind the drums, skidded to a halt and raised his rifle to fire. Yuri stood transfixed as the rifle came up, then the man staggered backwards, two crossbow bolts embedded in his chest and he collapsed into the Jerry cans. This time, Yuri needed no second telling. He scrambled through the hole in the wire and scuttled crab like over to where Alexei and Valery were waiting. Valery's arm curled protectively across his shoulders as they moved out, Alexei covering their escape.

"Did you arm it?" hissed Valery.

Yuri nodded. "Yes, yes," he snarled, "let's get the hell out of here. We only have a few minutes."

The Colonel appeared out of the night and led them off as quickly as he could through the grey moonlit landscape. The gunfire from the road was lessening in its intensity, but as they climbed past a wooded knoll and looked back, two trucks of troops were driving up from the west, their headlights adding to the searchlight from the north east tower. Onwards they stumbled, the minutes ticking by, as they tried to put as much distance between the compound and themselves before………………

The explosion, when it arrived, caught them all unawares in its rage and savagery. The air was initially sucked out of their lungs and then blasted back at them, throwing them backwards onto the forest floor in a heap of winded turmoil, as a towering ball of orange and red flame was hurled, rolling and tumbling up into the night sky. The initial bang was followed seconds later by an ear shattering boom. Trees were uprooted and flung outwards from the main blast area and they witnessed a momentary glimpse of flying drums, bowsers and buildings, before the ammunition store ignited. The six tanks parked outside the gates were bludgeoned across the road like so much chaff in a hurricane of destruction, tossed end over end into mangled heaps of twisted metal. Coupled with the petrol pyrotechnics, was the zipping and zapping of bullets and incendiaries puncturing the sky. The volume of noise assailed their ears and they cowered at its enormity. A hundred yards away to their right, a blazing horse cartwheeled down into the trees. Not more than fifty feet away, a rogue fuel drum crashed into a tree, pouring molten fire down through the branches. The sky was raining fire and the stench of burning flesh and petrol saturated their senses. They gawped, stupefied, as the volcanic like monster spewed its bile into the air. Sparks, bits of flaming trees, shrapnel and white hot shards of supercharged metal, peppered the ground around them. Small fires were breaking out everywhere, as the flaming debris ignited the trees and forest floor. Open mouthed, they neither moved nor spoke, just stared blankly at the unfolding spectacle. After what seemed like an age, the explosions subsided, leaving the vanished compound area smoking and burning as the fire burned itself through anything combustible that was left. A dense smoke cloud, drifted laboriously eastward on the breeze, the blackness of the soot filled canopy pitted with red and orange pin pricks of sparks, as it bobbed and curtsied its way across the moonlit grey sky.

The four of them looked at each other and let out a collective sigh of relief. Even Alexei was grim faced and quiet, as he led off back towards the island. Bringing up the rear, the Colonel allowed the explosive events to wash over him. He alone, had some idea of what had taken place not ten minutes ago. After all, he had witnessed many such military events and he prayed fervently that no human or animal had had to suffer as a result of the action, but knew, probably, that some had. He would need to tread carefully with his three young comrades. Even the normally unflappable and humour filled Alexei, could not fail to be touched by the carnage they had all caused and witnessed. Sudden death had a way of creeping into a man's psyche and he steeled himself against the tell-tale signs of fallout. He would need to be firm, but forgiving, during the next few days and nights. On they trekked, into the early morning mist, each lost within their own thoughts and demons. Finally, they arrived at the bay of the lake, un-loosed the boat and wearily paddled their way across to the island. The Colonel watched them warily, as the three young men stepped silently out of the boat and walked, like automatons up the steps and into the cave. He hung back, covering the boat with branches, giving them time and space. Then he too, entered the cave and took to his bed. The others appeared to be sleeping already, but he was not convinced. Eventually, he could no longer keep his eyes open and drifted off into a fitful sleep.

The Colonel awoke with a start. He had slept better than he had hoped and felt somewhat refreshed. He could hear Valery's breathing, which appeared to be relaxed and regular. Throwing back his blankets, he quietly moved into the outer cave. Yuri was fast asleep, but of Alexei, there was no sign. Worriedly, the Colonel passed the snoring Yuri and moved along through the outer entrance and into the morning light. He checked his watch, eleven-thirty. Where the hell was Alexei? After a brief search, he found him down by the water's edge. He glanced around at the Colonels approach, saw who it was and went back to staring across the water. The Colonel sat a few feet away from him and waited.

After ten minutes or so, Alexei said softly, "I thought it would be easy. Just go and blow up a petrol dump. And it was, until I actually saw it go off. Am I going soft Colonel, I'm worried because I feel quite bad about it."

The Colonel took his time, respectful of the youngster's pain and suffering before he replied. "Believe me Alexei, I do feel the same. Yes, I've witnessed things like it before and yes, I probably will again, but always, I feel for the enemy, as well as myself. Don't ever think that you are on your own in this. It's what makes us human. An animal sees only the end result, whereas, a human feels the end result. You will know when you don't feel anything that you've turned into an animal. That will be the time to worry."

After a while, Alexei turned to the Colonel and said, "Thanks Sergei, I do understand, but was having trouble coming to terms with it. Thanks for not patronising me."

The Colonel glanced at his young protégé, very aware of the fact that he'd called him by his first name and saw the tears coursing down Alexei's face. He smiled and Alexei smiled back, then Alexei lifted his hand and wiped away the tears. He nodded and the two of them sat and looked out over the water in a companionable silence.

After about an hour, the other two put in an appearance. The Colonel watched them as they approached, gauging their mood and mental state. The two men seemed relaxed and settled as they bantered between each other and then with a rejuvenated Alexei. Good, thought the Colonel, time to put this confidence to the test.

"What about all that gunfire from the road?" he began.

"Search me," muttered Valery, "it frightened me to death. I thought the game was up in no uncertain terms."

"I just froze," countered Yuri, "it threw me completely."

"Lucky for you both I reacted quickly," said a grinning Alexei, "otherwise we'd still be there now."

The Colonel then said, "Actually, it was me who caused all the commotion."

"What," answered the three of them together?

"You did what?" said Valery.

"I realised when I got there that the central guards were going to be a problem," admitted the Colonel, "so I decided to cause a distraction."

"Well thanks for letting us know," retorted Yuri heatedly, "what on earth were you thinking?"

"Actually, I was thinking of the success of the mission," replied the Colonel coolly. "Had anything happened to break the silence, like that sentry falling from the tower, the central guards would have been swarming all over you in seconds. I took a calculated risk."

"But surely," chimed in Valery, "you could have let us know?"

"How," replied the Colonel, "I was in position when you shot the two tower sentries. At that point I slung a grenade as far as I could into the field where the horses were, waited for it to detonate, then fired a shot at the main gate guards. They sort of twitched, so I had to sling another grenade, which bounced off the leading tank and exploded right outside the gate. Then I shot one of the gate sentry's in the head. That got their attention and I left them to it. It just meant that all you had to deal with was the clockwise sentry, which I saw you doing as I was getting back."

The three youngsters stared at him in disbelief. Then first Valery, followed by Yuri and Alexei, burst out laughing.

"You old fool," grinned Alexei, "shit, I almost wet myself when that gun went off. As it is, I guess it worked out pretty well."

"Sorry," said a mollified Colonel, "I know we said that we had to be silent to get away with it, but I reasoned that there wouldn't be too many people left to blab about it to the authorities, so I just took it upon myself to help."

Mid-afternoon came and went as the four went over the nights events in more detail. Eventually, the Colonel broached the subject that they had all been thinking about. What do we do now?

"Yuri," said the Colonel. "It's still your call and whatever path you chose to take, we'll follow. After all, we'd be rotting in some POW camp, or worse, if you hadn't come to our rescue. It seems only right that you come up with our future strategy and I'm sure you have an idea of the way we move forward now."

Yuri thought for a minute and then replied. "As far as I'm concerned, we just keep hitting them in every way we can. I have no idea where the war is, they could be in Moscow by now for all I know. What I do know, is there's a huge logistical stream moving east and it's arming and supplying their invasion

184

force. If we can help to stop this supply, by taking out lorries and wagons, then this must help. Shoot the horses, blow up the delivery drivers and their lorries, dismantle rail tracks, blow up trains and blow up bridges. Every time we do this, we stop that supply getting to the front. Harass them as they pass through the woods and fields. Wherever they go, have them looking over their shoulders, knowing that at any time, any place, we will strike and melt away into the woods and marshes. I can't believe that we are the only ones separated from the main fighting forces. There must be more. Maybe we could try and link up with them, pool our resources so to speak. But initially, just keep chipping away at their weakness, which is the supply trains."

The Colonel nodded. "And you Alexei?"

Alexei grinned and mused "well Colonel, you know I like a big bang, so I quite fancy whacking a train or a bridge, or both," he added. "I'm with Yuri, just keep chipping away."

Valery chose his words carefully. "I think we should broaden our area of influence. I'm with the other two, keep chipping away, but let's spread ourselves further afield. We have a perfect hiding place here, but I worry that if we keep doing things close to home, then sooner or later the Germans are going to notice that all these happenings are centred on a certain place. They could then saturate this area with troops and we'll be in the deep shit. This island is our refuge and sanctuary. We mustn't allow it to be taken away from us."

Everyone nodded their approval. "So, it's a surgical removal of the logistical stream from now on," concluded the Colonel. "We'll give it a day and then we start to broaden our catchment area. Yuri's right, every little thing must help. But I have to try and think of a way of utilising the Gruber scenario. It could prove more beneficial than any of you think, battles are not always won and lost on a battlefield. They can also be manipulated by intelligence. Leave it with me for now."

The foursome retired to the cave. The Colonel and Yuri rustled up a meal while Alexei and Valery, cleaned and oiled the Crossbows and rifles. Once they had eaten, all four of them made for an early night, as the events of the past few days were catching up with them. Valery did the final sweep of the surrounding area before allowing himself the luxury of a deep, dreamless sleep. Morning came, with surprisingly, no mist and after a quick breakfast, they got down to checking over the maps left by the previous owner of the cave. The maps showed all the paths, roads, railways and train routes through the marshes. The main roads were few and far between, nearly all dirt surfaced. Very few roads in Russia were of tarmac, the main mode of transport being horse and cart. There were lots of farms and villages, some hamlets and even a few small towns, within the marshes, but by far, the most common places of habitation were single or multiple huts or houses. The great rolling steppes of the Ukraine and what was formally White Russia, fell to the south and north side of the marshes respectively. Height was not an issue, until you reached the Urals, hundreds of miles to the east. They studied the maps long into the afternoon, trying to get a feel and an overall knowledge of the marshes and their intricacies, shown so graphically by the hand of Aleksander Dobrovolsky. Woodpecker Knoll would be their first port of call, as Yuri had intimated that the all-round view was such, that it was unsurpassed in giving them a three hundred and sixty degree view of the area. Maybe they would see something from there. Maybe they could figure out what was going on in the east.

The afternoon was upon them, when they finally finished poring over the maps.

"As I see it," the Colonel said, "we go prepared for staying away for a few days at least. We're well into July now and the weather should be good for camping, while we reconnoitre east and south. We'll need a pack each and provisions for three days. The pup tents will be enough by way of protection from the elements. We'll carry explosives and detonators, rope, binoculars and a blanket each. Yuri, you take a machine pistol as I will, as well as our rifles. The boys can take the Crossbows and also a scoped rifle each. How many bolts have you left Alexei?"

"Seven," replied Alexei. "We could do with some more, but where do we get them?"

"We make them," replied the Colonel. "While you were out the other day, I found a couple of moulds and even some prepared arrow heads, along with some strips of some sort of alloy. There are half a dozen shafts of rounded, planed wood and I also found Goose feathers for fletching. I figure we could make up another dozen at least. What we need is the stove firing up and then melt that alloy into the moulds. The shafts are green, so cut them to length, heat up the arrow heads, push a length of wood into the arrow head and plunge it into cold water. Contraction will shrink the head onto the shaft and apart from the feathers and the knock, we have a new bolt. Understood?" The three nodded. "Right, let's see how this stove fires up."

Wood was brought in and kindling and soon the fire was roaring in the hearth. "I'll go out and check where the stove pipe comes out," said Yuri, "make sure it's not causing too much smoke and fume." He disappeared outside and did a cautious tour of the island. All appeared quiet. The stove pipe was doing its job well, dissipating the smoke through the surrounding branches and what little wind there was, funnelled the fumes eastward. Hopefully, no one would associate the island with the smell, if anyone was close enough to pick up the scent. Satisfied, he returned to the cave and watched as the others went through the bolt making process. He joined in with the fletching as he had helped his father on many occasions, slitting the wood to take the feather and binding it with twine. Then he carved open the knock. By seven o'clock, another fourteen bolts were added to their arsenal.

"We'll move out first thing," said the Colonel, "hopefully the mist will aid our crossing."

Yuri then spoke up. "Actually, it's time I showed you where the other landing place is. We'll use that one tomorrow, as it's much better hidden than the bay of the lake."

"OK everyone," said the Colonel, "get the fire damped down, have a quick meal and let's get to bed. It'll be morning soon enough." The four men busied themselves with making sure all was ready for the next few days and then turned in. Before sleep, Alexei volunteered to patrol around the island, listening and watching. By the time he arrived back, the others were tucked up and fast asleep.

The morning came, misty and dank. After a quick breakfast, they tidied around, slung on their packs and accoutrements and made their way to the boat. The Colonel had cobbled together a hat from the deer skins and wore this much to Alexei's amusement. They paddled off through the clinging mist, Yuri guiding the way and made landfall on the north side of the lake. They hid the boat and Yuri showed them how to get through the thicket cordon, finally emerging between the giant oaks. The path was quiet and deserted. Yuri took point, with Alexei bringing up the rear and they made their way to Woodpecker Knoll. The sun was beginning to push its way through the mist, as Yuri crested the top of the knoll. The others spread out behind him, giving him space and time as he made his way to the centre and Grigori's grave. The flowers blushed in profusion around the small cairn and he paused to reflect on a life well spent, but taken from him too soon. The others came over and stood in silence around the tableau. Presently, Valery slipped his arm around Yuri's shoulder and guided him gently away from the cairn. Yuri was heartbroken, but fully appreciated the part his friends had played in their acknowledgement of his suffering. The bond between them was growing by the day.

Lying supine in the long grass between the pines at the eastern edge of the knoll, they scanned the area before them. To their left, the road was busy with heavy traffic, easily spotted by the tell-tale clouds of dust churned up by the military machine, heading north-east towards Minsk and beyond. Try as they might, they could not ascertain any clue as to where the war was being fought now. The steppe rolled forever onwards, with only the odd wood or copse to break the monotony of the grassy landscape. Apart from the road, there was no sign of men or animals, nothing disturbed the relentless rise and fall of the terrain. To the south, all seemed quiet over the marshes, still bathed in mist, but they did notice smoke rising from several points. They were too far away to hear or see the railway, either to the north or south, but they knew it existed and could get to either, by following Aleksander's maps. The difficult bit with the north was, they would have to cross the road. The west also proved quiet, back to where the compound used to be, but there were too many trees in the way, for them to make out what was left of it. After discussing the pros and cons of which direction to take, they decided to go east for a little while, before turning south. They knew, from the maps, that there was a rail bridge over the River Pripet at Kowel. The main line from Warsaw to Kiev passed through open country once it was past this point and they were looking to destroy the bridge and also try to cripple a train. Definite plans were impossible to make, until they could make out the lie of the land.

They came off the knoll and headed east along a fairly well defined path. The mist still clung to the fringes of the marshes, but as the sun climbed higher and the morning wore on, it gradually disappeared. They had travelled about three miles from the knoll when Valery, who was twenty yards ahead of the other three, suddenly stopped and went down on to one knee, searching the trees and ground around him. The others stopped, but he beckoned them forward. At this point, a path led out of the marshes to join up with their own track and Valery pointed to where many sets of footprints had come across through the grass from the north, then crossed the path that they were on and headed off down this other southerly path.

Valery shrugged. "Looks like whoever it was, had come from the direction of Minsk. The prints are quite clearly defined. Soldiers of some sort. It's strange that we didn't see them from the knoll. The prints are only a few hours old."

"I doubt whether Russians would be moving across open ground," reasoned the Colonel. "We have to assume, with the war being somewhere ahead, that this group were hostiles. However, we'll follow them south, to see if we can find out what they're up to. Alexei, you take point and the rest of us will follow in single file. Move out and keep your eyes and ears open."

Alexei moved off into the marshes, rifle slung easily across his forearms and the others swung in behind, Yuri bringing up the rear. The path wound its way around bogs and thickets, between trees and rock outcrops, always keeping in a generally southern direction. The tracks were fairly easy to follow, as no one had tried to disguise them. The morning wore on as the four men passed deeper and deeper into the marshes. They were making good time and had not seen or heard anything. Suddenly, a fusillade of rifle and automatic fire clattered out in the woods ahead. Immediately, the four hit the deck and crawled into cover. Alexei backed up to where the other three were hiding.

"What the hell was that?" he whispered. The Colonel shook his head. To their left, several deer bounded past and out of sight in an instant. The four waited for several minutes, conscious that the woods had remained silent since that one shattering, heavy burst of firing. The Colonel decided to move and spoke swiftly and concisely. "Yuri, you go to the left, Valery to the right, keep off the path and fan out, with ten feet between each of us. Alexei, you and I down the middle. No talking, hand signals only. OK?" The others nodded.

They fanned out silently into position, then moved forward together. The woods were quite dense here and movement was difficult. Slowly, they edged forward until Valery, on the far right, raised his hand. They all froze. Ahead was the sound of voices, German voices. Valery pointed to the path and made a sign of soldiers coming along it. The Colonel understood and moved further into the trees to join him. He looked over to where Alexei and Yuri were, but they had melted away and out of sight. Valery tapped him on the shoulder and pointed up through the branches towards the south. A thick plume of smoke was rising into the sky directly in front of them. They both looked at each other and Valery shrugged, then shook his head. Whatever was burning would have to wait. They both heard a distinct command, then the sound of feet coming up the path. They pressed deeper into cover as two soldiers hurried along the path, both carrying machine pistols. There was no doubt as to their unit, as both wore the SS insignia on their helmets. They were followed by twenty-four heavily armed SS troops, led by a very mean looking Stabsfeldwebel. They filed past in good order and disappeared back up the path towards the north. The four waited until they were sure they had gone, before holding a council of war, just off the path.

The Colonel whispered, "Spread out and move forward as quietly as possible. I have no idea what's ahead, but I don't like the look of that smoke and the gunfire had an execution sound to it. Be aware and take care. Move out."

Again, they spread out and ghost like, passed through the trees and scrub, until they came upon a clearing and saw what the SS had been doing.

Chapter 8 – The Cossacks

The scene spread out before them was stark and brutal. The burning remains of three houses and outbuildings, cast a sombre spectre over what was once, a small collective community. Death had come in several guises. The giant oak tree, in the centre of the glade, with its wide limbed arms spreading outwards from the main trunk, held the bodies of eleven Russian soldiers, all hung by the neck. To their left, laid in various forms of disarray, were the bullet riddled corpses of eighteen peasants. A pig lay to one side, its throat cut and still bleeding its blood into the soil, while scattered around were the remains of several goats and chickens. Yuri stepped out from the trees, followed by the others and gazed in horror at the scene. He moved cautiously across the clearing, the others fanning out behind him, making sure that there were no other signs of life or danger, before confronting the gory spectacle. Valery had slipped off to the right, while Alexei took the left, the Colonel stood in the centre, casting an unbelieving eye over the soldiers. Each man's hands were lashed behind their backs with barbed wire, as were their feet. A barbed wire noose suspended each of them by their necks, from the oak's limbs. Their wide open bulging eyes stared sightlessly ahead, their tongues hanging loosely over sagging chins. Death had not come swiftly to these men, their terror etched upon their faces. Several had urinated and defecated in their death throes, all were empty shells of once proud human beings. The peasant community had been lined up and executed without mercy. They ranged from parents and grandparents, down to children and even a baby of a few months. Women and girls lay with men and boys, the baby, head crushed by a rock, was faceless, a tangled mass of blood, bone and hair. Carnage.

The Colonel was the first to break the silence. "God help us all if this is what we are coming to," he uttered with a malevolence of shock and despair. "Soldiers defending their country, non-combatant farmers with their women and children. All eradicated by some cruel, sadistic monsters, who answer to no-one but their inhuman leaders. Where is the logic in all this barbarity?"

Valery was equally venomous. "Perhaps here, we are witnessing Russia's fate at the hands of these Nazi's. If you read Hitler's book, he preaches the genocide of all peoples that he believes are, in his words, sub-human. Is this the start of that genocide?" He stared uncomprehendingly about him. "Alexei, come on, they can't have got far, we can catch them, let's go get these murdering bastards."

"Stop," commanded the Colonel, "don't be so stupid. We're outnumbered six to one. There are

196

other ways to deal with this. Fill your mind with the scene and take it forward with you. We cannot take the fight to the Nazi's if we're all dead. Retribution will be served on these devils, including their leaders, of that, be in no doubt. But first, we need to utilise what strengths we have, in sabotaging their invasion."

Yuri then spoke with a quivering voice, "but why leave the evidence for all to see. They would know that they would be found out at some stage. Why not dispose of the bodies?"

Alexei answered quietly. "It's a warning. A graphic picture of what will happen to you, if caught harbouring soldiers. Who knows if the soldiers were here in the first place? They could have been brought from anywhere and this tableau staged for effect. I have a bad feeling, we have not seen the last of scenes like this."

The Colonel nodded, "I agree my young friend, but firstly, we have to give these people a decent burial. At least we can obliterate these horrors from anyone else coming to this place. It won't be much, a mass grave is all we can give them, but we must do it."

To that end, the four men began the unenviable job of digging a large grave and placing in it the victims of the brutality of the SS. Alexei and Valery found a site for the grave and began digging with their entrenching tools. Yuri helped the Colonel to get down the soldiers, the Colonel holding the bodies, while Yuri used wire cutters to cut the suspension wires. Each was reverently carried and laid out by the grave. After an hour, with Yuri and the Colonel also helping, Alexei and Valery had dug down deep enough and each body in turn was lowered into the grave, side by side. Then the three young men covered in the bodies and built up a mound of earth on top, while the Colonel fashioned a cross out of wooden planks from the houses. On the surface of one board, he scratched out the words, 'Here lie thirty bodies of sons and daughters of Russia, murdered by the SS. July 16th, 1941.' The cross was hammered into position at one end of the grave. Then the four men bowed their heads and stood in silence, honouring those buried. Finally, they picked up their things and took to the path, away from the horror and headed south towards Kowel.

The afternoon passed as they journeyed, ever deeper, into the enormous confines of the marshes. Aleksander's maps were a huge benefit in deciphering the terrain and being able to plot as southerly a course as possible. Knowing which way to turn, in a certain place, where the roads, paths and waterways criss-crossed the area, proved invaluable and they made good time. The memories of the morning weighed heavily on their minds and each man dealt with it in his own way. Mid-afternoon saw them crossing a main highway.

Studying the ground, they discerned that much heavy traffic had passed that way, the road running west to east. The inevitable piles of horse manure, showed passage had been recent and they wasted no time in moving on. They had already crossed several streams and small rivers and paused around five o'clock for something to eat.

"As I see it, we'll head east at the next river we come to," said the Colonel. "We must be twenty or more miles from where we buried the corpses. I hope to find the railway further south and east, but once we're at Kowel, there will be major bridges over the Pripet. Maybe we can destroy one of those? We'll have to wait and see." Once they were rested, they moved out and after another six miles, came up to the river that the Colonel had mentioned. This branch of the Pripet was quite wide, but the map had brought them to a single wooden bridge, which they crossed before turning east. The woods were quiet and dense, interspersed by rock outcrops and bogs, but the paths were relatively easy to follow. Dusk saw them closing in on habitation, as the sounds of people, animals and traffic became more and more apparent. They decided to camp well away from any form of path and sought out a quiet clearing, where they would not be easily disturbed. Tents were erected and as night drew in they ate a hot meal, courtesy of the Paraffin stoves, then rolled up in their blankets and slept until the coming of dawn.

Dawn appeared cold and misty. They consumed some biscuits and made coffee, mindful of the fact that they would be unable to see anything until the sun, hopefully, burned through the mist. After an hour, they packed away the gear and made their way back to the path. The pines dripped as the sun rose and they travelled east and a little south, hoping to find somewhere to overlook the town. The terrain was a lot hillier as they travelled cautiously towards the sounds of movement. A train whistled in the distance and they could smell smoke and see steam rising. It gave them a target to aim for and eventually, they crested a small ridge and Kowel was laid out before them. They looked at each other in disappointment. The town was crawling with soldiers. The road that ran parallel to the railway lines, in and out of the town, was full of heavy traffic, horse drawn as well as mechanised. They could just make out the railway station, with several engines huffing and puffing away. Through the binoculars, the station was a mass of human movement. Armed guards were patrolling the goods yards and lots of dogs, German Shepherds and Dobermans, were in evidence, their handlers separating and controlling what appeared to be civilians, before cramming them into cattle trucks. Then the train pulled out of the station and headed off west. Another train then pulled in and the same process was followed, more civilians loaded up and then it too headed off west. The second train had just disappeared from sight when another appeared from the west. It passed straight through the station at a fair speed and headed east towards the front. It was loaded with field guns, tanks and ammunition, with many troops in evidence, hitching a ride. The streets were also crowded, with troops coming and going. Why they should all be here, was a mystery to the four Russians. All the town had to offer to invading forces, was a road and railway line and possibly billeting for the night. So many troops didn't make sense, but they were there, in abundance and consequently, any form of sortie into the town here would be next to impossible. Dejectedly, they decided to try further east, where the railway and road crossed the river Pripet. Perhaps they might find something to attack there?

They moved out in single file, the sun now glorious in its intensity. Easing slowly and cautiously through the woods and marsh areas, they made their way towards the river. They travelled on for several miles, keeping well away from any form of habitation, until finally, they reached the river. Being summer, the level was quite low, with only a gentle flow to disturb the reed fringed edges. A path emerged from the woods leading off south and they followed it until they arrived within half a mile of the railway bridge. Through the binoculars it appeared huge, with three stone and concrete pillars, supporting the two railway tracks and the road. The pillars were a 'Y' shape, wide at the top, tapering down to a still formidable twenty feet circumference at the base.

"I'm not sure if we've brought enough dynamite for that brute," offered Valery, "and how the hell do we get to it. The place is teeming with guards."

"It does appear insurmountable," replied the Colonel, "what do you think Yuri?"

"I think we would be able to get to it," he answered, "We'll use the river. Notice how bits and pieces of debris keep floating down on the current. If we could fashion something out of logs that we could hide under, as well as keep the dynamite dry, then we'll just float down, hop off and set the charges. Once we're underneath it, we should remain undetected, even getting from one pillar to another. Thirty sticks of dynamite on each pillar should do the trick."

The Colonel looked sceptical. "It's an awful risk you're taking. They have lights on the top there and how will you get away?"

"Simple," replied Yuri, "just float downstream with the current. We could even pick up some flotsam from around the base of the pillars, to camouflage our passing."

"Well," said the Colonel grudgingly, "it might work. There's always me to cause a distraction while you're doing it. That would keep their eyes away from the water. What do you think?"

"It has merit," said Alexei, "at least then we'd know what you were doing, unlike last time," he added with a grin.

"Then I need to be on the other side of the river," replied the Colonel. "I'm too near to Kowel on this side and anyway, once it's blown, they won't be able to get to me on the other side."

"OK," said Yuri, "looks like we're going to get wet." They pulled away from the river bank, finding a concealed place to prepare. Firstly, they counted out the number of sticks of dynamite that they were carrying and it came to eighty. "Twenty-five per column with a few to spare," said Yuri, "that ought to do the trick."

"Sounds fine," said the Colonel, "we'll bundle them into three lots of eight. Then we'll rope them together at four foot intervals and you can tie the rope around each tier. Do you want long taper fuses or some mechanical ones, like the one we used at the compound?"

"It depends if we can get far enough away in the five minute time gap, before they blow," answered Yuri. "Can you increase the time factor Colonel?"

"Yes," he replied, "I can make it ten minutes."

"Then that's it," answered Yuri, "ten minutes will be fine."

"I hope there'll be enough light to be able to see enough to pull off the arming strip," said Alexei.

"Don't worry," said the Colonel," there'll be enough." Valery and Yuri found two pine trunks and managed to secure them about a foot apart with branches and rope. Then the hole in the middle was covered with fir branches, arranged haphazardly to give the appearance of trailing branches. They reasoned that the structure didn't have to look perfect in the grey moonlit water. The dynamite was carefully placed in a haversack, with the rope coiled around it. Then they made up a small raft for it to sit on, beneath the fir boughs. Valery was taking extra rope in case there wasn't enough. They could only estimate from where they were. Then they lashed three logs together. This was for the Colonel to traverse the river, with all their gear and get it safely onto the other bank. Valery had fashioned a paddle out of a strip of oak and the Colonel nodded his approval. All was ready for the coming night. Time to rest and try to make sure nothing had been forgotten. The rest of the afternoon and evening passed slowly, they daren't risk cooking food or moving about. At around nine o'clock, they lifted up the Colonels raft and carried it down to the shore. Earlier, they had spotted a way down to the water, where a small beach allowed the raft to be concealed. Once it became dark, the Colonel would paddle his way across the sixty yards or so to the other side. Once he was there, he would empty the raft and hide their belongings, so that they could be picked up later. They waited for full dark and around eleven o'clock, the Colonel pushed off for the far bank. The traffic crossing the bridge was lessening by the minute. A train had puffed its way west about half an hour ago, but it seemed that the road was becoming less and less busy. The soldiers were stopping for rest during the hours of darkness and the bridge was left to the sentries. There was a two-man machine gun nest at either end of the bridge and eight or ten other soldiers patrolled the ends and across it. The three watched the Colonel as he disappeared from sight into the shadows of the far bank. So far so good, they thought. Time wise, the three youngsters would get into the river at one o'clock, giving them enough time to drift down the current and be in position by one-fifteen to one-twenty. The main craft would then have to be sacrificed by sending it onwards downstream. They couldn't risk a nosey sentry noticing it go under the bridge and then not coming out. He may have sent someone down to investigate. But they would keep the small raft with the dynamite pack on it. They couldn't afford for the explosive to get wet.

One o'clock arrived. The three pushed out into the current, naked except for their underwear and socks. The Colonel had taken the rest with him. It was going to be a long cold night before they could get wrapped up again. Slowly, they edged their way south, gently moving with the current. The bridge loomed out of the darkness and as they neared, it assumed an aura of invincibility, so huge were its proportions. The three of them felt completely isolated and vulnerable to eyes and ears from above and so it was, with a feeling of immense relief, that they finally slipped unnoticed under the bridge, rescued the small raft with the explosives on it and sent their means of getting there off by itself towards the south. They had rehearsed what they would do, several times that evening. So, Yuri took one bunch of dynamite out of the pack and held it above water, while the other two swam gently around the ends of the pillar, taking the rope with them. Luckily, the rope was long enough and Valery tied a knot in it and then he and Alexei swam back to Yuri. The dynamite was suspended about a foot above the water level .One down, two to go. The three of them then moved to the central pillar, the little raft being pushed gently by Yuri. Again, they fastened the charges in place. Two down, one to go. All through the time they had been under the bridge, they'd been aware of the sentry's above. They could hear them tripping over the bridge, their boots ringing loud in the quiet of the night. Often, they stopped to gaze down into the water, at one time a cigarette butt fizzed itself to extinction in the

206

slow- moving current. Several times, the searchlights were brought into play, but never pointing too near to the bottom of the pillars. The three Russians knew that the last pillar would be the most challenging, as they had to move round the central pillar ends, taking the raft with them. As it was, the sentries were more interested in the sound of an oncoming train from the direction of Kowel and so the third pillar was made quite easily. Once the charge was in position, Valery stayed where he was, keeping the raft for cover when he moved off, while Alexei took the centre and Yuri the far side. At ten to two they were all in position, next to their explosives, detonators at the ready. They would arm the dynamite once they heard the Colonel kick off. Yuri pushed his detonator into the middle of the bunch and waited. Valery would leave first, after arming his detonator. Alexei would count to thirty after arming and then go. Yuri would be last, thirty seconds after Alexei. In this way they hoped that individual rafts of debris, floating downstream spasmodically, would be better than all going at once. He put his hand out and clutched a few branches. These he hoped would be enough to disguise his floating body, should prying eyes be cast downwards from the bridge. The seconds ticked slowly into minutes, the sound of the engine becoming louder in the distance. What if the bridge blew with the train on it? Was it that fanciful to expect?

Fifty yards from the end of the bridge, the Colonel lay in the scrub by the side of the track, his scoped rifle hunting for targets. Nothing was moving on the road or the rails, the last eastern bound troops and equipment had disappeared east almost an hour and a half ago. They would hopefully be camped some distance away. As the seconds ticked by, he knew exactly where his first shot would be aimed, at the machine gunners in that nest at the bridge end, then the searchlight. He reasoned that if he knocked the light out, some idiot might swing the one at the other end his way. That would leave anyone on the bridge in sharp relief. Two o'clock arrived. Zero hour. The Colonels first shot shattered the stillness, almost immediately followed by the second. The machine gun post was wiped out. The searchlight swivelled towards him and bang, the light shattered in a shower of crystal sparks. He rolled left and steadied. Bang. A sentry running across the bridge towards him collapsed in a heap. Again, he rolled left. Through the scope he could just make out running figures on the bridge. Bang, roll left. Bang, roll again twice left and in doing so, came up against one of the rails. Bullets were starting to fizz around him, one hit the rail and ricocheted off into the distance, but the figures on the bridge had hit the deck, conscious of the fire being directed at them. The Colonel waited, in no hurry to expose his position. The oncoming train by this time, was heading into view around a long bend from the direction of Kowel, a small light attached to its front. It was moving steadily and relentlessly towards the bridge, but was still maybe half a mile away. The Colonel decided to make his way back to the scrub on the right. Bang, roll twice to the right, steady. Bang, roll three times and into the scrub. Bullets were trying to search out his position, being aimed at the muzzle flashes. The Germans could not know what size of force was attacking them and were taking it steady. As it was, the Colonel held perfect position. Then a sentry got to the searchlight at the far end of the bridge and swung it towards him. The bridge surface was bathed in light. The Colonel had anticipated this and the defenders now provided an easy target. Bang. Roll to the left. Bang, roll again, then bang, out went the light, not by the Colonel, but by a soldier realising the defenders mistake. The Colonel rolled right again, hunting the cover of the scrub, knowing he had hit all three targets. Another three troops down and the light extinguished. Bullets zipped around him, but they were being directed at where they thought he was, rather than at him. He waited again. How long had it been since he began? Five, six, seven minutes? He couldn't think. Surely it won't be too much longer? Bang, he'd spotted a trooper creeping across the bridge, fired and immediately rolled left. Two bullets slammed into the scrub where he had just been. That was close, he felt the wind of them, time to move back. He rolled three times to the left and fired, then immediately rolled back to where he had been. Once more, he drew searching fire and he realised that the firing was becoming more intense. He squirmed his way backwards, trying to put as much distance between himself and the bridge before it blew. Slipping behind a boulder, he searched along the bridge with the scope. In the light cast from the front of the train, was a soldier running towards it, arms flailing, desperately trying to give a warning. Bang. The soldier collapsed and disappeared from view. Bullets again sang around his position, ricocheting off in a shower of stone chips. The Germans on the bridge were moving stealthily across and looked ready to launch a concerted effort to dislodge him. The train was coming closer and closer. He fired off two quick shots from around the boulder, which brought a withering salvo in reply. He squeezed himself into a tiny ball, trying desperately to hide from the crescendo of bullets peppering his position. His brain screamed danger, they'll be coming any minute, but at that moment, the charges went off.

From his position, the explosion was both muted and unspectacular. The centre charge was the first to go, followed a second or two later by the outer ones. The flash of light generated by the blast showed the bridge surface and the soldiers on it in shocked relief. Then nothing. The structure was still there. The soldiers ran stumbling and crawling for their lives towards an open mouthed, staring Colonel on the east bank. They almost made it, but slowly and imperceptibly, the bridge buckled. Giant cracks appeared across the surface, they grabbed frantically for a way out, before it teetered on the brink for a split second and then the eastern half of it toppled outwards and downstream, taking the petrified screaming soldiers with it, while the other half stayed in place, somehow balanced on the centre and far west pillars. Amazingly, the rails survived, sagging downwards in mid space and trembling as the train approached. The train, he'd forgotten about the train. Peering with the scope through the dust shrouded air about the bridge, he saw it approaching, heard the screech of brakes being applied and watched in growing disbelief as it edged, foot by foot onto the west end of the shattered bridge. The sound of tortured metal scratched into his brain and he shivered, involuntarily. Inch by painful inch it finally came to a hesitant stop. Most of its front length, almost three quarters of the engine, was suspended in space, above the expectant chasm below. Its' survival hung by a thread. And then, with an accompaniment of groaning tortured stone scraping apart, the rest of the bridge swayed, stumbled and finally slid off the severed bases of the pillars. The bridge surface crumpled, the rails snapped and pitched into the churning waters below, followed, almost serenely at first and then with a surge of gathering momentum, by the engine. It seemed to hang momentarily in space, before plunging downwards to its destruction, followed by the carriages and open topped cars behind, they being loaded with artillery pieces and tanks. The noise was horrific as tons of following metal collapsed upon itself, like the folds of a monstrous, metallic concertina, strewn haphazardly onto the now submerged, stricken engine. The resultant pile of twisted cars and carriages creaked and gouged their way together into a final resting heap. Miraculously, more than half of the train survived plus the Guards van. Many of the travelling soldiers were also milling around, shocked but thankful for their narrow escape. The engine driver and fireman had also managed to jump off before the train did its forward capitulation. By now, the great wave sent downstream by the collapsing bridge, had all but subsided, the hissing foam dissipating in its wake. Silence returned, punctuated by small shrieks and scrapes, as the pile of flat cars and carriages, settled into position.

The Colonel shook himself out of his stupor, as his senses returned to something like normal. The boys, he thought guiltily, where the hell were the saboteurs? He staggered to his feet, conscious of the pins and needles of returning circulation and mindless of the fact that he could well be spotted from the other side. He must be ready for the boys.

Earlier, they had formulated a plan to bring them all together again. He pulled out his torch and shone it with a hooded beam towards the south. He spelt out his initials, S.B. in Morse code using the flashlight. He knew there would be no reply, as they had no torch with them. Nothing. He waited a minute and then tried again. Come on Sergei, he thought, give them time. After what seemed an age, the three young Russians appeared out of the southern darkness, their socked feet slipping and sliding across the road and rail lines. They were shivering with cold and barely suppressed excitement at what they had achieved. But they were easy to spot, being naked in the moonlight and the Colonel hurried them into the scrub and trees and finally to where he had hidden their equipment. This consisted of a small hollow, surrounded by scrub and stunted pines and the three youngsters wasted no time in getting dressed. The Colonel stood guard as they completed their task and then they all loaded up their equipment and set off north along the river bank. He had watched the mayhem on the opposite bank, as officers rallied their stricken troops. Patrols were being sent out to the south and north, searching for survivors as well as hunting out the perpetrators. It wouldn't be too long before boats were launched and the river crossed. There was no time for the four of them to rest for the foreseeable future. They must put as much distance as possible between themselves and pursuit before morning came. Then the hunt would be on in earnest. The original plan was to cross back over the Pripet using the Colonels raft, but the opposite patrols made that course impossible. They would just have to head north along the eastern bank, trusting to Aleksander's maps. There were an awful lot of miles to cover before they could be safely ensconced in the cave on the island. The night passed slowly with them on the move, through the gathering mist and damp. On this side of the Pripet, the terrain was much more difficult to follow, being a series of rocky, tree clad outcrops and small wood choked valleys. The innumerable water courses through every single valley, made progress difficult and taxing. Consequently, by the time the sun started to put in an appearance, the Colonel reckoned they had travelled only five or six miles at the most. There were also tell-tale signs of pursuit. Alexei had noticed it first, when he had hung back while the others crossed a particularly choked up valley. The Germans had crossed the Pripet, obviously by boat or raft and he could hear and sometimes see them as they followed up behind. They had also brought along several dogs, which made excitable barking noises as they picked up the Russians scent. There was no doubt that the fugitives were being followed, but at the moment, they were keeping up a good lead. All that changed when they came to a dirt road running west to east. They had just passed the point where the course of the Pripet changed from a southerly to a west-east direction. The road was single track, but it was teeming with vehicles, horses and carts and foot soldiers heading east. The four settled into deep cover and waited. They were somewhere between the hammer and the anvil, having troops to the north and following troops to the south.

"Now what," said Valery, "we can't stay here for long? The soldiers on the road are unaware of our presence, but those coming along behind, have got us dead to rights."

"Then we'll go west," replied the Colonel. "If we travel counter clockwise to those troops on the road, hopefully we'll get to a point where the column ends. Maybe we'll be able to cross then and continue north. It's pointless sitting here and waiting for the following squad to catch up with us. Let's move out."

The others nodded their agreement and they moved off west. The woods along this side of the Pripet were quite dense and progress was slow. To the east, beyond where the column was travelling, the land rose into a multitude of rocky outcrops, on either side of the road, interspersed with stands of pines and oak. This left an avenue of open ground, on both sides of the road, which the column was taking advantage of, being able to spread out, not confined to the narrowness of the path through the woods. The prospect of being boxed in was not a very pleasant idea and they made better progress through the screening pines and scrub. They had travelled almost two hundred yards, when all hell broke loose. Bullets and shells crashed into the marching phalanx on the road. The German column was under attack. The four men scrambled for cover behind the trees and scrub. Bullets and stray Mortar shells buzzed, shrieked and exploded around them. What the hell was happening? Suddenly, half a dozen German troops were running towards them from the road. Yuri and the Colonel opened up with their machine pistols, while Alexei and Valery sought out individual targets with their scoped rifles. There was no time for the four of them to retreat, they were now heavily involved. To their right, another attack developed from the direction of the following group from the attack on the bridge. This was repulsed and beaten back. Mortars were now blasting down on the hapless column. Screams of injured men and horses mixed in with the crump of exploding shells and the hammering cacophony of misdirected ricocheting bullets. Then they all heard the unmistakable sound of galloping horses. Pounding through the woods to the north and flooding down the wide avenue, came a large contingent of Cossack horsemen, sabres flashing in the sunlight. The shelling ceased and was taken up by the battle cries of Russian soldiers as they left their places of concealment by the side of the road and hurled themselves, along with the charging Cossacks, at the remains of the beleaguered German column. Led by Yuri and the Colonel, machine pistols hammering out sudden death, the four fugitives fell on the rear of the column. Alexei and Valery, fixed bayonets to the fore, were wreaking havoc. The frantic hand to hand fighting that ensued was brutal and no prisoners were taken. Then, it was all over. Yuri, the Colonel and the two brothers stood amongst the remains of what was once a large German convoy, breath coming in great gasps as they surveyed their handiwork.

Yuri wiped away some blood trickling down his face and swore. "Shit," he gasped, "what the hell was all that about?" At that moment, several riders appeared from the head of the column, sabres still drawn and bloody. Another group appeared from the left, along with thirty or so Russian soldiers. They were grim faced and surrounded the four, guns pointing in their direction. The Colonel moved forward, so that he was stood facing the Cossacks that had first appeared. Alexei and Valery turned and faced towards the rear, Yuri coming up on the Colonels left flank. The four stood silently watching and waiting, the cries of injured men and horses, interspersed by single shots as they were dispatched, being the only sound above the steady crackling of the fires that raged through the column. It was a stand-off. Then, pushing through the Cossacks to the right, came a splendid figure on a large black horse, the air of command he exuded, evident for all to see. He pulled up, ten feet from the Colonel and gazed witheringly at the four fugitives, his men continuing to cover them in hostile silence. It didn't help, the Colonel thought, that here we are, in German ponchos, an assortment of boots, hats and pants and with German weapons. They have a right to be suspicious. His deer hide hat was pulled tight around his features, but he knew he had an ace up his sleeve.

Eventually, the bearded leader spoke, his voice deep and authorative. "Why do you make war on your own people?" he asked in halting German. "Are you deserters?"

The question hung in the air, nobody moved. Then the Colonel took a step forward, the movement bringing a rifle raising response from the men surrounding their leader. He stood, legs apart, machine pistol hanging loosely across his arms and addressed the gathering in Russian. "Gentlemen," he intoned gently. "We are not German fascists, nor are we deserters." He pointed out his three colleagues in turn. "I present to you Lieutenants Alexei and Valery Avseyenko and Private Yuri Petrovsky. I am Colonel Sergei Berezovsky and you, Major Pavel Lensky, late of the St. Petersburg garrison, should be ashamed of yourself, for not recognising your former teacher and commanding officer." He then removed the deer hide hat and peered, with a twinkle in his eye, at the bearded man on the horse.

"Sergei?" Lensky intoned, "Sergei, is it really you? Where in God's name did you come from?" The Cossack slid down from his horse and marched towards the Colonel. The two old comrades embraced and stepped back, both grinning hugely.

"I could ask the same question Pavel," replied the Colonel, "but we're awfully glad you did appear when you did. Our position was becoming a little hairy, to say the least."

"Sergei," the Cossack enthused, "this is a fantastic chance meeting and I know we have much to discuss, but time is very much of the essence. I have to get my men away from here before the Germans bring up support. You are most welcome to accompany us back to our camp, if you like. Go find yourselves a horse each while I organise our getaway."

The Colonel nodded. "Carry on Pavel, we would be most honoured to take up your kind offer." The Cossack smiled, snapped to attention and saluted the Colonel. The Colonel reciprocated and the Cossack turned on his heel, remounted his horse and trotted off.

"Sergeant," he ordered, "get those pack horses loaded up and destroy what we can't carry. Send out flanking patrols, we don't want to be surprised by any sudden unwanted arrivals. Move it."

The sergeant rushed off, berating his men and the Russians swiftly stripped the column of their needs, strapped it on to several pack horses and made ready for leaving. Yuri, Alexei, Valery and the Colonel, were brought horses of men who had been killed during the attack. Once mounted up, the cavalcade moved out, heading in a north-easterly direction on a well-defined path, leaving the remains of the German column, burning and completely wrecked. The four brought up the rear, Alexei and Valery hanging back and keeping a weather eye open for any sign of pursuit. Yuri and the Colonel rode along easily behind the snaking column, both deep in thought until finally, the Colonel spoke.

"So, what happened to you three after the bridge blew up?"

"Well," answered Yuri, "we stuck to the plan once the charges had been set. All that commotion you created, made getting away from the bridge fairly easy. We managed to find each other, Valery and Alexei waited until I arrived about a hundred and fifty yards downstream, in the centre of the river. We then made our way to the edge and managed to find a place to scramble out. It wasn't easy, the

220

banks were steep and rocky, but we got a grandstand view of the explosion and the arrival of the train. The whole event was staggering, in that it never looked like it was going to go and then, down came the west side. We're all of the opinion, that if the engine hadn't rolled onto the bridge, it would have survived, albeit, impossible to use again. When it finally did go, we just hugged each other with relief. Then it was a case of finding you and getting some protection for our feet. It will be a monumental task for them to replace it. It certainly will hold up rail traffic to the east. They'll have to use the branch lines, but that means a big detour."

The Colonel nodded, pleased that it had gone so well. "At least we're doing more than our fair share of blunting the enemy's capacity to wage war. I'm not sure what we'll find up ahead, but Major Lensky is a good man and a very able leader. We may be able to join forces, I'm still trying to find a way of utilising the Gruber situation. Perhaps something will come to me."

Their conversation was halted by the arrival of the Cossack Major. He chatted away to both of them before finally turning to the Colonel and saying. "It's rather fortuitous that you should appear at this moment. There's someone back in camp, I know you would like to meet. He was brought to us three days ago, as part of a rescue operation from a little town near Minsk." The Colonel looked perplexed.

"Sergei," Lensky said softly. "Yenisei is resting at our camp."

Chapter 9 – Yenisei

The Colonel reacted with amazement. "Yenisei, he's at your camp?"

"He is," replied Lensky, "a little the worse for wear, but still a formidable force. I need to leave now and get back to my men. I just thought you would want to know and could explain to your companions about Yenisei."

"Good God," spluttered an incredulous Colonel, "that I will Pavel. That I will." The Cossack Major then trotted off towards the head of the column, while an inquisitive Yuri stared uncomprehendingly at the obviously agitated Colonel Berezovsky. "Good God," he kept muttering, "Yenisei. He's still alive. Good God in heaven. Yuri, can you whistle up Alexei and Valery, tell them I need to speak to the three of you. Get someone else to bring up the rear will you."

"Certainly sir," answered Yuri, "I'll be back in a minute."

The three young Russians trotted up to where the Colonel was obviously deep in contemplation. They rode together for about half a mile in total silence, until the Colonel eventually spoke. "Tell me," he began, "have either of you ever heard of a man called Yenisei?"

The three young men looked baffled, but finally Valery said, "Yes, our father spoke of him, but surely, it's the name of a river?"

"That it is," replied the Colonel, "but it is also the name of a quite remarkable man". "At their obvious bewilderment, the Colonel carried on. "Yenisei is the embodiment of Mother Russia, a legend forged out of hearsay, myth and absolute truth. I do know his actual name, but he's always just been known as Yenisei. His family can be traced back to the eleventh or twelfth century. Their lands lie north and east of the great bend in the river Yenisei, thousands of square miles of Siberian steppe and forest and were bequeathed to his family by the Great Khan, as a reward for their help in conquering most of eastern and central Europe, at the head of the Golden Horde. His capital is Abakan and he rules an empire from there that even the Communists leave well alone. As an eighteen year old, he travelled with his father to Sitka, in what was then, Russian Alaska and was present at the sale of Alaska to the USA in 1867. His father had argued bitterly with the Romanovs over the sale and refused to believe the paltry two cents per acre, they were paid. He alone understood the vast resources of minerals, wood, furs and oil, that would, in this day and age, be a massive economic benefit. He never forgave the Romanovs and swore that he would never place himself, or his descendants, at their imperial disposal. His lands were virtually a republic of their own, in which trade, industry, agriculture and education, far exceeded that of anywhere in the Asiatic world. Yenisei, his only son, is an academic, teacher, universal historian and a great leader of his people. I met him twenty years ago, when he was in his eighties, so now he must be over a hundred years old. You will be well advised to listen to what he has to say, if you are granted the chance of meeting him. Without question, the man is a legend in his own lifetime."

The four riders continued on, each deep within his own thoughts. Yuri, although he had never admitted it, had heard of this 'Yenisei', being someone whom his grandmother had spoken of in glowing terms. It would be interesting to meet this man and Yuri could then make up his own mind about what was fact or fiction. They had been travelling now for over three hours and the afternoon sun had given way to a heavy downpour. Undeterred, they moved along, deeper and deeper into the eastern expanses of the marshes.

The Cossack Major trotted back down the line and swung in alongside the four. "There's not too far to go now," he said conversationally. "It's a small village that we've taken over. The original inhabitants welcomed us when we became detached from our unit on day three of the invasion. I suppose we give them protection from the Germans, but all in all, there are over four hundred mouths to feed, including my soldiers and Cossacks. Yenisei has thirty attendants with him, including his grandson and two of his great-granddaughters. As you can see, we need to feed them and our horses, if we are to keep harassing the fascist columns."

"So how can we help," enquired the Colonel? "Our base is many miles from here, very close to the River Bug. We have been hiding in a cave on an island, since Yuri rescued us from captivity, just before we were going to be handed to the SS. We could perhaps form something of a coalition and work out a strategy, beneficial to all our needs."

"That sounds like a basis to work with," answered Lensky, "but first, let's get you four acquainted with our camp and present situation. See that tree covered ridge over there? That is basically our camp. The wood itself is quite extensive, mainly oaks and pines, there's a lake at the east end for water and lots of natural defences in the form of rocks and boulders. You'll soon sort yourselves out once you're in there."

Slowly, the long column snaked its way through the scrub and stunted pines, finally coming out in a large field of long grass. The field was quite extensive, surrounding the 'L' shaped ridge on two sides. To the east was the lake that Lensky had spoken about and to the south, a jumble of rocky outcrops, precipitous valleys and virtually

226

impenetrable marsh. Yuri was captivated. This is a place to defend easily, he thought. Only two ways to attack it and both involved any would be assailant crossing a wide swathe of open ground. The column skirted around to the long side of the 'L' where a gently sloping angled path, climbed up the side of the ridge, much like an eye-brow track. The column moved through the prepared defences at the crest of the ridge and passed into the inner sanctum of the Cossacks hideaway. The pack horses were led off to the right where there were several wooden barns, skilfully blended into the oak and pine screen. Many men were in evidence, all heavily armed and curious as to why these four German clad individuals, were allowed access to their camp. Colonel Lensky rode through these searching eyes into a wide clearing, totally aware of the effect the four were having and grinned with delight. Then he slid down from his horse, handed the reins to a stable hand and marched to the centre where a fire burned lustily. He stood there as his sergeant called for all the men to assemble. Once everyone was within hearing distance, he told them of the successful attack on the German column, the ten pack horses of food and military hardware and the loss of several of their comrades. He thanked those who had been with him and told them they would soon be off again, hitting the invaders where it hurt.

He then introduced Yuri, Valery, Alexei and the Colonel. "These four Russians are under my personal protection. They helped us today and we will fight again together in the future. They are to be allowed entry to anywhere on this base and are to be extended every courtesy. Do you all understand?" "Yes Major," the throng chorused in unison. "Good," finished Major Lensky. "Dismissed."

The soldiers, workers, horse handlers and village families turned and went back to their business. Lensky turned to his four guests, who had got down from their horses and were stretching their legs. "Well gentlemen, please feel free to wander. We normally eat at around seven thirty, which is in a couple of hours. Familiarise yourselves with the lay out of the camp. My NCO's will happily answer any questions you may have. I must oversee the stabling and health of my horse herd, so farewell until later." With that, he turned on his heel and strode off towards the lake.

The Colonel looked around and marched over to the sergeant. "Where's the best place for us to pitch our tents sergeant," he enquired.

"Well," replied the NCO, "probably over there, under those two oaks. The family's living in the houses have children and animals which can be a bit noisy, so I'd steer clear of them. You will be eating with us though won't you sir?"

"Yes, thank you sergeant," replied the Colonel. "We'll get our tents set up and stow away our gear. Then we'll have a saunter around, see if we can help anywhere."

"Very good sir," saluted the sergeant. The Colonel relayed the information to the other three and they set about pitching camp. Their weapons needed cleaning and oiling but once done, they all decided to have a look around. The first visit was to the stables, where farriers and blacksmiths were hard at work, caring for the horses. Alexei and Valery were very interested, as they had done this kind of work for many years. They stripped off down to their undershirts and waded in, helping where they could. Yuri and the Colonel left them to it and made their way around the defences, chatting to the guards as they tried to understand the layout of Lensky's strategy. The Colonel was impressed and then was greeted by some soldiers he had known back at Minsk, before he was captured. They chatted and regaled each other with tales of their respective escapes. Yuri felt a little uncomfortable and made his excuses, saying he would meet up with the Colonel later. Leisurely, he wandered around the rest of the camp. Everyone was involved in doing some sort of work that would eventually benefit the whole cause. He acknowledged greetings from every place he visited, conscious that he would have to begin helping out at some stage. Eventually, he made his way to the lake, which effectively formed the defence on the eastern side of the camp. The rocky shoreline was where the women came to do their washing and several were scrubbing and rinsing. He waved a cheery hello to them as he passed and continued along the lake edge. A rocky outcrop barred his path along the shore and he moved inland, skirting the base, where he came upon three brightly painted caravans arranged in a semi-circle, behind the outcrop. Here, there were several men and women, busy with various crafts. He noticed the weaving and sewing of cloth and skins, the making of snow shoes out of alder and ropes of sisal and plaiting of leather. Old and young were busily attending to their chores, although they all smiled in greeting as he passed. He walked on, past the caravans and into the rocks and ledges that formed the south side of the camp. Here the guards were not as numerous and he soon discovered why. The southern side of the camp fell away into a myriad of gullies, tree and brush that formed an almost impenetrable screen. Bogs, marsh and trickling rivulets of water made passage a virtual impossibility. The whole area was just a gigantic mess and Yuri shook his head in bewilderment. Thank God I don't have to fight my way through that lot, he thought.

He turned then and retraced his steps, clambering down and over the rocks, until he heard a noise off to his right, coming from the lake. Inquisitively, he made his way over the boulder strewn outcrop, until finally, he peered out between two rocks and down to the lake. He gazed in amazement at a young woman, knelt on a rock by the water's edge. She was washing her hair, casting it into the water and then drawing it out to wring through her hands and wash away the droplets. Then she leaned forward, dipping her head into the water and raised it back out again. She picked up a towel from nearby and dried herself, then took her hair and wrung out the excess water, turning it again and again through her hands. Satisfied that as much water as possible had been removed, she picked up a comb and began to draw it through the thick, black strands. Yuri was spellbound, fascinated by the sight. She turned slightly to her left and he could make out her delicate profile. He stared at her, his jaw sagging in wonder. She was beautiful and he was smitten. He watched her intently, the sinuous movement of her body as she swayed from side to side, combing her lustrous hair. He mused upon the idea that he, at some stage, would meet such a lovely creature and fulfil his dreams of home and family. He smiled to himself, oh how I wish, he thought, but how do you reach for someone like this? His wandering thoughts suddenly clarified in his brain, as he realised, with a shock, that she was looking directly at him. She had tired of waiting for him to speak and had turned, expecting another soldier leering at her. She looked at him and her world turned upside down. With an effort, she regained her poise.

"So," she began in a soft, contralto voice, "do you always stare at girls while they're bathing?"

Yuri was aghast. "I wasn't, I was, I was not staring," he stammered.

"Oh, you were," she replied teasingly, "you've been standing there gawping for the last five minutes."

"No," he offered, "no, not that long at all."

"So, you do admit you were staring then?" she chided.

"No," he repeated, "I was not staring. I heard a noise and came to investigate. I was just making sure that you were OK, that's all."

"So, you hear a noise and you investigate it for five minutes. When were you going to say something, you obviously can speak?"

The heat was rising in Yuri's face, he could feel himself reddening, as she continued to smile serenely, her intransigence goading him. "Look," he blustered, "I'm sorry. Sorry for any embarrassment I may have caused. I must admit, I did not expect to find you where I did."

"But you were staring, weren't you," she argued, then mischievously added, "Are you some sort of voyeur?"

This final barb was too much for Yuri. His eyes narrowed and he waded into her. "Listen you little

232

peasant strumpet. I have apologised for any offence caused. Do me the courtesy of at least acknowledging my gesture, or is it beneath you?"

Her eyes flashed at the insult and she rose in one lithe movement. Bunching her tiny fists she marched towards him, until they were no more than a yard apart. Planting her feet astride, she leaned menacingly forward, eyes riveted on his face. "Peasant," she screeched, her eyes blazing "I am no peasant. How dare you, you big oaf."

"Well you are from where I'm standing," countered Yuri. "A lady would have acknowledged long ago."

"I have never been so insulted," she lashed back. "If I were a man I'd......

Sploosh. Their altercation ceased in a flurry of water, which thoroughly drenched them. Both spun around towards the source of their discomfiture, to be confronted by a small, gnarled, old man. In his right hand he held an empty bucket, the contents of which had shocked them into silence. "Children," he murmured, "you've ruined my afternoon nap. Your raised voices were making my head hurt. "You," he pointed to the girl, "go and help your sister."

"Sorry grandfather Yenisei," whispered the girl, now cowed with contrition. She shrank around him and disappeared towards the caravans.

The man now turned his attention to Yuri. "So, Yuri Petrovsky, how dare you shout at my great granddaughter? Perhaps you will be more discerning towards her in the future."

Yuri blanched, muttered an apology and slunk off across the rocks by the lake. Not until he was well away from the old man's wrath did he suddenly think, how the hell did he know my name? Yenisei chuckled to himself as he made his way back to his caravan. Alayna, his great granddaughter, was the apple of his eye. He had never seen her speak to any man, save for a few muttered phrases. Nor had anyone else. It wasn't that she was rude, just not interested. There had been so many men vying for her attentions, but she remained aloof, polite up to the point where they tried to ingratiate her a little too much. Then, she would flash her eyes in defiance, turn her back and walk away. Yenisei was concerned that she would never find happiness, but her older sister, Katerina, had assured him that Alayna had admitted to her that she just hadn't met anyone yet who remotely interested her. So, this Yuri must be something special. It will be interesting to watch the interaction between these two, he thought. He rubbed his hands in glee. Neither of them were aware of his presence, as he sat high in the rocks overlooking the lake. Sitting around watching the men and women work had bored him and he needed somewhere to think. He had picked up the bucket and filled it, they would need it later, but on his way back to the caravan, he had decided to go and sit for a while, the water would be returned later. He had seen Yuri approach, watched him as he took great delight in appreciating the beauty and demeanour of Alayna. Equally, he had realised that she was keeping an eye on Yuri through his reflection in the water. Yenisei had not missed the sharp intake of breath and the pleasure in her eyes, before Yuri realised she was watching him. The altercation between them both was civil enough to start with, but he was surprised at the way she baited and goaded Yuri. He in turn, had taken it all gallantly on the chin, realising that he was in the wrong, but he responded magnificently when she pushed him too far. The bucket of water had come into play before one of them said something they would later regret. If only all wars could be so easily squashed. Anyway, he now had to prepare his thoughts for the evening. What he had to say tonight, would surprise, but then hopefully stimulate the men of Russia gathered around him. Yenisei had seen much during his lifetime, but these young men had to believe that they could succeed.

Yuri was fuming as he made his way back to re-join Alexei and Valery. That stupid girl, he raged, setting me up like that in front of Yenisei. Mind you, she is the most gorgeous female I have ever seen and her blistering attack had been a joy to behold. He relented a little. Perhaps he would be able to lock horns with her again. At least he felt on an equal level, even though she was almost royalty. There was something electric between them, or was he just dreaming. Oh, sod it, he thought, plenty more fish in the sea. He wandered over to where Alexei and Valery were finishing helping with the horses.

"So, what have you been up to," asked Alexei gaily, "I've just shod four horses."

"Not much," replied Yuri, "I've done a tour of the camp and chatted to the guards."

"That's odd," interrupted Valery, "we heard you'd been fighting a woman." Yuri blanched. Merciful heavens, he thought, they know about it already.

"I merely had a difference of opinion with a common peasant girl," he replied, "nothing to write home about."

"That's not what we heard," laughed Alexei, "something about having to cool the pair of you off by dousing you in water. Must have been some argument."

Yuri bridled, "Go fuck yourselves," he spat out, his face crimson with embarrassment, then turned and stormed off.

Alexei turned to Valery and said with mock solemnity, "Shit brother, the boys in love." Then the pair of them became serious.

"Have we met this girl Alexei?" asked Valery. "Perhaps we'd better check her out before we say any more."

"I'm with you brother," nodded Alexei, "she may be an ogre with a cast iron backside or a beauty we need to see more of. Whoever she is, our Yuri's got a strong case of something strange. Have you ever seen him this far out of control?"

Valery shook his head. "Never Alexei, Never."

Yuri stomped back to the place where they had set up camp. The Colonel who was chatting to the sergeant, noticed Yuri's arrival. The black mood that hung like a cloak around his young features, warned off the Colonels initial approach and he bit his tongue, leaving Yuri to his anger. What the hell's got into him, he thought. Someone's rubbed him up the wrong way and no mistake. I wonder if the brothers know anything. At that point, Alexei and Valery returned from their work with the horses. The Colonel watched as they ignored Yuri and sat together talking. After a while, a soldier approached them and said, "Major Lensky sends his regards and would you all like to join him for something to eat. He wishes that you may stay after the meal for a council of war, as he wants to introduce you all to Yenisei and his party."

"Yes, thank you private. Tell Major Lensky that we will all be honoured to eat with him and to take part in the discussions later." The soldier saluted and hurried off to pass on their answer. The Colonel gesticulated to Alexei and Valery that they should leave. They nodded, got up and left him and Yuri.

The Colonel rose, made as if to leave, then tarried and said, "Yuri, I would not turn down this offer of food and company. You are one of the most important people in this camp and your presence and input will be sorely missed, if you choose not to attend. Control this rage within yourself, for everyone's benefit, but mostly yours." With that he followed after the two brothers. Yuri was touched by the Colonels obvious sincerity and concern. Damn it, he thought, this whole episode has wrecked my standing, with friends and colleagues. Put her out of your mind. She will still be there tomorrow. But what if she's there tonight? No matter, I will deal with it as it comes. There are more important things going on than my feelings. What's done is done, I cannot retract the things I have said, but I will be my old self tonight, at least on the surface.

The meal was a convivial affair. Yuri arrived later than all the rest, but was immediately welcomed into the throng. He was given a large helping of pork, potatoes and vegetables from the main cooking fire and searched around for his friends. The men and women of the camp were giving him the once over, he knew they would all be familiar with what had taken place. But no-one laughed, or pointed, so he felt better. At least, she was not here. That would have been hard to handle. But then, he thought, I wish I could see her again, try to put things right between us. I can't stop thinking about her, she was so lovely. He sidled over to where Alexei, Valery and the Colonel were sitting and offered a general 'sorry' to them. Alexei grinned in his usual mischievous way, stood up and made space for him to sit with them.

 Slapping him gently on the back he said, "No need for any apologies Yuri. We're just glad you're here". The others nodded in agreement and he sighed with relief. The last thing he wanted to do was alienate himself from his friends. Soon he was laughing and sharing in their conversation. The Colonel watched his young friend and welcomed the change in him. Major Lensky had filled in the details of his encounter with Alayna and he understood the boyish way in which Yuri had reacted, even though he had not met Alayna so far. Females are difficult at the best of times, he thought, but with a war on, doubly so. Once the meal was over, the majority of people drifted off to their beds or duties. Major Lensky walked over to the four Russians and said, 'If you would like to follow me, Yenisei is expecting us. He asked that we all go over to his caravan where he will tell us exactly what is going on with this war and where he feels our success or failure lies. Whatever the outcome, I'm sure you will find it all very interesting'. The four got up and followed the Major and also several senior NCO's. Yuri was apprehensive, hanging back until he could see that she was not anywhere to be seen. Relieved, but disappointed also that she was not there, he finally seated himself. However, Yuri was wrong. The drawn curtains of Yenisei's caravan twitched ever so gently, as Alayna, at one side and Katerina, at the other, watched the arrival of the men. Katerina had been told by Yenisei about the altercation between Yuri and Alayna and he had asked Katerina to watch Alayna's reaction to Yuri. She watched her sister surreptitiously as the men arrived. Alayna appeared anxious, her brow furrowed in perplexity, as the men arranged themselves around the table. Then Katerina saw her sister stiffen, the corners of her eyes crinkled into a smile, her lips parted slightly and she heard and witnessed the little gasp of delight as Yuri finally arrived at the table.

Alayna suddenly became aware of her sisters gaze and said quickly, "Grandfather Yenisei has a captive audience." Katerina nodded. Oh, no my little sister, you can't fool me, she thought exultantly. Grandfather Yenisei was right, you are besotted by this man Yuri. Now all you have to do is go out and snare him for yourself. That could be difficult, knowing how your initial meeting went. Love is not for the faint hearted. There were eight men seated around the table when Yenisei and his son made their appearance. The son, Stephan, was tall and slender, aged somewhere in his sixties. He took a seat close to his father but slightly behind. Yenisei was around five feet five in height, with hair a straggly grey beneath a deer skin hat. His facial appearance was mongoloid, round and smooth, which belied his age. He had a grey flecked beard, which hung tantalisingly down towards his chest. Dark deep set eyes peered out from behind thick bushy brows, the kind of eyes that could charm or terrorise a person. He walked with a slight stoop, supporting himself with a richly carved staff, his delicate fingers, almost feline in the way they caressed the wood. He bowed stiffly to all of them, before seating himself. He looked at each man in turn, searching for a clue to their thoughts. Then he began.

"Gentlemen," he said in his small, clear voice. "Thank you for coming. I am Yenisei. I have been asked to share with you my feelings about this terrible war that now engulfs us. Almost one hundred and thirty years ago, an upstart French dictator thought he would conquer Mother Russia. He believed that he could simply defeat our troops in battle, to bring about our decline and fall. Never was anyone so wrong, until this year. There is now another who would try to destroy us, a Germanic tyrant with a belief in his own infallibility. He originally spoke of peace between Russia and Germany and a pact was made between him and

Stalin. But, on June 22nd, the treaty was broken, not by Stalin, but by this Hitler. And so, we are assailed by the forces of fascism. We were almost totally unprepared, thanks once again to Stalin. The fascists smashed through our defences and are, as we speak, moving forward relentlessly on three major fronts. The northern army has, according to them, liberated Estonia, Latvia and Lithuania and is now encircling Leningrad, cutting her off from the rest of Mother Russia. The Finns have renewed their attacks on the Karelia and Leningrad from the west, siding with the fascists. In the south, the fascist army has almost reached Kiev, fifty percent of the Ukraine is almost lost to us. In the centre, Minsk and Smolensk have fallen and Moscow is their next target. Their new Blitzkrieg tactic, lightning war, has been a total success. Our armies have not been able to cope with the mass tank formations, even though we had three times as many tanks as they did at the start. Our air force was more or less wiped out in the first couple of days, the majority of our planes destroyed on the ground, lined up in neat rows for the fascists to smash to pieces. And our men? Conservative estimates at this time believe that three million troops have been killed, captured or, as you all are, displaced from your units. My friends, the situation is dire. France has fallen, the Low Countries, Scandinavia and Central Europe are under the Nazi heel. Only Britain retains its independence but for how long? The Luftwaffe bomb them by day and night. Can they survive? The Japanese sit in readiness on our far eastern border with Manchuria, as yet uncommitted to the fight. They desire a far eastern Asiatic empire and could attack our eastern front. Then we would be between the hammer and the anvil. The Americans sit on the fence, their Senate opposed massively to any incursion into a European war, the horrors of 1914/18 too entrenched in their minds. So, we are on our own. The only way out of this mess is by our own efforts."

Yenisei paused, searching the grim faces surrounding him. No-one spoke or reacted, each man deep within his own thoughts. Finally, the Colonel made a start.

 "If things are so bad, how can we stop this juggernaut?"

Yenisei sighed and continued. "We will do what we have always done in times of crisis. Trade space for time. The enemy expects us to fight pitch battles, to hurl our forces in defence of our land. But we will fight, then retreat and draw him in, set fire to our crops, butcher our livestock, destroy our homes, villages, towns and cities. We will do this to ourselves, leaving nothing for him to feed on, nothing for him to use against us. And our armies will chip away at his flanks, attacking in strength and then fading away into the east. In 1812,

Kutuzov did exactly this, as Alexander's main commander and his only real failure was not destroying the French as they crossed the Berezina River. However, only 90,000 men escaped back to Prussia, out of more than 600,000. This enemy comes with three million men, he has no more to call on, whereas we can muster thirty million, as and when we require them. Trade space for time. It will not be armies who defeat the fascists, it will be Mother Russia herself. His armies will move deeper and deeper into her endless rolling steppe. Supply and communication will become hopelessly extended. And then the autumn rains will come, turning roads into impassable glutinous mud, followed by the winter with its snow, ice and incomprehensible cold. And he has no protection from her, no way of understanding how to survive her, let alone continuing to fight. He will have to cross rivers, huge waterways that run in the main, north to south. We will attack him, then retreat over the rivers, destroying the bridges and fade into the limitless countryside. He wants battles, but we will only do this on our terms."

"So, what can we do to help our armies," said Valery.

"Imagine," replied Yenisei, "the fascists are like a three-headed snake. The heads are snapping away at our armies, while the body gets longer and thinner. To achieve success in his tank war, this

Hitler needs petrol. That petrol, along with the tons and tons of ammunition, food and medical supplies, can only be provided by his ever-lengthening logistical chain. We can also destroy his communications by sabotaging the telephone lines. That is where we can help. The head cannot survive if the body is continually ravaged. Destroy the lorries, kill the horses, cripple the airfields and the following army, not only has to walk to war, but also, carry its supplies on its backs. We hit the supply convoys."

The proceedings were interrupted by several of Yenisei's entourage serving tea. There were also small oat cakes and sweetbreads. The assembly chatted amongst themselves as the women fussed over the tea and food.

When they finally left the men alone, Yenisei began again. "My friends, you are all here due to good fortune and the grace of God. All of you have been touched by the enemy, some more than others. I have saved the most important facet of our survival until the end. For the last forty years we have endured civil wars and the curtailment of civil liberties. It's impossible to say how many died at the hands of the Communist takeover, or how many were incarcerated for their beliefs. Russia is not a complex civilisation. Eighty-five percent are peasants. The ruling class make the decisions and the peasants are coerced to comply. They don't know the difference between the proletariat and a manifesto. All they know is how to survive, as they have been doing for the past thousand years. In this way, they will succeed. The Communists are just another ruling class, but for the system to prosper, it has to be enforced by Commissars, the NKVD and other secret police departments. Some are shot, others dispatched to the gulags and so the cruel, relentless exploitation of the peasants continues. But gentlemen, we are faced with an even greater evil than Communism, in the shape of Nazism. Hitler believes that all Jews, Slavs and Gypsies should be exterminated, because the former are the root of all financial problems and the latter, sub human. He has already begun this extermination. In Warsaw, a ghetto has been formed, where Jews are subjected to criminalised barbarism. Men, women and children are being robbed, starved and violated, then sent away to internment camps. Here, they are murdered, simply for being Jews. In our land of peasants, they will be categorised as sub human and will be systematically butchered. Gentlemen, we face annihilation at the hands of these brutes, because we do not conform to their Aryan code. This annihilation will be carried out by Hitler's personal bodyguards, the SS and it has already started. Major Lensky, perhaps you could expand on this."

The Major nodded in agreement. 'My friends, what Yenisei says is true, we are to be annihilated. I have been witness to several examples of this barbarism. On one occasion, my men and I came upon a small hamlet. The male occupants of the hamlet had been hung, the women shot and the children had their throats cut. We counted twenty-four victims. On another occasion, we came across twelve of our soldiers, hanging from a tree. Then we came across a village. The men had been herded into a large barn, then the barn had been set afire. Any who tried to escape were shot. The women had been raped and then bayoneted, even girls as young as seven were subjected to this depravity. The babies had their heads crushed by rocks and rifle butts. And all were left for us to see. We counted fifty-seven charred or shot bodies in the barn and fifty-three women, children and babies. Colonel Berezovsky has also intimated to me, that he and his companions had found another hamlet further west, where the same bestiality had been committed. I cannot stress enough the danger we all face from these Nazis, even the non-combatants"

"So, Gentlemen," said Yenisei, "we need to be vigilant, to protect our own, here and wherever we find them. What happens in the east where our armies and countrymen fight for survival, is something we cannot influence. They must solve their own problems. We must solve ours. My friends, I hope I haven't depressed you too much, but the consequences of our actions will ultimately help our country. I have had the honour of meeting most of you since my arrival here. Major Lensky and his Cossacks whisked me away from danger before Smolensk came under siege. I'm afraid three caravans, with my entourage, are not conducive to waging war, so fortunately, we are hidden for the moment. The Major and I have known each other for many years and I also know General Berezovsky, who now is to be called Colonel, from our dealings with the Communist takeover. The Avseyenko brothers, I have not met before, but I know the family well and your grandfather was a staunch protector of the Romanovs before the Great War. You are both welcome here as officers of the Red Army and as personal bodyguards of Colonel Berezovsky. Finally, I come to this young man, Yuri Petrovsky."

Yuri's head came up and he stared at Yenisei. "Gentlemen, this man survived the initial attack in June, but lost his brother in the process. By his own efforts, he effected the release of Colonel Berezovsky along with the Avseyenko brothers, guiding them to safety. He then worked out the strategy to completely destroy a petrol and munitions dump and also a road and rail bridge near Kowel. Yuri, I knew your grandparents very well. Your grandmother came from Abakan, In fact, she was my brother's sister. That makes me a very distant uncle."

Chapter 10 – Betrayal

The rest of the assembly stood up and bade Yenisei goodnight. Alexei, Valery and the Colonel left Yuri with a 'see you later' wave and headed back towards their beds. Yuri's face was a picture. Disbelief, amazement and wonder flickered across his features.

"You're my uncle," he stammered, "why have we never met?"

"Oh, we have," replied Yenisei, "but you were very young. Your grandmother brought you and Grigori to my home near Abakan. She wanted to show you where she was born and to introduce you both to the beauty of Asiatic Russia. Do you remember that journey?"

"I remember travelling for weeks and weeks in an ancient caravan," confessed Yuri, "but I hadn't realised until now exactly where we went. What I do remember is meeting a lady who told me many tales of India and of crossing the Hindu Kush with magical accounts of Yeti's, Tigers and the Himalayas."

"That would be my wife," answered Yenisei, "she was the daughter of a Maharaja, who I met and fell in love with when I visited that country. She waits for me now back in Abakan."

"But what of you now," quizzed Yuri, "where can you and your entourage go in safety?"

"A moot point Yuri," answered Yenisei, "the journey to Abakan is some three and a half thousand miles and between us and it are an invading army of genocidal fascists. We will be more than lucky to survive, let alone return home safely. But we must do what we can, whatever the cost. I worry for the members of my party, especially the women, but I will try to protect them."

"This place seems as good as anywhere to hide in these difficult times," added Yuri. "The place that I found would be better, but it could not hold so many. You know that the Colonel, Alexei, Valery and I will do all we can to help, as will everyone else here."

The old man nodded his thanks and rose as if to go, then he turned to Yuri and beckoned him closer. Whispering, so as the words would not carry he said, "It would be a favour to me if you and Alayna could be a little less aggressive towards each other in the future. You are both so young and she is headstrong, like her mother. I wish only the best for her."

Yuri smiled his assent, "It will be as you say," he said, "We cannot be continually at loggerheads in such close proximity."

Then Yenisei spoke even lower. "Beware Yuri, this is for you and your companion's ears only. I am an old man and spend my time sitting, listening and watching the world going on around me. I believe there is someone here, who would sell us out to the SS. Call it a hunch and I don't know who it is at this time, but I'm sure there is a traitor in the camp." With that cryptic warning, Yenisei turned and made his way back towards his caravan, his son Stephan trailing him behind. Yuri was perplexed. He had felt elated with his association to Abakan and Yenisei's plea that hostilities between himself and Alayna should cease, but then, a traitor in the camp? Who? And how does Yenisei know.

Back in the caravan, Alayna and Katerina had watched and listened to all of Yenisei's talk and marvelled at the way in which he grasped and understood, the political and military situation. He was their great grandfather, a gentle but strict doting relative, especially in regard to their upbringing and schooling. To see him now, regarded so reverently by his peers, made them realise how little they knew of him and his influence over Russian affairs. Alayna had heard and understood the implications of Yenisei's revelations to Yuri and had been shocked to realise that this man was somehow related. All she knew was, he affected her in a way that no other had ever done and she was aware of the effect the implications were having on her mind and heart. Katerina had watched her sister and understood the emotions tugging and caressing her femininity. Such a time, she thought, for these two to have met. Perhaps they were fated to be thrown together like this, when all the world is going crazy. Only time will tell.

Yuri returned to his three companions in a deep and thoughtful mood. The Colonel and Valery had turned in, only Alexei was still awake. He nodded a smiled greeting to Yuri and continued shaving away with a knife on a piece of wood. Yuri debated whether to broach the subject of a traitor in the camp, but decided to wait until morning. Let's sleep on it he thought, we need to approach this issue together. With that, he said his goodnight to Alexei and climbed under his blankets. The morning would be here soon enough and he needed his sleep. Alexei continued to shave away at the piece of oak. He had it in mind to create a tank out of the wood and give it to one of the boys from the family's he had met yesterday. Good, basic, rustic folk, they toiled all their lives to try and provide a living for their dependants. And yet the Nazis would eliminate them all, for just being peasants. They were human beings, as everyone was, but these barbarians would destroy the very fabric of society and culture, a culture that had survived and prospered for thousands of years. How can all this wickedness be directed at such an easy target. We must see that it never happens, or life will be simply not worth living. He made a grim pact with himself.

I for one, will defend my people to the death, no matter what stands in my way. He sighed contentedly, put down his carving for the morrow and made for his blankets. Within minutes, the camp was silent, but for the snorts of animals and the quiet footfalls of the guards as they made their rounds of the perimeter.

Morning came with a gentle rain, the drizzle falling in a soaking haze as the camp became alive. Yuri was up early, filling a pot for coffee from the large communal fire that burned continuously in the central area. Women and children were fetching water from the lake, while the horse herders went about their early morning duties. Just a normal day, thought Yuri, but in such abnormal circumstances. The Colonel was up when Yuri arrived back at their billet. Alexei and Valery were grumbling their way out of their blankets and into the damp seating area beneath the oaks. Mugs were filled and coffee served. The four sat in convivial silence as they absorbed the awakening morning, watching the comings and goings of all associated with the camp. It was now well into July and the day to day process of preparing for winter was gathering pace. Forage and grain would soon need to be harvested, vegetables would need picking and storing, while the never-ending supplies of wood for shelter and burning would need to be sourced from an ever-increasing distance from the camp. Hunting parties were going out daily, bringing back deer, wild pigs, geese and ducks to supplement the farmer's livestock. Bears were killed for their furs and sometimes for eating. Everyone from the oldest to youngest had jobs to do. With so many mouths to feed, the daily gathering of supplies was tantamount to the whole camps general wellbeing. Soldiers were ever present and Major Lensky was busy with new duty rosters. Raids and attacks on the fascist supply trains would need to be co-ordinated and put into practice. So much to do and plan for, with so little time for rest. Suddenly, the general alarm sounded. Men, women and children vacated the camp area, fires were doused with water and all livestock hidden from view. The four young Russians hid within the oaks leaf covered mantle and waited. In the distance, a low hum emanated from the west, as their old friend, the Stork, trundled its way above the treetops. The tiny plane flew slowly eastwards, about a mile from the camp, then it banked and turned towards them. No-one moved. It continued on until it suddenly veered south and east, half a mile from the camp, following the far shore of the lake, until it finally disappeared towards the south. Silence returned to the camp and after a period of time where the hidden populace remained immobile, Major Lensky sounded the all clear.

"That little sod is becoming a pain in the arse," commented Alexei bitterly, "I thought he was going to come right over us, then he decided against it. It does make you wonder though, if this place, with all its people and livestock, must surely be a recognisable target from the air, the houses and barns can't all be hidden from view."

"That may be," granted the Colonel, "but there are so many of these hamlets and villages, they can't keep tabs on all of them. It must be signs of movement and congregation of equipment, but this area is so vast and we can hear him coming. He's obviously searching for insurgents, but let's face it, we could be anywhere."

"Well," countered Alexei, "he won't see much if he doesn't fly right over us anyway. Think we could knock one of those down Valery?"

"It's possible," said Valery, "if I hoisted you onto my shoulders at the top of a tree. It's a big enough target, but you'd probably miss."

Alexei grinned, "up yours brother," he said jovially.

"It's possible that he was warned off," said Yuri pointedly. The others looked at him questionably. He beckoned them closer and spoke in a low voice, telling them what Yenisei had told him last night.

"So, Yenisei thinks there's someone here who would betray us to the Nazis," said Alexei disbelievingly. "Surely we're watching each other all the time?"

Yuri nodded and came back with, "If someone had a reason to expose us and was waiting for something else to develop, or someone else to arrive, he could get a message to that plane. All it would take would be a torch, a smattering of Morse code and a position, somewhere on the outskirts of the camp."

"That would mean a soldier," broke in the Colonel. "I remember telling you before about the German espionage individuals like Gruber. The southern agent could be in this camp. Let's face it, we don't know where any of these displaced soldiers were found or how they were absorbed into this community. If Yenisei believes it could be anyone, then we cannot involve Pavel Lensky and his men, as equally, the insurgent could be one of them. All we can do is watch and wait, try to eliminate as many as possible. But this individual will not be easy to spot and he will have a very plausible cover story."

"Shit," muttered Valery, "that's all we need, a sodding spy. OK Colonel, what's the plan?"

"Like I said," the Colonel replied. "Watch and wait and hope that he makes a wrong move."

The weeks passed as July turned into August. Several raids were carried out on the Nazi supply trains, nothing major, just well executed forays, where plunder of food, ammunition and extra weapons, with maximum destruction of lorries and horses could be carried out in relative safety. The attacking force then faded away into the vast expanses of the marshes. They were also careful not to carry out these raids in close proximity to the camp, travelling well away from their immediate area. This meant three or four days away from home, but it was working and the Nazi columns were feeling the pinch, having to provide extra troops to guard against these attacks. But as Alexei said, it only takes one bullet in a petrol tanker and that's it destroyed, one grenade in amongst a team of horses and the field gun they were towing, now needs extra horses. Little by little and bit by bit, they were harassing the enemy, making it impossible for him to feel relatively safe, even though the supply columns were miles from the front and the main fighting. In short, they were vulnerable anywhere. Over the weeks, many stragglers, both families and displaced soldiers, had found their way to the safety of the camp and it was growing. Now the population was well over five hundred and it brought its own set of logistical problems, coupled with the on-going food shortages. However, they were becoming a potent, guerrilla force, welded into a resourceful and disciplined unit, thanks to the efforts of Major Lensky and the Colonel. Yuri, Alexei and Valery had been out on some of the raids, but they made sure that at least one of them was in camp to monitor the insurgent threat. That threat had so far been non-existent, making them believe that perhaps Yenisei could have been wrong. Yuri had not been able to speak to or make any kind of contact with Alayna, mainly because he was too busy with camp affairs. The Colonel had asked him if he would teach the recruits about bush craft and his days were spent honing the camps soldiers into an effective, ambushing force, able to hit a target with maximum firepower and then fade away into the impenetrable marshes. All aspects of direction finding by the sun and stars, the reading of maps and use of a compass, were drilled into the men, as were living off the land, camouflage and following a trail. Yuri loved it, but knew that the force was becoming too large. They would be better off splitting up with one half relocating in another area. He put this to the Colonel and the Colonel agreed, telling Yuri to take some time and to explore eastward, to try and find another base. With this in mind, Yuri and a dozen soldiers, travelled eastwards and southwards for a week, camping out in the woods. They found a couple of sites that would fit the bill, noted the locations and moved on. On their travels, they found more evidence of SS atrocities. Hamlets and villages burning, bodies strewn everywhere, soldiers hung and left in the trees to rot. The whole area was becoming a vast charnel house.

On his return, Yuri went back to training the new army personnel who had been arriving in dribs and drabs for the past month. They would go out in groups of ten or twelve and Yuri would push them hard in bush fighting and tactics. He returned back to camp one evening, tired and hungry, Alexei and Valery were off on a raid, only the Colonel was on the camp. He was met by Stephan, Yenisei's son. Yuri could see the worry on his face and thought that something must have happened to Yenisei while Yuri had been away.

However, Stephan was worried for another reason and said to Yuri, "it's Alayna Yuri, she went off this morning with a party of women and children hunting for wild roots and berries. There were six soldiers with the party acting as guards, but somehow, they became separated and the main party has just returned saying they'd lost her somewhere south of here. My father and I are very worried and we wondered whether you could go out and search for her."

"Of course, I will," answered Yuri, "you say she went south?"

"Yes," agreed Stephan, "off behind the houses over there. She's often doing this, going off on her own that is, but normally is home by this time. I would take it as a huge favour."

"No problem," said Yuri, "don't worry, I'll find her and bring her back safely."

"Thanks Yuri," said Stephan, "I'd go myself, but I'm not sure I would find my way back."

"That's OK Stephan," replied Yuri. "I know the area pretty well now, having covered most of it with the trainees. Don't worry, I'll find her."

With that, he picked up his rifle and with a parting wave, headed off into the tumble of boulders and scrub behind the houses. It will be nice to see her, he thought, maybe we can talk a little and resolve a few issues and maybe I can ask to see her a bit more around the camp. He carried on through the difficult terrain, his mood light at the thought of seeing her. The evening was cool after the warmth of the day, but he was tired and hadn't eaten since lunchtime. Scrambling down a rocky ravine he slipped and cracked his knee on a sharp rock outcrop, he swore and soldiered on. After a few hundred yards, the going became easier and he moved on quickly, although his leg was paining him and the Mosquitos were beginning to bite. He'd travelled about half a mile when he suddenly came up short. Something was moving through the trees to his right. Instinctively, he faded silently behind a tree and waited, his breathing controlled and even. Minutes passed then eventually, he saw the reason for his discomfort, as three large wolves moved into the small clearing ahead. He let out his breath in a long sigh and gave them chance to move on. They paid him no mind, seemingly intent on heading away to the south and he was able to move out, albeit in a direction away from their path. Where the hell was that girl? He was becoming annoyed, mainly because his leg had started to stiffen up, due to having to stand still and upright while the wolves moved past. He swore again, his demeanour souring by the minute. He reached the point at which the women, children and guards had become separated from Alayna and looked for tracks. Most were congregated in an area where wild onions and cherries were abundant, the trees having been stripped to their high branches. So, where the hell had Alayna gone? He scouted the area thoroughly, until he came upon a set of small tracks leading east into an area of scrub, ravines, small cascading waterfalls and tiny rivulets. Why would she come this way, he wondered, women have no sense. He followed the trail for a few hundred yards, dodging between the rocks and stunted trees, his knee now throbbing. Damn that stupid woman, where the hell is she? He stumbled his way down between rocks and scrub until he found himself in a small clearing. The tracks crossed the clearing, but had been joined by another set and this set had claws. A bear had picked up Alayna's scent and was following her. His concern now was acute, wolves, bears, the chance of a fascist patrol and she out there by herself. Does she not understand the danger in these marshes? Alarmed now and becoming more and more agitated, he blundered on, careless of the slippery rocks and snagging branches. A path suddenly diverted south, away from the main trail. Here there were signs of heavy boots. Was this somewhere he had brought the trainees? He couldn't remember, his anxiety outweighing his reasoning and he thrashed around manically trying to make sense of it all. Where were the bear tracks? They'd disappeared. And then he saw the small boot tracks, curving off into the boulders and scrub. Desperately, he followed the trail, until he came upon a large glade of oaks and pines. He knew now where he was and suddenly spotted Alayna, grubbing around under the trees, picking wild onions. He stomped over to her. She heard him coming and swung around to assess his noisy approach.

"Oh, it's you," she gasped sweetly, "are you my knight in shining armour, come to save me?"

Then she noticed the wild expression in his eyes and took a step backwards. Yuri just spluttered, threw up his arms in anger, spread his legs and glared at her.

"No, I'm no such fucking thing," he growled. His arm pointed menacingly at her, "you, you little idiot, what the hell are you doing out here on your own? Have you any idea the trouble you have caused to me, the party you were with and your family. And you just stand there like it's all a game. We're all worried sick about you."

"There was no need to worry," she countered defensively, "I can look after myself."

"Oh, so the wolves, bears and soldier footprints I've been following were just so much window dressing? I ought to put you over my knee and give you a good spanking."

"Just try it mister," she countered aggressively, "I'll chop you into little pieces, you arrogant brute."

The knife, concealed in her skirts was suddenly grasped in her tiny right hand, she set herself, her beauty masked by the malevolence in her eyes. Yuri had a fleeting glimpse of admiration for her obvious bravery and longing for her to somehow back down, but it was momentary, she had to be shown the error of her ways. With that, he took a quick step forward, slapped the knife out of her hand, she screamed in pain, her left hand gripping her stinging right. He then reached down, picked her up around the legs and dumped her unceremoniously over his left shoulder, her head hanging down towards his waist. She arched her back, fighting to drag herself away from his restrictive grasp when 'Slap', his right hand slammed down hard on her buttocks. She groaned, tears of pain rushing down her face, her little fists battering his back. 'Slap', another hard, open-handed source of torment. She wailed, eyes tightly shut against the pain and embarrassment.

"Be still," he commanded, "It's time to go home."

With that, he picked up the fallen knife and shoved it into his belt, well away from her grasping fingers, he didn't want her getting any ideas in her present state, slung the rifles over his right shoulder, picked up her sack of vegetables and moved off. He knew the way from here. Strangely, his knee was not paining him so much now and he felt a certain kind of exultance at the way he had dealt with her. She would have skewered him, given the chance and he loved her spirit and passion. He could hear her pitiful sobs as she allowed herself to be carried like some reward of conquest. As he walked he spoke matter-of-factly, hoping she would understand his concern.

"You see how easy it was to disarm you, how simple to dominate you. Had I been intent on rape, you wouldn't have stood a chance. Had I been a bear or wolves, again, not a chance. And yet you put me and your family through this hell because you assume, wrongly, that you can look after yourself. I will say no more on this, but please, try and stay safe."

With that, he lapsed into silence. Alayna continued to sob, the soreness of her buttocks, rubbing against her dress with each step he took. She gritted her teeth against the pain, but her only concern now was humiliation. Oh no, she thought, he's going to parade me right through the camp like this, how will I ever hold up my head again? She need not have worried. A hundred yards from the entrance to the camp, Yuri stopped and set her gently down, handed over the rifle, knife and sack and stood back waiting. She turned towards the camp, carefully avoiding his eyes and walked off, Yuri following a few steps behind her. The outer guards nodded a greeting as they passed, the men infatuated by Alayna's beauty. They walked past the houses and stables until Yuri spotted Stephan running over to them. He then moved away towards his sleeping area, gave Stephan a cheery wave and left Alayna to her uncle and Grandfather Yenisei.

Dumping his kit, he made his way over to the large communal cooking fire and got himself something to eat. He was ravenous and made short work of the stew that bubbled and hissed on the cauldron. Some of the new recruits came over and he spent a happy hour going over the week's events with them. He liked the easy way they fitted into the system here, but then he realised that one of them could be Yenisei's spy in the camp. Damn it, he thought, I've no idea who it could be, they all seem so innocent and their stories are so plausible. Perhaps Yenisei was wrong, although he seemed adamant. Eventually, he bid them good night and went off to find the Colonel, who was just arriving from a discussion with Major Lensky.

"Evening Yuri," the Colonel greeted happily, "I hear you found our missing Alayna. That girl is a real handful."

Yuri nodded, "that she is," he replied pointedly, "but she has lots of courage, even though it's misplaced in this hell we're having to live with. Anything to tell?"

"Nothing that won't wait until morning," admitted the Colonel, "I'm going to turn in and you?"

"Yes," answered Yuri, "it's bed for me too."

Tiredly, they both climbed into their blankets and were soon sleeping soundly. Out on the far defence screen, the guards were silently watchful. The darkness had fallen like a cloak around the sleeping camp and the guards ears were becoming attuned to the night time sounds. Vladimir Konchesko, late of Kowel, huddled into his greatcoat, wringing his hands together against the night chill. He had arrived in the camp about a month ago, his story being one of many such stories, from the early days of the invasion. At that time, the camp was much smaller than today, with only a couple of hundred men, plus the resident families. He smiled grimly to himself as he remembered the way in which it had been so easy to ingratiate himself into camp life, how simple to establish a rapport with the other soldiers. The arrival of Major Lensky and his Cossacks had worried him to start with, but he kept quiet and found that he was easily accepted as a displaced individual without too many difficult questions asked. In short, he was almost above suspicion. This suited him immensely, as he was without doubt, the most dangerous man in the camp. Vladimir Konchesko was the southern insurgent, his code name 'Rhine Maiden'. He had murdered a soviet soldier once he was safely over the Bug and had swapped his field greys for Russian brown. He spoke faultless Russian with a Georgian accent, much like Stalin. The rest, up to now, had been easy. The arrival of Yenisei's party had been of great interest to him, although he didn't understand the implications of Yenisei's position in the Great Russian structure. However, he discovered by talking and listening to others in the camp, that Yenisei was somehow of great importance. The arrival of Yuri, the Colonel and the Avseyenko brothers was the icing on the cake. Yuri, he did not know, but the other three were high on the SS's wish list. He had to get a message to them somehow.

The only way he could communicate with his superiors was Morse code, but the telegraph lines were continually being sabotaged by the numerous raids carried out by various groups from the camp. Therefore, he had to improvise. The arrival of the Stork earlier this week, gave him his first opportunity, flashing off a message to it while it cruised past. He had originally sent a coded message via the telegraph lines some weeks ago, informing Hauptmann Lientz in Minsk, that he was in the camp and would get information for him later. Basically, he divulged his identity to the little planes crew by torch and asked them to return tomorrow, at sunrise. His relief turned up at eleven and he snuggled down into his blankets, knowing that he would be awakened at four o'clock, ready for the early morning shift and the Stork.

Four o'clock came and his fellow guard shook him from his slumbers. The morning was chilly and damp, but there was no mist. He breathed a sigh of relief, mist could have been a real problem, but now he could concentrate on his task. His position on the outer defence, was in a corner where the woods joined the northern edge of the lake. Apart from his fellow guard, there was no-one else within twenty feet and he was confident that he could deal with this other guard when the need arose. Vladimir would raise the general alert and the other guard would stay, wrapped up in his blankets. That was how the alert worked. Nobody moved. He could hear the guard snoring now, some eight or nine feet away from him and screened by several trees. Vladimir sat back contentedly and watched as the light brushed the eastern horizon and the nightly shadows began to assume shape and texture. He fingered his torch in his jacket pocket. Not long now. Then he heard the tell-tale sound of an approaching propeller and he sounded the alert, a long, piercing whistle. The camp became alive, but only for a moment. All were awake, but no-one moved. The little plane drifted into view, just clipping the tree tops. It droned straight for the camp until it reached the edge of the lake and banked south to run parallel to where Vladimir was waiting. Taking a final careful look around, he flashed off a message to the Stork. The message consisted of a series of letters, singly and in pairs or triplets, which when de-coded, formed words and phrases. Satisfied that he had done as much as he could, he waited for Major Lensky to sound the all clear. Minutes passed, until the drone of the little plane disappeared off to the south. Perfect, he thought, now the die was cast. In two days, there would be an overwhelming attack on the camp. He hoped his training would be enough to keep him alive. If he could pull this off, the Fuhrer would be more than pleased.

The all clear sounded throughout the camp, as the occupants began to prepare themselves for another day. The Colonel was first out of his blankets, taking the large pot to the cooking fire, to fetch water for coffee. Yuri, Alexei and Valery were discussing the dawn's events when the Colonel arrived back with the pot. He busied himself with mixing in the grounds and pouring the hot treacly liquid into four tin mugs. There was nothing like morning coffee, even in the situation they all found themselves in.

"I don't like this at all," muttered Alexei, "that little plane is coming around much too often for my liking. Do you notice that he never actually comes over the camp, even though he must be able to see the houses and buildings?"

"I've thought the same for some time," acknowledged the Colonel, "he always comes from the east, then flies south along the edge of the lake. It's as if he knows not to approach, although how, I'm not sure."

"Perhaps we're all becoming paranoid," put in Yuri, "or maybe Yenisei's idea of an infiltrator could be true. What if someone on the outer defence screen is flashing the Stork a message and what if that someone has told them about Yenisei?"

"Shit," muttered Valery, "We'd better check this out. There can't be too many in a position to do what you say. Colonel, have a word with Major Lensky, he'll have the duty rosters for last night and maybe he'll remember who was on duty in the outer ring, on the other occasions that the Stork has put in an appearance."

The Colonel nodded his assent. "Yes, I'll do that," he intoned, "and let's just keep this between ourselves at the moment."

The Colonel hurried off to find Major Lensky, leaving the other three to drink their coffee.

"We're setting up a big raid on the airfield near Minsk," said Valery, "the Major reckons that we could take out a whole load of planes on the ground if we hit it at first light. I think his plan involves taking out the perimeter guards with the crossbows and then using the anti-aircraft guns in the outer emplacements to give the attacking force covering fire. The only real problem is that it's a good hundred miles away. It would take around two hundred and fifty of us to pull it off successfully, but I'm not sure it's a good idea now, given the morning's events and their possible consequences."

"I agree," said Alexei, "but it will be a shame if we don't. We could do with another major strike and that would really hit them where it hurts. Some of those airfields hold up to seventy aircraft of one sort or another, plus aircrew, guards and supplies, especially petrol. I could do with another big bang," he ended with a grin.

"You're incorrigible," laughed Yuri, "you'd blow up your own grandma, given the chance."

"Have you met my grandma?" threw back Alexei, "she'd probably supply the dynamite, eh Valery."

"You're mad," said Valery, "she'd give you a run for your money. Come on, let's go shoe some horses.

It'll help us to think." With that, the two brothers headed off towards the barns leaving Yuri to ponder.

Yuri was deep in thought when the Colonel arrived back. "I got the roster from Pavel," he said, "altogether, there's twelve possible suspects and you'll know them all, having done training with them. Over the last month there's been five times when the Stork has appeared and in most cases, the same men were involved somewhere along the outer perimeter. If I had to make a guess, I'd go for these three. Ivan from Odessa, Sergei from Stalingrad and Vladimir from Kowel. Of the three, Ivan and Vladimir seem the best bets, having been paired together several times. Do you have any choice?"

"Yes, I do know all three," answered Yuri, "Vlad and Ivan have been here for well over a month. Both came separately, joining up with other displaced soldiers along the way. If I had to make a choice between them, I'd go for Vladimir. He's more intelligent than most, in fact he's NCO material. Ivan's just a basic soldier, with no aspirations to being anything but a private, unless he's being particularly clever."

"Well," intoned the Colonel, "we'd better keep an eye on both of them. Maybe we're doing them a disservice, but if Yenisei's right, Vladimir could be our man."

"OK then," replied Yuri, "I'll be very discreet. I'm just going to have a wander around and see if I can pick up anything suspicious. See you later." Rising, he wandered off to do a tour of the outer defences. It's time to have a really good look at the way Major Lensky's set up the defences here, he thought. Then maybe I can come up with an idea for any weak points.

As Yuri began his tour of the defences, Hauptmann Lientz was sat at his desk, deep within the bowels of his headquarters in Minsk. He leaned back in his chair, satisfied that the war was going very favourably for the Nazi cause. Leningrad was surrounded, Kiev had fallen and Moscow was within reach, probably before Christmas. He allowed himself a smile of contentment, as he ticked off the SS's achievements so far. The Jewish situation was going nicely. Concentration camps were springing up all over eastern Poland and Heydrich's interpretation of Hitler's final solution was taking effect. Train loads of men, women and children were being sent to these camps every day. Russian prisoners were being put to work in the slave camps and where this couldn't be achieved, shot or hung where they were found. The 'Untermensch' were being systematically eliminated. The only thorn in his side was the repeated attacks of Russian partisans, who appeared out of nowhere to destroy his supply trains, only to melt away into the swamps and marshes. This would have to be stopped. He had two units of SS working out of Minsk, but they were too few to really make an impression. What he needed was information on the camps these insurgents were working out of, then he could bring other SS battalions into the equation. At present, they were needed elsewhere. There had been no word from two of his three spies, 'Kuhmo Wolf' and' Brandenburg Gate', but he had heard from 'Rhine Maiden'. Hopefully, all three would be in touch soon. His reverie was interrupted by a short knock on his office door, he called out "enter" and his orderly rushed into the room. The man came to attention in front of him, clicking his heels together and giving the Nazi salute.

"Herr Hauptmann, I have the communique from the navigator of the Stork."

"Yes, yes," growled Lientz apprehensively, "speak up Franz, what does it say?"

The orderly cleared his throat, Lientz glared at him, drumming his fingers on the desk top impatiently. "Sir," began the orderly, "the report states, five hundred plus insurgents, Ivan's five, fourteen and fifteen here."

With that, Lientz's eyes narrowed and sparkled. He rummaged around with the papers on his desk, selecting the one with the list of senior Russian military and political leaders. Ivan one was Zhukov, Ivan two Timoshenko and so on down the list. At five was General Berezovsky and fourteen and fifteen were the Avseyenko brothers. So, that's where you got to, he thought.

"Is that all?"

"Sorry sir, the report continues, request attack Friday, infiltrate north east corner by lake, I will pave the way. Abakan Zulu also present."

With that, the orderly stood silently waiting his next command. Hm, thought Lientz, Friday eh. Then the realisation hit him. "What did you say, what was that last bit?"

The orderly stammered, "Which last bit sir?"

Lientz surged to his feet, "After the attack request you idiot. What did you say?"

"Er, oh, er, Abakan Zulu also present, sir."

Lientz howled with joy, "Abakan Zulu. Good God Franz, get me a direct line to Heydrich now, now I say."

"I'm sorry sir," blustered the orderly, "all the lines to Warsaw are down. The partisans keep blowing them up."

"Then get on to the airfield and get me a plane," raged Lientz, "I have to be in Warsaw tonight, do you understand?"

The orderly saluted quickly, spun on his heel and made a hurried exit. Holy Mother, exulted Lientz to himself, Ivan's five, fourteen, fifteen and Abakan Zulu. This will guarantee my Iron Cross. Heydrich will be ecstatic. "Franz, Franz, have you got that plane yet?"

Yuri's tour of the outer and inner defences was going well. The men seemed ready and able, with a deep understanding of what was required of them at all times of the day and night. The west and north sides were the most heavily populated, with any assault on the camp most likely to originate from these directions. The east side was composed of the lake and so only posed a negligible problem. Behind the houses, to the south, were the jumble of ravines and thick brush, a difficult area for an attacking force and quite easily defended by a small number of men in strategically strong positions. If an attacking force broke through the east and north defences, then there was a secondary line, some twenty feet in from the outer ring and this was also heavily fortified. Any breach of the outer ring and the defenders could quite easily fall back to this line. All in all, Major Lensky had thought the whole thing through, to provide a considerable redoubt. If the camp was assailed by an overwhelming force, then a strategic retreat could be effected through the broken country to the south. Any following force would be pinned down as the vast majority escaped. Heartened by his overall understanding of their predicament, he went in search of Alexei and Valery. He found them hard at work in the Blacksmiths shop. Yuri loved the smells and sounds associated with shoeing horses, having worked in similar situations back at home with Grigori and their father, Joseph. Alexei and Valery were sweating profusely, the heat from the forge coupled with the warmth of the day was debilitating, but the two brothers revelled in the difficult work and the sometimes skittishness of the horses. So, Yuri gave them a wave and left them to their task. He then decided to go and seek out Yenisei, even though it meant the possibility of bumping into Alayna. Surely, she would not still be sore from their last encounter, after all, he had allowed her some dignity after her misdemeanour. But as he approached the caravans, she was nowhere to be seen, although Katerina was busy with a pile of laundry and waved him over.

She flashed him a smile and spoke with mock severity, "so Yuri, have you come to apologise to Alayna?"

"Apologise?" answered Yuri, "no, I haven't. I hope she understands what happened yesterday. It could have been a lot worse."

"Not according to her," answered Katerina sweetly, "she says you were very uncouth and uncivil to her, although uncle and Grandfather Yenisei both gave her a real telling off. I was hoping you two could be a little easier going towards each other, but she's adamant that you were just brutish."

"Brutish," exclaimed Yuri, "well, if you call giving her a good sm....", he stopped himself just in time, then added, "I was only thinking of her wellbeing," and left it at that.

Katerina smiled and nodded "well thank you for bringing my little sister back safe and sound," she leaned over and whispered conspiringly, "I know she was very angry when she returned, but I think it was directed at herself, not you."

With that she smiled again and Yuri hoped that he had grasped her cryptic message. Bloody hell, he thought, are we ever going to have any sort of relationship. God knows how much I want her. But he just said, "Thanks Katerina, is it possible to have a word with Grandfather Yenisei?"

"Of course," she replied, "he's down by the lake in the rocks by the foreshore. He often sits there so he can look out over the lake and the surrounding countryside. He's not anything like as active as he used to be." With that, she bade him farewell and Yuri walked off down between the caravans and into the rocks by the lake.

Yenisei was deep in thought, his head cradled on his arms as he stared out over the lake. Yuri thought he looked as if the world was weighing him down, such was the expression on his face, but he turned at

Yuri's arrival and his welcoming smile belied his age. "Welcome young man, welcome indeed. And to what do I owe this unexpected pleasure?"

Yuri was deeply touched by the effusiveness of the old man's greeting. "Well sir," he began, "I was wondering if you could spare me the time to go over a few points regarding the camp and our welfare. Major Lensky seems to have thought wisely about the defensive perimeter, but I'm concerned about the lack of any cover around your caravans. In the event of an overwhelming attack on the camp, it would seem that your position here is very exposed and I'd like the chance to address it."

The old man nodded, "firstly, my boy, do you think you could dispense with the sir and just call me Yenisei like everyone else?"

 Yuri shook his head, "It wouldn't be right sir and I would see it as disrespectful, especially for my elders and betters."

 "Then call me uncle," pleaded Yenisei, "sir makes me feel so old and somehow dictatorial. Would you do that for me?"

 "OK," replied a grinning Yuri, "I would be honoured to call you uncle."

 "That's better," said Yenisei, "it would make me very happy. As to the caravans, in the event of an attack, my party would make for the houses and outbuildings and help with their defence. The caravans are indefensible, therefore, we need to be prudent, in that we are non-combatants and civilians. We are more or less completely dependent on the camps soldiers for protection. There would appear to be no other way."

Yuri nodded, "well, I can think of nothing else that would guarantee your safety," he said, "the soldiers would be our last line of defence anyway. Let's hope it never comes to that." Yenisei stayed silent, mulling over his thoughts. Yuri took the time to study the approaches to the other side of the lake and where it joined the woods at the north and south corners. Those corners are our weak points, he thought and the lake itself could be a way in, but the night is never too dark to spot things on the surface. He made a mental note to bring it up with the Colonel and Major Lensky. His attention was suddenly focused on the rocks away to his right and his heart skipped a beat as Alayna came into view, walking along the lake shore. He became aware that Yenisei was watching him intently and he felt himself reddening.

"Go to her," Yenisei said gently, "she will be pleased to see you. Go on!"

Yuri was about to back down, but then he thought, why not? Let's see if there is still something worth rescuing from this seemingly doomed relationship.

With that, he climbed down from the high rocks and made for the lake shore.

She heard him coming and he stopped around ten feet away. Neither spoke, or made to move. They just stood looking into each other's eyes. Alayna had prayed for this moment, prayed that she could somehow rebuild the bridge between them. She stood silently, arms hanging by her sides, her dark hair ruffled by the breeze. She felt the ache in her loins as her heartbeat quickened, her breasts rose and fell increasingly with her breathing, which was becoming more and more ragged under his steady gaze. Her lips parted and she spoke but one word.

"Sorry."

Yuri covered the space between them in three strides, gathered her tightly in his arms as their mouths came together and their longing for each other was finally over. The kiss was fervent and passionate, awakening all their suppressed lust for each other, to the point where they both took a step back from the edge. Here was neither the time nor place. That would come later, as certainly as day follows night. This they understood, this they were prepared to wait for. So, they remained locked in each other's embrace as the heat relented, both knowing it would burst again into flames, at a time when there would be no restriction or need for self-denial.

"I thought I'd lost you," she whispered, the tears welling up within her eyes, "forgive me for being so headstrong."

"No, never think that," he replied, "I shouldn't have been so hard on you. I was acutely worried, so aware of what I could have lost, I wanted you so badly."

With that, neither spoke, just loved each other with their eyes. Up in the rocks, Yenisei breathed a sigh of relief. Thank God, he thought, that these two people have finally come together. He clambered down and made his way back to his caravan, Katerina saw him coming and he winked at her and smiled.

"Life is wonderful," he said, "I think I'll go for a lie down. Wake me later would you?"

Katerina watched him wander off, humming to himself, unsure as to why he appeared so jovial. Then from between the rocks that led down to the shore, Yuri and Alayna appeared, hand in hand. She gaped at them, unable to hide her joy and her face lit up seeing them together. Then she hurriedly looked away, allowing them their moment. Life was indeed wonderful.

The evening meal was in full swing when Yuri finally put in an appearance. Alexei and Valery nodded a greeting, both having heard about Yuri and Alayna's burying the hatchet, via the camp telegraph. Yuri picked up a plate and helped himself to a large slice of suckling pig and some vegetables, blissfully unaware that he was the focus of everyone's attention. He sat down opposite the two brothers, saw their questioning gaze and said, "What?"

"Nothing," Alexei ventured, "nothing at all." Then he threw back his head and laughed, slapping Valery on the back, who was also grinning hugely. Yuri reddened, knowing full well what was going on, but trying to appear unconcerned. He kept his head down and concentrated on eating. Thankfully, Alexei and Valery did the same. The Colonel strode up, shot Yuri a quizzical glance, saw he was unforthcoming and spoke to the three of them.

"Listen boys, the airfield attack is going ahead next Monday. That gives us two days to prepare as we'll be travelling late Friday, Saturday and Sunday, so any thoughts would be welcomed, OK?"

The three young Russians nodded, "Yeah, Friday afternoon would be good," offered Valery, "we could do with some crossbow practice beforehand and we'll need to carry four days rations as well as blankets, tents and weapons. Are we taking the horses?"

"Yes," replied the Colonel, "there'll be some two hundred plus men with horses and also several pack horses. We need to be able to move quickly, there's a long way to go."

"Well I for one need my beauty sleep," yawned Valery, "shoeing horses is tiring work. You coming Alexei?"

"You bet," answered his brother sleepily, "I too need to recharge my batteries." With that, they both climbed into their blankets and were soon sleeping peacefully.

Yuri and the Colonel spent the next half hour going over Yuri's assessment of the camp's defences. "Basically, it's the best we can do," Yuri said in completion, "we're as strong here as anywhere."

"Thanks for that Yuri," acknowledged the Colonel, "I think it's time we were both wrapped up in bed. See you in the morning?" With that, the Colonel made for his blankets. Yuri sat for a while going over the day's events in his mind, especially he and Alayna. He could not believe how lucky he was to have someone so beautiful love him. He decided now, that he would do all in his power to protect Alayna and her family, from anything and anyone. He was still fantasising about her as he slipped into his blankets and finally, fell into a contented, dreamless sleep.

Morning came wet and overcast. The relentless downpour splattered and drummed its heavy-handed way across the steppe and marshes, driven by a strong north-easterly wind. Thunder and lightning accompanied the steel grey clouds in a mad rush across the exposed expanse of eastern Russia. The epicentre of the storm hung over the marshes, its brazen tumult deafening and the horses suffered most, becoming difficult to handle and keep calm. Eventually, the storm passed, but everyone knew, autumn would not be long in coming. Everything was sodden, deep puddles everywhere and the many walking boots had turned the whole camp into a quagmire of glutinous mud. The miserable occupants huddled under any form of protection, waiting for the sun. Slowly, the skies cleared and the heavens exuded a brilliant, azure blue. Warmth returned, the dampness beginning to evaporate with it and the camp slowly came back to life. Preparations for the morrow began to go ahead a pace and by late afternoon, all was ready to be loaded onto the pack horses the following day. Evening brought a sombre mood to those who were leaving the following day. Raids were all very well, but the enemy was always an unknown factor. With God's help, they would all return in one piece. Yuri had been unable to get to see Alayna, because of the preparations going on. Not to worry, he thought, I'll see her tomorrow before we set off. He hated having to leave his new family, but the war dictated a soldier's duty and Yuri couldn't be an exception. Those who remained would have to tough it out. So, it was with a feeling of foreboding that the camp settled down for the night. On the outer perimeter, the guards maintained their watchful vigil, unaware that less than three hundred yards away, five hundred SS troops were moving silently into position. Only Vladimir, tucked up asleep in his blankets waiting for his duty to begin at four, knew anything of the hell about to hit the camp

Chapter 11 – Flight

Vladimir was roughly awakened at four, by a sleepy Ivan who was in a hurry to get to his blankets. "Nothing happening," Ivan conceded to Vladimir's quizzical question, "Quiet as the grave out there."

Vladimir nodded, thankful that the moment of truth was finally upon him. Many here would not see the light of another day and he would have to help some of them along, courtesy of his knife. Another hour and then he would start sending out the torch signal, but before that, he would have to eliminate Ivan and the other two guards who were close by. The sleeping ones would be easy, a knife in the heart, with his hand covering the mouth to stop any sound. Only the guard to his left, about eight feet away, could cause him problems, but he'd worked out a plan for that eventuality. The minutes ticked slowly by and he was increasingly aware of the shadows becoming lighter and more clearly defined, even though there was a considerable amount of mist covering the grass and trees. He checked his watch. Four forty-five. Time to kick off.

The guard to his left was his first priority. He leaned over towards him and went, "psssst". The guard rose up and looked quizzically towards him. Vladimir beckoned him with his hand, and the guard crept over, careful not to make any noise.

"What's up?" he whispered.

"Look," whispered back Vladimir, "over there by the lake. Can you see something moving?"

The guard, who was a large, full bearded man, strained his eyes to where Vladimir was pointing. "Where'd you mean," he asked, unsure as to what he was supposed to be seeing.

"Come over to this side of me," whispered Vladimir and the guard slid around him until he was looking out over the corner of the lake, Vladimir behind him.

"I still can't make anything out," the guard ventured, but it was too late. Vladimir's left arm swept around the guard's forehead and pulled back his head, exposing his throat. The knife in his right hand sawed across the guard's throat, cutting the carotid artery and severing his windpipe. Blood pumped from the lateral gash, the guard tried to scream, his mouth trying desperately to form sounds, but nothing would come and he sagged backwards, his life ending in a long, drawn out sigh. Vladimir froze, unsure as to whether anyone had picked up the guards final death throes, but all remained quiet. As silently as he could, he moved the inert body out of the way and tried to get his breathing back to normal. Shit, that was harder than I thought, he mused. Next, he moved onto the sleeping Ivan, dispatching him with a single thrust and then to the other sleeping guard, who he also dispatched cleanly. Shaking with suppressed excitement, he crawled back to his post. The adrenaline was pumping now and it took three deep breaths to settle his nerves. Picking up the torch, he flashed off a single word, 'now'. He waited, hardly daring to breathe for what seemed like an eternity, until he saw an answering hooded flash in return. The SS were on their way and he was the gatekeeper, unlocking the camp and letting them in. This is what he had been trained for, this was his moment of glory.

He could just make out the camouflaged figures, crawling through the grass, in a long, snake like line. The first to arrive was a sergeant, a huge bull of a man with flat reptilian eyes over a large nose.

He grunted a greeting to Vladimir, whispering, "Your jobs done now. Hauptman Lientz wants you unharmed, so keep out of the way while we do our jobs."

Vladimir nodded, thankful his role was now complete. There were almost a dozen SS troops within the perimeter now. They looked mean and deadly. He pointed out where the perimeter guards would be and then faded into the undergrowth, down by the lakeside. This will be easy, he thought, then 'Bang', a single shot shattered the stillness far to his left, followed by the harsh staccato chatter of one of the heavy machine guns. The guards on the western perimeter had spotted the incoming SS troops crawling through the grass and opened up with everything they had. 'Boom', one of the large calibre field guns blasted away at the incoming SS, then another. The SS Sergeant cursed, their surprise had been only fleeting. But the SS were very close before being spotted and a concerted rush hurled them into and through the outer perimeter defences. The defenders had to abandon the field guns, shoving a hand grenade down the barrels to render them useless, all except one, near the western corner. Its defenders had been overwhelmed in the initial rush and the field gun fell intact, into the hands of the SS. The camp was now alive with firing, shots and ricochets flashed everywhere, as the two groups of protagonists, fought out their duel to the death. But the SS were inside the perimeter, where Vladimir had let them in and were able to take out the guards on the northern side from the rear. The fighting was brutal and chaotic, until the surviving defenders fell back behind the secondary defence line. Dead bodies were everywhere, wounded men screamed in agony and still the SS surged forward in a relentless phalanx against the camps defenders. But the inner defences were holding firm. They and the SS were locked in a battle of attrition.

Yuri, Alexei, Valery and the Colonel had piled out of their blankets at the first hint of trouble. Bullets were whining and zapping everywhere and the shouts of the defenders and attackers alike, rose steadily over the escalating crescendo. From their place at the centre of the camp, they could see figures running from the houses and buildings, making for the broken country behind the houses in the south, all bent double, trying to minimise themselves against the chattering fusillade. Some fell, women and children included, as Major Lensky's escape plan was put into effect. Yuri ran towards the caravans in a panic, but a near miss had him diving for cover behind one of the numerous piles of logs, scattered around the camp centre. Breathlessly, he strained his eyes to see and saw Yenisei's party making for the outbuildings, several women in the breakneck rush for cover. Unable to tell if Alayna was one of them, he heard the Colonel yelling his name and realised suddenly, that the defenders needed him, she would have to try and escape without him, at least for now. He jumped up from behind the pile of logs and made a zigzag dash for the Colonel. He arrived safely in a cloud of water spray as he dived into cover behind a tree. Looking across to his left, he saw Major Lensky with his senior NCO setting up a machine gun nest, behind one of the piles of logs. Half a dozen men and the machine gunner, were positioned to counter any breach in the northern, inner defences. Lensky ran across to another pile of logs and beckoned another six soldiers and a machine gunner. This should counter any breach from the west. Alexei and Valery were helping and cajoling the defenders of the north defences, making their presence felt wherever it was needed. The Colonel was searching the trees, looking for snipers, the scope on his rifle, slowly quartering the area to his front. So far, nothing, but there would be, Yuri had no doubt.

Suddenly, there was a tremendous explosion and a gap around six feet across appeared in the western defences.

"They've turned one of the field guns," yelled a horrified Yuri to the Colonel, "someone couldn't have destroyed it when they fell back." Yuri stared at the gap. Directly in line was the machine gun nest with the seven soldiers and Pavel Lensky. He yelled at the major to get away, but it was too late. The major shot a glance over the pile of logs, then 'Boom'. The last thing Pavel Lensky saw was the muzzle flash, before the heavy shell smashed into the logs and wreaked its havoc. When the smoke cleared, nothing remained. Men and logs had been scattered to the four winds.

The Colonel, his face ashen at the loss of his friend and the doomed soldiers, swung on Yuri. "Go get a squad together," he commanded, "get around the southeast corner and take out that fucking gun. It's going to murder us."

Yuri sped off, ducking and diving in and out of cover until he reached the soldiers in the southeast corner. 'Boom', went the gun again. This time the outhouses were the target, shattering into so much matchwood, pigs, horses and human body parts being flung into the air. Yuri quickly gathered a dozen men together, thinning out the defensive wall as much as he dare. He told them what they were going to do and the men nodded in agreement. They understood the implications if the field gun was allowed to continue. They made their way around the southeast corner, conscious of the fact that they were now behind the SS. The horse handlers were putting down a steady stream of fire, their rifles targeting the SS from the side. They waved the squad forward, laying down a heavy covering fire as Yuri and his men fanned out below the ridge leading to the camp. 'Boom', the field gun fired again, the shell blasting one of the houses to smithereens. Fires were raging, the outhouses and houses were aflame. The caravans were also burning as Yuri and his squad breasted the rise and fell upon the SS around the gun emplacement. Surprise was complete, the Russians machine guns exacting a terrible revenge. Two grenades down the barrel and the gun was wrecked, the barrel shattered and the firing pin blown apart. Yuri led his men into the breach, laying down a concerted fire to left and right. He left six in the breach, while he and the rest moved south towards the horse handlers. Caught between the two fires, the SS ran, but the Russians were having none of it, chasing and butchering all who tried to flee back to the west. Elated by their success, he turned his men again back to the breach. They were holding out, maybe they could beat off this attack?

His thoughts were instantly shattered as a roar arose from the lake side. The SS had circled round, shown the way by Vladimir and fell upon the Russian rear. They moved with steady purpose, rolling up the north flank. Alexei and Valery were in danger of being isolated, but then Yuri saw the Colonel, pistols in both hands, walking into the oncoming SS. Left hand pistol, 'bang', right hand, 'bang', he calmly waded into the fray, alternating his weapons as he went. The SS faltered, then a bullet took the Colonel in the left shoulder, sending him lurching to his left, his right arm clutching his wound, his face grimacing with pain. But the Russians seized the chance to vacate the defences and fell back in good order towards the burning buildings, using the log piles as cover, then dropping back as the covering fire increased. Yuri and his squad backed off through the breach, circled around to the south and picked up the horse herders. The horses were rearing and snorting, maddened beyond reason by the noise and tumult. Covered by Yuri and his men, the handlers cut free the horses restraining bonds and shooed them away from the camp, allowing them the chance to escape being captured by the SS. Then the whole squad moved towards the crackling, blazing buildings. They arrived on the SS's right flank and opened up in a fusillade of fire. But the SS were calm and methodical and returned the fire with a vengeance. Yuri was losing too many men, so he pulled them back towards the paths into the broken country, hoping to circle round and help the retreating defenders from a different position. All the civilian families should be long gone, he thought. Then he heard a shout of alarm. Running towards the sound he came upon a group of several people, struggling to carry wounded. He ran up and was confronted by the sickening sight of injured men and women, trying to make their way through the rock-strewn terrain.

"What happened," he demanded of them, "why aren't you all well away from here?"

"It was the shells from the field gun," one replied, "we were taking refuge, waiting to leave, when the shell hit and the roof fell in. There are still some people left in there now, those from the caravans."

Yuri needed no second telling. He raced headlong for the burning houses, fear gnawing at his heart. He burst inside the first house, the smoke and flames choking him and making him cough and splutter.

"Alayna," he yelled, "Alayna, where are you?"

The flames continued to crackle, falling beams and debris crashed around him. He ran to another house, this one a smoking ruin and on to another.

"Alayna," he cried, "where the fuck are you?"

Then he heard it, above the tumult of battle and the roar of the flames. A plaintive "Yuriiiiiiiiiii".

Desperately tearing at the smashed beams and crumbling walls, he vaulted through a window opening, into the space inside. She was trying to lift a huge beam, but her efforts were useless, she hadn't the strength. Yuri ran over, picked her up and hugged her, but she broke free and pointed.

"There Yuri," she wailed, "Katerina."

Yuri looked where she pointed. The beam had fallen and trapped Katerina's legs. She was still alive. But not for long. Alayna was back trying to lift the beam off her sister's legs, but Yuri knew, there was no hope. Both legs and her lower body were smashed to a pulp, how she was still alive was impossible to say. He dragged a sobbing Alayna away and then knelt down and looked into Katerina's eyes. Her grey, ashen, contorted face was a mask of agony, her lips pleaded with Yuri to end her torment. He nodded gently, pulled out his pistol and shot her in the head. No more would she have to suffer. Alayna screamed and ran to her sister, but Yuri stopped her, holding her tightly to him. After a few moments, her sobbing eased and he tilted her head and looked into her eyes.

"I had to do it," he said tenderly, "she was suffering unspeakable agony."

"I know," was all she said.

"Is there anyone else?" demanded Yuri. "Alayna, is there anyone else?"

She tore her eyes away from her dead sister and mumbled, "Grandfather Yenisei is over there, I think he and uncle were also hit."

Yuri left Alayna and scrabbled over the twisted and smouldering timbers, in the direction she had pointed. Two charred and unrecognisable bodies lay side by side in the smoking ashes. Stephan was on his knees, rubbing his head gingerly, blood oozing from wounds on his head and his arms. Of Yenisei, there was no sign. Yuri put his arm around Stephan and his head slowly rose and he looked uncomprehendingly at Yuri's concerned expression.

"Are you all right," enquired Yuri?

"I don't know," answered a clearly concussed Stephan. "I guess I'm still alive, although everything's so fuzzy and my heads buzzing. Where are the others, Yenisei was with me."

"I'll take a look around," answered Yuri, "will you be OK?" Stephan nodded groggily and Yuri began to search again. He found Yenisei laid against the remaining wall, eyes closed as if asleep. Yuri gently shook the old man and slowly, the eyes opened and a faint smile passed across his face.

"Yuri," he said quietly, "am I in heaven?"

'No uncle, but you've been in the wars," Yuri answered, "do you think you can stand up?" The old man reached his hand out towards Yuri and Yuri helped him to his feet. He swayed, as the blood began to course back through his veins and he held on to Yuri for support, but eventually, he was able to move under his own steam. He and Yuri then scrambled over the remains of the outside wall and into the light.

Stephan had also made it outside the confines of the shattered house and at Yuri's question he said, "I'm OK, I just need to move about a little."

Yuri left him and Yenisei together and returned inside for Alayna. She was slumped on the floor, the tears flooding down her tortured face. Yuri bent down, gently raised her to her feet and guided her outside to her uncle and Yenisei. They had been joined by two of Yenisei's party, a small, serious woman with a bloodied arm, wrapped in a shawl and a man who Yuri recognised as one of the blacksmiths from the forge. He suddenly realised that the battle was still going on in earnest. He moved along past the burning buildings and peered around the end of the line. The SS had pushed back the defending Russians to a line just in front of the broken ground to the south. Yuri realised he and his new party were separated from the others, by a line of SS troops. They had not spotted Yuri, but he knew their position was untenable. The noise was still almost deafening with lulls every now and then. He strained his eyes to see just where his friends might be and he saw the Colonel, left arm covered in a blood-stained bandage, organising the defensive retreat. Something must have made the Colonel turn and he looked straight at Yuri. Their eyes held for a few seconds, then the Colonel turned, threw back his head and shouted to no-one in particular above the deafening noise of battle.

"The island, go to the island."

 Yuri heard and understood. He was on his own, with five non-combatants. They must escape under their own steam. His path now laid out for him, he made to return to the others, alarmed at their inability to understand the danger they were in. Come on, he thought to himself, they've been through hell and are not used to fighting. He paused by the body of a Russian soldier. The man's eyes stared upwards from a horror filled face, Yuri bent down and closed them. He knew the man, but for the life of him, couldn't remember his name. He sighed an apology as he went through the man's belongings. A few rounds of ammunition and a knife. Yuri pocketed them, picked up the man's rifle and pack and moved on. Another fallen victim caught Yuri's attention and he rescued the rifle and pack, they would come in useful later, he thought, but we have to leave now. With that in mind he approached Stephan.

"Stephan," he began, "we need to get away before the SS realise we're here. That means moving everyone out now, do you understand?"

Stephan nodded and Yuri was pleased to see that he was beginning to respond. "Look," he explained, "I'm going to have to lead, I'm the only one who knows where we're going. So, can you bring up the rear, watching for any pursuit?"

He handed Stephan the rifle and pack. "Can you use one of these," he said. Stephan nodded. "Make sure you keep me in sight and keep them moving, OK?"

"Yes," breathed Stephan, "but are these the only ones left? Alayna is here but where is Katerina?"

"I'm sorry Stephan," said Yuri gently, "I'm afraid she didn't make it. She's gone to a better place, one where she will not feel any more pain. Do you understand?"

The older man looked haggard, his face a mask of remorse. "These are terrible times Yuri," he confided, "so many gone, so few remaining. But I suspect I need to look after the living. There's nothing I can do for Katerina except honour her memory."

Yuri flashed him a look of concerned gratitude and turned to the others. "It's time to move out," he said, "follow me and don't worry, I know where I'm going, but we have to go now."

With that, he handed the other rifle and pack to the blacksmith and with a reluctant but seemingly steadfast Stephan bringing up the rear, got everyone to their feet and started off, towards the lake side. They moved off with a collective sigh, no-one wanting to have to go, but all realising the danger of hanging around. They started in abject silence, all aware of the horrors they had witnessed. Yuri led them slowly down towards the lake side and then across the uneven boulders into the screening trees. He glanced back to see everyone moving resolutely, if slowly and tried to make up his mind as to the right way to go. He knew that the island lay to the west, but at the moment, their path in that direction was blocked by the SS. Even if they succeeded in circling their way around the lake, firstly east, then north, sticking to the tree cover, they would have to cross the path on which the SS arrived at the camp this morning, when they moved from a northerly direction to the west. He could not be sure that there was not a rear guard somewhere to the north. However, going south was impossible, what with the broken country and the SS following the retreating Russians. It had to be north and then west and it had to be done soon. His mind now made up, he turned to look over his flock, only to see Yenisei pitch forward onto his face, Alayna rushing to his side. Yuri ran back to where the old man lay. At his age, the walk and the day's events were just too much for him. Alayna was all concern, gently shaking her inert great grandfather. Yuri brushed her aside, picked up the old man in his arms and turned to go. He looked over the others, concern written all over their faces.

"Come on," he said roughly, "we have to go, now."

The others shrugged, including Alayna and they set off again.

Yuri was aware that the old man was reviving, he opened his eyes and said in a feeble voice, "leave me my boy, I'll only slow you all down."

"Quiet uncle," Yuri replied gently, "be still and silent. I will not allow the embodiment of Mother Russia to perish while I have him in my care." Stoically, he strode on, the rest following behind him like so many automatons.

The going was relatively easy, a clearly defined path snaking its way between the trees and marshes. They were now moving north, the sounds of battle diminishing with every stride as the pursuers doggedly tracked the pursued. His little party were doing well, even though they all appeared beaten and unconcerned for the future. At least Stephan was in the right frame of mind, conscientiously checking his rear and shooing along his charges in front of him. Yenisei, although small and light, was beginning to strain Yuri's arms and back. Probably a hundred miles to go, he thought, perhaps three days, if all goes well. The sun was now nearing its zenith as the party turned westwards. Directly in front about a mile away, running in a north/south direction, was the path that had brought the SS to the camp this morning. Yuri stopped everyone once they were within a few hundred yards of it, put Yenisei down gently to allow him to rest and crept off by himself to study the layout and the proximity of any insurgents. He got to the path and saw the many boot prints heading south, but there was no sign of a rear guard as such. He listened intently and searched the surrounding woods, but nothing appeared problematic. Satisfied, he made his way back to the others, but the party had been seen. Vladimir had watched them vacate the camp from his position in the trees by the edge of the lake. He recognised Yuri and saw him carrying a small person, but at that moment, he was unsure as to who the person was, or the make-up of the party, although some looked like females. So, he decided to observe them from a distance. After all, the small person could be the man from Abakan and the SS wanted him badly. He had made his way swiftly to a point where he could overlook the small group and now he knew for certain. It was the little man from Abakan and also his great granddaughter. He purred with satisfaction. She, he would love to de-flower. He could almost feel his hardness pushing into her, but first, there was the matter of the others, especially Yuri. The blacksmith and his ugly friend would be easy and the one at the back looked incapable of too much resistance. Get rid of Yuri and the rest were his. He salivated at the thought. Firstly, let them think that they've got away. Yuri can't stay awake for ever, then a knife between the ribs and I have the gorgeous Alayna to hump. I may even give the ugly one a good seeing to if she begs me not to. With all this in mind, he made his way to where the paths crossed. No doubt they would be heading north towards Minsk or Kharkov, trying to join up with their soldiers, somewhere in the field. He would choose his own time and place. He could wait.

Yuri arrived back where he had left the others and was concerned with what he saw. All of them, including Stephan, looked exhausted, even though they'd only travelled a few miles over easy terrain. This was going to be harder than he had initially thought. The carnage of the morning was having a debilitating effect on all of them. There was only a small amount of water spread over two canteens, plus several biscuits. There were going to be a lot of hungry people between here and the island. But they must press on, putting as much distance as possible between them and the SS.

"Right," he said commandingly, "everybody up. Stephan, get them moving. We've got to cross the path ahead and we must do it quickly and try to leave as little evidence of our passing as possible. Do you all understand?"

They had stiffly got to their feet, but they all nodded in agreement, albeit, grudgingly.

Yenisei waved away Yuri's offer to carry him, "I can manage for a while my young friend and Alayna can lend me her arm."

Yuri nodded, "OK," he said, "keep tight to me and as silent as possible. We'll stop again in a few miles or so." With that, the company moved off. They reached the path and hurried across, Yuri shepherding and cajoling them and made off westward through the trees. That was the hard bit, Yuri thought to himself. Now let's put as much distance between us and the SS as we can before nightfall. He led off, keeping to a reasonable pace and the others filed along behind him. They made good time over the next five miles or so, the terrain being helpful to swift travel. But then came a series of bogs and thick scrub and they were reduced to wading up to their knees through the glutinous mud filled bogs, while the dense bushes of scrub clawed at their clothing. Yuri had lifted Yenisei over the worst of the bogs and rocky places. He dragged them all onwards, knowing that pursuit could come upon them at any time. But eventually, he had to call a halt. The one suffering most was Yenisei, the old man was out on his feet, his breathing shallow and ragged. Alayna tended to him, giving him a little water and a couple of biscuits. The others made do with collapsing by the wayside, giving their tired limbs the benefit of rest. Yuri looked them over, pleased that they had managed to get this far, but he knew that they couldn't take much more today without a full nights rest.

He had, for some time, been concerned that all was not as it would seem. He had first got this feeling, many miles away, a feeling of not being alone, of being watched by unseen eyes. Initially, he shrugged it off as him being paranoid, but the feeling persisted, until he thought he had heard a twig snap, somewhere to the party's rear. This made him doubly concerned. If someone, or something was indeed on their trail, he needed to know before the light gave way. But what should he divulge to the others. In their present state, it would only make them even more hysterical and frightened, not a good thing to do. So, he sidled over to Stephan. He alone would be an ally and he needed someone to guard the others while he was away, checking out his hunch. Stephan understood and agreed to watch over them. Yuri handed him the machine gun and spare drums, he wanted to travel light, his trusty knife would be his protection. Then he waved a curt goodbye to Stephan and slipped away unseen and unheard into the undergrowth, while the others were resting peacefully.

Yuri knew his way around the woods, having hunted for game all his life and he moved with a woodsman's sense of his surroundings. He moved with the wind, which was luckily blowing from the south east, as he slid his feet forward, searching for tell-tale twigs or roots that could expose his whereabouts to any listener. He'd travelled about five hundred yards back in the direction they'd come from, when he detected movement and froze behind an oak. Whatever was out there was not friendly he thought. If it were a man on the run, he would have hailed the party some distance back, safety always being in numbers. A bear would probably not have followed them for so long, unless really hungry, but wolves were a different proposition. They would follow a scent for hundreds of miles, if they believed a kill was possible. But Yuri had a vague suspicion that this predator was human and so it turned out to be. The man slowly came into view and Yuri recognised him. Vladimir. Shit, thought Yuri, is he the one who gave us away, or is he just tracking us for safety's sake. Whatever the reason, Yuri was suspicious. This would have to be handled carefully and with as little fuss as possible. He slid out the knife, if Vladimir was bent on selling them out, then Yuri would have to be very careful. He had to know, he couldn't just kill in cold blood. Vladimir closed on the tree behind which Yuri was hiding, rifle slung across his arms, unworried and confident. He knew the party were not far ahead and was slowly and gently moving up to a point where he could observe them without being spotted. He passed the tree unconcernedly when Yuri jumped out and grabbed him from behind. The rifle clattered to the ground as Yuri kicked into the space behind Vladimir's knees, effectively bringing him down, then Yuri was astride him, knife tickling Vladimir's exposed throat. Vladimir's face exuded shock and fright at Yuri's sudden relentless attack.

He garbled his words, pleading for mercy, but Yuri held him tightly, refusing to remove the knife from Vladimir's throat. "Listen you piece of shit," Yuri growled, "Why follow us, eh? Why not join us so we can all go on together? Maybe it was you that unlocked the camp for the SS this morning, so maybe I should slit your gizzard."

Vladimir's bulging eyes begged to differ. "I didn't let them in," he wailed, "it was that traitor Ivan. I was asleep and only survived by the skin of my teeth. You've got to believe me."

"Well, I don't," snarled Yuri, "Ivan hadn't the wherewithal to collude with the SS and I saw the roster. You had the four o'clock shift, you lying bastard."

"No, no we changed," wailed Vladimir desperately, "he had the early watch."

Yuri relented, apparently satisfied. He stood up allowing Vladimir to do the same and stood back. "It was you all right," he said gently, "so pick up you knife and let's settle this, once and for all."

Vladimir winced, unsure as to what to do, but his ego outweighed his caution and his face suddenly contorted. "Yes," he snarled, "I let them in. That bastard Ivan didn't know what hit him, or the other two. The SS will be dealing with your three buddies back there and once I've stuck you, that bitch whore Alayna will welcome my dick inside her. The Abakan freak, I'll give to Hauptman Lientz."

Yuri smiled, but not with his eyes. He circled warily, keeping away from Vladimir's right hand, which held the curved, Arabic blade. Vladimir lunged suddenly, catching Yuri on the back foot and Yuri had to move quickly to his right to avoid the slicing blade.

Vladimir laughed, his lips curled in contempt. "Cutting you up will be a pleasure," he growled.

Warily, the pair circled, both lunging and parrying successfully, until Vladimir spotted the tree roots, sticking out of the ground behind Yuri. His eyes narrowed in realisation and a grim smile edged his pursed lips. With a rush, he lunged in, Yuri parried and backed away, he lunged in again and Yuri's heel struck the exposed tree root and he staggered backwards, losing his footing and fell against a tree, his knife hand now back trying to arrest his fall. Vladimir rushed in, arm aloft to deliver the killing blow when 'bang', a shot rang out. The bullet took Vladimir in the mouth, exiting through the back of his head and throwing him backwards in a crumpled lifeless heap.

Yuri recoiled, scrabbled around and looked into the steely eyes of Yenisei, not five yards away. In his tiny hands, the smoking rifle seemed huge and oversized, but it was held rock steady. "I am no freak," he muttered, then seeing Yuri's astonishment said, "Thought I could be of assistance. Stephan was reluctant to leave the others. The girls had no idea so I just wandered off. I had a hunch something was amiss. That traitor was my nemesis, no one else's. Thank you for exposing him my boy."

Yuri gaped as the little man beamed and said with the merest hint of irony, "carrying the embodiment of Mother Russia must have tired you. Shall we join the others?"

With that, he turned and moved off. Yuri was speechless. The man is a marvel, he thought. Where does he get his strength from? He shook his head in admiration, picked up the inert Vladimir and pitched the body into the bushes. No burial for you, you fucking arsehole, let the wolves have their fill. But he did go through Vladimir's clothing, looking for anything to tie him in with the SS. He found a few papers and shoved them into his pockets for later. He took off the boots and there, in a secret side pocket, were several other papers. He glanced at them, unable to understand the German words. Its times like this I could do with the Colonel, he thought. God knows, I hope he, Alexei and Valery are OK. Then he stripped the body of anything useful, picked up Vladimir's expansive pack and set off, straight into the arms of Alayna.

She clung to him, her tears cascading down her beautiful face as she checked him for any wounds or abrasions. "Grandfather Yenisei told me everything," she said, "why couldn't you tell me before you left? I was worried sick once I found you were gone and desperate when I heard the shot. He said he had dispatched an evil spirit, a stain on the patchwork of Mother Russia."

Yuri nodded, "He certainly won't be bothering us again. Uncle Yenisei sent him to the hell he deserves. But now, we have to hurry away. That gunshot would have been heard for miles around. We still have a long way to go before we can be reasonably safe and night will soon be upon us."

The pair walked back to the others, everyone was pleased to see Yuri's return, but he ordered them brusquely to their feet and set off towards the west into the now setting sun.

After another five miles, Yuri called a halt. He had spotted a couple of caves, off the main path and in a sufficiently high position to overlook the surrounding area. The daylight was fading fast and after a meal of biscuits and a few sips of water, they arranged themselves as best they could, under the caves roofs. Everyone was completely exhausted. Yuri tried to stay awake, to be their only guard, but finally fell into a fitful, troubled sleep. His dreams were interspersed with demons and dragons, breathing fire and smoke. Vladimir's blasted face flashed before his eyes, but then Alayna appeared and Vladimir, along with all the demons and dragons, faded away in her embrace. Then he slept in peace, her virtual hands gently stroking his brow. Morning came in splendid beauty, the sun rising magnificently into a cloudless sky. The party awoke stiff and sore, but sleep had done its work and the mood was one of relief to be alive. Yuri, appalled that he had slept so long, was however adamant that they should set off without delay, having many miles still to go. He badgered and cajoled them into movement and the party set off before the day was past five o'clock. They walked down the long morning, taking a few breathers along the way. By lunchtime, Yuri reckoned they had travelled at least thirty miles, but he only allowed them a short break for the lunch period. The rest of the biscuits went, but they were able to refill the canteens from a gurgling stream of sweet water. They marched on into the afternoon, but they all could sense a change in the weather. Sure enough, after a couple of hours, the skies clouded over on a brisk, north easterly wind and the rain began. It poured down in soaking sheets, the path becoming treacherous and slippery, consequently, there were many falls and trips. Yuri knew that they would have to stop soon, so he scanned the forest for signs of somewhere to spend the night in reasonable dryness and safety. Eventually, he spotted a small hut, probably a hunter's cabin. On inspection, it turned out to be just such a place, the door opened scratchily on ancient leather hinges, but inside was dry. The sod covered roof of branches, made for a haven away from the clutches of the incessant rain. The party slumped down, anywhere they could, exhausted by having to battle through such a continuous downpour. In one corner was a hearth and Stephan and the blacksmith put together a small welcoming fire, while Yuri prowled around the hut, searching for reasonably dry wood. He brought it inside and the fire was banked, many hands reaching out to its welcoming heat. Yuri rummaged around in Vladimir's pack and came up with a cooking pot and several tins of meat and vegetables. The pot was placed on the fire, the tins opened and the contents heated thoroughly. The party then enjoyed their first meal in three days, raising their spirits as they dried out with the comforting heat from the fire. Then, they settled down for a good night's sleep.

Yuri asked Stephan to take the first watch, then Yuri would relieve him at two. Two o'clock duly arrived and Stephan shook Yuri awake.

"Nothing to report," he whispered, "at least the rain seems to have stopped."

With that, he huddled down against the cabin wall and drifted off to sleep. Yuri took a walk outside. The rain had indeed stopped and the moon was casting its ghostly luminescence through the trees. Yuri listened and watched, his ears picking out those small sounds that betrayed the many creatures who enacted the life and death struggles of the night. He noted these in his mind, but was unconcerned about anything problematic that might be hanging around. He estimated that they had travelled about sixty miles so far, tomorrow should see them very close to or actually on the island. With luck and an early start, he saw no reason why not. Soon, he should start to recognise familiar terrain.

He woke them all at five. Grudgingly, they grumbled out of their slumbers and after a quick breakfast of biscuits and water, they vacated the cabin, leaving it as they had found it, for someone else to benefit in the future. The fire had been doused with water, their recent presence here disguised to all but the trained eye. They set off in good spirits, the early morning light and subtle. Twelve o'clock saw them break for a long rest and Yuri was ecstatic. He knew he was not far from his island. He was beginning to recognise the landscape. The little group was starting to open up to each other. Alayna and Giselle, the lady from Abakan, who was more or less Stephan's personal servant, were chattering away gaily. Yenisei and the blacksmith, Ivan, were deep in conversation about the pros and cons of the forging process. People are right, thought Yuri, there are an awful lot of Ivan's in Russia. That's why the Germans call us that collectively. I suppose it all comes from Ivan the Terrible, that malevolent icon of Russian folklore. He could have given Genghis Khan a run for his money. His musings were suddenly interrupted by a distant sound, a sound that reverberated down through the marshes. Shit, he thought. Dogs. He had heard it before. There was no mistaking the high-pitched yap of Doberman's on the scent and they were not far away.

"Up," he yelled at the seated party, "dogs are on our scent. There's not far to go to the island, but we're going to have to run. Move yourselves."

The party responded quickly, snatching up their possessions and hurrying off, Stephan bringing up the rear. Yuri led them at a brisk trot, trying to put as much distance between them and their followers as he could. But Yenisei was not up to this sort of pace and a cry from Alayna after a few hundred yards brought Yuri skidding to a halt. The old man was breathing heavily, his florid face bathed in a sheen of sweat.

"He can't go on like this," said a concerned Alayna.

"Don't worry," countered Yuri, "I'll carry him, as I did before."

With that, he picked up his uncle and continued his steady trot along the path. The miles slipped slowly by, the sound of pursuit gaining little by little by his calculations and every so often, Yuri would bring the pace down to a walk, helping the others with a little walking relief. Eventually though, he had to stop for a longer rest, carrying uncle Yenisei was wearing out his arms and back. But he was not too unhappy, for he had spotted Woodpecker Knoll. A mile, two at the most, he thought. However, the sounds of pursuit were becoming more evident. They would need luck and providence if they were to reach the island undetected. With that in mind, he tried to forget his aching arms and got them to their feet and off again.

A mile away, the German sergeant pondered over his squad's involvement in this chase. He knew there were six people in front, three of them probably female, judging by the size of the footprints. He was getting mightily sick of the incessant amount of times his dog unit was being called upon to hunt down perpetrators on the run. Four days ago, he had been in Minsk, having just returned from rounding up insurgents between Minsk and Kharkov. It had been an endless merry-go-round since the Barbarossa invasion, of tracking down the enormous amount of unattached soldiers, separated from their units and, when banded together, causing havoc with the supply trains. Their latest venture had been to assist the SS in a raid on an insurgent camp, somewhere to the south east of where he was now. The SS had moved out of Minsk last Thursday, but he and his dog unit, didn't get their orders until late Thursday evening. They met up with the remnants of the SS, close to a lakeside camp and were told by a brutish sergeant that the four main suspects for capture in their attack had somehow escaped their clutches. Therefore, the SS were adamant that the dogs were required to sniff out any sign of these four and whoever was with them. Then they heard the shot from the woods towards the west and investigating that shot, was what had led them to this place in time. He could see the dogs were champing at the bit, wanting to be off and running and guessed they sensed that their prey was close.

"Corporal," he called, "are you ready to release them?"

"Jawohl Herr Feldwebel," the corporal replied. "Time to see what we have flushed out." The corporal released his Doberman's and the dogs sped off, the sergeant and the troopers trotting along behind them as quickly as they could.

Yuri heard the release of the dogs in a panic. He knew they had been let loose, by the way the yapping suddenly increased in both frequency and volume. Shit, he thought, here we go again. He pounded on, regardless of the ache in his arms and the sound of breathlessness from the party behind him. The gap appeared where the path to the island diverged from the main and he blundered through it, catching his foot on an outstretched branch, which brought him and Yenisei crashing to the ground. He managed to protect his uncle from the full force of the tumble, but badly scratched and bruised his own arms, legs and back. He scrambled achingly to his feet, dazed and in severe discomfort, staggering initially along, but gaining strength from the sound of the dogs. The two giant oaks appeared on his left and he skidded to a halt, waiting as the rest caught him up. Before him was a huge puddle, courtesy of yesterday's rain.

"There's a way between these trees once we slosh through the puddle," he gasped, "everyone hold hands and follow me. Uncle, you'll have to walk too. We need to get to the boat."

He led them through the deep puddle and between the seemingly impossibly spaced trees and bushes, until they reached the clearing on the other side and he spotted the boat. He waved them over, as he dragged the little craft out from its hiding place and one by one, fitted them in. Stephan was in the prow, the rest packed like sardines in the middle, with Yuri just managing to dovetail in at the stern.

"Keep as still as possible," he commanded, "we need to get around to the other side of that island in front."

With that, Stephan pushed off, Yuri paddling away furiously from the rear. The boat was perilously low in the water, not being designed to carry so much weight, but little by little, they passed around the east side of the island and ran the craft up onto the southern beach. Stephan managed to haul himself out and he held the boat steady, as the others and finally Yuri, collapsed on the rocky shoreline. But Yuri knew they were not safe yet. He groggily got to his feet and dragged the boat into hiding next to the raft. Then, with Stephan's help, replaced the screening branches. The boat and raft were hidden from all but a close-up inspection. Then he cajoled the rest to their feet, clambered up the rock steps and led them across the open space towards the front of the cave.

"Wait here in the opening," he told them, "I need to check on the dogs."

With that, he set off in a crouched run, across to the north side of the island, leaving the others to rest and recover. Once over the edge of the perimeter, he crept slowly through the trees, until he could clearly see the opposite bank. There were raised unintelligible voices from the pathway, but the dogs seemed to have gone past and were yapping further along to the west. Good God in heaven, Yuri thought, we might just have made it.

On the path, the German sergeant hailed the corporal back to him. He was bent over, his hands on his knees, fighting for breath. "What's going on corporal?" he asked enquiringly, "the dogs seem to have lost whoever they were chasing."

"It looks that way," replied the corporal exasperatedly, "they definitely appear less concerned than they were. I saw them have a good sniff around both sides of that puddle, but then they seemed to lose interest, maybe the water has masked the scent. We're almost back to the starting line on the River Bug, it can only be a few miles."

"Yes," answered the sergeant, "If you remember, we were here on the second day of the invasion, chasing somebody who also gave us the slip. Put the dogs back on their leashes. We'll keep going until we hit the river, it's possible they're still in front of us. They can't be far ahead, but they seem to have vanished for now. I did think we were getting close and we'll keep trying. Organise the men will you. Let's get back to a steady march."

The corporal saluted, called the squad back together and after leashing the Doberman's, the unit marched off towards the west. "God knows where we'll sleep tonight," the sergeant conferred to his corporal, "Some of those bloody partisans, blew up the last place we had by the Bug. What is it all coming to?"

Chapter 12 – Re-Group

Yuri waited while the German unit vacated the path on the north side. He could hear them talking but didn't understand the language. However, it appeared that they had not been able to find a trace of them and the unit moved off towards the west, eventually being lost to hearing. Yuri's relief was palpable. He had somehow managed to get five non-combatants of various ages and sex, onto the island in safety, despite the best efforts of a spy, the SS and Wehrmacht to apprehend them. Perhaps now they could take stock of the situation and decide on a course of action. Firstly though, he needed to introduce them to Aleksander's cave.

He made another quick circuit of the eastern end of the island, searching and listening for signs of trouble, but he was aware of nothing out of place. So, he made his way back to the now recovering party. They were sat roughly within the caves entrance, but as of this moment, had no idea what lay beyond the supposed back wall. It was time to introduce them.

"Well," he said conversationally, "what do you think of my island?"

The five members of the party exchanged dubious glances before Stephan came up with, "at least it's out of harm's way. I was hoping it would have been a little bit bigger, the cave that is, but we should be able to make do."

Yuri grinned, he couldn't keep them guessing any longer, so he said, "Actually, you're sitting in the front entrance, not in the actual cave. Let me show you the way in."

Happily, he motioned them out of the way while he moved to the back of the entrance. Putting his hand on the latch on the right side, he pulled open the hide bound door. The little gasp of astonishment that rippled round the others faces, made him smile gaily to himself as he reached forward, picked up a candle from the cupboard behind the door, lit it and turned towards them.

"Ladies and gentlemen," he said with mock solemnity, "welcome to my house."

Turning, he walked into the main cave, the rest following behind. Excited gasps and comments followed him into the high-ceilinged centre, where he lit another candle and stood facing them. "This is the main central room of the cave. As you can see, the man and his wife who owned this before I came along, made many changes to where you now stand. Water is fed to the sink over there by pipes from a series of pools on the roof above. The stove has a chimney that exits, by pipe also, through the roof above. To my right, behind another hide door, is a bedroom with two single beds. The bedroom also has a fireplace with the flue joining the main stove behind me and a bench which the previous owners used for writing and drawing. They were both committed naturalists, studying the flora and fauna of western Russia. Their legacy is one of far reaching quality. Around the walls are various tools, weapons and implements. On the floor over there, is what we stole from the German's camp, when I managed to rescue Alexei, Valery and the Colonel. Also, there are several large jars with lids for curing meat. All in all, the cave is a splendid work of genius."

"I had no idea," spluttered Stephan in awe, "how could we have expected anything like this. It just beggars belief."

Yuri smiled, savouring the moment, then asked, "And what do you think ladies. Do you think you could live here in this place?"

Alayna and Giselle shrugged expansively, exchanging happy glances. "It could be made into a very comfortable place," enthused Giselle, "internal water, so unexpected, and all these helpful pots, pans, cutlery and crockery. Wonderful."

Alayna looked around speechless, "I don't know what to say," she said finally, "it's too much to take in."

Yuri smiled happily. "Then please be my guest and look around at your leisure. I was thinking that the side bedroom could be for the ladies, it will give them that much more privacy, the four men sleeping in here. There are two converted stretchers over there and we could rig up another two. What I have to emphasise and I can't say this strongly enough, is that we are still in a war zone, even though the major fighting is hundreds of miles from here. The main road and rail links from Warsaw to Minsk are about five miles away to the north, as the crow flies, whereas eighty miles to the south is the railway and road to Kiev. There are hundreds of paths and thoroughfares through the marshes and enemy patrols have regularly been seen on the eastern side of the lake. In other words, our safety is in not being seen or heard. A regular watch must be kept throughout the day and there's always a chance of the Stork flying over, so nothing can be left outside for them to see. Anyone going across to the mainland needs to be monitored. There is a boat and a raft which we can use, but we have to make sure they are hidden at all times, whether here on the island, or in the two mooring areas, which I will show you, on the mainland. All will be revealed regarding the immediate area, once we're settled in here. Any questions?"

The party exchanged glances, all shaking their heads. "Then please, feel free to look around and change anything you want. I know there will be things we need to do to make this place work for us.

Stephan and uncle Yenisei, could I have a word outside please?"

The two men nodded their acquiescence and followed Yuri out into the evening light. Yuri had been dreading this moment for some time. He had to tell them about Katerina. So, he took a deep breath, turned and faced them and said in a faltering voice, "I haven't been able to tell you, due to the journey we have just undertaken, but I found Katerina in the shelled- out building, before I found the pair of you. Alayna was there, trying to lift the huge beam that had fallen and crushed Katerina's legs and lower torso. I pulled Alayna away, but even between us, we couldn't have moved the beam. I knelt by Katerina and she was somehow, still alive, even though her blood was everywhere. But she was in severe pain and suffering terribly. She implored me to end her life, to stop the agony she was experiencing. I took it upon myself to take out my pistol and end her suffering. I couldn't live with this knowledge and not tell you. Alayna saw me, she knows and understood. I hope you can understand too."

Yuri then lapsed into silence. Stephan and Yenisei looked at each other, both reliving the horrors of the shattered house, until finally, Yenisei spoke.

"I cannot attach any blame to you Yuri. Had I been put in the same position, I'm not sure I could have carried out such an act of mercy, knowing who she was. Thank you for telling us, we appreciate what you did for her. You are truly a remarkable young man."

He then turned and walked out into the fading sunlight. Stephan moved over to Yuri and put his arms around Yuri's body, drawing him close and squeezing him tightly. "Bless you Yuri," he said in a broken voice, "my brother will be told of my niece's passing. Thank you for your courage and humility."

With that, he moved away and joined Yenisei, the pair of them remembering a life well spent, but cut short by this grotesquely ugly war. Yuri relaxed a little, he had said what he wanted to say and he hoped he had helped to give them closure. Now he needed to make sure Alayna could grieve for her sister. He left the two men outside and wandered back into the main cave. The women were nowhere to be seen, obviously in the side bedroom, but Ivan, the blacksmith, was studying the tools on the wall.

 "He must have been a clever man, the previous owner," he said with grudging admiration, "some of these objects have been carved and finished off beautifully. I mean, look at these cupboards and the way he attached things to the wall. Quite remarkable."

 "Have you seen the weapons he made," added Yuri, pointing to the remaining crossbow and long bow. We made good use of the other two crossbows, but I fear that they may now be lost. I doubt whether Alexei and Valery saved them from the attack on the camp."

"Well," answered Ivan, "I could always make some more. There's wood for the stocks and plenty of metal about to make the frame and trigger mechanism. I just need use of the fire and stove. That would be where the previous owner did his smelting."

"That would be great," enthused Yuri, "we also need more snow shoes and maybe even skis and poles. Anything you feel might help us, I for one would be pleased to endorse. We also need some beds rigging up for tonight. I'll check in the packs we brought, there may be a camp bed or two in there. Thanks Ivan, keep looking around and see what you can come up with."

Turning, he picked up Vladimir's pack and pulled out the contents. Spare shirts and underclothes, great coat, socks and wool mittens, a poncho, binoculars, compass, wool jumpers, fur cap and a leather aircraftsman's cap, cooking pot and stove, a tent and one metal tubed foldable bed, with six inch feet. Brilliant. He would be OK sleeping on the floor tonight, he was used to being on the ground when in the camp. So, he helped Ivan make up the tubular bed, pulled out some blankets and things to be used for pillows and stood back satisfied.

Stephan and Yenisei returned from outside and Yuri showed them the beds, "pick your own," he told them, "and get settled down." Just then, the ladies came out from the bedroom, both chattering about what they had found. Alayna hurried over to Yuri and threw her arms around his neck and kissed him.

"It's wonderful Yuri," she said gaily, "but Giselle and I are tired so we're off to bed. See you all in the morning." With that and a cheery wave, the pair of them scurried off, closing the door behind them.

Yuri saw that everyone was settling down, so he picked up his blanket and pillow and bade them goodnight. Then he went outside for a final tour of the island. The stars were evident in a clear, blue-black sky and a slight breeze ruffled the branches of the pines and alders. He climbed up to the top of the rocks at the west end and gazed around, listening and watching for any signs of danger. The breeze was out of the east and he thought he smelled smoke, but was unsure. There was no sound from the Warsaw to Minsk road and no signs of light apart from a crescent moon hanging palely above. It was difficult to imagine anything more beautiful and peaceful, but he knew that not many miles away, people were dying. And what of the Colonel, Valery and Alexei? Where were they tonight and were they OK? Being in such close proximity to Alayna would be interesting in the least. He would have to see how that panned out, but he knew that he was yearning to be alone with her. Tomorrow, he would show them all around and begin providing food and wood for the coming months. It would be impossible to move from here, there was no way they could go to Abakan, for example. Between them and eastern Russia was a whole army and the SS. He thought deeply about the SS. A fanatical group of psychopaths, Hitler's own personal bodyguard. And they were the instruments of his policies, his overriding ambition being to wipe out whole nations, creeds and cultures. A dangerous and morally corrupt monster, that only total resistance to and commitment to defeat whatever the cost, would be acceptable and just, for any decent, law abiding human being the world over. Hitler had brought the free world to the brink. He and his sadistic henchmen must be eradicated before it was too late.

With that last thought, he gave the area a final scan, before making his way back to the cave. As quietly as he could, he opened and closed the hide door and made ready for sleep. The cave was quiet, only a gentle snoring from Ivan could be heard. Yuri relaxed, snuggled down into his blankets and fell into an exhausted sleep, his trusty knife laid within easy reach. He became aware gradually, that morning was upon him and careful to make as little noise as possible, he peered myopically at his watch in the dim light. He couldn't believe his eyes, ten thirty was as late as he had ever slept. He grinned to himself, no-one else was moving either, so he was not the only one guilty of over sleeping. We were all exhausted, he told himself. Let them sleep on, it's what they need, young and old. But then he saw Stephan beginning to move and decided that now was the time to have a look around outside. He raised himself and stood up stiffly, bending and flexing his whole body, then with a satisfied yawning stretch, he opened the outer door and stepped out into the light. The sun, blinding in its intensity, shocked him into complete awareness. He raised his hand, squinting through outstretched fingers, until his eyes became accustomed to the glare. He searched around, still well within the confines of the outer entrance, but saw and heard nothing untoward. Then he moved out into the rock and tree covered open area in front of the cave and breathed in the morning air. He loved the morning, even though this one was a lot later than normal for him to just be rising and so he took his time. He completed a full circuit of the island, but nothing disturbed his tranquil mood. Birds were singing, insects buzzing around and tiny puff-ball clouds rode serenely across the heavens. He made his way down the steps to the little bay where the boats were. A fish plopped in the vastness of the lake in front of him. Fish? He'd forgotten about the fact that fish would be in the lake. Another source of food had just presented itself and he admonished himself for not having thought of it before.

Squatting down on his haunches, he watched ducks and geese sailing across the clear water in their never-ending search for food. The abundance of nature in this part of western Russia, never ceased to amaze him.

His reverie was interrupted by the appearance of the rest of the party, all deciding that they would venture out to take the morning air. He waved to them, beckoning them to come and join him by the water's edge. Ivan was the first to navigate the steps, followed by the others. Yuri noticed that Alayna looked particularly lovely this morning, her dark combed hair falling in wavy abandonment across her shoulders and back. She spied him looking and gave him the benefit of her most glorious smile. He grinned back, acutely aware of her sensuous body, as she glided down the steps towards him. Alayna chuckled to herself. Oh, my handsome hero, she thought, he of the lust filled eyes and a head full of erotic fantasies. You could devour me in an instant, of that I have no doubt. But my instinct is to make you wait, to let this ardour build, until we are both ready to devour each other. Then, you will know how much I want you, how much I desire you and how much I need to be a woman, your woman. This is my first time and a quick romp in the woods is not on my agenda. I, alone, will decide where and when. Do not worry, my darling, I also cannot wait too long. Be patient, all will be well. So, she sat down beside him, gave him a quick peck on the cheek and said wistfully, "Yuri, this is so beautiful." He was nonplussed with such a curt welcome, expecting more than just a peck and it threw him for a second. Then he regained his composure, but she had sensed his frustration and she smiled to herself, satisfied that her plan was now in operation. Wait, my love. It will be so worth it.

He showed them all around the island, but not the area where Anna and Aleksander were buried. He wanted to save that until later, to try and lure Alayna down there where they could be alone. He had to be near her, with no-one else around. So once the tour was over, they all repaired back inside the cave. Yenisei was most interested in looking over the Dobrovolsky's drawings and writings and Yuri showed him where they were. On his insistence, Yuri took the boxes outside into the sunlight for Yenisei to peruse at his leisure. Ivan was keen to start on a new crossbow and to get together materials for some snow shoes. Alayna and Giselle were re-arranging the pots, pans, cutlery and crockery, giving them all a thorough wash before leaving them to dry. That left Yuri and Stephan, so they decided to saw and chop some logs, to at least get started on preparing for the weeks and months ahead. The work was hard, but enjoyable. Soon they had amassed a large pile which they stood in the front cave entrance to keep dry. The girls then announced that the evening meal was ready and the party sat down to a full meal, the first for a good few days. All through the meal, Yuri had tried to catch Alayna's eye, but she skilfully avoided his direct glances without appearing to do so. Once the meal was over, the men went back to their tasks, the women clearing up and putting things away. Then, as the evening was drawing in, Alayna stepped outside and spoke to Yuri.

"You haven't shown me the west end of the island," she chided, "Do you think we could have a look now?"

Yuri responded with, "of course, if you'll just walk this way." He took her hand and they both sauntered up to the top of the ridge in the islands centre. The air was cooling now, but the sun still shone down, westering slowly, the shadows long and distinct. He showed her the steps down to the lower level and taking her hand, he gently led her down to the bottom. They walked out together onto the sun dappled promontory, both of them acutely aware of the nearness of each other. Yuri moved out across the open green sward, knowing here was a sacred place. Alayna's hands lifted up to her face and she gasped, "Oh Yuri, what a beautiful spot. Over there, is that where the Dobrovolsky's are buried?"

His eyes followed her pointing finger and he nodded, "yes, that's where they both lie. I buried Aleksander there myself, next to his wife. She had died in 1939 and Aleksander died sometime early this year."

As he spoke, he carefully guided her towards the two graves and they stood in silence for a little while, drinking in the beauty of the place that Aleksander had chosen for his wife and himself. Alayna leant against Yuri, sure that he understood how impossible it would be for anything to happen here on the island, being too sacrilegious against Aleksander and Anna's memory. He felt her body against his and sighed, there will be another way to resolve this, he thought. Alayna smiled to herself. She ached with a passionate longing for his touch. It will be soon, my love, be patient. Yuri was also remembering that the death of Katerina was still high in all of their thinking. He would bide his time, lending his support where he could. She would need his love and understanding. So, he put his arm around her waist, she responded the same and the pair of them sauntered back to the cave in a companionable silence.

August slipped slowly by. September arrived with many days of heavy rain, mixed with a little sleet. The party were now well established in the cave. Repairs and additions to the structure had been carried out, most of them to make life easier when winter struck. Ivan had made Yuri a bed out of alder boughs crossed on a pine frame. He had also been able to create another crossbow to go with the one remaining, along with a couple of dozen bolts. With Yuri and Stephan's help, he had made more chairs and extended the table. The girls had washed all of the bedding and clothing, using the lake as a giant washtub. They had also stitched skins and furs into wearable clothes, hats, trousers and gloves. Yuri's main job had been the procurement of wood for burning, shooting game for eating and salting it away for the coming months. Stephan had used his skill to catch several hauls of fish from the lake, which varied their diet and kept their precious stocks of protein high. Yenisei was content to burrow deeper and deeper through Aleksander and Anna's drawings and writings, his mind reeling with the diversity of the content. He was also interested in the maps of the area and marvelled at the accuracy of the handmade drawings of their immediate surroundings, which included all tiny streams, bridges and paths which were too small to feature on the main maps. Yuri did most of the hunting. He was easily the best woodsman that they had and using the crossbow, brought back a never-ending supply of geese, deer, wild pig and bear. The earthenware pots were filled to capacity, the girls had dressed the meat and salted it down. All in all, preparations for the coming winter were going well. Every three or four days, the three men and the girls, leaving Yenisei alone with his paperwork in the cave, took the boat across to the bay through the reeds. The girls went hunting for vegetables and berries, while Yuri, Ivan and Stephan sourced wood, dragging it back to Aleksander's hut, where Ivan and Stephan cut it into six foot lengths for transporting across to the cave on the raft. The trips were self-protecting, the men keeping their eyes on the girls and each other, while they busied themselves with their jobs. During the almost three weeks they had all been on the island, they had never seen or heard anything of the Nazi's, apart from the squadrons of planes that regularly plied between their airfields in eastern Poland. But these were becoming increasingly fewer and fewer, as the Nazi's probably built or took over more captured Russian airfields, bringing them closer to Moscow and beyond. However, Yuri was adamant that they should be vigilant at all times and that nothing was to be left at the end of a working day, for unscrupulous eyes to witness.

The weather recently had been awful, days of rain and high winds. It helped, in a way, as the downpours masked the noise of sawing, chopping and hammering. Aleksander's hut had come in for a makeover, the roof had been strengthened and where there were walls, battened tight against the high winds that were now sweeping down from the north. It was a really snug, dry place, where the sawing horse came in for much use, as Yuri, Stephan and Ivan, spent many days building up the party's reserves of sawn timber. The sawn lengths were piled methodically against the sides of the hut, leaving a reasonable space in the centre for the sawing horse for future cutting. Ivan had fashioned a screen of alder boughs to cover the entrance, where only a close inspection would reveal the contents inside. Wood was being sourced, further and further away from the hut, they didn't want to thin out the nearby timber, as this would be left for ease of use when the winter really set in. Their forays into the marshes had seen evidence of wolves and bears, the wolf pack being a large group of fourteen or more. On several occasions, Yuri had come upon carcasses stripped to the bone. He found a pair of what were probably cattle skeletons, easy pickings for the ravaging wolves. The discoveries heightened his concern about there being a large pack in the area, even though this group seemed more aligned to the southern marshes. But apart from tracks from these wolves and many other animals, he had failed to see anything remotely human. The war was being fought far away from here. What was happening in the east? He had no way of knowing, but he was beginning to hanker after more action, being concerned that he wasn't doing anything to help the Russian cause. And what of the Colonel, Alexei and Valery? Were they still alive, or captured or hanging on in some remote place. He knew the Colonel would try to get to the island if he could and the thought made Yuri more settled in his mind, if not completely happy with the situation. What he did know was that they couldn't support any more individuals within the cave. What he didn't realise, was that he was helping the Russian cause. Yenisei was a massive target for the SS and Yuri, by keeping him safe, was doing the war effort a huge service. His thoughts turned often to Alayna. When the party had first arrived on the island, he couldn't wait to be at her beck and call. However, the closeness of her every day without being able to be alone with her, was filling him with frustration and his mood was becoming short tempered and morose around the times they were all together. He took his spite out on the day to day tasks, joyfully smashing down trees with the double handed axe and hauling the logs to the hut, courtesy of the yoke sled. She was not helping either, to his mind. He could feel her eyes on him at various times of the day, but whenever he faced her, she offered him that beguiling half smile that she was becoming so adept at using and then looked away. Yes, there were a few kisses from time to time, but they were quick pecks, nothing to show if she was feeling the same, or indeed hurting as he was, so, he now felt more like a brother, rather than her lover.

But Yuri had no idea of the pain that Alayna was suffering. She too was losing her nerve. Her initial decision to try and exploit their close situation, had evaporated by the end of the first week. It was taking all her resolve not to drag him into her bed at night, even though she knew that this would be disastrous. She had a hunger and only he could satisfy the longing. As far as she knew, no-one suspected her inner torment. But Giselle knew and also Grandfather Yenisei. They watched and waited, hoping that somehow, she and Yuri could settle the matter. As it was, the opportunity presented itself while she and Giselle were out with the men, collecting fruit and vegetables. The men had gone off into the woods looking for more trees to fell and Giselle had turned to her and said, "Why don't we go and see what the men have been up to in the hut. It's probably a real mess in there."

With that, they made their giggling way to the hut and stepped inside. The hut, if it could be called that, was surprisingly large and spacious, although the logs piled up around the walls, were beginning to encroach on the space in the centre. The sawing horse stood towards the rear wall and the place smelt of fresh sawdust and seasoning logs, not at all what they had expected. They looked around for several minutes before Giselle made to leave, saying on her way out, "yes, this would be perfect," before disappearing outside. Alayna's brow furrowed, wondering what she was talking about, when realisation suddenly hit her. Good God, she thought, this would be perfect. My boudoir, away from prying eyes. We could be alone and undetected here. Why haven't I thought of here before? With that, she gazed around the inner space, a plan forming in her head. What she needed was an excuse for her to be here and how to get Yuri to come to her. She racked her brain, but nothing would come. Then she thought, don't be stupid, you're female. You'll come up with something. Holy mother, let it be soon. She went outside, deep in thought, as she made her way back to Giselle and the vegetables. Giselle watched her and knew her cryptic message had worked. But for Alayna, she was none the wiser, only now focused on making it happen, and soon.

Two days later, Alayna was ready to put her plan into action. The men had finished logging for the moment, giving themselves some time to spend around the cave. Ivan was making some pan supports of tempered steel from the remaining bits left by Aleksander, while Yuri was helping Yenisei and Stephan, piece together the information from the maps and drawings. Yenisei had also discovered Gruber's papers and documents which the Colonel had tried to decipher, a month or so ago. The morning had begun normally enough. Yuri was first to rise making his daily tour around the island to listen and hear. The day was bright and warm, an Indian summer which they all knew would be probably, the last of the really good days before the onset of autumn and then, the winter. When he came back inside for tea and a bite to eat, he noticed that Alayna was deep in conversation with Giselle. Alayna had decided to tell Giselle her intentions, needing an ally while she tried to sneak away to the hut. Giselle had smiled and told her that she was well aware of the way her and Yuri were feeling and Alayna was astonished that it had been so noticeable. Giselle also told her that it was Grandfather Yenisei who had first broached the subject with her, being very aware of the unspoken friction flying around the two of them whenever they got close to each other. Alayna was gladdened by Grandfather Yenisei's attitude. If he was in favour, then she knew she had his blessing. He had told Giselle that the war could end everything for them and that they should grasp every moment, while they were able. Alayna knew that Yuri would be upset when he realised she was not on the island and would come storming across the lake to find her. She wanted him that way, fired up, his eyes blazing with passion and his temper on the boil when he found her. But first, she had to make her getaway. She disappeared off into the side bedroom to prepare herself. The pack she was taking was all ready to go. She smoothed down her dress, combed out her hair and waited for the signal from Giselle.

After about five minutes, Giselle appeared. "They're all involved with the map making," she whispered, "I'll move the pack to the outer entrance for you. Once you've got past the men, you're on your own."

She squeezed Alayna's hand in farewell, picked up the pack and disappeared off into the main cave. After a couple of minutes, Alayna put her head cautiously around the door. Grandfather Yenisei caught her eye, jerked his head towards the outer cave and said to Yuri, "look, my boy, here is the place where our last camp was, but where did you come from to get there?"

Yuri bent over the drawings, his whole concentration on the paths and streams where he, the Colonel, Valery and Alexei had met up with Major Lensky's attack on the supply train. So engrossed was he, that Alayna was able to slip past him to the door, pick up the pack and move quietly outside. Once free of the confines of the cave, she hurried down to the landing area, launched the boat and paddled off towards the reed bay. Once safely across, she tied up the boat and made for the hut. Once inside the hut, she made her preparations and waited nervously for him to discover her escape. She wanted him to be mad, but not too mad. Holy mother, she suddenly thought, what if he is so incensed and simply takes me? Could I stand that, for my first time? She now began to shake with trepidation, the bright sunlight unable to warm her suddenly oh so cold body. No matter, the die is cast, she thought. What will be, will be.

An hour had passed when Yuri first realised that he hadn't seen Alayna for some time. He had been so engrossed in Yenisei's questions, he had somehow become aware that she was not around

. "Where's Alayna?" he asked generally. The men looked at each other, shrugged and collectively shook their heads.

"Er, no idea," muttered Yenisei non-committedly, "have you seen her Giselle?"

"I think she said she was going over to the mainland to look for fruit and berries."

"What," boomed Yuri, "she's gone over there by herself? Good God, do none of you have any sense. We never go off singly, especially the women."

With that, he stormed out of the cave and made for the landing. Stephan and Ivan were about to follow when Yenisei said placatingly, "leave him to it, he'll find her soon enough."

The two men shrugged in agreement, realising that Yuri would be best at sorting out Alayna. "Anyway," said Yenisei blithely, "the boat would be gone and unless he takes the raft, he's going to have to swim."

Yuri was indeed having to swim. The raft was too cumbersome for one to navigate, so he stripped off down to his army trousers, pulled off his boots and socks and dived head first into the lake. The impact

344

of the cold water did nothing for his mood, which was by now in overdrive. Visions of wolves and SS patrols flashed through his mind, as his strong stokes bore him swiftly across the lake and through the reeds into the bay. There was the boat, neatly tied up, but where the hell was Alayna? Scrambling wetly ashore, he called softly, not daring to shout too loudly. There was no reply and he ran off in the direction of the area around the hut where the girls had previously found fruit.

"Alayna," he called again, where the hell was that stupid woman. Then he saw the hut, with Alayna standing in the entrance. Relief flooded over him as he stalked over to her, his wet hair flowing in the air as his body dripped and dribbled. He was wet and he was mad. But as he approached her, she turned her back on him and moved inside the hut. Piqued by her seemingly uncaring attitude, he stomped right up to the entrance, peered inside and stopped dead. She stood facing him, her arms down by her sides, her hair perched high on her head, held in place by a single, decorative pin. Her lips were parted slightly and she appeared totally serene and beautiful. However, she was trembling inside and she touched her tongue to suddenly dry lips. He stood there and dripped, not a word was spoken, but he saw in her eyes that now was the time. Suddenly, his father's words spilled into his brain. 'Be gentle,' he had said. 'Take your time, but be positive. She will guide you, especially if it is her first time.'

She smiled enticingly, raising her hands to her dress buttons and slowly undid each one, until the dress was fully opened. Then in a single, flowing movement, the dress fell to the floor. Yuri was stunned, he had never seen a woman naked before, especially one so beautiful and so ready to offer herself to him. He breathed deeply, wanting to savour the moment, his eyes wandering all over her nakedness. Then she raised her hands above her head, pulled out the pin and allowed her hair to fall. She shook out the locks which cascaded into a dark halo, framing her exquisite face. Yuri gawped, he had never believed anything could be so erotic. Then he too, discarded his trousers and stood before her, allowing her the same. As he gazed at her, she felt her trembling body relax, but his eyes were having an alarming effect on her breathing. Her breasts rose and fell with increased regularity as he moved towards her, never taking his eyes away from hers. She sighed inwardly, her whole being on the brink, then his arms reached around her waist and drew her to him. She felt his hardness taut against her belly, and her hands groped for his head as their lips came together, in a long, deep, smouldering kiss. She gasped hoarsely as his lips and tongue ran flutteringly around her face and neck. Then he reached down and picked her up gently, moving towards where she had laid out the blanket for them, his eyes promising everything. Bending at the knees, he lowered her to the floor, his eyes still totally focused on hers. She stretched herself luxuriously, parting her legs to allow him entrance and lay, hardly daring to breathe. She felt him move inside her, gently probing and her hymen parted. Years of horse riding had stretched it to breaking point and it finally gave with just a small hint of pain. Now she was ready and she moved her hands down to his taut buttocks and pushed him fully into her. She moaned with growing pleasure as he began to move inside her, building momentum and adjusting his position. She could feel his hot breath on her cheek and he grunted as a spasm coursed through him. They were now rising gradually to that higher plane where the seas meet the sky and the waves roll endlessly in rippling motion, a spiritual place, where ecstasy reigns supreme. Her inhibitions fled before the joy that pulsed through her veins. She lifted herself to him, synchronising her urgency with each thrust and drove him on, ever faster and more furious in her abandonment. Her ragged breathing, torn from deep within her throat and punctuated by small, high pitched wails, were having a profound effect on Yuri, as her hands dug into his hair, such was the power of her commitment. He was also within the grip of the deafening torrents that thundered in his ears and willed him onwards. She felt the heavens opening and the wave that minutes ago had seemed so far off, was now steadily and remorselessly pounding towards her, the towering foam flecked head, rising with each passing second. And then, as it seemed that nothing could get any more pleasurable for either of them, the wave peaked, teetered on the edge for a cataclysmic moment and then crashed down upon them. Alayna's body went rigid. Her legs wrapped themselves tightly around his waist, her back arched while her hands raked across his back and from somewhere deep within her being, a sound welled up that shattered the brooding stillness of the hut. Yuriiiiiiiiiiiiiiiiiiiiiiiiiiiiiiiiiiiiiiiiiiiii, she wailed, the banshee sound of sexual triumph pummelling the air, as the ripples of joy swept relentlessly over her again and again. Yuriiiiiiiiiiiiiiiiiiiiiiiiiiiiiiiiiiiiiiiiiiii, a second time, as she thrashed around in the grip of unbelievable ecstasy. He responded with moans of his own as he hit the short strokes. She felt him pause and stiffen, then his heat exploded inside her and he cried out, ravaged by his own incredible feelings. Then little by little, his ardour subsided. She still clung on tightly, refusing to allow him to relax, as her internal muscles wrung the last dregs of passion from him. Slowly, she began to descend from the heights, her whole body tingling and pulsing with pleasure from every pore. Eventually, she relaxed, opened her eyes and saw him gazing down on her. He bent his head and kissed her, but this kiss held no passion, only love for her. He smiled, made to speak, but she placed a finger on his lips. She just wanted to love him with her eyes. Then, a mischievous smile touched her lips and she twitched again her internal muscles. He groaned his discomfort and she started to giggle uncontrollably. The pair of them shook with mirth, until she finally removed her legs from around him, sliding her feet down the backs of his legs and allowing him his freedom. He tiredly manoeuvred himself from her and rolled onto his back, she turned towards him as his left arm slipped behind her head onto her shoulders and drew her to him, his right hand caressing her tumbled hair. She lay across him, her hands gently stroking his chest, both now breathing freely.

After a few minutes spent basking in the afterglow of fulfilment, she sighed heavily and said, "Do you remember the first time we met, down by the lakeside?"

"Oh, I do," he replied gently.

"I thought I'd lost you then, before I'd even found you," she confided. "I behaved so irresponsibly, so out of character, because you stirred me so."

"It's as well uncle Yenisei threw that bucket of water over me," admitted Yuri, "I could have said something I would have regretted."

"Threw over both of us," she corrected, "I was ready to thump you."

He laughed out loud at her revelation and she nipped him and giggled. He yelped in pain and said seriously, "the second time, in the woods, would you have really stuck me with that knife?"

She paused for a few seconds, before replying with, "Oh no my darling, I couldn't have hurt your beautiful body." He breathed out a long sigh of relief, but she continued mischievously, "however, I was extremely angry and provoked. Perhaps I could have." She left the words hanging in the air, before falling into a fit of giggles.

He leaned his hand down and slapped her playfully on the rump. "Oh, God no, not again," she said hoarsely, "the second slap in the woods was so sexual, so domineering, I could have done it there and then."

"It's as well we didn't," he murmured, becoming serious again, "I was so worked up, it would probably have been all over in seconds, I would have hurt you and damaged us for ever." With that, they lapsed into silence. She snuggled deeper into his arms, safe and sound within his warm embrace.

Eventually, they became aware that they would need to get back to the island, their long disappearance would be worrying the others. So reluctantly, they dressed themselves and leaving the hut to its memories, they made for the bay and the boat. Their feelings for each other were now complete, they had matured as adults. Both understood the implications of the morning and although they didn't know it, their whole outlook had changed. Gone was the tenseness between them, banished to the four winds, leaving a glow of contentment and an acceptance of each other. The war was still the overriding concern, that would not go away so easily, but they now could look ahead to a future of togetherness, no matter how fleeting that may be. A final long kiss on the shore before they stepped into the boat and paddled for the island, cemented their resolve and both could not wait for their passion to be unleashed again, although it was not the overriding necessity it had been before. Yenisei was sat outside when they beached the boat and climbed the steps to the central area. He looked from one to the other and realised, they had finally become as one. He smiled a greeting, Alayna blushed prettily and her eyes were cast downwards, away from his searching look as she continued on into the inside of the cave. Yuri held out his hand to his uncle and shook the proffered hand in return. No words were spoken, but Yenisei absorbed the feeling of peace emanating from Yuri's eyes. He nodded in acquiescence.

Inside the cave, Ivan was finishing his work, helped by the ever-willing Stephan. Giselle looked up from the sewing she had been doing and smiled at Alayna's blushing entrance. Alayna glided through the main area, gave Stephan a kiss on the cheek and went into her bedroom, followed by a deeply curious Giselle. She pulled the door closed behind her and the two girls embraced, Alayna pouring out her thanks for her friends help and advice. The details of the morning she kept jealously to herself and Giselle would have had it no other way. So, now they spoke of other things, of what Giselle had been doing and how to fill the rest of their day. Outside, Yuri had entered the cave and heaped praise on Ivan's new pan holders. Stephan showed him how these would sit around the fire and stove allowing ease of cooking for the girls. Yuri was impressed and hoped the girls were too. No mention was made of his storming exit earlier, the two men happy that it seemed to have been resolved amicably. So Yuri went back outside to talk to Yenisei, there being no sign of the girls. He figured that Giselle had been somehow involved with Alayna's exit this morning, but whatever her involvement, it didn't really matter. Yenisei was deep in thought as he approached his uncle.

He motioned Yuri to sit and after a while he confided, "I've been looking into the papers you got from this Gruber. Can you remember if there was any sign of papers hidden in his boots, like there were in Vladimir's?"

"I can't ever remember looking," answered Yuri truthfully, "but I've got them here. I swapped my own with Gruber's after I'd killed him, his were far superior to mine. I'm afraid they have been soaked on a couple of occasions, but if papers were wrapped in something water resistant, perhaps they'll have survived. I changed them for some I stole from the compound when I released the Colonel and the brothers, they're these I'm wearing now. The others are inside, I'll go and get them."

Thoughtfully, he went back into the cave and dug out his old boots. Taking them outside, he pushed and prodded at the inner lining until lo and behold, he found a secret compartment, just like Vladimir's. There were the papers, wrapped in a cellophane packet. Gently, he opened the packet and pulled out the papers from inside. They were damp, but appeared OK.

He handed them to Yenisei who said, "Just as I thought, more or less identical. It would appear that both Gruber and Vladimir were issued with the same material, which contains codes and cyphers. I can translate some of the German words, but I can't understand all of it, especially the way the codes are laid out."

"We need the Colonel for that," said Yuri with a shrug. "If he were here, we would have a way of manipulating the SS. As it is, we're really none the wiser."

Yenisei nodded and went back to his thoughts. Yuri was silent for a moment and then said, "If the Colonel is still alive, I know for certain he will make his way here. I've been expecting him for a couple of weeks now, but something is obviously holding him up. If he doesn't arrive in the next few days, I will probably go and see if I can find him, before the weather turns for the worst."

"That might be a possibility," concurred Yenisei, "but hopefully, he'll come to us."

The afternoon was disappearing fast. Yenisei and Yuri continued their conversation for a while, but no real plan regarding the papers was forthcoming. Once they had all had something to eat, Yuri took the island tour before settling down for the night. He climbed to the top of the west ridge and stared off into the distance. Where are you Sergei he thought, are you surviving or are you in dark peril? He sniffed the wind, sensing a change on the way. Tomorrow would be stormy, he could feel it in his bones. Just then, Alayna came out of the cave and skipped gaily up the ridge towards him.

She came to him and he held her close, then kissed her and said, "I may have to leave in the next few days. I'm going to have to find out what's happened to Alexei, Valery and the Colonel."

He saw her concern and then the inevitability of their situation sobered her. She nodded and clung to him, wishing it could all be different, but knowing that he must do what he must do. "I'll wait for you my darling," she said quietly, "God will be with you and he will bring you back safely to me."

Tragically, she knew she was deluding herself, this senseless war would ruin all of their dreams. But she kept her peace and remained clinging to him as they watched the light fall from the sky together.

About twenty miles away to the east, a haunted figure limped his way towards the island. He would not reach his destination tonight, so he searched for somewhere to be dry, out of the coming storm. The Colonel sighed deeply as he thought about what lay ahead. He had no way of knowing if anyone had made it to the island, but he knew he had to find out, one way or another. He was travelling the same path that the party had used almost three weeks ago, although he did not know it. He limped on, the pain in his injured leg bothering him as the miles racked up, but he could find nowhere to spend the night. Then, after a couple of further miles, he spotted the cabin in the woods. This will do, he told himself and made his way warily through the trees. The door creaked a little as he opened it to find a snug, dry room, away from the coming rain. He knew he wouldn't be able to sleep much, being too aware of pursuit from behind. He was pretty sure that he had no humans following him, only the pack of wolves who had picked up his scent, many miles to the east. The last three days and nights had been a constant worry, trying desperately to dodge the pack and he was reaching the end of his strength. Only the hope that Yuri was indeed on the island, kept him going. I'll rest here for a few hours, he thought, then once it starts raining, I'll move out. He knew the rain would mask his scent and he also knew a few tricks to outwit his wily followers. They couldn't get to him while he was in the hut, so he made a small fire and gathered together some long branches. Fire was one of the few things that wolves were afraid of and he made ready, just in case. There were a couple of dry biscuits in his pack and he munched on them while he waited. Slowly the day waned, the light fading from the sky, but he heard the wind increasing from the west, the fire gutted and he heard the first droplets of the storm pattering on the roof. Another hour he thought, then I'll go. He leant back against the cabin wall, forcing his eyes to remain open, but it was a fruitless task, he was too exhausted. His chin dropped to his chest and he slept. The wind keened eerily around him, the rain sluicing down in driven torrents, but he slept on regardless.

He was awoken at three, by the thing that he was dreading most, the howl of a nearby wolf. He staggered up, his limbs stiff and sore from being in a cramped position, but he knew he had to move, or die. The howl was answered by several others and he estimated them to be less than half a mile away. Panic overtook him now, he had to leave and leave fast. He flung open the door and was hit by the full blast of the wind and the driving rain. No matter, he thought, just get away from this place. He made his way to the path and looked carefully around. Lack of a moon meant there was very little light and he strained his ears for any unnatural sound. Go, his mind told him, go. He set off at as fast a limp as he could, wanting to put as much distance between himself and his pursuers. The poncho he had donned as he left the cabin was doing its job, but his head was sodden, his hair and beard matted and streaming in the teeth of the pouring rain. He dare not wear his hat, he needed to be able to hear and the hat would only impede both vision and hearing. He staggered on, the keen threnody of the wind doing its utmost to delay his progress. He was lost within a living hell of wind and water. Mile after sodden mile he staggered, grinding his teeth against the pain in his leg and also the old wound in his shoulder, that he had received during the attack on the camp, seven weeks ago. The sky was becoming lighter and the rain seemed to be lessening. Where the hell were those wolves? He searched the woods and path behind him. Nothing. And then he became aware of eyes, moving relentlessly through the gloom. They were not more than twenty feet behind him. He looked around everywhere, panic rising in his throat. If they surrounded him, there was no chance. He saw

357

nothing but the eyes behind him that were now closing imperceptibly, until he could make out the silhouettes of four, huge wolves. The leader moved towards him, certain now of a tasty meal. But the Colonel had other ideas. Allowing them to move closer, he put his hand inside his poncho and pulled out his pistol. He aimed at the lead wolf. 'Bang', the leader collapsed, blood pumping from a wound in the throat. The others whined and dashed around, uncertain now that their leader was down. 'Bang', another shot, and another wolf hit the path, coughing out its last breath. The others, whinged and whined around their two fallen colleagues, uncertain and smelling the blood and death that was now filling their nostrils. More came out from the trees. Good God, he thought, there's at least fourteen of them. The Colonel moved backwards, eyes transfixed on the snarling, pandemonium going on between the remaining wolves. His only hope lay with an assumption that might just work. As far as he knew, a leaderless pack was unacceptable in wolf culture. One of the others must now assume the mantle. He watched them hesitate and prowl around each other and saw that three of the would-be kings, were sizing each other up. There was a pause and then the three tore into each other, ignoring the Colonel in their bid for supremacy. He backed off further until he lost them around a bend in the path and then he turned and hurried off as quickly as he could. What he didn't see, was the rest of the pack falling ravenously on their two downed brothers. They would be busy eating for quite a while, as well as settling the leadership issue. He took the proffered respite and soldiered on, surely it couldn't be far now?

Yuri awoke with a start. He listened intently as his eyes became accustomed to the darkness of the cave. Had he heard something, or was he dreaming it? The gentle snores from the others told him that nothing had caused him to wake inside, so whatever it was must have been outside. He pulled on his boots, grabbed his rifle and binoculars and as silently as he could, opened the outer door and stepped outside into the outer cave entrance. The sky was overcast, but the rain seemed to have lessened, the wind however, still blew strongly. He pulled his jacket tighter around his neck and made carefully for the landing area. The wind was whipping the lake into waves and troughs as he carefully looked all around. Nothing. Was his mind playing tricks? He then ascended the ridge on the southern side, keeping as close as possible to the screening trees. Nothing to the west. The wind battered his face and his eyes smarted with the driven rain. Then he crept down the northern side of the ridge, angling for the northeast corner. Gingerly, he passed between the pines, trying to make out the northern shore. He searched the north side, where the trees and reeds reached the water. He stopped suddenly, aware that something or someone was standing near the reeds close to where they beached the boat. He adjusted the binoculars for a better view. There was someone and even through the clinging mist, he made out the unmistakable outline and features of the Colonel. He had returned as Yuri knew he would.

Chapter 13 – The Colonel Returns

Yuri stood up and showed himself, the Colonel saw and responded to his wave. Yuri held up two hands, ten fingers. The Colonel nodded, that would be how long it would take Yuri to launch the boat and get across the lake to him. Yuri was elated, the Colonel had found them and he couldn't wait to find out what had been happening since they last parted. He removed the branches covering the boat, shoved it out into the lake and jumped in. With a few deep paddling strokes, he was around the eastern edge of the island and making for the northern landing area. As he approached, the Colonel moved lamely towards the incoming boat and Yuri was appalled at the Colonel's appearance. His clothes were ragged, ripped in many places and his left leg was obviously bothering him. His gaunt face spoke volumes, wrinkled and careworn and his eyes were set deep into their sockets. Here was a man who had suffered and was still suffering. Yuri jumped out and helped him into the boat, the older man groaned as he shuffled into his seat.

"Sorry Yuri," he offered gingerly as he settled into the boat, "I'm not too good at the moment."

"Don't worry Sergei," answered Yuri, "we'll soon have you sorted once we're back in the cave."

As quickly as he could, Yuri pushed off, the Colonel unable or unwilling to paddle, but Yuri was more concerned over his friend's obvious mental and physical state. He paddled around the east side of the island and made landfall in the little bay. Jumping out, he dragged the boat into the screening trees and then helped the Colonel out of the boat. Between them, they managed to stand him upright and with Yuri supporting him, scaled the steps up to the central area. As they crested the top, Stephan appeared from the cave and hurried over to offer his assistance. The Colonel was on his last legs and Stephan and Yuri had to virtually carry him into the warm confines of the cave.

Inside, the others were up and about, the two girls having just come through from the side bedroom. Ivan immediately built up the fire and the Colonel was placed on a chair in front of it's now roaring flames. He shook with cold and tiredness, as if in the grip of fever, but all knew that his clothes would have to be changed. Giselle filled a pot with water and put it on to boil, while the men stripped the clothes from him and pulled off his boots and socks. His body was a mass of cuts and scratches, most of it being superficial. The concerns were his left shoulder and his left thigh. The shoulder was the result of being shot on the day of the attack on the camp. It had been roughly bandaged, but the bandage was now hanging off, held on only by dried blood. Yuri prised it away, revealing a puss filled wound at the front and an exit wound at the back which appeared cleaner. Giselle came over and using a strip of clean cloth, began to wipe away the dried blood and puss surrounding the wound.

"I've had some experience of dealing with this kind of wound Colonel," she told him "and so if it's OK with you, I'll carry on."

The Colonel nodded resignedly, then winced as she wiped, emitting a low groan and he sighed deeply. "Sorry," he kept saying in his stupor, "can't really help."

"Shhh", whispered Giselle, "no need to speak, but I must make sure that the wound is clean and free of debris."

The Colonel nodded weakly as she cleaned and cleared around both sides of the wounds, then Alayna brought over the now hot water. Dipping the cloth into the water, Giselle coaxed the remaining blood and puss from around the bullet hole, which was now showing purple and brown-black bruising. The skin had begun to heal a little, but she could see where the bullet had chipped the shoulder bone and she knew that she would have to search for any remaining fragments.

"This will hurt Colonel," she said softly, "but I must do my best to clean it. Would you like something to bite on?"

The Colonel nodded and Stephan produced a piece of thick deer hide, which Alayna placed between the Colonels teeth. She motioned Yuri and Stephan to hold onto him, while she sterilised a knife over the fire coals. Then she expertly opened the wound and started digging around inside. The Colonel stood the pain for a few moments, but then with a shriek of pain, collapsed unconscious, still supported by Yuri and Stephan. Little by little, she recovered several pieces of bone fragments and once again, wiped the wounds with hot water.

As she dabbed it dry, she looked up and said, "Grandfather Yenisei, could you get me some of that ointment from the medical box, a clean bandage and the rest of that Brandy that we have."

Yenisei nodded and went to get the things she required. Giselle again shoved the knife into the coals of the fire until the blade glowed red hot. While it was heating, she poured Brandy over the two wounds, dabbing it dry with a clean cloth. Then she placed the flat side of the knife blade over each wound, cauterising them and stopping the blood flow. Once this was done, she motioned Alayna to put ointment onto the wounds and refit a new bandage, while she had a look at his thigh.

The thigh looked ugly. Again, the bandage surrounding it was old and filthy and once it was prised away, revealed two deep cuts, where a bayonet or knife had probably been driven through. Thankfully, it had missed the bone and artery, but it was inflamed and a deep purply-black on both sides.

 "All we can do is clean it," said a concerned Giselle, "and apply Brandy and ointment after cauterising it. I sincerely hope that it's not turned gangrenous."

With that, she carefully cleaned away the dried blood and dirt and poured over the Brandy, dabbing it dry with a clean cloth. Then she cauterised the wounds, applied the ointment liberally and finished by bandaging the thigh tightly. The inert, slumped Colonel was beyond pain at the moment, but he would suffer once he came around. Yuri and Stephan dressed him with difficulty in fresh clean underwear, then a shirt and trousers. Between them, they lifted him up and carried him into the side bedroom, where they placed him in the nearest bed. Alayna covered him with two warm blankets and a fur skin cover. They left him sleeping in peaceful unconsciousness. It was now up to his body to respond to their treatment of the wounds. The Colonel was a strong individual and hopefully, would make a full recovery. Only time would tell.

The Colonels dramatic entry back into their lives, had a sobering effect on everyone. Clearly, the war had taken its toll on him and he barely had a chance to speak, before lapsing into pain induced oblivion. Yuri had no idea how he came to be in this way, apart from the bullet wound in the left shoulder, that he had witnessed first-hand. Thankfully, there was no mention of Alexei and Valery, surely he would have said something if anything had happened to them? But then, bad news is not something you want to disclose unless you can embellish it. Anything that the Colonel has to say, thought Yuri, would have to wait until he was capable of doing it and that meant waiting until he was sufficiently able to do so. The next twenty-four hours would be vital, if he was going to pull through his present crisis. Alayna had tidied up the things used in treating the Colonels wounds, the old bandages had been consigned to the fire and the ointment put away for another time. She saw the anguished look on Yuri's face and her heart reached out to him. She went over to him and put her arms around his neck, gently stroking his hair with her fingers.

"He'll be OK," she said compassionately, "he's a strong man and a fighter. Giselle and I will monitor him on an hourly basis. He's in my bed and he can stay there for as long as it takes. I don't suppose Ivan and Stephan could build another bed for me to sleep in tonight, Giselle will stay with him in her own bed. I promise I won't try to seduce you," she ended with a gentle smile.

Yuri smiled back, "I know you wouldn't," he chided, "those moments are reserved for us alone. Here would not be appropriate. But I wish I knew more about Alexei and Valery. Seeing the Colonel in this state makes me wonder if he's the only casualty."

"Don't worry my love," she implored, "think good thoughts and go and find some work to do, it's no use brooding on something you can't change."

Then she reached up and kissed him. He responded, eternally thankful that she was here with him and able to share his darkest thoughts.

"Yes," he said finally, "I will get some work done. We could still do with more wood. Thanks for being here for me." She smiled an answer, stroked him gently on the cheek and turned away to get the Colonels clothes together for her and Giselle to launder.

Yenisei came over to Yuri and said, "He'll be fine Yuri, don't worry, we'll look after him and God will give him strength. Perhaps when he's fit enough, we could talk to him about the two spies we turned up. I think the papers we found will be most interesting to someone who can read German. Maybe there'll be some way of using what we have against the fascists and the SS."

"You could well be right uncle," agreed Yuri, "but first, we need more wood. Stephan, would you and Ivan care to join me in ferrying some logs back to the hut and then over to the island. With the rain having abated, we should take advantage of this window of opportunity." Stephan and Ivan nodded their agreement and the three men bade farewell to the ladies, dragged out the raft and paddled their way over to the bay in the reeds.

Once they had landed and made fast the raft, Yuri decided to have a scout around the area, while Stephan and Ivan busied themselves with the crosscut saw.

"I'll be back in a couple of hours," said Yuri, "then we can go and fell a few more trees and drag them back here. There's plenty for you to be getting on with while I'm away. It might be a good idea though to do the sawing within the log store. It will keep down the noise"

 "Sounds good to me Yuri," replied Stephan, "Ivan and I will have a nice, steady time of it and we'll keep a good lookout."

Yuri nodded his assent, shouldered his rifle and adjusted his binoculars, before moving off towards the south. He was keen to see if he could pick up any tracks, either animal or human, so he planned to walk for an hour before returning in a westerly circle, back to the hut. The wind was still fairly brisk, blowing across his right shoulder and he felt reasonably happy that his scent would not be picked up by any wild animals. The trees were beginning to lose their leaves, as their autumnal colours turned from a rich green to several shades of red and brown. The days were becoming increasingly shorter and shorter and two mornings ago he had noticed a faint tinge of frost around the lake edges. It would not be long before winter made its way into the equation. The recent rains had swelled the pools and bogs that littered the marshes and the path itself was constantly flooded and muddied with thick oozing goo. He was beginning to really like this part of western Russia, with its diverse flora and fauna, so different to where he had grown up around Kazan. The memories plucked at his heart. He hoped all was well with his family, knowing that he had been unable to tell them about the loss of Grigori. That was a painful task for the future. His musings were interrupted by the sight of several deer tracks, which crossed the path and moved off westwards. It showed the fighting had moved away from this part of the world, when the native animals, so caught up in the tumult of invasion, decided to move back from where they had been driven. He carried on, crossing small rivulets and wider, streaming torrents, made deeper and wilder due to the recent rains. The main streams had wooden bridges in the most part, affording easy crossing and he carried on south as the morning wore on. He reached a point where the path he was travelling, was bisected by one running east to west and he turned to his right and followed it. He had a good idea of where he was, having traversed most of this area in his searches for food and timber. All was silent within the confines of the woods, only the wind disturbing the clashing branches. This path had been travelled by many people recently and he found lots of tracks, mostly made by boots. However, he also spotted dog prints and surmised that the German patrol who had chased them a few weeks ago, had also passed this way. There were also ruts made by tyres of horse drawn vehicles, all moving towards the east. The fascists were still having to re-supply their attacking forces as best they could.

He checked his watch and realised that he had been travelling for just over an hour, it would soon be time to head north and back to Stephan and Ivan. He carried on, keeping to the hard areas of the path wherever he could, new tracks only made it easier for inquisitive eyes to see and decipher. The northern path opened up to his right and he moved onto it, listening and watching all the time. He could hear a woodpecker hammering away at some productive tree, searching for grubs. All the wildlife in the area were acutely aware of the coming of winter and prepared themselves accordingly. He stopped suddenly, his instincts detecting a presence, but he was unsure as to what. Melting into the screening trees he waited, his whole being focused on sight, sound and smell. Then he sensed smoke, just a whiff, but enough to put him on his guard. In the position he was in, the smoke could not have come from the island, the wind being in the wrong direction. He moved cautiously forward, alert for any sound or movement. The path wound around to the left and as he turned a shallow corner, he found the source of the smoke. Instinctively he waited, unsure as to what lay ahead, but after a few minutes, he realised that no other stranger was present, at least, none that were alive. Cautiously, he approached what had probably been a gypsy caravan, all that was left were the axels and wheel hubs, which had almost collapsed in on themselves. The remains of the caravan were so much ash and charred metal. But he could smell the sickly aroma of burnt flesh, emanating from the smouldering heap. Circling around through the surrounding trees, he tried to ascertain what tragedy had enfolded here. Once he had passed around to the northern end of the remains, he came across tracks, deeply visible in the mud. Soldiers had been here and not long ago. They had come, destroyed the caravan and headed back towards the north.

Feeling more secure now, he approached the still smouldering remains. It was evident that the attack on the caravan had been swift and brutal. Three corpses were laid within what had been the caravan's living space, burnt horribly to a crisp. Male, female, age? He couldn't be sure. But then he saw a sight that would haunt him for the rest of his life. Hanging from two trees, about fifteen yards into the wood, were the remains of four children.

Their ages would be from five to eleven, Yuri estimated. They had been hung by their necks with barbed wire and left to the mercy of the elements, but their bodies had been ripped apart by wolves, who had obviously jumped up and tore at what they could reach. The churned-up wolf printed mud around each hanging corpse, was testament to the wolves savage attacks. Only the heads and tops of their torso's now swung pathetically in the wind. Even their hands and forearms had disappeared. Yuri retched, the sight hammering its message into his brain. The SS had been at their most brutal again. How could anyone do this to children? What sort of society bred this kind of sick psychopath? Uncle Yenisei was right, the SS were eliminating the 'Untermensch'. Tearing his gaze away from the horror suspended before him, he tried to decide on what to do. He couldn't leave them there, but he had no way of burying them. He would have to return to the island and pick up a spade or shovel. However, he couldn't in all honesty involve anyone else in this most gruesome of tasks. A sight like this was not for the faint hearted and he wondered if he would ever be able to rid it from his mind. He wandered back to the path and headed north, careful to leave no sign of his passing. After about two miles, a small path opened up to his right, the boot tracks disappeared off north-westerly, heading towards the river. The trees and scrub closed in on him, as if to allow him protection from the evil to his rear. He had a task to do and he would do it without help from anyone else.

After about half an hour, he arrived at the place where the path he was on joined the path running east to west. This was the path he had used that first day, when all this catastrophe had begun. Wearily, he turned right and after about ten minutes, spotted the small path heading south to the bay of the reeds. He approached the hut, where he could see and hear Stephan and Ivan hard at work. Stephan saw him first and waved him over.

"Glad you're back," he said heartily, then noticing Yuri's pallid expression, he enquired concernedly, "are you OK, you look like you've seen a ghost?"

Yuri shook his head and replied, "No ghosts Stephan, only what were once real people." He then told a horrified Stephan and Ivan what he had found. They both baulked at his watered-down description of the caravan site and he finished with, "I need to get a spade, return to the spot and give those youngsters a decent burial." At their offer of help Yuri replied, "Thanks, but I wouldn't want you to see what I have just seen. Give me a couple of hours and I'll put those kids to rest, all I need is a spade and some wire-cutters which are back on the island, don't worry, I won't be long."

"Hang on," said Ivan, "there's a spade here in the hut, I brought it over here last week and you can have my wire-cutters, I carry them around in my pack." He hurried off to get the things, returning and handing them to Yuri. "Are you sure we can't be of assistance?" he asked helpfully.

"No thanks Ivan," replied Yuri, "It's OK, I can cope." He picked up the spade, shoved the wire-cutters into his belt and made his way back to the caravan in the woods.

Yuri's journey back through the woods was made with a heavy heart. Unanswered questions rampaged through his brain and he was not looking forward to the next couple of hours. But he knew he must be strong for the children's sake and this helped to psyche him up for the grisly task ahead. After forty minutes or so, he once again stood at the carnage site. He wept inwardly as he cut each of the kids down and laid them to rest in a grave deep in the woods, where the flowers grew in profusion, as the sun smiled down through the branches of the alders and pines. He knelt for a long time, his mind in prayer, for the lost lives of four children who would never have the chance to grow to maturity. They had committed no crimes, except that of being in the same area as the SS. His job done, he bid them a final farewell and returned to the burned-out caravan with its three occupants, charred beyond recognition. There's nothing for it, he thought, I'm going to have to bury these people as well. Sadly, he dug another grave close to where the children lay and dragged the corpses over to it as best he could. Finally, he stood back and said another prayer for all seven individuals, hefted his spade on to his left shoulder and trudged back to those waiting for him. The day was fading fast as he made his weary way down to the bay of the reeds. Stephan and Ivan had long since returned to the island with a full raft of logs, so he was marooned here. He was wondering what he should do to attract one of the party to bring back the boat, when through the entrance to the bay it appeared, Alayna paddling, along with Uncle Yenisei. They pulled up against the shore and Yuri was able to get on board and settled, before they pushed off for the island. No-one spoke as they made the short journey across the water and beached the boat.

"Thanks for that," said a downcast Yuri, "I didn't know how to attract your attention."

"Alayna was watching from the ridge," said Yenisei. "Once Ivan and Stephan returned and told us what you were doing, she watched for you returning along the path."

"I couldn't have you swimming back," Alayna said with a gentle smile, "we knew you'd had an awful day. There's food on the table, when you're ready." Then she reached out her hand towards him, he took it gratefully and the three of them climbed the steps and made their way back to the cave with its aura of calming serenity.

The rest of the party greeted Yuri with a mixture of compassion and relative understanding. They were eating and engaged in light conversation, but all were aware of his situation. He sat down heavily and Alayna brought him some stew with a couple of slices of bread. He ate hungrily, suddenly realising that it had been some time since he had last eaten. He listened to the quiet banter around him and after a while, began to join in, as the pall of tragedy in his head began to diminish. Ivan and Stephan had been very busy, cutting and chopping logs. They had made two trips across from the bay, each time loaded with a mass of ready timber for the stove and fires.

"Has anyone seen anything of the Colonel?" enquired Yuri.

"We found him awake about an hour ago," answered Giselle, "he had a little stew and bread, then went back to sleep. The effects of his wounds were apparent and he was clearly suffering, but there was no sign of bleeding through the bandages. We also gave him a cup of Brandy, which we hope may alleviate the pain somewhat. I'll sleep in there with him tonight, he may need me to adjust his position, or get him something."

"That's fine," replied Yuri, "did anyone build up another bed?"

"Yes," replied Stephan, "Ivan and I knocked one up when we returned the first time with a load of logs, after we'd spoken to you. I'm sure Alayna will be comfortable on it."

Alayna nodded and smiled. "I'm sure I will," she said "and thank you, both of you," to Ivan and Stephan.

"Well," said Yuri, "I'd better do a sweep of the island before settling down. Fancy a walk Alayna?" She smiled gloriously in reply and Yuri picked up the binoculars before the two of them left. Outside, the wind had eased right down. The pale, setting sun hung like a burning wheel over the western forests. Yuri shivered as the sight brought back memories of earlier in the day. Alayna sensed his torment, moved closer to him and put her arms around him. She squeezed him tightly as he reciprocated.

"Was it really so bad, my darling," she asked gently.

"Worse than you could ever imagine," he replied hoarsely.

"Then you must tell me if the pain becomes too unbearable," she added, "we could talk it through whenever you feel the weight dragging you down. I don't want to make you divulge anything you're not ready to admit, but know I'm here if you need me."

Yuri pulled her tighter to him, feeling her steady heart beat through his chest. He held her this way for a few moments longer before saying, "Thanks Alayna, I can't really describe how I'm feeling, but knowing you're here, fills me with joy and more comfort than you will ever know."

With that, he released her from his tight embrace, took her hand and between them, they climbed up to the top of the ridge. The country around was silent, the shadows lengthening from the west. The past weeks had seen the war fade from their immediate surroundings and then, within a day, it had all come flooding back. The arrival of the injured Colonel and now the discovery of more SS atrocities, had sharpened Yuri's resolve. Alayna now shivered, for she understood that her man would not take the last twenty-four hours lightly. He would demand justice and that meant putting himself back into danger.

She wanted to scream, to implore him to stay safely with her, but instead, she simply said, "Whatever you decide, I will support you one hundred percent. I love you and I don't want to lose you, but you must do whatever it takes to bring peace to our lands."

He saw the pent up emotion in her eyes and died inwardly. She would be impossible to leave, but leave he must and in those few short sentences, he knew she had laid herself bare.

"Let's enjoy our time together now, while we can," he said softly. "The war will be upon us again, soon enough." So they left the ridge and walked together down towards the cave. How many millions had been in their position over the centuries? A man, a woman and a parting into danger. They both knew that some came back together, they also knew that many didn't.

When they were safely back inside the cave, they prepared for sleep. Giselle had already moved in with the Colonel, the others were getting ready. Yuri moved Alayna's bed so that they were laid across from each other, close to the outer door. He wanted to be near her, but resisted the temptation of being too close. Sex was out of the question, with too many people in such close proximity and he needed to be able to hear anything problematic outside. With that thought in mind he placed the beds about a yard apart, close enough, but not overly so. The darkness after the candles and Paraffin lamps were snuffed out was intense. He reached out for her hand and lay there, connected to her. Feeling her strength pulsing through him, helped to banish the feelings of doom that crept unannounced into his mind. His last thought before sleep overcame him, was that he loved her and she loved him in return. It was enough.

Yuri came out of his slumbers with a start. He listened intently and heard the Colonel groan in pain, Giselle, gently admonishing him.

"It's all right Sergei," she spoke soothingly, "sleep and the body will look after itself. We're all here, don't be afraid." With that, the grunts of pain lessened and after a few more minutes, silence once again reigned. Yuri laid listening in the dark, trying to discern its secrets. But nothing seemed out of place, so he settled back down and drifted off again. He awoke with the dawn, glowing dully through the deer hide door. He felt refreshed and alert. He had heard no other sounds from the Colonel as the night progressed and hoped he was settled and regaining his strength. As silently as he could, he turned over and peered across to where Alayna was still sleeping softly, snuggled deep into her blankets, her hair like a sleepy ebony storm across her pillow. He was gladdened, just to look at her. As softly as he could, he pulled on his boots, picked up his jacket and opened the outer door. He looked back at her and realised she was awake. He bent down and kissed her.

"I'm just going for a look around," he whispered, "no need to get up yet." She answered him with a smiling yawn and stretched herself expansively.

"Don't be too long," she said sleepily. He nodded and stepped out into the early light. A heavy dew clung to the grass and trees and his feet made little noise as he completed his island tour. A thick, cloying mist surrounded everything and the silence was made even more intense by its ghostly cloak of invisibility. Somewhere out in the lake, a fish plopped its greeting to a grey, motionless morning. Yuri shivered, it was time to get back inside.

As he neared the cave entrance, he became aware of a commotion going on inside. He pushed through the outer door and into the candle lit interior. Alayna had left her bed, as had all the others and were now congregating around the entrance to the side bedroom. He could hear Giselle talking soothingly to an obviously irate Colonel, who was raging at everyone and anyone who he could vent his anger on.

 "What's happening?" asked a bemused Yuri, "is Sergei having a seizure?"

 "He seems to be losing his mind," answered Stephan from inside the open doorway, "for the last five minutes he's been delirious, ranting and raving and threatening anyone who tries to get near him. Perhaps you could try and reason with him."

Yuri pushed past Stephan and Ivan and moved into the bedroom where Alayna, Yenisei and Giselle were trying to address the wild ramblings of the Colonel. Sergei's face was demonic and his eyes rolled relentlessly around in their sockets. A dribble of spittle eked out from between his lips, as his mouth tried to form words, words that had no apparent logic or continuity.

"Heydrich," he spluttered, then, "Romanov's" then, "all as bad as each other," followed by, "wolves, I'm being eaten by wolves, save meeeeeeeee".

Yuri took command of the situation in one decisive movement. He pushed past a clearly horrified Giselle, grabbed the Colonel by the shoulders and then back handed him across his face. The Colonel reacted to the slap as if shot. He stared at Yuri, comprehension beginning to return to his bloodshot eyes. His body lost its rigidity and he lay back onto his bed.

"Yuri," he croaked, "what, why?"

"It's alright Sergei," gentled Yuri, "you were having a bad dream, a nightmare. Do you remember?"

The old man shook his head, "I remember nothing," he admitted, "apart from the fact that you hit me. Did you really hit me Yuri?"

"You were shouting and raging at everyone Sergei," said a relieved Yuri, "They couldn't understand why you were so aggressive. You have been my mentor for a good many months now and I know how you conduct yourself. This was totally out of character. I hit you because you were in danger of demeaning yourself, in front of your friends, those who love and respect you. It was only a lapse, due to your condition. Now, Giselle is here, she will look after you, as she has been for the last couple of days. It's time for rest now. We'll talk again later. Do you feel calmer now?"

The Colonel nodded, "Yes Yuri, I feel calmer. I'm sorry Giselle if I was being disruptive. I do appreciate what you have been doing, what you have all been doing for me. I just need rest."

With that, he closed his eyes and within moments was sleeping peacefully. Yuri motioned to the others to leave him and the party moved back into the main interior of the cave.

"Thanks for that Yuri," said a clearly relieved Giselle, "I just couldn't cope with him. He had been restless all through the night, one minute being hot and perspiring, the next cold and shivery. I tried to keep pace with his wanderings, but that last episode was beyond my control."

"It's just the fever within him," answered Yuri, "that coupled with the fact that he's not in control of his own destiny at the moment. He's relying on others and it's something he's never had to deal with before. I think he'll be OK from now on, but if he does lapse again, you know what to do."

"I couldn't possibly hit him," said an appalled Giselle.

"Oh, I think you could," answered a positive Yuri, "remember, it's for his benefit, we're secondary to his long-term recovery. You can make the difference, you are making the difference. If he needs more encouragement, then you can administer it, OK?"

Giselle smiled tentatively, "I will try," she said, "for Sergei's sake."

"Good girl," said Yuri confidently, "we all need the Colonel back to as he was before. Let's all carry on with this thought in mind. With our help, he will pull through."

The rest of the party nodded in agreement and began to return to the things they were going to do before the Colonel's aberration. Alayna gave Yuri a squeeze and a 'well done' smile as Giselle slipped back into the bedroom to keep a closer eye on her patient. Ivan and Stephan, who were becoming inseparable in their allocated tasks, started to get their gear together for another foray in the lumber business. Yenisei was deep in thought, as he tended to be these days.

"Are you OK uncle?" asked Yuri, "you seem absorbed in the complexities of some ideas that may or may not affect us all. Are you waiting for the Colonel to shed light on them?"

Yenisei smiled and said, "Ah, Yuri, the complexities of life are so far reaching. Yes, a fit Sergei would be most welcome, but I'm focusing on surviving the next six months. Winter is almost upon us and we are still ill prepared. Bear with me, my boy, we shall discuss it when Sergei is back with us. Now you be off and see if you can rustle up some game, perhaps even some potatoes?"

"Good God," said an exasperated Yuri, "I'd completely forgotten about potatoes. There may be farms or smallholdings about the area where they have been cultivated. I'll have a look today while I'm out. Why have I totally disregarded the obvious?"

He shook his head in bewilderment. Yenisei slapped him on the back. "Well, we've remembered now," he said pointedly, "better late than never eh?"

Yuri laughed and moved over to where Alayna was organising the making of more winter clothing. "More furs and skins would be helpful," she replied to his questioning look, "We will all need to keep warm and dry."

"Listen," he confided, "I'm going to the east side of the mainland today. I'll be after game, but I also want to check around the area to see if anyone else has been travelling or hiding nearby. I'll be back around five and I'll take the boat, Ivan and Stephan will have the raft. Keep your ears and eyes open if you go out."

"I will my darling," she said gently, "be careful and safe journey."

He kissed her, picked up his gear and with a parting wave, headed off down to the bay. Stephan and Ivan had just pushed off and were paddling the raft over to the bay in the reeds. The mist had evaporated in the sunshine and the day appeared cloudless, if but a little cool. He dragged the boat out of its hiding place, launched it and stepped in, settling himself towards the rear. He made good progress and was soon finding his way through the scrub surrounding the oaks on the path, having beached the boat and secured it. The path was devoid of any watchers or walkers, whether animal or human. He hefted the pack onto his back and set off towards the east. After about fifty yards, he spotted the fork between the trees that led southwards, the path running alongside the eastern shores of the lake. Today he was carrying the crossbow, as well as the rifle, and across his shoulders was the yoke. He could balance two carcasses across this and he was after deer or wild pig, a bear would be a bit heavy. Studying the ground as he went along, he saw plenty of old tracks, most only a hint after the recent rains. The air was definitely cooler, but the sky held promise of a decent day. He carried on through bogs and clearings, the leaves on the trees turning browner in readiness for the season to come. His thoughts returned to the Colonel, who was really going through a bad patch, but maybe he was now over the hump. Giselle was showing a more than close attentiveness towards Sergei, which appeared additional to just friendly concern. She would be a good twenty years younger than the Colonel, but Yuri knew that love could be forthcoming between many age groups. With the uncertainty of their situation, as with he and Alayna, he perceived a bond between the two of them. Perhaps Alayna might know something, after all, she was in closer proximity to the pair of them than he was. He would have to ask her.

The morning was almost done when he approached the house that Valery and Alexei had passed and mentioned, all those months ago. As before, the house was abandoned, but he rummaged around the area surrounding it and came across a few clamps of cultivated potatoes. Why he had not thought about finding potatoes before, he couldn't think. But now, here was a source of nourishment and he immediately began to uncover the soil from around them. The crop was a good one and he soon filled the hessian sack he had brought with him for just this purpose. Satisfied, he left the rest for another day, hid the full sack by the side of the path for his return and carried on towards the south. It wasn't long before he reached the wider path which ran from east to west. There had been much traffic along its length and he studied the ground for clues as to what had been moving along it. Horse hooves and wheel tracks were much in evidence, as were booted feet. The convoys of stores and supplies from Poland towards the front appeared to be still quite frequent, judging by all the discernible signs. This was worth remembering, as their supply of perishables such as flour and tinned goods, were ever becoming less as they worked through them. Perhaps they could mount a raid on the supply trains? It was worth considering and he would put it to uncle Yenisei at the earliest opportunity.

The afternoon drifted on, as he scouted around along the wide highway. Soon he would need to return and he had come up with no fresh meat so far. Time to concentrate on the immediate problem. He back tracked to where the northern path joined the one he was on and headed off back towards his sack of potatoes. He had noticed several places where deer had crossed and re-crossed this path and he also knew where he could find wild pigs. He travelled on, through the now innumerable bogs, surrounded by dense scrub and impenetrable foliage. He could remember where the most recent deer tracks were and made steady progress towards them. Far off, he heard the hammering of a woodpecker, always a salve to his mind, remembering where he had buried Grigori. He arrived at the house in the woods and picked up the hidden potato stash, always alert to the possibility of stumbling over something unpleasant. After another few miles, he spotted where deer had crossed and decided to try his luck with them. With that in mind, he stripped off most of his gear and hid it behind some screening rocks, away from prying eyes. Then, armed with the now fully compressed crossbow, a bolt fitted in place, he drifted into the deeper woods. He had not gone far when he came up short. Something was stirring up ahead and he moved cautiously forward, sniffing the air. The trees were close together at this point and he ghosted between them, his senses alert with anticipation. Suddenly, he saw a flicker of movement. He froze, straining with peripheral vision, to discern where and what caused it. Before him were several deer, cropping the lush grass that carpeted the woodland floor. Regulating his breathing, he raised the crossbow gently into position, aimed at a suitably large doe and let fly. His aim was perfect. The doe collapsed in a heap, it had been a clean kill. The rest of the deer scattered, they would not settle again for some time, thought Yuri. He moved over to the doe and hefted her onto his shoulder. The crossbow had done its job again, the silent killer. Back at the path, he tied the doe's forelegs together and hooked them over one side of the yoke, while the sack of potatoes balanced his load on the other side. Making sure he was still alone, he loaded himself up and headed for home. The deer skin would make wonderful soft, warm leggings for Alayna and for Giselle too. The meat would be used over the next few weeks. The afternoon slipped by as he made his way north. After three or four miles, he came to the area where he knew wild pigs roamed. The load was a painful burden to his back and a pig would add to it, but he decided to look anyway. He hid his gear by the side of the path and stepped into the trees to his right, knowing that the pigs liked to hang around a small lake about three hundred yards from the path. His crossbow was loaded and ready and he made slow and cautious progress through the thick foliage. The pigs were drinking and rolling around in the mud, oblivious to his stalking presence. However, two were standing guard, sniffing the wind as he approached. They were becoming restless, probably because they were picking up a hint of his scent, from a wind that was blowing slightly towards them. Yuri decided to take a long shot, almost seventy yards. He knew the crossbow was powerful enough for the distance, the hardest thing was to find a place that offered a clear shot, without spooking them. He ghosted through the trees to his right, trying to keep his scent away from them, until he found a position where he could guarantee a clear strike. The two guard pigs were still acting skittishly, so he decided to go for one of them. Slowly he took aim and loosed off. The pig went down without a murmur, the others charging off with a succession of grunts and squeals. Good, he thought, another clean kill. He dragged the pig back to the path and hung it by its tied forelegs to the side with the bag of potatoes. Once he'd loaded himself with his gear, he lugged the yoke into place and this time, made for home.

The journey back to the island was straightforward, if backbreaking. He had to take a few respite breathers, to ease his sore limbs, but made it across the lake as the clock struck six. Alayna was there to meet him and she cooed excitedly at the deer, pig and potatoes. "You have been busy", she remarked happily, "I was hoping you might find me some doe skin".

"How's the Colonel," asked Yuri.

"Actually, he's improving," she replied, "he ate some more at lunch time and Giselle thinks he might have something tonight."

"That's great," enthused Yuri, "I hoped he would make progress today. I suppose the main thing is to get his bandages off and see what that reveals."

"Yes," Alayna replied with a hint of concern, "but he's been talking a little with Giselle and making sense."

Yuri nodded, satisfied that the Colonel was at least showing signs of coming out of his delirium. He and Alayna carried the potatoes back to the cave and then he returned for the pig and deer. He hung the two carcasses in the outer cave. Tomorrow, Stephan and Ivan, would begin the task of butchering them. All of a sudden he felt hungry and moved into the main cave where the others were congregating for a meal that Alayna and Giselle had prepared. Stephan and Ivan talked of having a good day. They'd felled eight trees and dragged them back to the hut, where they had stacked them with the rest that were already there. All being well, they would finish cutting them into useable lengths tomorrow, then they would stack them inside the hut. The hut would then be full to the brim. Yuri was impressed and told them of his day, the clean kills of the deer and pig, the finding of the potatoes and a search of the area to the south, which had revealed no immediate problems. He re-affirmed to everyone, that the wide paths from the river Bug towards the east, were being well used on an almost daily basis. They would need to keep a constant eye on the woods around the island, as there was always a chance that someone could head north from these paths, as the SS had done before.

Giselle left the table and took some food into the Colonel. After a while, she emerged with a happy smile and said to them all, "He's eaten all I took in and he appears to be settled and coherent. He asked if you could drop in and see him Yuri, I think he has things to tell."

Yuri was suddenly serious. He got up and disappeared into the side bedroom. The Colonel was laid down, his head resting on a thick pillow. He smiled tentatively at Yuri's concerned expression, his face still taut and drawn, but he was beginning to show a little colour. "I'm sorry not to have told you before," he began in a quiet hoarse voice, "but Alexei and Valery were fine when I left them. Perhaps tomorrow I could give you a more comprehensive overview of the days after we parted."

 "That's OK Sergei," Yuri replied gently, "I now know all I need to for the time being. It's great to see you making progress and looking so much better."

The Colonel nodded slightly, "Well, I still feel like shit," he whispered, "but Giselle has been wonderful."

 "She'll keep a good eye on you," promised Yuri, "now get some rest and we'll see what tomorrow brings."

He gave the Colonel a parting smile and went back into the main area. "He's coming along fine," he told them, "and Alexei and Valery are both well."

 "That's really good news","" said Yenisei, "I like those two boys a lot. Do you think we could all get together tomorrow Yuri and have a council of war? There's things I think we need to thrash out, otherwise I'm not being much use. Everyone else is doing something to further the cause, but all I do is think and plan. I suppose it's a kind of easy job for an old man, but I would welcome all your inputs."

Yuri laughed at Yenisei's put down of himself. "That fertile mind of yours has been in overdrive ever since we arrived back here," he said with a sincere smile, "I think we all could benefit from what you have to say."

"Then tomorrow it is," laughed Yenisei, "we'll see just how fertile I have been. Anyway, I'm for sleep now, I'll see you all in the morning."

Stiffly, he got up and went over to his bed, the rest of the party also deciding to join him. Yuri did his nightly tour of the island before turning in. Once the outer door was closed on his return, he slipped off his boots, snuffed out the final candle, leaned over and gave Alayna a kiss before snuggling down into his blankets. Tomorrow would look after itself, he thought, now I need some sleep.

Morning came with the sound of heavy rain splattering against the outer door. Yuri awoke and grimaced to himself. He was not keen on leaving his nice warm blankets, but he had to go and have a look around, he couldn't become complacent. Tugging on his boots, he slipped into his poncho and crept out into the outer cave. The rain was certainly coming down heavily and he pulled a fur cap out of his inner pocket and placed it over his head as he moved off from the outer caves protection. The steel grey sky reflected from the puddles, cold and pitiless in its stark demeanour. It lashed his face as he circumnavigated the island and he was glad to see nothing out of the ordinary, as he arrived back at the cave. The others, apart from Giselle and the Colonel, were all up when he arrived back inside and he could smell the heady aroma of fresh coffee, bubbling on the stove.

"Looks like its set in for the day," he said disappointedly, "still, we can always do jobs in here, out of the rain."

The others nodded their assent, as Giselle came out of the side bedroom. "How's the Colonel?" asked Stephan as Giselle picked up a mug and filled it full of coffee.

"Actually, he had a very quiet night," she replied, "he's awake and demanding coffee, so I think he's improving. I didn't have to get up to him at all during the night. I think today we should have a look at his wounds and maybe put on fresh bandages."

"That's a good idea," said Yuri, "it's been a few days since he was last checked out. When he's ready, give me a shout and I'll come and help you get him out of bed."

"Thanks Yuri," she replied happily, "I'd better give him his coffee now before he starts getting grumpy."

She disappeared off into the side bedroom and the others sat around the table chatting. "I have something for Sergei," said Ivan, "it's something I knocked up the other day."

Reaching over, he produced a crutch that had been standing against the wall. "I hope it's the right height for him," he said hopefully, "but it should help him to get about, if only for the short term."

"That's wonderful Ivan," said Yuri, "I'm sure it will be fine, it certainly looks good."

Stephan hefted the crutch and then passed it to Yenisei. Yenisei was admiring the beauty of Ivan's work when the side bedroom door opened and out stepped the Colonel, leaning on Giselle for support.

"Sergei," Yuri said happily, "it's great to see you up and about. How are you feeling?"

The answer came from Giselle who was taking great care of the Colonel as he hobbled across to the nearest chair. "He's a lot better, but he won't stay in bed any longer. I won't be responsible if he has a relapse."

"Nonsense woman," grumbled the Colonel, "just prop me up in this chair and stop you're fussing."

Giselle glowered at him. "Ignore him," she admonished to the others, "he's just old and cantankerous."

"Less of the old," the Colonel snarled in return, then his mood softened, "my nurse says I have to be good," he said gently, "and as she is always right, I'd better conform."

Giselle gave him a withering glance as he seated himself more comfortably on the high- backed chair, but her eyes softened as she settled him and said, "the first thing we need to do is remove your bandages. Now you can chat away to your friends while Alayna and I do this, but no histrionics and no sudden movements, otherwise, it's back to bed for you my lad."

The Colonel grunted and shrugged, shaking his head in resignation. Ivan then produced the crutch and handed it to the Colonel. "Now that is a truly fine gift Ivan," said the Colonel happily, "I will use it whenever I need to get around, especially going outside."

"That will not be in the near future," Giselle retorted, "one step at a time Sergei, now sit here." He sat back in the chair and allowed her and Alayna to raise his left leg and support it on a stool. Then they began to remove the bandage.

"Maybe you can you fill us in with what happened after we were separated at the camp," said Yuri, "Uncle Yenisei has a lot of questions for you, but that may have to wait until tomorrow?"

The Colonel nodded, his face becoming more serious as he began. "All in all, we were lucky to escape with so few casualties. Having said that, we

397

did lose one hundred and fourteen men, according to the roster. The defence plan worked reasonably well, but we could never have predicted that the SS would get into the camp so easily."

"That was courtesy of Vladimir," butted in Yuri savagely. "However, he eventually met his doom."

The Colonel nodded as he digested the information and then continued. "As it was, the western guards spotted the main attackers crawling through the long grass and the alert was sounded. But they were already inside the north-eastern corner in large numbers and if it hadn't have been for those brave defenders in that area, who virtually gave their lives for the rest of us, we would never have had a chance to prepare and we would probably have been overrun. The worst thing that could possibly have happened, was the turning of that damned cannon. Had it been able to get off another four or five shots, we would have been in deep trouble. Every shell tore our defences apart. Once you had destroyed it Yuri, we fell back in good order. The horse handlers scattered the horses and made good their escape, while we concentrated on getting the families and Yenisei's party out. By this time I'd taken a bullet in the shoulder and I was feeling pretty groggy. Alexei and Valery got me away from the main fighting and they made sure that the rest of our men, protected our rear. The SS were very strong, but we came into our own once we got into the broken country to the south. It took less of us to hold them up and eventually, after a few hours, their attack ground to a halt. By this time, the vast majority of us had travelled quite a distance from the camp and we made for the other camp you previously told me about Yuri. Once there we were able to lick our wounds and take stock."

During his discourse, Giselle and Alayna had removed the bandages on his thigh and shoulder. Amazingly, both wounds were showing positive signs of recovery. Gone were the bluey-black bruising and puss on his shoulder and his thigh had lost its inflamed greeny-black appearance. The skin was beginning to knit back together in all four wounds, so the girls decided on more of the same. Ointment was spread on each and fresh bandages applied. The Colonel seemed able and willing to carry on, so he took up the story again.

 "After a few days, we returned to the old camp. The SS had removed and buried their dead, it's impossible to say how many casualties they suffered, but I'm inclined to think that we hurt them badly. They'll think twice about trying to storm one of our camps again. We buried our dead in a mass grave, there were too many to try to bury them individually. However, we did bury Katerina, I think you probably knew about her demise and a couple of Indians from your party Yenisei who were burnt beyond recognition. We were told by one of your staff that they were both doctors."

Yenisei nodded gravely and sighed deeply, "they came to us at Abakan many years ago," he said sadly. "Their family and my wife's family were related and they did much to build and run our hospital. They will be sadly missed."

"We torched the whole place when we left," continued the Colonel, "as a mark of respect to all those who fell. The past weeks have been spent getting back to some sort of normality. Alexei and Valery have been constantly going out on raids, seeking out the SS and executing them wherever they can. They are both committed to searching out these demonic killers, as I am and they keep finding more and more examples of their atrocities. They send their best to all of you, by the way. As far as news of the actual war is concerned, it is still going badly for our forces. By various ways and means, I have been able to ascertain that we are still taking enormous numbers of casualties, whether dead, captured or displaced, as we are. Leningrad is still totally surrounded, Kiev has fallen and the fascists are moving towards Stalingrad and Odessa. In the centre, they are only a stone's throw from Moscow. Many citizens have left and Stalin is beginning to rip up our factories and move them east behind the Urals, where they will be re-established, out of the enemy's reach. Concentration camps are springing up everywhere, there are at least six around Minsk. In Minsk itself, the SS have established a Ghetto for the Jews, similar to the one in Warsaw. There are about four thousand trapped in the Ghetto at the moment. The SS have built a barbed wire barrier around the Ghetto which they patrol constantly. However, there are no fixed guards as such and some Jews have managed to escape when there are no patrols present, by crawling under the wire. They then make their way to join up with the partisans. There is a Communist brigade active in Minsk, led by a man called Hersch Smoliar. He liaises with the partisans in the marshes and between them, they have a budding relationship developing. It would appear that the SS are a mixture of men from different organisations like the secret police and the Waffen SS, they being the protective wing of the Nazi Party. Many foreigners have joined the Waffen SS as a means to do what they enjoy, murdering and terrorising people. Their job is to follow behind the Wehrmacht's main thrust and murder civilians, especially Jews, by shooting. For this they are known in Germany as 'Einsatzgruppen', literally for our purposes, "death squads."

"There are very few positive things to report. However, the number of displaced persons is increasing steadily. There are thousands now in the woods and marshes and significant steps are being taken to weld these ex-soldiers into some sort of partisan brigade, an almost regular fighting unit, its job being to harry or destroy, supply lines, telephone lines and the transport system. I suppose it's the same as we have been doing, but on a grander scale. Lastly, I come to myself. I left Alexei and Valery in charge and set out for here about a week ago. The initial part of the journey went well, but then I was ambushed by a group of five soldiers, who I managed to see off, but not before one of them had got his bayonet into me. I left three of them dead, the other two just disappeared off into the woods. It shows that not all the displaced individuals are fighting back. Some, like these, have taken to banditry, thinking only of themselves. Then my scent was picked up by a pack of wolves. Somehow I managed to evade them, right until I was only a few miles from here. I shot two of them and the rest ripped their former partners to pieces, deciding that a free meal was better than a man with a hand gun. I was running on empty when I arrived at the northern landing area and hoped that you, Yuri, would still be doing your early morning recce of the island. Otherwise, I hadn't a clue as to how I was going to make you aware that I was here. Had you not been on the island, I don't know what I would have done."

The Colonel lapsed into silence, as the others digested his vivid account. Yenisei was the first to offer a reply.

"It would appear Sergei that we are most fortunate to be all here together again. You have had your share of hardships as we have. Yuri was magnificent in guiding us all away from the camp that day and bringing us here to this magical oasis. It was he who exposed Vladimir for what he was, although I had the honour of putting a bullet through the cretin's brain. We managed to relieve him of his papers and other documents. In his boots, we found what are probably codes and cyphers. Because of this find, we looked in Yuri's old boots and found similar papers regarding Gruber. I have studied these and although I have a limited knowledge of German, I think this Vladimir Konchesko was really Hans Liebermann. Does that ring any bells with you?"

The Colonel was suddenly fully alert. "Did you say Liebermann, Hans Liebermann?" Yenisei nodded. "Then, my friend, it would appear that you have eliminated 'Rhine Maiden', the southern insurgent. Yuri disposes of Kuhmo Wolf and now his uncle gets rid of Rhine Maiden. What is it with this family, are you just lucky or what?"

Yuri and Yenisei looked at each other and laughed. "This is great news," enthused the Colonel. "When we were trying to identify Gruber, Liebermann and whoever 'Brandenburg Gate' is, earlier in the year, I had no idea that they would succumb so quickly. It is indeed fortunate that you both were able to do what you did. Mother Russia is a profoundly safer place now that they are eliminated."

"I would also like to mention another pressing matter," said Yenisei seriously. "If we are to stay here through the winter, we really need to try and increase our stocks of tinned food, medical supplies, flour, coffee, tea, sugar, salt and if possible, butter. On the other hand, I think I should try to get back to Abakan, the main reason being that my presence here puts each and every one of you in mortal peril. As I said before, I have read through Gruber and Vladimir's papers and if Sergei interprets them as I think I have, then we must return east before winter sets in properly."

Giselle called a halt while she fussed around the Colonel, fetching him water and some bread with butter to eat. He chewed methodically, nodded his assent and said, "Those papers you were talking about Yenisei, do you have them? I'm starting to feel a little tired and my nurse is becoming more and more agitated, so to please her, I'd better go for a lie down. I can still read for a while though can't I?"

Giselle frowned and tutted, but then seeing his pleading expression, relented. "Just for a while then Sergei, but you must remember you need to build up your strength. An hours reading for a full meal tonight, deal?"

The Colonel shrugged playfully and replied, "Do we have any pork and perhaps some potatoes? I'm feeling hungry, but I wouldn't want to put you out."

"Away with you," she scolded, "don't try my patience. The sooner you're up and healing, the better it will be for all of us. Now, do I have to ask you again?"

"No, no, I'm going, as if I wouldn't," he answered grumpily and stood up, balanced himself on the crutch and turned to leave, Giselle following after him, but not before she'd given the others a quick, satisfied smile.

After the bedroom door closed behind them Ivan said, "They behave like an old married couple. You don't think that.................?"

Yuri shrugged, grinned and said to Alayna, "I think that something is in the wind, don't you?"

"Yes," she replied, "I'm more than happy for them."

The rest nodded their agreement and moved off to begin doing whatever they had planned to do. Yenisei beckoned Yuri to him and together, they walked outside into the cave entrance. The rain was still hammering down, the sky showing no remorse for its continued presence. Yuri was perplexed, wondering what was to come. Yenisei seemed tired and old, as if the weight of the world was on his shoulders. It boded ill for all of them.

"Yuri", he began, "I'm sorry to have to tell you this but…………."

His words were interrupted by a commotion going on inside the main cave. Yuri threw back the door and hurried inside to see the Colonel hobbling towards him, in a highly agitated state. Giselle was not far behind him calling, "Sergei, what are you doing, you need rest."

"Rest," the Colonel muttered, "there'll be no rest for us for some time. Yenisei, I presume you know what I'm talking about?"

Yenisei nodded, "then it's as I feared," the old man said bitterly. "My translation was correct."

"What the hell's going on," demanded Yuri, "and what is so important about a translation?"

Yenisei shrugged and sighed. "Perhaps we'd all better sit down and listen to what Sergei has to say," he said pointedly. "Things are moving out of our control. I'm not sure that I fully understand what Sergei has found out, but it affects us all."

The others arranged themselves around the table, Giselle making sure the Colonel was settled comfortably before he began. "I've read and re-read the papers that we obtained from Vladimir and Gruber and there are several points to discuss.

Firstly, I have four sheets pertaining to a list of codes. The Nazi's have devised a simple system of one, two or three letters to signify various words and phrases. They are organised in random sequences, where the receiver of a message could only translate what the message says, if they also have a copy of the code. I'm presuming that there are only four of these code sheets spread between the three insurgents and their senior handler. Any message the insurgents send, can be translated by the handler, but only him. OK so far?' The others glanced at each other, then nodded and the Colonel continued. 'The first two sheets contain everyday words and phrases like 'I', 'you', 'me' or 'five', 'five hundred', 'woods', marshes' etc. The third and fourth sheets, contain prominent Russians with their own identifying group of letters. They call the military 'Ivan's'. For example, Ivan 5 is General Berezovsky, in other words, me. Ivan 14 is Alexei, Ivan 15, Valery, the Avseyenko brothers. Zhukov is top Ivan with Timoshenko second. The accompanying letter codes are, for example, PT, which is Ivan 7 or XLY, Ivan 8. There is no logical order in which these letters appear. The fourth sheet is the one which contains the real horror of the Nazi system. There are ten names on this sheet, mostly academics and senior party leaders, but number 4 is Mikhail Korsakov, apparently a Siberian Warlord, who we all know as Yenisei. His code is Abakan Zulu. It also reads; 'known to be in the

407

Minsk area at outbreak of Barbarossa, travelling in several garishly painted caravans."

The Colonel paused to allow his last statement to sink in, then he continued. "At the bottom of the page it reads; [the SS are to eliminate all high-ranking members of the national government, the armed forces and prominent citizens, especially Jews, after interrogation. All persons on these lists will be targeted and exposed by Kuhmo Wolf, Rhine Maiden and Brandenburg Gate, to allow this purging of the Soviet system. Any associated family member will also be interrogated before being shot]. We know that Vladimir used this code system to flash a message to that Stork that was often seen around the camp. The SS knew that Alexei, Valery, Yenisei and I were in that camp. They also know that we all escaped and are still at large. You can be sure that they will now double their efforts to locate us, especially since they have displayed posters offering up to one hundred thousand Roubles, for information leading to the arrest of any of us. Our own people will be more than tempted. We can trust no-one."

With that, the Colonel lapsed into silence. The others all occupied by their own thoughts. Eventually, it was Yuri who spoke.

"So," he said, "it looks like it's up to me. I am not on this list, so am not a named target. Yenisei, Ivan, Stephan, Giselle and Alayna must be spirited away to the east before anything happens to change that. Uncle Yenisei, do you know what we should do?"

The old man was sat with his eyes closed, a look of bleak resignation on his face. Then he opened his eyes and with a grim smile said, "I fear you are right, my boy. I was thinking that the quickest way to Abakan would be by plane. Do you know where I could get one?"

Yuri was startled by his uncle's flat question. "A plane," he said incredulously, "who would fly it if we could get one?"

"I could," replied Stephan, "I've been flying for years. German planes are not so different to Russian ones. It's a definite possibility."

"But where the hell would we get one?" retorted an irritated Yuri.

"Steal one from the Germans," answered the Colonel quietly. Yuri began to reply and then decided against it. Getting to his feet he paced around the room, his mind in turmoil.

"We just go and commandeer a plane and fly it over five hundred miles of hostile country, knowing that the skies are dominated by German fighters. And when we get to where we are going, our own people will shoot us out of the sky because we're displaying the swastika. It's madness, utter madness."

"It may be madness, my boy," said Yenisei gently, "but once the winter sets in, we won't be going anywhere."

"Look," said the Colonel, "the fascists are not in Moscow yet, as far as we know. Getting to Abakan would be impossible, no plane has that sort of range. But we could get beyond Moscow. That is our first priority, delivering our non-combatants into safety, wouldn't you agree Yuri?"

"Most definitely," answered Yuri, "but I still don't know where we can get a plane."

"You need to speak to Alexei, he wants to hit an airfield," said The Colonel, "mind you, you'll have to go and see him by yourself. I couldn't make it and won't be able to for quite a while."

Yuri thought it over, looking around the tense, worried faces and finally, came to a decision. "OK," he said softly, "I'll leave in the morning. Meantime, get ready to leave here. We know it's over one hundred and fifty miles to Minsk, so you need to be prepared and ready to leave when I get back. I'll try and sort something out while I'm away and hopefully, I'll bring some support back with me."

Chapter 14 – The Escape Plan unfolds

The morning came slowly out of a grey, brooding sky. The ragged clouds scudded airily across the heavens, driven by a cold north-westerly wind, the threat of more rain imminent. Yuri shivered as he completed his tour of the island. He had not slept well, his slumbers interrupted by nightmares of catastrophe. Their situation had turned from one of merely staying put to see out the winter, to one of having to flee eastward on a hair brained scheme, based on the acquisition of an aircraft. But uncle Yenisei's right, he thought ruefully. They could never simply walk through a war zone, not with their personnel, or stay here, with the risk of being sold out for a handful of Roubles. At least they would have a chance this way. His main concern was once the plane was airborne, then German fighters and flak guns would come into play. And once in Russian-held territory, how would the plane land in safety? So many if's and buts. Firstly though, he had to get to Alexei and Valery.

He opened the door into the main cave and stepped inside. The others were all up and preparing for the day. There was coffee brewing on the stove and its welcome aroma filled his nostrils. However, the mood in the room was muted and tense.

 "How's the Colonel, Giselle," Yuri enquired, "Did he have a good night?"

"Good enough," she replied, "and he's insisting on getting up today. I think he wants to start planning our departure with the other men."

Yuri nodded his understanding. He became aware that Alayna was hovering at his shoulder and she said gently, "I've packed plenty of food for your journey, plus a complete change of clothing. How long do you think it will be before you return?"

"I would prepare for two weeks," he replied, "and only if things go to plan." He spoke to the room in general. "Whatever you do, keep regular tours of the island. The SS can be anywhere at any time, so make sure you're not caught unawares. If one of you would be so kind as to ferry me across to the mainland, I'll be on my way. Don't forget, if we don't leave tracks, or make noise of any kind, or allow ourselves to be seen here, then no-one can be aware of our presence. Take care, I'll be back as soon as I can."

With a parting nod to the room, he hefted his pack, picked up his rifle and made for the door. Ivan was going to ferry him across, so with Alayna in tow, the three of them went down to the islands landing area. Ivan dragged out the boat while Yuri and Alayna said their goodbyes. She clung to him tightly, fearing the worst, then with a final kiss, she allowed him to climb into the boat. He raised his hand in farewell as the boat slid around the eastern edge of the island. Then she ran back up the steps and across to the north side, just in time to see him land and disappear into the screening trees, while Ivan returned the boat to the island. God speed, my love, she thought tearfully to herself. God speed.

Yuri strode along the path at a good pace. He had listened and searched for any signs of hidden enemies before stepping out and now, he moved with alertness and purpose. He was not a fan of protracted goodbyes, so he had deliberately got going as soon as he was able. The Colonel had furnished him with Aleksander's maps, which he, Yuri, Yenisei and Ivan had pored over yesterday afternoon, working out Yuri's best route. Of course, the hardest part of his departure had been saying goodbye to Alayna. It appeared that they would never be allowed to be together for long, but at least he had a definite goal to aim for, a safe return to her as soon as he possibly could. Until then, he would hold her close in his mind and spirit. The morning passed slowly by, the rain holding off at present. After a couple of miles, he had come across the place where the Colonel had faced down the wolves, the path and surrounding woods slashed and torn up as a result of frantic fighting, with scattered bones left hither and thither. He would have to remember that the wolves could be anywhere and so be on his guard. He had nodded a greeting to Woodpecker Knoll as he passed, Grigori's memory still weighing heavily on his mind. The morning passed into afternoon as he stopped for a rest near a branch in the trail. The rain, which had held off throughout the morning was now falling steadily, from a windswept iron grey sky. He was not too concerned about the rain, as it would help to wash out his tracks and scent. His only aim that day was to put as much distance between himself and the island as possible. He saw nothing and heard nothing, just the sound of his heartbeat and the odd footstep over stony ground. Evening came with no let-up in the rains relentless drive and he began to look out for somewhere to hole up for the night. He found it where a stream crossed north to south. He followed its winding confluence northwards for about five hundred yards and there, well-hidden within scrub and pines, he found an overhang under a small knoll, facing south and out of the wind and rain. After a quick, cold, meal he wrapped himself tightly into his blankets and fell into a tired sleep.

Morning came gently, the rain had eased overnight and the sky was a picture of washed out blue with the odd puff ball cloud sailing south-westwards. He breakfasted on water and a few biscuits before making his way stealthily back to the path. He paused there to sniff the wind and have a quick look at Aleksander's maps. Keep heading east, he thought. Yuri was young and fit and figured that he could walk at about five miles an hour normally, but with him having to be careful and in some cases, keeping off the main track through the woods, he reckoned he was doing about three miles an hour. That meant, that yesterday he had completed at least thirty miles. If he kept on at this rate, he would be at his destination sometime late tomorrow afternoon. However, he was under no illusions as to what might be standing in his way, so he resolved to tread carefully. The morning merged into afternoon as he marched on. He was now in more recent familiar terrain and he recognised several areas where he had been, when he had been training the recruits at their last Camp. His thoughts suddenly turned to Pavel Lensky, blown to smithereens by that rogue field gun. He had liked the man and knew he would be missed. He shuddered at the thought, here one minute, vaporised the next. Pavel would be avenged, Sergei would make sure of that. The afternoon wore on and he was becoming increasingly aware of other boot tracks, which were prevalent on his path and also those which merged in on paths from the left and the right. Whether they were friend or foe, he had no idea at this time, but it made him more aware of others using the same route. This was SS country, as he was pretty sure that he was almost due south of Minsk. He now searched around for somewhere to spend the night and found another overhang, deep in the trees and away from prying eyes. He ate greedily of the provisions packed for him by Alayna, washed it all down with water and was tucked up in his blankets as the sky became dark.

Morning saw him up with the sun and after a quick breakfast of biscuits, he once again set off on his journey. The morning mist clung to the trees making progress damp and cold, with visibility down to twelve or fourteen yards. Eventually, the sun burned through and he continued on, as the morning passed into afternoon. He halted for a brief rest around two o'clock, but was keen to press on and didn't waste too much time, easing his tired limbs. The miles were slowly ticking by and he was on schedule.

His progress was interrupted by the sudden interruption of gunfire from the north-west. He froze, unsure as to where all this cacophony was kicking off, but he knew that he was too exposed here on the main path. He ghosted into the trees, the noise still hammering away somewhere to his left and behind. Machine gun fire punctuated by single rifle rounds and the distinct 'crump' of mortars, battered away at his ears. Someone, somewhere, was having a pitched battle and he didn't want to get caught up in it. With that in mind, he moved silently through the trees, making for a vantage point to give him a better view of the terrain to the north and west. By now, the firing was becoming more sporadic and eventually, after another few minutes, died out altogether. Silence returned and with it, the fear of the unknown. He crested a small knoll and peered out from behind some screening pines and scrub, his scoped rifle searching for targets or signs of movement. The afternoon hung heavily in the air, as he searched for clues to his situation. Half an hour ticked by into an hour. Nothing. Perhaps whoever it was, had gone north or west or east or somewhere, apart from here. Then a distant movement caught his eye. He adjusted the scope slightly, using it as a monocular and scoured the woods to the west. There, through the trees, came a cavalcade of men, some on horseback and some on foot. There were several pack horses and two pairs hauling wagons. Within the group were what appeared to be citizens, including women and children? They moved purposely towards the path he had just vacated. Yuri panned the scope around the horsemen and walkers, looking for familiar faces. He knew this was a raiding party and sure enough, a single horseman snapped into focus. He grinned happily. Valery was leading the group. Satisfied that no-one else was following them, or that his position was vulnerable, he made his way back to the path and waited.

After about ten minutes, he spotted the party coming into view along the path. There were six horse riders at the front of the column, one being his friend. When they were about twenty yards away, Yuri stepped out from behind a tree. The riders stopped and stared, as Yuri held up his hand in greeting. Then the leader spurred his horse forward with a whoop. He clattered to a stop beside Yuri and a beaming Valery jumped down and embraced his friend.

After much back slapping and hugs Valery spoke, "Shit Yuri, you frightened me to death walking out like that. The others, are they OK?"

Yuri nodded, "Yes, even the Colonel. It was touch and go for a few days, but he seemed to be well on the mend when I left. Where's Alexei?"

Valery laughed, "Alexei has a new lady friend." At Yuri's quizzical look, he added with a twinkle in his eye, "she's fifteen hands high, shits in great piles and can run anything off its feet."

"A horse," said an astonished Yuri, "Alexei has a horse?"

"Not only that, he's forever swanning around the country righting wrongs, like that English Robin Hood. That's where he is now, robbing the fascists to give to the poor Russians." He then put back his head and laughed uproariously. "Anyway, let's get you safely away from here and back to our camp, then you can fill me in with all the gory details." Unhurriedly, Valery vaulted astride his horse and shouted, "Corporal, a horse for mister Petrovsky if you please."

"Right away sir," replied the corporal and within a few seconds, brought a black filly along for Yuri.

"Beats the hell out of walking," said Valery, "just blend in with everyone and let's be off. I want to be in camp before nightfall." Yuri did indeed blend in, as the party headed off westward. He called a greeting to some of the soldiers he had known from the old camp and settled in beside Pavel Lensky's old sergeant, who he knew quite well.

To Yuri's question the sergeant replied, "We've been on a people collection mission that turned into a bit of a raid. For a week or more we've been helping the Minsk partisans, in spiriting away as many Jews as possible from the Ghetto. They tell us when and basically, we turn up to keep the SS off their backs, while they make their escape. The Lieutenant was keen to get as many out as possible, like we did four days ago. We were successful and got away quietly, then one of our scouts reported a supply train moving up towards Minsk from one of the smaller roads that criss-cross the area. Well, we couldn't turn down the chance of some free booty, so we ambushed it and what you see here is the result of that ambush."

"Is this a new idea, this freeing of the Jews?" asked Yuri.

"It's something we started when the Colonel discovered that the Ghetto existed," replied the sergeant. "We try to get out women and children as much as possible, but the men who come over to us are fantastically brave fighters. They have the same philosophy as we do regarding the SS. Kill the bastards wherever and whenever we can. I don't think the fascists have enough men to properly patrol the Ghetto, so we, with the help of the Minsk partisans, get them out once the patrols have gone past. Our last two snatches have produced sixteen men, twenty-six women and thirty-two children. They come to us quite freely, the alternative being sent to Poland to the concentration camps, or being shot trying to escape. There are over four thousand in the Ghetto at the moment, but its rising fast." The sergeant left Yuri then and went back to check over the column.

The Column travelled on, through woods and bogs. In places the path was only just wide enough for a wagon to pass and after a few more miles, they halted.

The sergeant trotted up and said, "we need your horse now Yuri. The Lieutenant decided weeks ago to hide the wagons in a clearing, well off the main trail. If we need them in the future, then we know where they are. It means that we have to walk and carry for the last few miles. There's also three horses in the rear, dragging branches of scrub to wipe out our tracks. It works quite well, especially after the rain. You'd never know we'd been there."

Yuri got down and went to load up his little filly. What a good idea, he thought, both hiding the wagons and disguising their trail. Imaginative. Once the wagons had been emptied and the majority of goods loaded onto the horses, Valery led the column off in the direction of the new camp. Yuri was carrying whatever he could, as was everyone else including the Jews. They were a mixture of women and children with a few men. They looked terrified, but stuck to their task stoically. God knows what the future holds for ethnic groups like these, thought Yuri. If we don't stop them, the SS will murder everyone east of the Bug. After a few miles, the woods opened out into a long meadow of tall grass. Across the meadow, the land rose steadily until it topped out on a long ridge. Yuri recognised it as the place he had come upon when out training the recruits from the previous camp. Within the woods on top of the ridge, was a small community, several houses, barns and buildings. The fields surrounding the ridge had been used for grazing livestock and horses, but the animals were now kept within the boundaries of the defences of the new camp. As with the old camp, a track led at a gentle steepening angle along the side of the ridge, before entering the camp itself through a fortified gap in the trees. The column moved like a huge snake across the meadow, up the track and onwards into the main camp area. As Yuri entered the camp he was amazed at its size. The Colonel had said that there was over five hundred here and Yuri knew he wasn't kidding. Temporary shelters were built or being built to augment the original houses and out-buildings. Everywhere, men and women were hard at work, either building, tending the cooking fires, looking after stock and horses and generally making sure the place was habitable. It was a huge undertaking, but the people were making it work. The sergeant and corporal looked after the storing of supplies and dispersal of horses, barking out orders and supervising the transition from a returning raiding party to settling down for the evening. Valery had disappeared and of Alexei, there was no sign, so Yuri wandered around familiarising himself with the general layout and chatting to the many soldiers that he knew.

Eventually, a soldier walked up to him and said, "The Lieutenant would like you to join him for the evening meal, if you would just follow me."

Yuri nodded and followed the soldier, meandering between groups of soldiers and civilians, who were all at some stage of eating. Valery was seated outside his command post, with several of his NCO's. He thanked the soldier and beckoned Yuri to follow him a distance away from the rest, so they could talk freely and privately. A young girl brought each of them a bowl of steaming stew, with several slices of bread. They both ate hungrily for a while, until the sound of galloping hooves, heralded the arrival of a troop of Cossacks, headed by Alexei. The troop dismounted and handed the reins to a group of handlers who led the horses away. Then Alexei stalked over to where his brother and Yuri were sitting. Alexei's expression turned to one of delight, as he recognised Yuri sitting with his brother. Yuri stood up and embraced Alexei, both of them happy to see the other.

"When did you blow in?" asked a curious Alexei, "I hope you've been well looked after?"

"I met up with Valery this afternoon, on his way back from the raid," countered Yuri, "it's all a bit new here, but I can see you've both been hard at work. The Colonel, Yenisei, Alayna, Giselle, Stephan and Ivan send you both their best. This is the third day since I left the island and I'm here to pick your brains and request some help."

"I'm intrigued," answered Alexei, "according to Valery, me and brains don't really get on. I'm more into off the cuff, so to speak."

"Amen to that," muttered Valery, "but seriously Yuri, what have you got in mind and how may we help?"

"Well," began Yuri, "the problem is Yenisei, the two girls, Stephan and Ivan. I'm sure you know about the reward posters and this increases the risk of them staying here. If any of them got into the wrong hands, especially Yenisei or Alayna, I'd never forgive myself. I have to get them out of here and that means getting them to the other side of our lines, which is probably Moscow. We know that winter is closing in. Yenisei would not be able to walk the distance in good weather, let alone with snow on the ground. The only real way to do this is by plane. The Colonel reckons that you, Alexei, would be more than willing to have a go at one of the airfields and if we did, we'd steal a plane and fly the five of them out of here and hopefully, to safety beyond the reach of the SS. Stephan is a pilot and he says he could fly whatever we could come up with. I need help to transport them all to the airfield and it has got to be soon. The island, for all its isolation, is becoming untenable, with a hundred thousand Roubles up for grabs. I wouldn't trust anyone, in this camp or otherwise, they'd sell their mothers for that sort of reward. Could we perhaps launch a combined strike on the SS headquarters at Minsk, at the same time as hitting the airfield? Whatever we do, I desperately need both of your inputs."

The two brothers looked at each other. "Fuck," muttered Alexei, "what a proposition. The strange thing is, it's not outside the realms of possibility. A combined strike is a solid idea and holds water. I think we could come up with a suitable plan, don't you Valery?"

Valery nodded his agreement, "we've been looking at some sort of attack on SS Headquarters and it could combine really well with a plan for the airfield, even getting some more Jews out of the Ghetto. The more I think of it, the more audacious it sounds. What sort of time frame are we looking at?"

"Ten days from today," answered Yuri, "I would be looking to fly them out overnight, to give us the protection of darkness. Do you think you could organise something within that time scale?"

"Ten days is good," answered Valery, "we have the manpower, so it's a definite go. Do you think Sergei will go with you?"

"Not a chance in hell," laughed Yuri, "he wants to be involved with the partisans. He has a vision of it growing into brigade strength, even a whole army, a fifth column so to speak. On the other side of the battle lines, he'd be just another Colonel, subject to the will of his Communist chiefs. He likes the freedom of movement this situation offers."

"OK," said Valery positively, "I'll sort out something with my NCO's and then get back to you. Do you want everyone to be aware of your flying out?"

"Not by any stretch of the imagination," said Yuri, "like I said, I don't know who we can trust. What I would like is a handpicked squad to return with me to the island, to help with our passage and give us added support and firepower, in case of trouble. As it is, our journey will take us about five days. I think we will travel a lot by night, to reduce the chance of being spotted. There's a lot of open country away from the marshes and I'm acutely aware of that Stork that's forever flying around. Is there anyone who knows the terrain we'll be travelling through?"

"Some of the locals may know," answered Alexei helpfully. "I'll have a word, discretely of course."

"We'll need a place where we can meet, whenever both parties are in position," said Yuri, "but I'll leave that up to you."

"OK," said Valery, "give me some time to prepare a plan. When are you looking to head back to the island?"

"Tomorrow," said Yuri, "whenever we can tie up a suitable schedule."

"Right," said Valery, "I'll see what I can put together." With that, he got up and strode off to where his NCO's were finishing their meal.

"So how are things back at the island," asked Alexei conversationally, "have you married that incredibly gorgeous Alayna yet?"

"When have I had the time to get married, you nutcase," laughed Yuri, "mind you, I will whenever this sodding war is sorted out and if the churches ever open again." Yuri told Alexei about the way they had prepared the cave for the forthcoming winter, the salted meat, the wood for burning, more snow shoes and Ivan's new crossbow.

"I suppose the crossbows went missing after the attack on our last camp," asked Yuri.

"Actually no," replied Alexei, "luckily, we found them when we returned to bury our dead. I had an inkling of where they might be and lo and behold, there they were, beside a shattered tree stump where we were camped. The SS took any rifles and machine pistols that were laid about, but missed the crossbows completely. That's something I needed to ask you, do you have any more bolts back there?"

"Yes," replied Yuri, "Ivan made up another twenty odd. I can bring them with me when I return if you want. I was sure the crossbows would have been lost forever."

"It just shows how you miss things when you're not looking for them," answered Alexei, "I'm glad Ivan has some more, I've got through quite a few recently." Then he explained to Yuri what he had been doing since the attack on the old camp. "Valery and I tend to split the day to day running of the camp between us, he does his thing and I do mine. He's been fixing up the camp defences and organising new recruits into the roster. The Colonel and he worked tirelessly securing the ridge here and trying to learn from the deficiencies of the old camp, you know, what worked and what didn't. It's tied him down in some ways, but he does go out on the occasional sortie, as he did today. We're getting more and more Jews in the camp, which isn't a bad thing actually, as they're so anti-fascist. We've augmented quite a few of the men into the system, even though they're not really soldiers as such. I can't imagine what sort of hell it is within the Ghetto, but they give an extremely vivid account to anyone who will listen. But I've been on my own quests, nobbling the SS wherever I can. We're still finding many examples of atrocities and I more or less scour the countryside, hunting down their hit squads. That's where the crossbows are so useful. We sneak up on them, dispatch a couple and then fade away into the woods and marshes. I would imagine the price on my head has now doubled. Have you seen anymore examples of their barbarity?"

Yuri nodded. "I found the burned out remains of a caravan, in the woods about ten miles south of the island." Yuri explained the gruesome remains he had found and his subsequent burying of the bodies. "I told no-one about what I'd actually found, back at the cave. You can't describe to a neutral just what these fiends are capable of. I don't think I will ever forget that sight."

Alexei put his arm compassionately on his friends shoulder. "You and I," he said vehemently, "have seen things that no-one should ever have to witness. That's why I have to dispose of these animals, whenever I can." Then he became the boyish Alexei again. "It's time I introduced you to Sophia," he said with a twinkle in his eye. "I give her a bag of oats, some hay and she gives me the ride of my life. What other woman could do that, eh?" Then he threw back his head and laughed, Yuri joining in.

"You idiot," said Yuri laughingly, "but thanks, I understand and appreciate it."

Alexei grinned, "I've got to go and see a few people and run a few errands," he said, "you'd better find somewhere to lay your blanket for the night."

With a parting wave of his hand he rose and moved off into the camp, leaving Yuri to find somewhere to sleep. The camp was becoming quiet as most people were taking to their blankets. Yuri found a place under an oak tree and spread out his blankets, using his poncho as cover. There was no sign of his two friends, so he snuggled down and went to sleep, his thoughts, as always on Alayna.

Morning came in mist shrouded gloom. Above him, he could just make out the serried ranks of clouds as they brushed the tree tops, heading south-west. All around him was damp and chill as he stowed away his blankets. The camp was coming to life and he could hear the clink of pots and mugs, with the unmistakable aroma of brewed coffee hanging in the air. He pulled his own mug from his pack and wandered over to the nearest fire, where a wizened old lady was decanting coffee to all around her. He thanked her and chatted away to the men who congregated around the fire, seeking its warmth on such a late September morning. After a while, he wandered down through the camp, getting a feel for the people thrown together in the midst of this war-torn part of western Russia. Soldiers and farmers, heroes and villains, who knew which was which? There were good and bad here, he knew that, but they were all having to live together, at least for a while. He passed the Jewish camp, even here, they were detached from the rest, as if they carried some mysterious disease that would infect all who came into contact with them. Men, women and children, a collage of bleak, frightened faces, staring stonily in their grief and hardship, unable to trust anyone but themselves. Yuri shook his head. What are we coming to? He thought.

Just then, the corporal marched up. "If you'd like to follow me sir, the Lieutenants are waiting to see you," he said.

Yuri nodded and replied, "Carry on corporal," The two of them marched off through the gathering mayhem of the increasingly busy and hardworking camp. It's good to be back, thought Yuri. The work, the camaraderie, the feeling of contributing to a worthwhile cause, with its basis in a tightly-knitted community.

Alexei and Valery were sitting around a large table. The corporal and half a dozen soldiers were sat or grouped around and Yuri noticed that there was no-one else within probably fifty yards of the table. These then, were the most trusted of Valery's and Yuri was aware that he was within the inner sanctum of the camps hierarchy. Valery nodded a smiling greeting and immediately got down to business. He made sure that all were grouped closely around the table and began.

 "Gentlemen, we are planning a joint venture between ourselves and Yuri's party. This event will take place on October, 9th and we will be targeting the SS Headquarters in Minsk and the airfield, east of the city. This airfield is small, basically a non-military base, where the fascists house a couple of Storks and several transport aircraft. Our sources have informed us that these planes are used for reconnaissance, the transporting of SS troops and also for the personal usage of Hauptman Lientz, when he visit's Warsaw, to speak to Heydrich in person. The plane he uses is a Junkers JU-52, one of their old bombers, that has been converted into a troop transport or a platform for paratroopers. It's a quiet airfield, the larger military airfield being twelve miles away to the north-west. The plan, which is still in its most basic form, is to hit the SS

Headquarters with everything we've got, at precisely the same time as the attack goes in at the airfield. Yuri, you requested a squad to take with you to your base camp and these men here are those chosen. You will be able to fill them in as you go along and also co-operate with Colonel Berezovsky. Corporal Kurnakov will be your second in command. Within your force, are four Jews, who I will introduce you to later. Two of these men, have intimate knowledge of the terrain over which your party will be travelling. They will be your guides and you can trust them implicitly. The four still have families and relatives within the Ghetto. The precise point at which our two forces come together, has been worked out between the Jews. They will lead us to the rendezvous, as yours will lead you and your party to the same place. Only they know this location. We have a wagon, that should fill the needs of you and your party and my sergeant has gone to get a couple of horses. This particular wagon has rubber tyres and will provide a quieter mode of transport than solid wheels. If you and Sergei can do your part, we will meet again on the evening of the 9th. God speed to all of you."

With that final pronouncement, the proceedings broke up. Yuri glanced around at his squad, all looked ready for the task ahead. There were six, displaced regular troops and Yuri knew each of them.

Corporal Kurnakov moved over to Yuri, saluted and said, "I'll assemble the men at the camp entrance. We'll be ready to leave in fifteen minutes."

"Very well corporal," replied Yuri, "I'll get my things and we'll be off." The corporal saluted and hurried away to make sure all was ready for leaving. Alexei beckoned Yuri to where he and Valery were talking to a group of four men, obviously, the Jews.

On Yuri's arrival, Valery said, "Yuri, meet Avi, Jacob, Moshe and Ben. They have all volunteered to come as part of your force. Integrate them into your plans as they are desperate to strike back at the fascists in any way. They know of Yenisei and understand how hard it is to be imprisoned within their own land."

Yuri shook hands with each of them. He looked into their eyes and saw a ready determination. He nodded to Valery, "they will be fine," he said. The four Jews hurried off to join up with the others who were congregating by the gate.

"These are my most trusted men," said Valery quietly, "you can't be awake all the time. We'll meet again on the 9th."

Yuri embraced Valery and Alexei, shook hands and moved to the hesd of the formed-up column in front of the gate. "OK corporal," he said, "let's move them out."

The column moved off, spreading out into a skirmish line as they reached the bottom of the angled roadway leading from the camp. They passed across the meadow and Yuri gave a final wave to Alexei and Valery, before disappearing into the trees.

After several miles, they spotted the sergeant with the wagon. "These two horses are good workers," he said, "just keep them on a tight rein. Pieter here will drive the team."

Yuri thanked him, as Pieter climbed up onto the seat, then with a wave, the sergeant trudged off in the direction of the camp, while Yuri's party moved out along the path. He had three days to get back to the island.

The morning passed quickly, the only sound being the soft clip-clop of the horse's hooves as they pulled the gently rolling wagon along the tortuous path. Yuri had positioned himself at the front, mainly because he knew where he was going, with the corporal bringing up the rear. One of the Jews and a soldier had taken up point duty and they ranged well ahead of the group on the lookout for danger. The others were tucked in behind Yuri, spread out and alert. The soldier who was managing the team of horses seemed competent and knew his way around a team. The wagon was covered with a tarpaulin, stretched around iron supports, with covered entrances at both ends. Along each side of the interior were wooden benches, with an open area down the middle. At the moment, this open area housed the men's packs and cooking utensils, freeing them up while they walked. Early in the afternoon, Yuri called a halt, to give the horses a feed and the men some time to rest their feet. They had crossed the main path heading north/south a few miles back, so Yuri knew they were almost parallel to their old camp. The two point men had returned when Yuri and the others halted and reported that they had not seen or heard anything troublesome throughout the morning. Tracks were everywhere in evidence, but they all seemed fairly old.

The horse handler, Pieter, came up to Yuri and said, "The black is the one to watch, he's very astute and can smell trouble a mile off. He'll let you know if it's a machine, human or animal. With humans, he's quite easy going, but if he smells animals, like a bear or wolves, he becomes very agitated. The pair of them are quiet in tense situations, not being liable to snort or whinny, but if bears or wolves are close, they get pretty skittish. You'll notice he walks with his head down, but if it comes up sharpish, watch his reaction and his line of sight."

"Thanks," said Yuri, "I'll bear that in mind." After twenty minutes, they were all back on the path, heading due west. The afternoon continued apace as the group made good time. The journey was giving Yuri time to think. The schedule was going to be tight, even though there would be nine days left after today. Problems could arise from any quarter and he was only too aware that fate could turn fickle at any moment. One step at a time, he thought. The afternoon passed into evening and the skies turned grey. The swollen clouds bore down on them, on a strengthening north-westerly wind and they were soon engulfed in a heavy downpour, lashing onto their backs. They had made good time, so Yuri whistled up the two point men and told them to look out for somewhere to bed down for the night. After another mile or so, he saw the two men beckoning them forward. To the north was an area of stunted pines, with a trail that threaded between them into a small clearing, about fifty yards from the path. Yuri was going to set up a perimeter, but decided against it. The men were all tired. They would leave the horses to warn of any danger. The rain still lashed down, so a cold supper beckoned. The men ate in silence, each with their own thoughts, then found a place to sleep, three inside the wagon and the rest laid under it, or in tents. The horse handler unhitched the horses, gave them both a rub down and some food, before tying them securely to a couple of trees, his own tent and blankets, pitched close to his charges. Yuri curled up in his blankets, the rain beating down on the wagon roof and drifted off to sleep, satisfied that the day had gone well.

Back at the camp where they had left from that morning, two men were deep in conversation. The pair were the escaped duo that had been seen off by the Colonel, a couple of weeks ago. Once they had stopped running, they had made their way back to the camp and re-established themselves as displaced soldiers. It seemed as though they had been accepted by the garrison and helped around the camp, even going out on raids. The original five had thought that the Colonel would be an easy target, as they had seen him leave the camp by himself on some mission to the west. They had heard about the rewards and knew that former General Berezovsky would bring a good price from the SS. So, the five had managed to sneak away from the camp and lay in wait to spring their surprise. But the trouble was, it backfired dramatically. Three of the five were dead, the older man becoming a tiger when attacked. They had only managed to stick a bayonet in his leg, before he dealt expertly with their uncoordinated attack. Now they both blamed everyone but themselves, as all cowards do.

"I don't like the way that jumped-up lieutenant looks at me," said one to the other, "he's a fucking pain in the arse and needs to be brought down a peg."

"Couldn't agree more," his mate replied, "we should shop him and his fucking brother to the SS.

Two hundred thousand Roubles for the sodding pair. But where the hell did that little group head off to this morning?"

His friend leaned closer and said conspiringly, "you remember that little shit, the old relic from Abakan. I reckon they've gone to meet up with him. I don't know who that Yuri character is, but I had heard that he was sweet on the relic's niece or something, you remember, the one with the tits, always washing her hair in the lake."

His cohort nodded. "I remember her," he said, "I'd give her a good seeing to, mark my words. But what's the Abakan relic got to do with anything?"

"He's also on the SS's reward list," replied his mate. "Look, whenever this Yuri or Berezovsky take off, it's always west. That's where he was going when we ambushed him and that's where that Yuri was coming from when we picked him up after the raid yesterday. Somewhere west. Now that should be something that the SS would pay handsomely for, Yuri and Berezovsky somewhere west and the shit kicking brothers, here in the camp. Tomorrow, we're out of here. I'm sick of being ordered about. Let's slip up to Minsk and have a word with the fucking enemy. You with me?"

"Too right I am," his friend spat back, "the wars lost anyway, so let's get cosy with the SS and make some new friends and a load of cash."

The sun rose in a cloudless sky, the nights rain a distant memory. However, the ground was saturated and even minimal movement around the camp churned it into a sticky morass. After a quick, cold breakfast, the wagon was hitched up and driven back to the path. The squad moved out in reasonable spirits, at least the path was relatively clear, apart from a few giant puddles. Yuri was blissfully unaware that fate was conspiring against them, as he hurried the squad westwards. If possible, he wanted another thirty miles under his belt before they made camp again. The sun sparkled off the wet leaves and grass, almost blinding in its intensity. The air was cool, but still pleasant for the end of September and the squad carried on, content but alert. The midday break saw them almost halfway through their journey, the next few hours would be crucial, in making it to the island by tomorrow evening. Onward through the afternoon and into the evening with not a problem of any kind, the miles racking up behind them. Eventually, Yuri called a halt, at a place where a side path angled off to the south and after half a mile or so, the two point men guided them into a clearing, a good distance from the main path. They were all tired and Yuri decided to build a fire and therefore, have a hot meal tonight. He could see the men welcomed this and they all helped in readying a fire, collecting wood and warming through the tins of meat and vegetables. They ate hungrily, last night's cold offering a thing of the past. They also brewed up some coffee and the men sat around, smoking and chatting until the sun went down. With a bit of luck, thought Yuri, as he settled into his blankets, we'll make the island by tomorrow afternoon.

Morning once again saw them up early and on the move after a cold breakfast. The sky was relatively clear with a few clouds, but it didn't look too bad for the next few hours, if not more. They pressed on, the countryside basking in the late autumnal sunshine and stopped for a midday break, just short of the cabin, where Yuri and the others from the camp attack, had stayed for that night several weeks before. Yuri was content, they were doing really well and another couple of hours should see them there. As they sat around chatting while they rested their legs, the black horses head suddenly came up and it peered off back towards the way they had come. The squad were instantly alert, fading into the trees and brush on either side of the path, the horses and wagon being moved quickly into the trees. For a moment, Yuri could see nothing and then he heard the tell-tale throb of a propeller. That fucking Stork, he thought ruefully. Somebody needs to put a bomb under it.

"OK boys," he said, "It's our old friend the Stork, come to pay us a visit. Everybody keep still and out of sight."

The little plane droned overhead at little more than tree top height, the pilot and co-pilot clearly visible from the squads concealed position. It skirted to the north and then turned towards the south, criss-crossing the path they were travelling. Eventually, it headed off west towards the River Bug and the sound ebbed away into the distance.

"That black of yours certainly knows its stuff," said a relieved Yuri to Pieter. "Had we been on the move, a few moments like he gave us could have been priceless."

Pieter beamed and nodded, pleased that he had been of use. "OK," said Yuri, "back on your feet and let's get to the island before that sodding thing comes back."

The squad re-formed and moved out, but now everyone was keeping a close watch on the black and the sky. Twelve miles later, Yuri was back in familiar territory, the island just a short trip across the water.

The hard thing now will be to attract the attention of someone over there on the island, thought Yuri. Then he remembered what the Colonel had done when he had last arrived, that is, stand by the shore and wait for somebody to do the island patrol. With that thought in mind, he settled the men down for a rest, while he moved through the oaks and scrub to the shore. He didn't have to wait long. Almost immediately, a hand appeared through the screening branches of the alders along the northern edge and as he stared he recognised Ivan, waving at him. He waved back in reply and after five or six minutes, the boat appeared around the eastern edge of the island, Ivan and Alayna paddling towards the beach. Taking his time to savour the moment, he watched her as she neared the landing area, her smile radiant as the boat was beached and she and Ivan stepped out. She ran to him, throwing her arms around his neck and they were locked in a fierce embrace for all of a minute, the slightly embarrassed Ivan looking anywhere but at them.

Eventually, Yuri stood back and said, "So, you didn't miss me then?"

She aimed a playful punch at his head without connecting, stamped her foot and retorted, "just a little my darling, nice of you to return, eventually," the last word said with emphasis. Then she collapsed into a fit of giggles. Yuri laughed with her and turning to Ivan, shook him warmly by the hand.

"Everything OK back on the island?" asked Yuri pointedly.

"All shipshape and ready to leave," answered Ivan jovially, "Sergei is a lot better and he and Yenisei have been busy. So, are you alone?"

"Good lord no," answered Yuri, "I have eleven with me. Can you and Giselle cook for eighteen tonight Alayna?"

"You know we can," said Alayna blithely, "whether you get anything is another thing."

She jumped quickly out of the way as Yuri's boot made for her rump and giggled her way back to the boat. "Hang on," said Yuri, "I haven't finished yet. Ivan, could you take Alayna back and pick me up from the bay in the reeds later. I need to settle the men down for the night and was going to suggest to them that they pitch camp behind the hut. They'll be well away from inquisitive eyes and there's plenty of grazing for the horses. Can you give me about half an hour?"

Ivan nodded and got back into the boat, Alayna sensible now as she said, "Tell them supper will be at seven, all will be most welcome."

With that, Ivan and Alayna paddled back across to the island while Yuri returned to his men. "Corporal," he said, "get the men together and follow me, I'll show you where you can all bivouac for the night."

The corporal nodded, formed up the men and they trooped off behind Yuri, the wagon bringing up the rear. Yuri showed them where the path deviated southwards and led them to the area behind the hut that they used for wood storage. "If you want, you can use the hut as a sleeping area. It's rainproof and with a bit of manoeuvring, could probably house most of you. I have to return to the island, but supper will be served at seven and you're all invited. If you could remember to bring your mess tins, cutlery and a mug with you, it would be very helpful. The horses can be accommodated around the back. Any questions?" The sea of unconcerned faces and shrugs of approval told Yuri all he needed to know. "Right," he said, "make yourselves at home. I'll be back at six, see you then." With a parting wave, he walked off towards the bay, where Ivan was waiting patiently for him. The corporal set to, organising everyone for the night.

The short trip over to the island was covered quickly. The boat was beached and hidden away in the screening trees. Yuri was first up the steps and into the cave, anxious to assess the situation. He need not have worried. The party were all busy preparing a meal for everyone, both of the girls in the thick of it, but they all stopped and hailed a greeting as Yuri walked in. Yuri grinned, happy to be back with his new family again. Even the Colonel was up, but he was sat at the table, poring over some paperwork.

He beckoned Yuri over and said, "Nice to see you back safely. I hope our two brothers are well and not trying to win the war singlehandedly?"

"They're both fine Sergei and send their best. They reckon you're getting old if you can't see off robbers and wolves without being stuck with a bayonet and almost eaten."

The older man grimaced and snarled, "Pair of clever buggers, Stalin would do well to learn from them, getting old indeed." Then his face broke into a grin, spread out the sheets he had been reading and called Yenisei over.

The old man slapped Yuri on the back and sat down opposite the Colonel. "Thanks for getting me away from those two women," he whispered, "This is much more my line of work."

"I heard that," said Giselle, "and we'll need that table soon, so don't think you're there for the rest of the day." Yenisei chuckled and blew her a kiss, she responded with a stuck-out tongue. The Colonel became serious and spoke directly to Yuri and Yenisei.

"When are you looking at leaving Yuri, we're ready to go whenever you like."

"The day after tomorrow," answered Yuri. "That should give us enough time to be in position on the evening of the 9th."

"I hear you have brought some help with you," said Yenisei, "and also a wagon."

"That's right," admitted Yuri, "the wagon is about the size of one of your caravan's uncle, with a tarpaulin cover and rubber wheels. It's more than adequate for our needs."

The old man nodded happily as Yuri continued. "There's six soldiers with Corporal Kurnakov in charge. You'll know them all Sergei and they were handpicked by Valery. There are also four Jews, escapees from the Ghetto, who are ready to fight for their countrymen. Two of them have intimate knowledge of the woods and paths, north of the main Minsk highway and they will guide us to the rendezvous point on the 9th. All four are very capable, especially Avi and Jacob who show excellent signs of leadership and woodcraft. Between them, the eleven are a significant fighting force and will be invaluable to our plans. Valery is organising an attack on the SS Headquarters in Minsk and probably an attempt to release more Jews from the Ghetto, at exactly the same time as we hit the airfield. This should provide us with the time needed to secure the airfield and get us airborne."

The Colonel nodded his agreement and the three of them lapsed into silence, thinking through what Yuri had said, while the clatter and smells of cooking carried on around them.

Eventually, the Colonel spoke. "It sounds good," he admitted contentedly, "Yenisei and I have come up with a few wrinkles of our own, to try and aid our quest. As you know Yuri, I've been trying to come up with something involving 'Kuhmo Wolf' and we think we may have just the thing. Basically, there are two problems as I see it. Firstly, getting a message to the SS in Minsk when our boys keep hitting the telegraph lines on a regular basis. To that end, before I left them, I instructed Alexei and Valery to leave the lines alone, until we had put the communication theory into practice. Hopefully, the fascists will have repaired them in time for us to use them. Secondly, how to use 'Kuhmo Wolf' to our advantage regarding our escape? Yenisei and I have come up with a plan that involves sending the SS bogus information, telling them that we will attack the military airfield, some twelve miles north-west of Minsk, during the night of the 9th. If it works, it will draw away the bulk of their forces, leaving us to grab a plane at the other smaller airfield and for Alexei and Valery to do some real damage to their Headquarters. What we don't want, is for that JU-52 to bugger off to Warsaw and by seemingly going for the military airfield, we create the illusion of our airfield being safe from attack."

Yuri blew out his cheeks in agreement, "Yes," he said, "I think that could just work. The problem is of course, Alexei and Valery know nothing of this plan and it may throw them into confusion if they see the SS moving out."

"That's as maybe," agreed the Colonel, "but both of them are sufficiently capable of thinking on their feet, should the need arise. Are we agreed?" Yuri and Yenisei nodded. "Then it's a go," said the Colonel.

The three of them chatted away until the girls insisted that the table be used for serving supper. Yuri, Ivan and Stephan took the boat and the raft over to the bay in the reeds, to pick up the squad. Once they were all aboard, it was a relatively easy task to ferry them all over to the island. Pieter, the horse handler was a little upset at having to leave the horses, but Yuri assured him that he would bring him straight back across, once supper was over. It was no easy task getting everyone inside the cave, eighteen people tended to fill it out, but with a little management of what resources were available, they were all able to sit in relative comfort and tuck into the meal that the girls had prepared. There were two huge roasts of pork and a haunch of venison. Then boiled potatoes, onions, turnip and freshly baked bread, with plenty of butter. The squad were amazed at the size of the inside of the cave, asking question after question while supper progressed. The story of how Yuri came upon it and had since developed it, with plenty of help from willing hands, was covered and re-covered as the meal disappeared before them. Yenisei was in deep conversation with the four Jewish men and Yuri was pleased to see that all the squad were now on first name terms and intermixing with the rest. The Colonel sat close to Giselle, she being aware that he was still in need of rest and relaxation, both of which, he was never going to get in the near future. He, on the other hand was watching Yuri, as he moved between the assembled guests, chatting easily with the common soldier, Jew and the academic brain of Yenisei. He hadn't realised before, that Yuri was such a natural leader, commanding respect from all levels of society. He had seen the way the corporal saluted him and how Yuri coped with the weight of command. Yet he had no official rank or training. He was just a natural, with a cool head in a tight situation and he possessed the ability to make decisive decisions, when they were most needed, in the heat of battle. Yenisei had pointed this out to the Colonel long ago, but it was now that he glimpsed the charisma of one born to lead others. He must write to Semyon Timoshenko and get Yenisei to deliver it, once Yuri and the others were safely behind the Russian lines. Mother Russia needed leaders like Yuri Petrovsky.

The brandy was produced and mugs filled, the food having totally disappeared. Once everyone had a brandy in their hands, Jacob stood up and called for quiet.

"Gentlemen, after such a wonderful meal, please raise your glasses to the cooks, two more beautiful of which, I have never had the pleasure of dining with. The cooks."

The men toasted the now highly embarrassed ladies and then gave them a heavy round of applause. The Colonel waited until the noise subsided and then got to his feet.

"Ladies and gentlemen," he began, "we come together at this most distressing time, affecting all our lives. The fascists are still in the ascendancy and over the next week, we must strike a blow for freedom. If you would be so kind as to meet here tomorrow lunchtime, myself, Yuri and Yenisei will go through our plans for the next six days. Until then, it only remains for me to again, thank our cooks and our hosts, for such an elegant evening, given in the midst of all the horror going on around us. I fear it may be the last such evening for some time. Sleep well and God be with you."

The men finished off their brandies and moved outside and down to the landing stage. The evening had been one of nostalgia, for remembering old and happier times. They were silent now, as they were paddled back to the bay of the reeds. On arrival, there were many mumbled messages of thanks to Yuri as the squad marched off to their beds.

Yuri tarried awhile with Corporal Kurnakov. "Get them bedded down quickly," said Yuri, "if you want to set a perimeter, then do so, whatever you feel safest with."

"I'll do that sir," the corporal replied, "good night and we'll see you tomorrow lunchtime if not before. Would it be OK if I send out some scouts in the morning?"

"Good idea," said Yuri quietly, "don't wander too far though."

The corporal nodded, then saluted. Yuri returned the salute and the corporal marched off to organise his men. Stephan and Ivan had already paddled the raft back to the island by the time Yuri left. He would leave worrying about the future until it happened. At least he would get to spend a little time with Alayna tonight before bed.

Yuri awoke from a dream filled sleep, feeling anything but ready for the days ahead. His mind was filled with a deep foreboding and no matter what he tried to alleviate this feeling, it still continued to rankle. The whole escape plan was based on too many imponderables. Having said that, he thought, what other options do we have? If it was at all possible, Yenisei, Stephan, Ivan, Giselle and Alayna must be taken out of the equation. Their capture and subsequent torture at the hands of the SS, didn't bear thinking about. Get it through your head, he demanded of himself, make it work. He arose and slipped on his boots, picked up his rifle and stepped outside. The morning was cold and damp, with rain in the air. The wind had picked up overnight and the lake was being lashed into foam filled wavelets, besprinkled with leaves and fallen branches. As he crested the ridge at the west end of the island, he searched for any sign of his squad, but they were well hidden from his view and he knew the corporal would have everything under control. Nothing else was causing him concern, so he made his way back to the cave. The others were busy with packing away their sleeping gear, but the stove was brewing coffee. Alayna brought him a mug full and offered a verbal salve to his woebegone expression.

"Try not to worry, my darling," she said gently, "we're all responsible for our own actions and everyone realises the risk we take staying here. Therefore, our only course is to try and escape, so that we can make all our lives more bearable. If we're safely out of harm's way, then the soldiers here can concentrate on waging their partisan war, without recourse to looking after civilians. I love you and I want you with me, but you have to do your duty for all of us. Only then will you be content, knowing you did everything you could." She kissed him lightly on the lips and moved over to where Giselle was preparing bread for baking. Yuri digested her words and felt better. She trusted him to do the best he could and, he thought, there's nothing else a man can do. So he fought down the negativity befouling his mind and determined to carry on regardless.

All through the morning, preparations went ahead for the journey over the next few days. The girls roasted more slabs of venison and pork that would be taken with them to eat cold. The newly baked bread would have to suffice, for today and for the journey. Life on the road would be hard, but not too unbearable. There was always the tinned goods and biscuits, that each man would be carrying, but really food, was secondary to their survival. They would do what they could. After lunch, Ivan, Stephan and Yuri took the boat and raft over to the bay in the reeds and picked up the squad. The men were in good spirits and keen to discover what the Colonel had to say. Once safely inside the cave, everyone was handed tea or coffee and once settled, the Colonel stood up and addressed them all.

"Ladies and Gentlemen," he began, "we are here to show you the plan for our journey to the airfield. We have five days to reach our destination by the evening of the 9th. Tomorrow, we must try to be on our way by eight o'clock at the latest as we need to cover at least twenty-five miles before dark. I have a drawing here of the basic route we are to take, up to the point where Avi will assume the leadership and guide us to the rendezvous. We also have Aleksander's maps and drawings that are proving

453

invaluable." He held up a large sheet of paper which Ivan and Stephan held while he continued.

"As you can see from the drawing, we travel east for about eighteen miles before turning north. This path, is one that I have not used before, but Avi and Jacob assure me, that it takes us directly through woods and large areas of scrub to the main road. We know that here, the woods are very close to the road on both sides and this is where we will cross. If all goes well, we will make camp for the first night, a few miles north of this place. The next two days will be tricky, in as much as we're heading north-east through patches of woods where open areas will see us exposed to air reconnaissance and obviously, ground forces. To eradicate this problem, we are going to have to travel under the cover of darkness, until we can reach a deeper forested area. There will also be two rivers, the Szczara and the Neman, plus any tributaries to cross. Hopefully, our Jewish guides know the best crossing points and will then be able to utilise the last two days in getting to our rendezvous. We will be travelling as swiftly and as quietly as possible and we all need to trust and assist each other, to make this work. Any questions?"

The Colonel gazed around at the sea of faces. Everyone seemed satisfied with the details that would unravel as the journey progressed. He couldn't detect any feelings of trepidation, only a collective determination to see it through. "Then I shall see you all in the morning," he said finally, "until then, prepare and get a good night's rest."

The meeting then broke up. The soldiers returned to the mainland while the rest began a thorough estimation of what would be needed for the journey. Yuri suddenly remembered the crossbow bolts wanted by Alexei and approached Ivan.

"I've got at least twenty-four," said Ivan in reply to Yuri's question, "if you like, I'll bring the moulds with me. Alexei will be able to find another blacksmith capable of producing more. I can't see much point in leaving them here, if no-one is going to be able to use them."

"Good idea," said Yuri, "slip them into your pack and we'll get them to Alexei somehow."

Everyone was fitted out with a pack, even the two girls. The tinned goods, medical supplies and spare ammunition, with much of the cold meat and bread would be stowed under the benches of the wagon. Each man and woman would carry a weapon and grenades and dynamite sticks were also packed. Water containers would be filled en-route. Yuri made sure that the two crossbows were ready. He would carry one, while Ivan took the other. The evening meal was a quiet affair, each person concentrating on their own thoughts. All were in bed early, as Yuri finished his tour of the island. He fell asleep with Alayna's hand in his, with all concerns regarding tomorrow, locked away within his mind.

Chapter 15 – Minsk

The morning arrived cold and misty, with a keen frost. Yuri was up with the sun, as usual and went for his early morning tour of the island. The crisp, frosty conditions crunched under his feet as he crested the ridge and swept the area with his binoculars. There was nothing to worry him, as far as he could tell, as he tried to penetrate the clinging mist shrouded trees. All was peaceful, there being no wind at all, as if nature was holding its breath. He shivered as he breathed in the stillness. It was time. Back in the cave, everyone was busy with last minute preparations. Stephan and Ivan would take the girls over to the landing area north of the island, Ivan returning for all the remaining packs and extra luggage for the journey. Then Ivan would return a last time for Yuri, Yenisei and the Colonel and the boat would finally be left hidden in the reeds and branches of the landing area. This, they had decided earlier, would be its best place of concealment and also, if any of them returned in the future, they would have access to the island. The transfer of people and equipment went to schedule and Corporal Kurnakov had his men ready, waiting and loaded up, by the time Yuri passed through the gap between the two oaks.

The corporal approached Yuri and said, "We're all set sir, I've sent Avi and Jacob to scout well ahead, I hope that was OK?"

"Very good," replied Yuri, "move them out will you corporal."

The corporal nodded to Pieter, the horse handler, who took up the reins and with a click of his tongue, moved off, the rest strung out in front and behind. Yenisei and the Colonel rode in the wagon with Giselle, the rest walked for now, including Alayna. Yuri took a long last look at the place he had called home for the last three and a half months, until it faded from view in the mist. Will I ever see it again, he thought, maybe, but for now its Minsk and then Moscow.

The corporal set a brisk pace as he led the party eastwards along the path. The mist cleared as the morning progressed, but the sun was conspicuous by its absence, being masked by brooding clouds. The wind had also picked up and before much longer, a gentle but persistent rain moved in across the marshes. Yuri was not too concerned as the rain would help to obliterate their tracks, but he was also aware that the rain could turn to snow, it being not uncommon in early October. This was one thing he wanted to avoid if possible. In the rain, tracks were swallowed up by mud, but laying snow was a different matter. He had voiced his concerns to the Colonel yesterday.

The Colonel had shrugged and said, "The weather is something we can't predict Yuri, if it snows, we'll have to put up with it." Lunchtime arrived without a hitch and Yuri halted for a breather and to feed the horses. Twelve to fourteen miles by his reckoning, right on schedule. The party were wrapped up within their own thoughts, each conscious of their situation and the fact that they were exposed to any malicious eyes. But there was an unspoken resilience that Yuri saw in their determined faces. After half an hour, he was keen to get them moving again and they formed up on the new path, which headed north towards the main road running from Warsaw to Minsk. The rain was still persistently falling, but they moved steadily forward at a good rate. The scouts were foraging well ahead of the main group, with two soldiers bringing up the rear and the Colonel had declined to travel in the wagon, relying on his crutch while he exercised his healing leg.

In the SS Headquarters in Minsk, Hauptmann Lientz was busy at his desk, when there was a sharp rap at the door.

"Enter," he called out brusquely and Franz, his orderly, entered the room. Lientz tore himself away from the papers he had been reading, adjusted his position in his chair and demanded, "well Franz, what is it?"

The orderly saluted smartly and began, "Sir, the two prisoners we have been interrogating have come up with some interesting information regarding Ivan's 5, 14 and 15 and the man from Abakan, Mikhail

Korsakov. They say that after the SS attacked the insurgent's camp, Korsakov and a Yuri Petrovsky, escaped with four civilians connected to Korsakov, two of them being women and headed west. As you may remember, Feldwebel Huth and his team, with the two dogs, lost contact with them close to the River Bug and they assumed that they had somehow crossed the river and were hiding out on the Polish side. However, General Berezovsky left the insurgents new camp a few weeks ago and also headed west. According to the pair downstairs, they tried to overpower him, but he managed to escape. They followed him for a while, but lost him in the same area as the Feldwebel had done previously."

Lientz nodded, stood up and beckoned Franz to the large map pinned to the wall. He pointed to the area in question and said, "we always seem to lose track of whoever we are chasing around this point, they must be hiding somewhere in this area. Don't forget, someone blew up the compound near to this place, after Berezovsky and the Avseyenko brothers were spirited away. I always thought it was Gruber who had effected their escape, but I can't see him blowing up the compound. There's something more to this area than we're seeing and it's time we put a stop to all this speculation, once and for all."

Franz was silent for a moment and then said, "The prisoners also added that Petrovsky appeared in their camp a few days ago, talked at length to the Avseyenko brothers and left the following day with six soldiers, four Jews and a wagon. They also headed west."

"Interesting," murmured Lientz, "Jews now becoming fighters. The wagon can only be for transport, so who are they picking up and where are they going. If I read this right, it would appear that Petrovsky, with a group of soldiers, has gone to pick up Korsakov, Berezovsky and the civilians. Do they have a target? What the hell does all this mean?"

Franz shrugged and shook his head. "Right," said Lientz decisively, "get Feldwebel Huth and his team into that location now. Then get two squads of SS to the area via the main road. Call the airfield and get them to put up the two Storks. We'll blanket the marshes and woods, south of the main road and try and flush this party out. I'm sick and tired of being taken for a ride by these damned Russians and their Jewish friends. Himmler is due to visit in a few weeks and I want this place locked down and secure. Off you go Franz, get this thing moving."

The orderly saluted, turned on his heels and rushed off to do his masters bidding. Lientz returned to his chair. So, he thought, somewhere to the west is it? Well, this time we're coming to get you. And just where the hell is 'Rhine Maiden' or 'Kuhmo Wolf'? I need information.

Yuri was at this moment, feeling vaguely optimistic about crossing the main road and putting some mileage between the island and their camp for the night. The rain still persisted and it was becoming colder, with some sleet mixed in with the rain. The afternoon was passing, but they were making good time. The Colonel had reluctantly agreed to get back into the wagon at the insistence of Giselle, his leg having had enough of a workout. Alayna walked with Yuri, the pair chatting quietly about what may or may not lie in their near future. Their progress was interrupted by a sudden hiss of alarm from Pieter, the blacks ears had come up and he was looking over towards the east. Yuri got the wagon off the path and into deep foliage, the others melting into the trees. They listened and watched until the unmistakable sound of a single engine plane grew steadily from the east. The Stork was back. The little plane droned over their heads heading west and continued on towards the river. But suddenly, almost at the limit of hearing, it turned and made its way back towards them.

Yuri and the Colonel looked at each other, "did they see us?" asked a concerned Yuri.

The Colonel shrugged, "I don't think so," he replied warily, "but I wish he'd piss off back to where he came from." The Stork continued to circle around their position, sometimes coming close, but then turning away. "It's doing a general search of the area," the Colonel said suspiciously, "I've never known it stick around for this long before. I think we're getting out of this location just in time."

Finally, the little plane swung off southwards and the sound disappeared, only to be followed a couple of minutes later by the same sound coming down from the north. Yuri was uneasy, two Storks quartering the area seemed to him like their position was known to the Germans. Surely there was no spy within the party? Could it just be coincidence?

The Colonel grimaced as the Stork passed overhead and turned to Yuri, "I don't like it one little bit," he said worriedly, "if you ask me, they're following the lines of the pathways. For whatever reason there's two Storks above us and I can only think there will be troops in place on the ground before much longer. We've got to get across the road tonight, there's no question about that now."

With that, the Colonel lapsed into silence, while the second Stork continued to drone around above them, everyone staying still and quiet. Eventually, it too moved away westwards and the party were able to continue, albeit in a sombre mood.

A couple of miles had passed them by as they trudged on, but after an hour the Storks returned.

They almost caught them unawares, but the black did its job and the rear scouts shouted a warning, otherwise they would have been caught in the open. As it was, there was barely time to vacate the path, before the two planes droned overhead.

The Colonel was livid, "fucking Storks," he ranted to no-one in particular, "that was a close one. Hopefully they're low on fuel for today and are heading for home. All of a sudden, this area is becoming a fascist playground."

He shook his fist at the disappearing planes and spat vehemently in the stodgy puddles. "I'll be damned if we're not on the other side of the main road by tonight. This journey is becoming a nightmare."

Once again, the party dragged itself back onto the path and walked on into the rain. The evening brought a respite from the problems overhead, the Storks must have returned to their base and the rain finally petered out. However, the end of the day was cold and damp, with the clouds much in evidence and the wind still strong from the North West. The miles were stacking up behind them, as they approached the main road. Corporal Kurnakov halted the column and strode back to where Yuri was standing beside the wagon. The Colonel and Yenisei were sitting in the back as the corporal came up.

"Bad news," he said to all within hearing. "The scouts report that the road is very busy, in both directions." He picked up a stick and began to draw in the mud by the side of the path. "Where the path meets the road, it's on a long incline from west to east. Before the incline, which isn't too severe, is a hill and the fascists are experiencing great difficulty getting up the hill and along the incline due to the rain turning the road into a morass of thick gluey mud. They are having to push and drag all motorised vehicles up the hill and across the incline. There is also a certain amount of refugee traffic trying to head west, but they are caught up in the general pandemonium. The fascists horse drawn carts and wagons are faring a little better, but in most cases, the horses are being unhitched from their carts and wagons once they've reached the end of the incline and are being taken back to help pull the motorised vehicles up the hill and part way along. The whole movement of transport is taking an age to complete. Hopefully, the remnants of the column, will wait overnight at the bottom of the hill for another try in the morning, while the rest, who have made the summit, will continue onwards towards Minsk. The scouts have gone back to keep an eye on the situation and will report back when there is a chance for us to cross. I've sent one man to the top of the hill and another to the end of the incline. These two will relay the situation at either end, to the rest of the squad, who I'll take forward to the edge of the tree line. If the rest of you could just wait here, off the path obviously, I'll get the situation back to you as soon as possible. We're about a mile from the road here, so it's just a case of waiting it out."

The corporal hurried off with his six soldiers, while the rest gathered around to wait for the moment to cross. Alayna and Giselle broke out some cold meat and bread with some mugs of water. Yuri approached the two Jews, Moshe and Ben and asked if they would keep an eye on their rear at say, about five hundred yards. The two were keen to help and Yuri was happy that they would be alert and able to cope with any circumstance that might arise.

Once they had gone, he, the Colonel, Yenisei, Stephan and Ivan held a discussion. "Apart from the Storks, we've made good progress," began Yuri, "with a bit of luck, we'll be across and well away from here long before midnight."

The Colonel agreed, "Yes," he said grudgingly, "I must admit those planes scare the shit out of me. If it wasn't for that black, we'd have been spotted easily, so really, we've done very well."

Yenisei was more cautious, "I don't want to alarm the ladies," he said quietly, "but I have a bad feeling about today, as if someone had put their finger on our very position. We know that Vladimir was a

German working within the camp, who sold us out very badly and many lives were lost. I have a feeling that someone else could have dropped us in it, especially with the reward posters. There's not a hope in hell that the fascists would pay up for information, but some of our simple soldiers could be persuaded, never having dreamed of money like that before. I, for one, will not be happy until we're well rid of this area and much further north and east."

Yuri and the Colonel nodded their agreement just as events, once again, began to spiral out of control. The first hint of anything awkward was the rapid arrival of Corporal Kurnakov with the six soldiers.

 "Sir," he gasped out to Yuri, "get everyone away from here now. There's a twenty-man SS patrol coming down the path and they're not far behind us."

Yuri was galvanised into action. "The wagon," he shouted to Pieter, "get it turned around and head back the way we came. There's a side path off to the east about a mile back. Move!"

The wagon was swung around, both horses excitable, but Pieter held them in firm control. Yenisei and the Colonel scrambled back inside the covers and with Yuri leading, moved off south at a brisk pace. Moshe and Ben appeared out of the trees some way along the path and Yuri hurriedly explained the situation as they made for the side path. Once there, Pieter swung the horses into the narrow aisle and headed off east.

Yuri ran to Corporal Kurnakov, "take four men and get into a position opposite here in the woods. If the SS come up the side path, get in behind them. We'll be about five hundred yards along there and we'll have them in a crossfire."

The corporal nodded, "understand sir," he said. The corporal and his men melted away into the trees and brush on the west side while Yuri and the other two soldiers headed east to the wagon. When he arrived, he sent the two soldiers into the trees on the left while the two Jews went to the right. Yenisei and the Colonel were prone under the wagon, both with rifles pointed back the way they had come. Stephan and Ivan had taken up a kneeling position behind each wheel. Alayna and Giselle were helping Pieter calm the horses, both of which were reacting to the scent of panic emanating from the fleeing group. However, Pieter was an old hand at horse handling and between the three of them, the pair settled, and the black especially ceased trembling, its breath finally becoming even. Yuri slid into the wagon, his rifle ready to the rear, but he was watching the reaction of the black. The minutes dragged on, until finally, the black's ears pricked, its head came up sharply, but with a soft coaxing voice, Pieter calmed and settled him down. By then, Yuri had the scoped rifle nestling against his shoulder and was searching for the SS. The squad marched purposefully southwards down the main path, looking neither to left nor right, apart from brief glances into the trees on either side. They marched totally unaware that yards away, sudden death lay waiting, as they focused only on the path ahead. Twenty men, armed to the teeth and heavily laden, with an aura of being chillingly prepared for anything. They passed the side path with barely a glance and continued southwards. Within a few minutes, they were gone.

The relief from everyone was palpable in the extreme. They had avoided a fight, which they couldn't have hoped to have won convincingly and had remained hidden and silent. Now was the time to ride their luck and head back towards the road. The wagon was turned with a little difficulty and the party headed back to the main path. There, Corporal Kurnakov and his men re-joined the main group.

"Back to the road corporal," said a relieved Yuri, "we'll be in the same spot where we were earlier. Moshe and Ben will do a holding role to the rear. Let's hope there's going to be no more surprises tonight."

The corporal grinned and saluted. "I'd just got back to the tree line, when these two trucks appeared from the east. They both stopped opposite our position and the two squad leaders, one from each truck, had a chat by the side of the main road. Then the lead truck carried on westwards, while the other one disgorged its troops. We got back to you as quickly as possible. Where the other truck was heading I have no idea, but it could be that they've gone down towards the River Bug. My feeling is that both squads will come together at some point and there could even be a third or a fourth squad somewhere between us and the island. I fear we're leaving too many tracks, but we can't be too pedantic within the time frame we have set. Let's just hope they're not very good on the scent."

The corporal saluted again and hurried off to join his men, Yuri's mind working overtime on the possibilities facing the group. Pieter moved the horses along at an easy pace and they reached the place where they had stopped earlier after about an hour. "Now we wait again," said Yuri tiredly, "we've got to cross tonight, whatever happens. Would you be prepared to keep going right through the night?"

The Colonel, Ivan, Stephan, Yenisei and the two girls looked at each other, shrugged and nodded.

"I think you're right," said the Colonel. "Again, that SS squad seemed to be heading for a definite rendezvous with someone or something. I think we should try to get as far away from here as possible."

"Corporal Kurnakov said there were two trucks on the main road and one went further west," said Yuri worriedly, "he thinks, as I do, that the SS are sweeping the whole area we've just passed through. My real concern is that they will team up with the Wehrmacht section who have the dogs. We're leaving a scent trail a mile wide with the horses and all of us. That's why we have to keep going through the night. The four Jewish lads know the woods ahead really well, even in the darkness. They've hunted here since they were kids and guarantee they can lead us exactly where we want to go."

The group lapsed into silence, each with their own thoughts. The evening ebbed into darkness, the wind still ruffling the trees as they waited for the corporal to return.

After an hour or so, one of the soldiers appeared. "With the corporal's compliments sir," he said softly, "could you all move forward to the tree line by the road. He believes the way across will soon be practicable."

Yuri nodded, gave the thumbs up to Pieter and the group moved forward. After about a mile, another of the soldiers appeared. "Just wait here sir," he said, "the corporal will be along in a minute. The road is now passable."

The cavalcade halted, the tension gripping everyone. After a few minutes, the soldier beckoned them forward. At the tree line, Corporal Kurnakov stepped out of the shadows. He motioned to Yuri to join him and the pair went forward through the thinning trees.

"I've had the signal from the man at the top of the hill," said the corporal guardedly, "I'm just waiting for the man at the top of the incline to respond."

Yuri nodded, ready for the crossing. "There," said the corporal, "see the light?"

Yuri strained his eyes to the east, "Yes, I see it corporal," he said, "get your men across to the other side and into position. We'll wait for your signal, one flash only."

The corporal nodded, gathered his men together and in a crouched run, they splodged their way across the main road and into the screening trees on the other side. After a few minutes, Yuri saw the single light flash.

"OK Pieter, bring the wagon in at an angle and try and cross on a sideways run, rather than straight across. Whatever happens, keep moving. The road looks pretty messed up."

Pieter nodded, clicked his tongue and the pair of horses pulled the wagon out of the screening trees towards the road. The gradient was gently downwards until the road was reached, everywhere was just a sea of mud. Tyre tracks, wagon wheel tracks, footprints and hoof prints, were all haphazardly speckled across what once had been a dirt road. Running down the centre, were two deep grooves where the assorted traffic had tried to make its way east and west. The moon loitered palely through the encompassing cloud cover and there were also signs of frost forming. It would be a cold night ahead. The wagon slithered and skidded across the clinging morass until Pieter finally, with a supreme effort on behalf of the horses, dragged his way out of the mud and into the trees beyond. The party waited there, giving the horses a breather and waiting for the two Jews from the top of the hill and the end of the incline, to catch up.

 "Get us away from here for a few miles Avi, then we'll have a discussion about where we see ourselves by the end of the night," said a relieved Yuri. "We're gambling that you know exactly where you are going, even in the darkness."

Avi grinned, his teeth showing grey in the soft light, "don't worry," he said candidly, "Jacob and I know these forests like the backs of our hands. We won't get too far ahead, just keep coming on at a good pace."

Avi turned and moved onto the semblance of a path that headed northeast and with Jacob by his side, trotted off into the darkness, while the rest of the party pulled into line behind them. Corporal Kurnakov and four of the soldiers ranged in front of the wagon, while Yuri and the other two brought up the rear. Ben and Moshe continued to hang back as a rear guard, the others rode in the wagon. The miles and time slipped slowly by. The sky cleared as they travelled, leaving the odd scudding clouds flowing swiftly across the heavens, while a million stars twinkled in the black firmament. When they stopped for the discussion, the crescent moon bathed the area in a pallid glow. It was obvious that everyone was tired, even the horses appeared sluggish and reluctant, but they needed to be far from here by sun up.

Everyone gathered round to hear what Avi had to say. "The going from here is undulating, many small ridges and long open valleys, but not as marshy as we've been used to. We'll be exposed from time to time as we cross these open areas, but Jacob has chosen the spot where we need to be by the coming of the sun. By our reckoning, that will be another twenty-five miles. String yourselves out across the open areas, we'll try and leave as thin a trail as possible. After fifteen miles I'll call a halt, it'll be where we make the first river crossing, but I can't emphasise enough the need to get to Jacob's stopping point by four to four thirty. Just make sure we keep nicely grouped and if anyone needs to stop, we all stop, understood?"

There was a chorus of nodding heads, no-one wanted to waste energy by talking. So, they formed up in a long line and moved out. The endless night stretched out before them, frost now turning the ground into a crunching sea of ice. Tired limbs stumbled and slithered their way across the moonlit wastes, everyone's heads drooping and swinging from side to side. Yenisei, the Colonel and the two girls slept intermittently in the rocking and rolling wagon as the hours and the miles slipped slowly by. One o'clock passed then two o'clock when Avi called a halt. All the men flopped onto the ground, regardless of the cold and frosted surface. They were almost at the end of their tether. After twenty minutes, Yuri got them back on their feet.

Avi appeared and whispered quietly. "Up ahead is a bridge. It's wooden and a bit rickety, but it's clear of the enemy."

Once again, they moved out. The bridge was crossed with no problems and Yuri moved them all on again, driving himself and the others towards the limit of their endurance. Eventually, when all were certain that they could go no further, they reached Jacob's resting place. It was a small glade, screened by trees and rocky outcrops, with a couple of oaks in the centre. Yuri gazed around through sore eyes and pronounced it good.

"This is excellent Jacob," he said with as much enthusiasm as his tiredness could muster, "everyone get bedded down, we'll sleep away the daylight hours and continue tonight."

The men needed no second bidding, as they laid out their tents and blankets, crawled into them and were immediately asleep.

The Colonel slid down from the wagon and said, "I'll look after the two horses Pieter, I know what I'm doing. You get yourself some sleep. Yenisei and I will stand guard, we've had a fair bit of rest while we've been travelling and the girls will help."

Yuri nodded blankly and he and Pieter rolled out their blankets under the wagon and were soon snoring peacefully. By two o'clock, all of the men were awake. The sun graced them with its presence throughout the morning, which helped raise the spirits of all of them. The girls and Yenisei had been busy, courtesy of the paraffin stoves and there was a hot meal for everyone with bread, coffee or tea. The Colonel had stood guard duty, keeping his eye on the surrounding area and leading the horses to fresh grazing around the camp perimeter. The pair were now roped to trees and were munching away at the long, coarse grass. While everyone was eating, he returned and pronounced the area secure, as far as he could see.

"It's been a quiet morning," he said thankfully, "no sign of man or beast. I did see a Stork again, way over to the south, but it came nowhere near our position. Hopefully, they're still concentrating on the area south of the main road. We can all relax a little this afternoon, because tonight is going to be another walk in darkness. However, we should make the forest after a few hours travel, then it's up to our Jewish guides as to how far we go before stopping for sleep. It could be that we could sleep from two o'clock onwards and then spend the rest of that day travelling, the forest providing us with cover. What do you think Avi?"

The tall Jew shrugged and said, "We've made good time so far. I would rather make up my mind later tonight. The closer we are to Minsk the better, in my view. We can always find somewhere to hide and I would rather have more time at or around the rendezvous than dawdle our time away in between."

My thoughts entirely," answered Yuri, "you make the decision Avi, but I would also rather be there and in position. Anyone else think differently?"

The rest nodded in agreement, no-one wanted to tarry in case something or someone caused a hold-up. The final decision would be left up to Avi tonight.

Feldwebel Huth was becoming agitated. He and his squad had arrived at their agreed rendezvous with the two SS patrols earlier in the morning, but of either patrol, there had been no sign so far. They were, had they known it, beneath the two oaks opposite the island and the Feldwebel was keen to pass on the information his unit had found out. His orders were to follow the paths he had used previously to get to the position he was now in. He and his squad had overnighted in the hut, used in the past by Yuri and the fleeing civilians and latterly, the Colonel. The SS were being ferried three quarters of the way by truck on the main road. They would camp out last night and were then to spend this morning searching the paths and area to the east and west of the island. When Huth's unit passed the northward leading path, used by Yuri's party yesterday, the two Dobermanns immediately started to become agitated and very interested in the northern path and all the way to the southern path, west of the island. Huth decided to reconnoitre down the western path and the dogs led them to the wood store, hidden deep within the screening trees. The store was very cleverly hidden and was difficult to spot, but the dogs strode right up to the door. Ha ha, he thought. This is where they've been hiding out. His unit made a thorough search of the surrounding area, finding the remains of campfires and where tents had been erected. They also spotted wheel tracks and where horses had cropped the grass. All he needed now was the SS and the dogs would follow the scent and tracks northwards, where the party had obviously travelled over the last few days. He was not best pleased when two o'clock passed and there was still no sign.

"Can you see anything yet?" he barked at Schmidt.

"Nothing yet sir," the private replied. Schmidt was high in the oak tree with the Feldwebel's binoculars, trying to spot the SS patrols coming up from the south.

"Damn their lateness," the Feldwebel muttered to himself, "The fucking SS are a sodding law unto themselves." He kicked absent-mindedly at a rock and sent it scurrying across the path.

The minutes ticked slowly by, until Schmidt cried out excitedly, "Here they come sergeant, coming up both paths. They'll be here in ten minutes or so."

Hurriedly, Schmidt scrambled back down the tree and stood waiting with the rest of his unit. Huth was uneasy. He detested the SS, they frightened him a lot and he knew his men felt the same. So, with some trepidation, he waited for their arrival. The two squads marched up the path towards them, one from the east and the other from the west. As both groups came to a halt, he brought his unit sharply to attention and they all gave a vociferous 'Heil Hitler'. The SS also snapped to attention and chorused the same in return.

"Well Feldwebel," the senior Oberleutnant commanded in a deep gravelly voice. "Have you come up with anything we can use?"

Huth nodded, "Jawohl Herr Oberleutnant. We found where they had been hiding out, it's down the path behind you, cleverly screened behind the trees. The dogs took us straight there this morning."

He smiled inwardly at the sudden look of annoyance on the Oberleutnant's face which was followed by, "Show me."

Huth's mouth dropped open, "but Herr Oberleutnant," he protested, "surely we should be allowing the dogs to follow the scent trail."

"I wish to see the place where the Ivan trash managed to hide from you so many times in the past." The last few words were delivered ever so sweetly, but Huth felt the barbed comment strike home.

"Well, well of course," he spluttered, "if you would just follow me sir."

With that, he and the SS went back to the wood store, all the time he was conscious of the fact that they were losing any advantage they might have gained, by getting on the party's trail immediately. Eventually, the Oberleutnant was satisfied, but somewhat maliciously instructed his troops to set

480

fire to the store and throw any equipment found into the lake.

"They won't use this to hole up in again," he said with a grim smile as the flames took hold. Then the three squads marched off eastwards. At the point in the trail where the path turned north, the Feldwebel made to go that way but was halted by the Oberleutnant.

"Why are we going this way?" The Oberleutnant asked belligerently.

Huth blanched. "Well sir, the dogs are keen to follow it north. Look at them sir."

The dogs were straining at the leash, but the Oberleutnant was unconvinced. "My squad and I came down that path last evening," he retorted, "we saw and heard nothing."

"Perhaps they had gone off on one of the side paths. Over there, the wheel marks are clearly shown," offered an exasperated Huth, "look at the dog's sir!"

After fifteen minutes of haggling, Huth finally got his way from a clearly reluctant Oberleutnant. They all headed north, but the afternoon was passing. Actually, they made good time and arrived at the main road as the sun finally slipped over the horizon. The Oberleutnant called a halt and ordered the three squads to prepare for sleep.

"We'll catch them up tomorrow," crowed the Oberleutnant. "Tonight, we need rest."

Huth was mollified. They would need daylight to scan the road and see just where the wagon and the party had crossed. The dogs had guided them past all the side trails except one. Closer inspection had revealed that the party had indeed used this path and Huth felt exonerated, because this side path was clearly where the party was, when the SS had passed yesterday. Not so clever now, Herr Oberleutnant, he thought mischievously to himself.

As the SS were going into camp, the party were preparing to leave. The afternoon and evening had been spent in lazy contemplation and they were now ready to hit the road. Yuri had spent the time with Alayna, something he could never have envisaged twenty-four hours ago. The others left them to each other, most casting envious glances at two people so obviously in love. Yuri though, was fascinated by the interaction of Giselle and the Colonel and he said as much to Alayna.

"Yes," she answered to his question. "There are strong feelings between them and a bond is developing. I'm not sure if Giselle will come with us, or stay behind with Sergei. It will have to be up to them when the time comes."

As darkness fell, the party prepared to move out. Their formation was the same as the previous night, with Corporal Kurnakov and four soldiers leading, while Yenisei, the Colonel, Giselle and Alayna travelled in the wagon. Yuri, Stephan, Ivan and the other two soldiers brought up the rear. Avi and Jacob scouted ahead and showed the way, while Moshe and Ben lagged behind Yuri, protecting the rear. The night was clear and cold and before long, the ground began to freeze. Avi led them across open ground and through dense thickets of scrub and trees, always angling northeast towards the airfield and Minsk. The moon shone brightly in its starlit heaven and all was peace and quiet, save for the horse's footfalls and the gentle creaks from the wagon as it rolled from side to side. The miles stacked up and when Avi called a halt, it was just after midnight. The twenty minute respite gave everyone a chance to ease their aching limbs, before they once again took to the road. Avi had told them that they were about an hour away from the forest and after crossing a long valley, the trees ahead stood out starkly against the black, star sprinkled night sky. When they entered the forest, the difference in light intensity was immediately apparent. But it was also a little warmer, the trees keeping away the wind and the forest floor was only sparsely frosted. However, the cavalcade slowed down noticeably, as the shadowy silence seemed to hem them in. Avi led them for another four or five miles before calling a halt.

It was around two thirty and the night was noticeably cooler. Gone were the clear skies of an hour ago and in its place, a thick layer of heavy cloud. The ghostly moon did its best to lighten the way, but it was becoming harder and harder to see.

"My idea would be to camp here for the rest of the night," said Avi, "the light is becoming very bad and Jacob has found us a place off the main path, about a hundred yards from here. We can continue once the morning is well under way, at least we'll be able to see where we're going."

"Sounds OK to me," admitted Yuri, "lead on Jacob, the horses could definitely do with a rest and I think we're all pretty tired."

Jacob led them to where the trees thinned a little. The wagon slipped easily between the towering pines and after about three hundred yards, the trees opened up into a small glade, perfect for their means. Tents were pitched, blankets spread out and before long the party was bedded down. Pieter found some good grazing for his pair of horses, tying them securely to a couple of tree trunks. He then pitched his tent close to them and was soon asleep. Two of the soldiers were given the first watch of three hours. They would be relieved, just before sun up. Yuri was satisfied that they had journeyed as far as they could have. Going on would have been a risk that they didn't have to take. Avi's advice was good, daylight would be much easier.

The two soldiers were wrapped up against the late night cold. Theirs was the first watch, but they weren't too unhappy about it. They wandered around the camp as quietly as they could, listening and watching for anything out of the ordinary. The party had been asleep for an hour when the black's ears pricked and it scrabbled to its feet, followed by the other. The snort of alarm brought Pieter rolling out of his blankets and he made for his two skittish charges. The black was quivering and pawing the ground, its eyes fixed on the trees to the North West. The nearest guard slid over to join Pieter and whispered, "What's wrong?"

Pieter shook his head. "The black's acting like it's some sort of animal," he replied equally quietly, "could be a bear or wolves. You'd better wake the officers."

The guard slipped away and shook Yuri awake. "The black's acting up," said the guard to Yuri's questioning look, "Pieter thinks it's an animal, the way it's reacting."

Yuri was out of his blankets in a flash and padded over to Pieter and the horses. Both were now very agitated and Yuri could see the concern in Pieter's face. "What's out there Pieter?" he asked worriedly. They were answered by the howl of a wolf to the northwest, which was closely followed by an answering howl from the northeast.

"Bring the horses closer to the centre of the camp," said Yuri, "I'll get the rest up and prepared."

The second guard had come over to see what all the commotion was about and he helped Pieter and the other guard move the frightened horses. The camp was coming alive, everyone was up and armed. The black still looked off towards the north, rolling its eyes in fear. Another howl drifted down on the wind, closer this time and then all hell broke loose in the trees to the north of the camp. There was a roar of pain, followed by the sound of fighting beasts, growls and snarls and the crashing of savage animals locked together in mortal combat. Another howl of anger and the screams of something in agony was wrenched out of a throat in torment. The scrub and low foliage towards the edge of the glade was shaking violently, when suddenly, with a roar of pain, a large bear burst through the trees and raced madly into the camp, followed closely by at least eight wolves, all hell bent on catching up with it. The moon had broken through the cloud ceiling, enough to see the bear and wolves approaching. The bear was oblivious to the man shapes before him, his only intention was to flee the bared teeth just yards behind him. He careered onwards, straight at Ivan who was crouched with his rifle and bayonet, thrust out in front of him. Ivan knew he was doomed, even as he plunged the bayonet deep into the bear's chest. The shock of the charge hit Ivan in the belly and he fell backwards, the rifle and bayonet still welded tightly to his hands. The bear loomed over him, one huge clawed paw lashed at Ivan's exposed face and throat, almost tearing his head off. Ivan finally let go of the rifle, the butt thudding into the ground, the bear being skewered by the bayonet and then the first wolf jumped onto the bear's back while another grabbed its exposed right leg. It screamed in agony as another piled onto its back and the weight of the three falling animals, shoved the bayonet, through the bears ribs and out of its back followed by the rifle barrel. The rest of the wolves piled in for the kill, guns crashed and bayonets hacked at the melee covering the bear and Ivan. Suddenly, it was all over. Two of the wolves limped slowly away into the trees and were bayoneted by one of the soldiers. The others and the bear, had been hacked to pieces. The camp was in chaos, the frantic horses lunged and bucked at the scent of bear, wolves, blood and death. The speed and savagery of the last four minutes had left everyone in complete shock. Then the realisation that Ivan was embedded under all the bloody carnage, galvanised them into action. The shredded wolves were dragged off and the bear pulled away. The blacksmith from Abakan was ripped to pieces, his head almost decapitated and his face, hardly recognisable, such had been the fury of the attack. Two or three of the men retched at the sight of so much gore and the accompanying cloying scent of blood. The Colonel dropped down from the back of the wagon and gazed all around him, Yenisei surveying the scene from the wagon, close to tears. Everyone was numb and speechless, until the Colonel took control.

"Yuri, get a burial detail formed. Avi, take Jacob up the path to the east, Ben, you and Moshe go west. If anyone heard this commotion, they'll be coming to investigate. Giselle, you and Alayna get some coffee on and some food. The rest of you, form a circle around the camp and face outwards. We may have got away with the noise, but I wouldn't count on it. Stephan, help Pieter to move the horses upwind of here and away from the killing ground. It's over, so let's not dwell on it. Move!!"

The Colonel's words and commanding rhetoric, snapped them out of their stupor. Everyone in the party had a job to do and went to it. The dead animals were carted into the brush and dumped, out of the way. Yuri and three of the soldiers dug a deep grave for Ivan, who was laid to rest with his head facing east. Once the grave had been filled in, the party gathered around the spot for a moment's reflection. Prayers were uttered and thanks given for a life well spent. Ivan would be sorely missed and his legacy would be their escape, which he had helped to fashion. Morning had crept up on them and the day was cloaked in cloud as the hours ticked by. A gentle rain dampened the grass, beginning the process of washing away the remnants of the past few hours. The four Jews were back from their scouting, having found nothing to alarm them at the moment. So, the horses were hitched up to the wagon and the party vacated the clearing and hurried back to the path. Avi set a brisk pace to the east and before long, the clearing was just a distant horror-filled memory, albeit, tinged with deep sadness.

The path began to rise quite sharply and after a few miles, they topped out on a long ridge, high above the forest which stretched out interminably to the north, east and west. Through his binoculars, Yuri could easily make out the main road to the south, with its endless stream of vehicles and horse drawn wagons. To the northeast was the large military airfield, with its connecting road leading to Minsk, somewhere to the east behind the tree screen. About twelve miles beyond the military airfield, was the smaller, civilian airfield, which was their goal. Avi gathered all the party together just after lunch, to explain the next few hours. Everyone was there except Ben and Moshe who were quite a distance back, keeping an eye out for any pursuit.

"This afternoon, we will cross the road," began Avi, "and make for the rendezvous point. If all goes to plan, we'll meet up with the others around tea time. That will give us a few hours to prepare for our attack on the airfield. Once we come down from this ridge, we'll be quite close to the road, where we'll see just what we have to do to get across it. Jacob and I will reconnoitre the situation and get back to you. Just keep coming on as you are. Any questions?" No-one answered. "OK," said Avi, "let's move out."

The party formed up in their usual file and stepped out along the path. The rain was still persisting, with no sign of a let-up in sight. Gradually, the path began to taper downwards and the going levelled out over a few miles. Yuri was bringing up the rear, when a noise behind him made him turn quickly, rifle aimed and ready. He breathed a sigh of relief however, as Ben and Moshe came jogging down the path. He halted the party to let them catch up, but was concerned by their news, once they arrived.

 "We're being followed by a large SS patrol and they appear to be about fifty strong" began a breathless Moshe, "they're about fifteen miles back, but heading right for us. They've probably followed us from the main road and they have two dogs, Dobermanns by the look of them."

The party digested the new information. More trouble, that seemed to have dogged them from the very outset of the journey. Yuri looked grim, but the Colonel spoke.

"I have an idea," he said candidly. "We're not far from the airfield now, so I think it's time we abandoned the wagon and walked from this point. Would you be up for that Yenisei?"

The little man from Abakan nodded, "I will be fine," he said.

"Good," said the Colonel, "Avi told me earlier, that there's a side path about half a mile from here, which leads to the military airfield. I think we'll take the wagon up this side path and leave it where the woods end, close to the airfield. That way, the SS and their dogs will follow the wagon and not us, hopefully. We'll abandon the wagon there and Pieter can take the horses back through the woods by foot, if that's OK with him?"

Pieter grinned and said, "My horses will be fine now, but I would love to get them back to the Russian camp. The black is priceless."

The party nodded its agreement. "Then that's what we'll do," said the Colonel decisively, "get everything out of the wagon that we might need and then we'll head off. Corporal Kurnakov, can I have a word please?"

The corporal nodded and trotted over. He and the Colonel were in deep conversation for several minutes. The corporal looked bemused and then grinned hugely. He nodded and went to help unpack. Everyone loaded themselves with packs, weapons and accoutrements. They all made a huge fuss of Pieter and the two horses, everyone saying their goodbyes. When all was ready, they moved off to meet Avi and Jacob. Half a mile on, the side path appeared, the wagon turning into it and with a wave from Pieter, disappeared off along it, Corporal Kurnakov and a couple of soldiers going along to give support if needed.

"What was all that about," asked a curious Yuri, "I mean, with Corporal Kurnakov?"

"Oh, nothing too serious," answered the Colonel, "I've just asked him if he can watch out for the SS coming along behind us. He'll join up with us later."

Yuri was mollified and said, "OK," in reply. The party walked for another few miles before Jacob appeared.

"Avi says to move up now," he said positively, "the road is clear at the moment and he thinks we should be able to cross."

Having digested this positive information the party hurried on, until they began to approach the thinning tree line and the road. Avi met them and asked for a couple of soldiers to head off to the left and right, to give them the thumbs up for crossing. Evening was now upon them and the grey, shadowy sky, showed no signs of the rain lessening. Yuri and the Colonel watched the two soldiers disappear along the road. Both turned and waved to say the road was OK. The party then made their way across and were soon deep within the trees on the other side. The Colonel, however, had stayed back with Moshe and Ben and the two Jews were helping the Colonel rig up a line to the telegraph wires that ran alongside the road. The Colonel was sending his message to the SS Headquarters in Minsk. After several minutes, he pronounced himself satisfied, de-rigged the line and the three of them hurried off to join up with the rest. The party had travelled a couple of miles before the Colonel and the two Jews caught up with them.

At Yuri's questioning glance he admitted, "I've sent a message to the SS Headquarters in Minsk, using 'Rhine Maiden'. I don't think they know that Vladimir's dead, so I thought I'd save 'Kuhmo Wolf' for another day. The gist of the message was, that we're going to attack the Military Airfield tonight and that Yenisei, Valery, Alexei and I are leading the attack. I'm hoping that the SS will send out a big squad to apprehend us, thus leaving the centre of Minsk unprotected for Alexei later. What I didn't tell you before, is that I've asked Corporal Kurnakov to precipitate an attack between the SS following us and the SS coming from Minsk. If he can get between the two forces once it gets dark, and shoot at both sides, I'm hoping those following will think it's us at the airfield. Conversely, the SS at the airfield will believe they're under attack from us. What do you think?"

Yuri gawped, shook his head and burst into laughter. "I love the way your mind works," he said happily, "the SS shooting themselves up. Whatever will you think of next?" He trotted off then to join Alayna. The rendezvous would not be far ahead.

Avi and Jacob guided them onto a side path that opened out into a small glade. The first person Yuri saw was Valery.

"You made it," said an enthusiastic Valery, "how was your journey?"

Yuri embraced his friend and told him their story, the days and nights of travel, the bear and wolves debacle, Ivan's demise and the fact that the SS were hot on their heels. He then reiterated the Colonels coded message, the fact that Minsk would be almost devoid of soldiers when Alexei's attack went in and also the SS shooting each other up at the Military Airfield, hopefully. Valery took it all in and nodded his agreement.

"Sergei's a clever sod," he said ruefully, "he's a damned good leader and no mistake. I'm really sorry about Ivan, he was a good man and a patriot. Well, you've had a torrid time. Maybe now, it's time to get you all out and away, once night descends upon us. Let's get our heads together and I'll tell you what I've planned." With that, the pair joined the rest who were taking a well-earned breather.

At the SS Headquarters in Minsk, Franz had decoded the Colonels message and was rushing downstairs to Hauptmann Lientz's office. He rapped on the door, listened for the perfunctory reply and then entered. Lientz was in a foul mood, having heard from Oberleutnant Schaefer this morning that the party had been discovered, but not apprehended.

"Well Franz," he said grumpily, "I hope you bring me some good news for a change."

Franz hesitated and then said, "Good news and bad news I'm afraid sir. We've received a message from 'Rhine Maiden.' Lientz's mood brightened. "Apparently, Berezovsky, Korsakov and the Avseyenko brothers are planning a big raid on the Military Airfield……… tonight."

"What," screamed Lientz, "call out the guard at once. Get eighty men mobilised and on their way to the airfield. Do it now Franz, do it now."

Franz scuttled off, he didn't need a second telling. Lientz was beside himself. Sodding Ivan's, he thought broodily, God knows where they get the cheek. Attack the Military Airfield? Shit, what's the fucking war coming to. By then, Franz was putting his master's orders into place. Four truckloads of SS were dispatched forthwith, leaving a skeleton guard to defend Minsk City centre. The Colonels plan was beginning to work.

Valery gathered everyone around and laid out the night's proceedings. "In about half an hour, we'll all move up to the outskirts of the airfield. You'll be pleased to know, that the JU-52 is there and we're pretty sure it's fuelled and ready for take-off. I've had several of my men watching the comings and goings there for the past three nights and I think we've got the timing pretty well sewn up. Yuri, you and I will have the task of nullifying the perimeter guards, with the crossbows. They're sticklers for the same time changeover of guards and the substitution is at seven thirty. The rest of us will take over the place once the two gate guards are eliminated. Once we're in the control buildings, silence won't be an issue. We've just got to make sure no-one sends off a distress call. The group who are flying out will stay together outside the airfield, until we make the base secure. We'll give you the signal, then it's up to Stephan to fly you out of here. The attack will go in at eight o'clock. At the same time, Alexei will begin his assault on SS Headquarters in Minsk. They will also try to free up another batch of Jews. I do have a request for the flying out party. Would it be possible to take some of the Jewish contingent with you, perhaps a dozen or so women and children? It's only a small amount, but they've drawn lots and are happy with the result. Please let me know and I'll arrange the details. We leave here in, er, fifteen minutes."

The meeting broke up, Valery heading off to organise his men. The flying out party discussed the question of the Jewish women and children coming with them and unanimously agreed to take them. Then they all readied themselves for the final push and moved out towards the airfield.

The small group of four horse drawn wagons and a single field gun trundled slowly along the main road towards Minsk. In the lead was a German Lieutenant, resplendent upon a grey mare. His poncho was dripping from the continuous rain, but the grey didn't seem to mind, stepping along quite jauntily. The wagons slithered slowly along, the German handlers slouched in their seats, allowing their horses to make their own pace. To the casual observer, it was just like any other German column from any day, during the last three months. But on this occasion, the casual observer would be wrong. On the leading grey horse was a tall Russian Jew. He had been chosen to lead the column, because he was fluent in spoken German. Behind him, each wagon held five Russian soldiers plus the horse handler, all kitted out in stolen German uniforms. The final wagon pulled a seventy-five millimetre field gun and watching expectantly out of the back covers was Alexei. The column continued its laborious journey through the outer suburbs, until a commotion broke out up ahead.

The man on the grey shouted back to the handler in the first wagon, "somethings up Pavel, there's a bunch of fascist trucks baring down on us, light's flashing, horns blaring. You'd better tell the Lieutenant."

The message was passed back through the wagons until Alexei, who had heard the distant tumult, stuck his head out of the last wagon. "Fucking hell," he said vehemently, "what in shit's name's going on."

The trucks continued to charge towards them and Alexei feared the worst. "We'll just try and brazen it out," he yelled to the wagons in front. If they want us, we're dead anyway. Just act dumb."

The trucks plunged towards them, the handlers having to take evasive action and bump up onto the kerbs, to allow the oncoming trucks free passage. Without as much as a wave from anyone, the four trucks howled past and hurtled down the road away from the city. Alexei tried to repair his thundering heart and said to no-one in particular, "Bloody hell that was close. Where the fuck are they off to. I hope it's not that fucking airfield we're using tonight, or our guys are in it right up to their necks. Let's look on the bright side, perhaps Hitler's had a change of heart and has proposed marriage to Churchill."

The rest of the wagon laughed at Alexei's ribald comment. Trust the Lieutenant to come up with a beauty. Calmly, the column moved gently on, through the suburbs and into the main heart of the city. Their target tonight was SS Headquarters. They were going to free a few prisoners and then blow it up. The time was approaching seven forty-five when the column halted in the street, just past the headquarters. Fifteen minutes, thought Alexei, then its crossbow time and bye-bye fucking SS.

Back at the Military Airfield, Corporal Kurnakov and his two soldiers were in position in the woods. They were waiting for the arrival of the following SS squad and were beginning to wonder where they'd got to. The corporal's position put him halfway between the abandoned wagon in the trees to his left and the perimeter of the airfield to his right. The three men had watched with grim interest as the four trucks skidded to a halt, disgorging their troops, just inside the perimeter gates. Their officers had quickly organised them into a formidable line, facing south, where the expected attack was going to come from. After a few minutes, they were hidden and ready. But the corporal knew where they were. The darkness was almost total, the moon being swallowed up by the thick rain sodden clouds, but he continued to sweep the woods with his binoculars and in the end, he spotted movement. It was time now for him and his two soldiers to get into the trench that ran partway across the open ground. Crawling on their bellies, rifles across their arms, the three men moved slowly out into the open, only the trench sides hiding them from any watcher to left or right. After about thirty yards, the corporal risked a look through the tall grass to his left. At first, he detected nothing and then he spotted troops moving towards him across the field, not fifty yards away. He motioned to his men to be ready, they had already decided to shoot at the following troops firstly, and they moved into position, rifles poking through the long grass. The corporal had a final look, forty yards away and coming on slowly, aimed and squeezed off his first shot. The two soldiers fired a split second later. The following troops were in complete shock, three men were down, what was happening. Then another three shots, but they were aimed in the opposite direction, or were they? The gunshots echoed away into the distance, everything was still for a second and then both groups of SS opened up on each other through the darkness. The corporal and his two men crawled madly back along the trench, bullets whizzing and whining over their heads and made it safely back into the trees. Heavy machine guns were being brought into action from the airfield, along with the harsh cough of mortars. The following SS had taken cover and were giving back as good as they were taking. But the corporal's job was complete and he and his two soldiers headed off, to join up with Valery's group attacking the other airfield.

Valery and Yuri crept forward on their bellies, until they were about twenty-five yards from the perimeter fence. All was quiet, only the guards moved as they patrolled the outer fence. Two men in total, one on a clockwise route, the other, anticlockwise. Here we go again, thought Yuri, more circular guards. Valery checked his watch and held up ten fingers. Yuri nodded in reply, ten minutes. Yuri was going to take the anticlockwise guard and he moved off to Valery's right, hoping to get into position before the guard hove into view. Valery was taking the clockwise man. Once Yuri took out the guard, he would return to Valery and between them, they would see off the two gate guards. That was the plan. The seconds ticked by, then several shots sounded in the distance, far to the west. The shots were followed by a furious fusillade. Someone was really having a go. Yuri grinned in the darkness. Well I'll be damned, he thought to himself, Corporal Kurnakov's done it. SS fighting SS, hope the boys get away OK. He concentrated on his own problems. His view was good and he knew he had to be accurate. His crossbow was the new one that Ivan had made back at the island and Yuri was determined to avenge his lost comrade and friend. The seconds ticked by, where the hell was the guard? Maybe the racket over to the west was bothering him. However, before too long the guard plodded into view. Yuri relaxed, let out his breath slowly and let loose. The man died instantly, a crossbow bolt embedded in his throat. He gave the still body a cursory glance and then made his way back to Valery. They met outside the main gate, the two guards distracted by the pitched battle going on in the west. They were chatting to each other and pointing, trying to make out what was going on.

Valery tapped Yuri on the shoulder and whispered, "You take the one on the right. I'll count to three and we fire on three. Right?"

Yuri nodded and took up position, then Valery counted, one, two three. The two guards died never knowing what was taking place to the west. As they went down, Valery's squad joined him from behind and moved quickly to the gate and were soon inside, vanishing into the gloom. The flying party joined Yuri as they waited for Valery's signal. The minutes passed until eventually, the quiet was shattered by several shots, followed by several more. Silence followed and seconds later, a soldier appeared, beckoning them onto the airfield. This was it, the time had arrived.

Alexei scratched his balls as he waited for eight o'clock to come. The men were getting restless, being exposed out here in the city centre, with German troops wandering about. Alexei hawked and spat, not long now. He paused for a few moments and then nodded to the Jew, acting as the Lieutenant.

The man looked at him, "Now?" he said enquiringly.

"Now," muttered Alexei.

The acting Lieutenant took a deep breath and barked, "Right you motley bunch, out of the wagons and form up here."

The soldiers jumped down from the wagons, formed up along the pavement and stood in the 'at ease' position. Alexei, as sergeant, yelled, "Attention." The troop came quickly to attention and Alexei deferred to his Lieutenant. "All ready and correct sir."

The Lieutenant nodded, "right Feldwebel, move them out." Alexei barked out the order and the troop marched purposely down the street and around the corner, the Lieutenant in front with Alexei and the troop marching behind. SS Headquarters was a three-storied building, standing within its own gardens. It was an eighteenth century masterpiece, which took up a whole block, it having been the Mayor's residence before the SS took over. The building was surrounded by a colonnade of pillared columns, reaching upwards to the second floor. This allowed the second floor to have its own walk around balcony and it was here that Hauptmann Lientz had set up his command offices. The third floor was the communications area with several dishes and aerials clustered about the roof. Below in the basement, was a substantial wine cellar, which the SS had converted into an interrogation room and prison for politically sensitive prisoners. Leading from the main gate was a wide pathway with stone steps lifting up from the gardens to the pillared colonnade. The main entrance to the building was along the colonnade and around to the west side. The entrance was directly opposite to the SS barrack block, where the majority of the troops quartered. This was another substantial building, where they ate, slept and rested. Surprisingly, neither building had received any damage, when the Germans had bombed the city during the first weeks of the invasion. Neat, bordered gardens surrounded the Headquarters building on all sides and it was enclosed by a ten-foot high stone wall. The pavements surrounding the wall were heavily blanketed in barbed wire coils and at each corner, there was a machine gun nest. The main gate, which the Lieutenant was now approaching, stood outwardly open towards the street and was guarded by two sentries with a duty Feldwebel also in attendance. Within the gate entrance, were two sentry boxes, one to each side, with a red and white wooden barrier barring entrance. Alexei licked his suddenly dry lips. Here we go, he thought grimly.

The Lieutenant marched purposely forward, an air of leadership emanating from his brisk walk. Be bold, be brave and be confident, he told himself, you will be a very German Lieutenant. As he approached the gate, the duty Feldwebel moved out from behind the entrance and stood waiting for the Lieutenant to arrive. The two guards brought their machine pistols to bear and stood either side of the Feldwebel, albeit, a little behind. The Lieutenant strode up, stopped, clicked his heels and gave the straight arm salute. The rest of his squad, at Alexei's command, halted. They stood rigidly to attention, gave the same straight armed salute and chorused, 'Heil Hitler'. The Feldwebel and the two guard's reciprocated.

Confidently aloof, the Lieutenant unhurriedly surveyed the Feldwebel and then pronounced, "My name is Lieutenant Dolman of the 351st Army Battle Group. I have been sent by Herr Heydrich to escort six Jews that you have in your possession, back to Warsaw. Hauptman Lientz knows I am coming. Here are my papers and my orders." The Feldwebel hesitated, unsure as to who this mysterious Lieutenant was.

The Lieutenant saw the uncertainty and barked, "Feldwebel, my papers." The Feldwebel took the proffered papers and orders and quickly scanned through them.

"They appear in order," he answered suspiciously, "but I will.............." His words were cut off by an altercation going on across the street to his right.

Two men had staggered out from a side road, about fifteen yards from the gate and across. They were obviously drunk, both were singing loudly and very badly, and as they staggered along, the two guards moved around the still to attention soldiers, for a better look. Once they saw how ridiculous and inebriated the couple were, they relaxed and even smiled a little. The soldiers manning the machine gun posts at the east and west ends of the Headquarters, were also watching the drunken sideshow. All eyes were on the pair. The two guards at the gate died silently, each with a crossbow bolt through the throat. The two Jews, in the house opposite the gate, had practiced all week to perfection. The two guards fell backwards to be caught by Alexei's soldiers. The Feldwebel made to step forward, a cry of alarm forming on his lips, but the Lieutenant was too quick for him. His left arm snaked around the Feldwebel's head, his hand covered his mouth and the knife hidden up his right sleeve dropped. He grasped the handle and plunged the knife into the Feldwebel's back three times.

The Feldwebel died in his arms, as he whispered vehemently in the dead man's ear, "that was for my Christina, you lump of SS shit," before dragging him into the left-hand sentry box. The other two guards were dumped in the right sentry box. All remained quiet, no-one else had noticed the events at the main gate, as the two drunks continued onwards up the street. Alexei searched the windows of the Headquarters, a shape passed by one on the second floor, but no alarm was raised. Two soldiers quickly posed as the gate guards, the barrier was lifted and the Lieutenant strode through and into the manicured gardens, followed by the rest of his troop. Alexei scanned the street out front. The men in the two machine gun nests were unconcerned, their view of the gate entrance being masked by the doors. Alexei glanced along the street to his left. His men in the last wagon were ready. They would soon be in action.

Alexei sauntered off through the gardens, up the stone steps and around the corner of the Headquarters building. He strode unhurriedly along the walkway until he arrived at the main entrance. His men were inside the large vestibule, the Lieutenant haranguing the desk orderly. The orderly was a very officious man, keen to fully ascertain the reason for the Lieutenant's visit. He asked for more identification and the Lieutenant beckoned him forward, stretching over the desk to see the papers produced. He peered at them myopically through thick lensed spectacles and shook his head. The Lieutenant had had enough. Again, his left arm swept around the orderly's head and shoved it hard into the desk surface. The knife appeared in his right hand and he drove it with great force through the orderly's exposed neck, severing the spinal column and exiting out of the man's throat, to embed itself in the desk.

Alexei sprang into action, "right," he ordered, "you all know what to do. Go."

He and four Russians padded softly down the stairs towards the basement while the others ditched their captured uniforms and started to set the packs of dynamite, which they had brought with them. Alexei halted at the stair bottom and peered around the corner. The room was laid out before him, prisoners manacled to the walls in various poses, all had been ruthlessly beaten. Halfway down the room was a table and on the table was a naked woman, her arms and legs tied to the four table legs. Standing in front of her was a huge SS jailer. He was mocking and taunting her, spittle dribbling from the corners of his mouth and as Alexei watched, he dropped his trousers and made to climb onto the table. His intention was obvious and Alexei reacted as only Alexei could. In five long silent strides he was across the floor, the man unaware of his presence, due to his insatiable lust for fornication. Alexei didn't falter, he just plunged the bayonet again and again into the man's back. The man's mouth dropped open and he whimpered. Alexei stepped around him, noticed his still hard erection and grabbed it with his left hand while the bayonet in his right, hacked it off. The brute gawped through fast closing eyes and Alexei bunged the severed penis into his sagging mouth.

"Chew on that you SS shit," said a triumphant Alexei. The assembly of manacled prisoners cheered and most spat in the jailer's direction.

Suddenly, there was a harsh clatter of machine guns from above. Alexei knew that in the next few moments, all hell would be let loose on the SS. He grabbed the jailers keys and he and the four other Russians unchained the prisoners from their manacles. The woman, a strikingly pretty Jewish lady, was also untied and given some clothes to hide her nakedness.

She thanked Alexei profusely, "that would have been the fourth time he had violated me," she said by way of explanation, "he was a sadistic brute, but the female SS jailer was worse. She should be the one for you to bring to justice, but she's over in the SS barrack block."

Meanwhile, back on the street, the awaiting Russians sprang into action. At the first sounds of shots, a hail of fire emanated from the buildings across the street from the main gate. The two machine gun nests were nullified instantly, but that was only for starters. The men in the last wagon, now readied the seventy-millimetre field gun. Between them, they pushed and hauled it around the corner and the gunner took aim at the entrance to the SS barrack block. By this time, SS troops were beginning to respond to the shooting in the Headquarters building, by flooding out of the entrance. 'Boom.' The field gun roared, rocked back on its wheels and the shell destroyed the barrack block entrance, taking the SS troops with it.

"Reload," yelled the gunner, the others ejecting and then loading a new shell while the gunner spun the wheels and found another target.

"Ready," the loader yelled. 'Boom', the target was the second floor of the barrack block. Then the gunner changed direction, his comrades dragging the gun around until it faced the Headquarters.

"Ready," yelled the loader. 'Boom', went the gun and the shell careened through the central second floor window in the Headquarters.

"That's it," yelled the gunner, we've no more ammunition. Toss two grenades down the pipe and let's get out of here."

The others needed no second telling, the grenades were dumped down the barrel and the Russians were off like scared rabbits. Back in the Headquarters basement, Alexei was busy. Most of the prisoners could walk, but a few were too far gone and had to be assisted and in two cases, carried. At the insistence of the Jewish lady, the two Russian's who had blabbed to the SS about the whereabouts of Yuri, Yenisei and the Colonel were summarily executed by Alexei. She had heard them telling their secrets and hated them for it. That was before they had been chained up and tortured. The traitors had received their reward, a bullet in the back of the head, instead of a handful of Roubles. Hurriedly, the soldiers and released prisoners ascended the stairs and arrived in the vestibule. The scene was chaotic, dust and smoke lay everywhere. The SS above were dropping grenades down the stair well and the Russian soldiers were having great difficulty holding them back until the shell from the field gun more or less took out the second floor.

"Out," yelled Alexei, "make for the main gate. Keep the prisoners moving and protected. Move."

Then a soldier appeared out of the storeroom behind the shattered desk, with the orderly still skewered to its surface. "OK?" asked Alexei questioningly.

The man nodded. "Two minutes," he said. Alexei and the remaining soldiers vacated the building as quickly as they could, running pell-mell along the colonnade, trying to dodge the odd bullet coming out of the SS barrack block. But the Russians in the houses across the street from the main gate were putting up a withering hail of fire and the whole squad, with the released prisoners, got out and away down the main street, with only a few minor wounds, before the dynamite in the store exploded.

The noise was deafening, with a huge column of smoking debris thrown hundreds of feet up into the air, followed by a roaring flaming pinnacle. The windows, for a thousand yards around, shattered into a billion fragments of rapier like shards. Alexei beamed to himself. Now that's what I call a big bang, he thought. Up yours Lientz.

At the airfield, the party had made their way to the aircraft. In the western distance, the sound of firing continued, with the unmistakable 'crump' of exploding shells, as the SS slugged it out between themselves. The JU-52 looked huge to Yuri, who had never flown before. There were also four Jewish women and eight children, all looking extremely frightened. Stephan was first up the steps and made his way into the cockpit. After about ten minutes he pronounced himself ready. The plane had enough fuel for a flight to Moscow, although it would be close. He started the main central engine as the rest prepared to board, then the two wing engines burst into life.

Valery embraced everyone, tears in his eyes and hurried them forward to the plane. "You must hurry," he said urgently, "time is of the essence. Yuri, tell Stephan we've lit up the runway you're to use. God speed and come back and see us one day, don't forget about us."

At that moment, there was an explosion away to the east in Minsk. "That's my little brother," shouted an exultant Valery, "he's just blown up the SS Headquarters."

Yuri and the Colonel gawped, then laughed along with Valery. "Give him our best," said a delighted Colonel, "Yuri and I will be back after Christmas once we've got Yenisei and the girl's home. Bye for now."

With that, the Colonel and Yuri boarded the plane, being the last to embark and closed the door. Stephan gunned the throttles, the chocks were released by a couple of soldiers and the plane lumbered slowly away from its parking area and lined up at the head of the lit runway. Valery saluted, then waved frantically at the little figures waving from the windows as the plane built up the throttles. Stephan then released the brakes and the plane sped along the runway, faster and faster as the throttles were opened and then, when Stephan was ready, he pulled back the joystick and the plane rose elegantly into the air. As he gained height, Stephan turned the aircraft from its take off line which had been westward and swung it around to a south easterly heading. Valery and the soldiers below watched as it disappeared into the night, until the sound of the propellers had gone. Then they set fire to the Storks and the buildings and headed for home.

Stephan was beginning to come to terms with the planes vagaries, not least the fuel system.

Everything was written in German and he called on the Colonel to translate for him, so he better understood what he was dealing with. They were now passing over the south-west corner of Minsk and from the port windows, they gazed down at the carnage wreaked by Alexei and his men. Fires blazed all around the Headquarters site, the building itself, was just so much rubble. The plane was still climbing, cloud cover being at less than a thousand feet and Stephan was keen to get the plane above the clouds, once Minsk was safely out of the way. He turned gently to port and settled the converted bomber onto a north-easterly heading, still climbing upwards towards the cloud ceiling. At nine hundred feet, the plane was swallowed up by the thick cloud and what little light there had been, was lost. The passengers were experiencing various states of terror and euphoria. The children cried incessantly, arms locked around their mothers. Alayna, who had flown several times before and Giselle, tried their best to pacify the children's dread and eventually, the crying and terror lessoned for them as they became more used to the planes erratic movements. Yuri was in paradise, the trepidation before the plane took off, had been surmounted by a wave of delight.

He smiled happily at the Colonel saying, "This is fantastic, so different to what I was expecting. That feeling of pressure in the pit of your stomach when you first take off, was just mind blowing. What a fantastic experience."

The Colonel laughed at his obvious pleasure, "Don't worry Yuri, wait until you come in to land. That's also a fantastic experience."

Yuri nodded contentedly, "by the way Sergei," he enquired, "I didn't think you'd be coming with us. I thought you would want to stay with Valery and Alexei."

"So did I," admitted the Colonel, "but then, I think I will be needed before we make Moscow. I'm not sure what the reaction will be of the military, to a German plane wanting to land on one of their airfields. I have a few tricks that may be of help. Let's just see how it pans out."

Thoughtfully, he lapsed into silence. At two and a half thousand feet, the plane suddenly cleared the cloud ceiling and was plunged into moonlight. It even brought smiles to the drawn faces of the children as they could see the vastness of the skies around them. Yuri was exultant, this was so much better than he had ever imagined. The stark whiteness of the clouds below him, the purple-blackness of the distant horizon and the myriad of stars above filled him with awe. Alayna had returned to his side and she squeezed his arm and encouraged him to keep looking about him. What could be better than flying through this splendour with the woman I love, he thought.

The plane flew on, the hours drawing slowly by, as mile by mile, they neared their destination. The Colonel had gone to sit with Stephan up in the cockpit area and he chatted to him as the time marched on. There had been no sign of pursuit, but that didn't mean that they were home and dry. Nothing was predictable in this war-torn land. The children and most of the adults dozed as the plane cruised along, their lives in the hands of Stephan as he caressed the controls. But the Colonel was apprehensive, it was all going too well. After five hours, the cloud below them thinned and eventually dispersed altogether. They flew through a world of grey, nothing distinct or evident below, the shadowy steppe, rolling endlessly eastward. Stephan's first real point of interest came when they were six hours into the flight.

"Look down there," he shouted to the Colonel, "I think that's the River Oka near Kaluga. If it is, we're on track. Another hour should see us within sight of Moscow."

The Colonel nodded his agreement. At least the lack of cloud was allowing them line of sight, even though he was concerned at their exposed state. Onwards they flew, the miles being swallowed up, until the Colonel decided that it was time to make contact with the Russian military at one of

Moscow's airfields. He had already discussed the possibility of having to contact the Russian airfield with Yuri, Stephan and Yenisei earlier. They had left it up to him, to try and get them landed safely.

He settled himself, plugged in the radio lead, donned the other pair of headphones and spoke in a clear voice into the radio mouthpiece." Moscow airfield, Moscow airfield, I am former General Sergei Berezovsky in command of a stolen German JU-52 aircraft. We are not hostile, I repeat, we are not hostile. With me on board are six women, eight children and three males, one of whom is Mikhail Korsakov, who you may know as Yenisei. My credentials can be checked by contacting General Timoshenko or Beria at the NKVD. We are fleeing the fascist forces around Minsk and request a landing at a Moscow airfield. I repeat, we are not hostile. Do you copy?"

The line went quiet, only small bursts of static interrupting the silence. The Colonel fought down his impatience, he had to remain calm. The plane flew on. Nothing came back through the airwaves.

The minutes ticked by and then, "Unidentified aircraft, you will be shot out of the sky as soon as you cross the Moskva. Turn back, you are not welcome here."

The line went dead. The Colonel was not too dismayed, at least he was getting an answer.

"Moscow airfield, Moscow airfield. Please pass on these messages to Timoshenko, Beria, Zhukov or Stalin. They are codes that only ten people in our country know about. They will confirm my credentials. Firstly, 'The shores of the Black Sea are riven with failure', secondly, 'The Ides of March come gently to the Caucuses', and thirdly 'The Archangel succumbs to the Mongol hordes.' Do you understand?"

The line continued to be quiet with only the annoying hiss of static puncturing the airwaves. Finally a curt "understood" and the line went dead.

The plane flew onwards through the morning skies. The Colonel began to sweat as the minutes slipped agonisingly by. He knew there was no use in rushing them. Their fate was now in God's hands.

After ten excruciating minutes, the caller was back. "Unidentified aircraft, General Timoshenko has two questions. One, 'The Archangel succumbs to the Mongol hordes,' refers to what?"

"That would be the assassination of Rasputin", replied the Colonel.

"Secondly", said the voice, "what is the name of General Timoshenko's youngest daughter's dog?" The Colonel was stumped. Damn, he thought, what the hell was it.

He racked his brains, then he suddenly remembered, "The dog's name is Borrisy."

"Wait one moment please," came the patient reply.

The seconds ticked by and then, "General Berezovsky, please make your heading twenty degrees to port. You are about to cross the Moskva."

The Colonel was ecstatic, "we've convinced them to allow us to land," he shouted down the fuselage, "We'll be landing in fifteen minutes."

Then the voice suddenly returned, "General Berezovsky, we have scrambled ten Yak fighters to cover your descent. This is in response to six bandits being spotted about twenty-five miles behind you and gaining fast. The airfield should be visible in about five minutes. Good luck."

Again, the line went dead. Shit, thought the Colonel, I knew it was too good to last. The fascists must have picked up on our voice traffic. Six bandits, probably ME-109's.

"Stephan, get this thing on the deck as soon as possible. We have visitors behind."

Stephan blanched. He crossed himself and began the long descent towards the airport. Ten minutes at the most, he thought apprehensively. Come on you beauty, don't let me down now. The airport came into view as ten Yaks roared past them heading west, looking to engage the approaching enemy fighters. Downwards the JU-52 crept, the airfield looming larger and larger through the cockpit window.

"Hold on everybody," yelled the Colonel, "we're on our way in. Touchdown in two minutes."

Stephan had delayed dropping the wheels until the last possible second, to give them more approach speed. Now they were in position, he lowered the wheels and eased the joystick backwards. Then, as the wheels touched, he pushed forward hard on the joystick and slammed on the brakes, cutting the engines as soon as he could. The plane slowly decelerated and finally, came to a shuddering halt.

"Out, out, out," yelled the Colonel as he hobbled for the door, while Yuri disengaged the latches, swung it open and jumped down. The Colonel knew that they were not safe yet.

"Stephan, leave it," he bawled, "get out now."

Hurriedly, Yuri helped everyone onto the tarmac and the party tumbled off the plane as quickly as they could, just as a covered truck screeched to a halt alongside. Four soldiers jumped down from the back of the truck and helped the women, children and Yenisei aboard. Yuri and Stephan threw themselves onto the tailgate and into the trucks interior, dragging the hobbling Colonel in behind them. The driver had the truck already moving and he crunched the gears, taking off madly for the safety of the concrete bunkered hangers, all of two hundred yards away. The party peered out of the back of the truck and watched in horror at two ME's barrelling onto the airfield from the right, at treetop height. The airfields flack guns sent up a furious fusillade, as the ME leader focused on the JU-52. A three second burst was enough for the JU-52 to disintegrate in a cloud of sparks and flying wreckage, as his wing man, who was about a quarter of a mile behind the leader, angled towards the fleeing truck. Twenty yards, ten and then the truck passed beyond the concrete threshold and skidded crazily to a halt as the ME's cannons ripped huge holes in the tarmac and peppered the concrete walls across the entrance. The flack guns thundered back at the two ME's at point blank range and succeeded in bringing down the leader, who was hit just behind the cockpit. The plane did an over end loop and slammed into the ground at the edge of the airfield, the other escaping for the moment. The party hugged each other. They had finally arrived safely in Russian held territory.

Lightning Source UK Ltd.
Milton Keynes UK
UKHW02f0825110318
319210UK00004B/218/P

9 783710 332050